An author of more than ni[...]
adults with more than sev[...]
Janice Kay Johnson writes about love and family and
pens books of gripping romantic suspense. A *USA Today*
bestselling author and an eight-time finalist for the
Romance Writers of America *RITA*® Award, she won a
RITA® Award in 2008. A former librarian, Janice raised two
daughters in a small town north of Seattle, Washington.

New York Times and *USA Today* bestselling, award-winning
author **Lisa Childs** has written more than eighty-five
novels. Published in twenty countries, she's also appeared
on the Publishers Weekly, Barnes & Noble and Nielsen
Top 100 bestseller lists. Lisa writes contemporary romance,
romantic suspense, paranormal and women's fiction. She's
a wife, mum, bonus mum, avid reader and less avid runner.
Readers can reach her through Facebook or her website,
lisachilds.com

Discover more at millsandboon.co.uk

CRASH LANDING

JANICE KAY JOHNSON

HUNTED HOTSHOT HERO

LISA CHILDS

MILLS & BOON

First Published in Great Britain 2024
by Mills & Boon, an imprint of HarperCollins*Publishers* Ltd
1 London Bridge Street, London, SE1 9GF

www.harpercollins.co.uk

HarperCollins*Publishers*
Macken House, 39/40 Mayor Street Upper,
Dublin 1, D01 C9W8, Ireland

Crash Landing © 2024 Janice Kay Johnson
Hunted Hotshot Hero © 2024 Lisa Childs

ISBN: 978-0-263-32223-1

0324

This book contains FSC™ certified paper and other controlled sources to ensure responsible forest management.

For more information visit: www.harpercollins.co.uk/green

Printed and Bound in the UK using 100% Renewable Electricity at CPI Group (UK) Ltd, Croydon, CR0 4YY

CRASH LANDING

JANICE KAY JOHNSON

For Pat aka Alexis Morgan, an amazing friend and
plotting partner

Chapter One

Gwen Allen inhaled the powerful smell of hot jet fuel as she walked across the tarmac toward one of the two helicopters parked near the long, low building that served as the base for EMS Flight, the helicopter rescue service she worked for. Her small rolling suitcase bumped along with her, and her enormous tote bag weighed heavily on her shoulder.

Her home base with EMS Flight was just outside Seattle, but she'd spent a week visiting a good friend from college in Yakima, Washington, on the dry side of the Cascade mountains. The very dry side. Heat radiated off the paved surface and it felt as if it were baking any exposed skin to leather. Within her fire-retardant Nomex suit, she was even hotter. She'd enjoyed a few days of sunshine—Seattle was having an unusually cool July—but she wouldn't want to live and work in this climate. Imagine how blistering August and September would be! Still, she was glad she'd been able to borrow the suit and a helmet from the locker of a nurse who was taking maternity leave.

Eyes on the two Bell helicopters painted with the familiar red and green stripes against an overall white, Gwen felt like skipping. A week ago, she'd gotten lucky enough to hitch a ride over with a coworker driving to Spokane, almost to the Idaho border, but she'd planned to either buy an airline ticket or hop a Greyhound bus for her return. Wonder of wonders, a guy in base dispatch had called yesterday to let her know they were transferring a helicopter to her base on a temporary basis to replace one that would be out for much-needed maintenance. Someone had mentioned she was in Yakima and planning to travel back at about the right time. Did she want a ride? She'd be alone with the pilot, no patient to monitor.

Of course, she could have afforded to pay for the trip home, but this way, she could tuck a few more dollars into her dream fund.

Only, to her puzzlement, an ambulance had just pulled up behind the Bell 419 helicopter she thought was supposed to be her ride, and as she watched, EMTs from the ambulance unloaded a patient packaged on a backboard and transferred him or her to the helicopter.

Nobody at all stood by the second helicopter. Probably that pilot had already done his preflight and retreated back into the building, and she was heading for the wrong one.

She took out her phone to check the time. They were supposed to lift off five minutes from now.

She'd been a paramedic with EMS Flight for two years now after working on an ambulance and in the emergency department at Swedish Hospital in Seattle. She'd studied hard for the certifications required. She loved her job and the adrenaline boost with every rescue. The thing was, among her coworkers, she liked order and the certainty she could absolutely rely on them.

If that was her helicopter, the pilot had probably taken a last-minute restroom run, something she'd just done, too. In prep for the flight to Seattle, she'd restricted her fluid intake, too. She was fussing. Not like they were in any hurry.

The patient was now on board the helicopter right in front of her, the door closed. The rotors weren't turning yet, so she presumed the man in the Nomex suit sewn with the company patch was the pilot. The other guy wore chinos and a denim shirt open over a T-shirt. Who was *he*? Friend or family of the patient?

She'd almost reached them when they noticed her. The second guy moved fast to intercept her. His body language was weirdly aggressive enough that she had the sense he was blocking her.

"What are you doing out here?" he demanded.

"Is this the helicopter going to Seattle?"

"Who are you?" he asked impatiently.

By most women's standards, he was handsome. Sandy brown hair, square jaw, tall, nice shoulders. Gwen did not like the cold, verging-on-hostile way he was eyeing her.

"A paramedic with EMS Flight," she said shortly. She tapped the logo patch on her shoulder that said EMS followed by a bird in flight. "Who are *you*?"

Instead of answering, he turned just enough to wave the pilot over. "Bill?"

This man, somewhere around forty years old, was friendly looking, thin, with military-short hair, which didn't surprise her. Many of the pilots were ex-military. Knowing the training and experience they brought with them inspired a level of trust in the nurses, EMTs and paramedics who relied on their expertise.

She held out her hand. "Gwen Allen, a paramedic with EMS Flight, but out of Seattle."

"Oh, ah. We were told the nurse scheduled to fly with us couldn't make it. We were just talking about what to do."

"You're the pilot?"

"Yes. Sorry. Bill Thomson."

"Then…this isn't the helicopter being transferred to Seattle?"

"Yeah, it is," he said readily. "That's our end goal, but we, uh, kind of got hijacked." He nodded toward Mr. Unpleasant. "Law enforcement. I'm new with EMS Flight, but I'm told we try to help out whenever any LEA asks for help."

That was true, but law enforcement agencies typically called when they had a severely injured victim that needed quick transport with expert care. They didn't "hijack" a flight.

"So," she said, still trying to understand, "you don't have a nurse or paramedic, but you do have a patient?"

"That's right."

"We don't need a medical attendant," Mr. Unfriendly said. "We're transporting a man who had surgery some hours ago. He's stable. I'm assured there's no reason to expect a problem. I'm an agent with the Drug Enforcement Administration, and we want him moved to Seattle, get him checked out so he can be transferred to where he belongs."

The distaste and heightened hostility in his voice made it seem as if this patient was, if not dangerous, someone whose crimes were contemptible. A recent arrest, presumably.

Bill's phone rang, then hers. She glanced at the number. Dispatch. She let the call go to voice mail, but saw that Bill had half turned away and was talking on his phone, his gaze staying on her. He gave her a nod.

She concentrated on the circumstances. This wouldn't be the first time the patient her team had rushed to pick up was someone who'd be placed under arrest—if he survived grave wounds. She'd given her all to save the life of many a street criminal.

"What kind of surgery?" she asked.

"He took two bullets."

She waited. No more information was apparently forth-coming.

"If I'm going to handle his or her care on this flight, I'll need to know more."

"His. But I told you. We don't—"

"You do," she interrupted, making sure there was no give in her voice. "The company does not allow a helicopter carrying a patient to take off without trained medical personnel on board." She shifted her gaze, raising her eyebrows. Fortunately, Bill had ended his call. "Isn't that right, Bill?"

"That's what I was just telling Agent Kimball," he agreed with a sidelong glance at his companion. "That was dispatch on the phone," he added. "I've only been with the company a month, though, and have never run into a situation like this. Er, Agent Kimball plans to fly with us."

"Salazar needs to remain under supervision by a law enforcement agent," Kimball said. "If he breaks free, you couldn't handle him."

"Okay," she said. "Where are you taking him?"

"The university hospital in Seattle."

The teaching hospital in Seattle was definitely where you wanted to go if you had any unusual problems. But if this guy had come out of surgery in good enough shape that his surgeon had anticipated no problems and okayed a long and uncomfortable helicopter flight, why send him there?

For someone who liked to be prepared, she had a lot of qualms: Was there even a trauma bag on board? If so, who had packed it? Before they lifted off from the ground, she could hustle to do some of her preflight checks, but there were half a dozen tasks she always completed at the start of her shift so there were no later surprises. She started running through potential issues in her mind. Had the levels of oxygen in the tanks been checked? Unexpectedly running out *was* a major crisis. Plugs and inverter functioning? Were they stocked on batteries for handheld devices? This would be an unusually long flight. EKG patches…

She cut herself off. The pilot had seen the patient, so she wasn't relying a hundred percent on Agent Kimball saying the guy was in peachy keen condition. The EMTs on the ambulance must not have been concerned, or they'd have waited to do an in-person handover.

And, hey, she'd not only get a free ride home, the company would now have to pay her for her services. That made her feel a little more cheerful. No reason to think there'd be any issues.

Famous last words, a voice whispered in her head. She ignored it.

"Fine," she said. "Then let's get on our way."

There was a short silence that felt…odd. Gwen didn't know how to read it. Neither man looked at each other, yet she had the weird sense that they were conferring, anyway. Maybe she *didn't* want to get on this helicopter, especially without having done her own preflight check.

Except…there was a patient who needed her. Besides, working with people who were new hires or pains in the butt wasn't out of the ordinary, and cops she dealt with at accident or crisis sites were given to being dictatorial with the medical team, wanting to give orders when that was no longer their place. The fact that she found DEA agent Kimball annoying was no reason to refuse to do her job *and* get a free—no, paid!—ride home.

"Works for me." Bill sounded agreeable, and his wink at her was reassuring, hinting that he, too, found Kimball difficult.

"Fine," Kimball grumbled. "What's one more?"

Normally, if she were heading a team, she'd ride up front

next to the pilot, in part to watch for potential hazards in the air and at a landing site. Of course, in that case, there would also be a nurse or EMT at the side of the patient.

Even as they walked the short distance to board the helicopter, she made up her mind: she was staying in back with the man who definitely needed monitoring and might need intercession. Agent Kimball could sit up front, where she mostly wouldn't be able to see a face that radiated impatience and irritation as much as the vast paved tarmac did heat.

Maybe, it occurred to her, he'd been relegated to what he considered to be scut work and resented it. After all, how challenging was accompanying a semiconscious, restrained man? She could give him a break.

RAFE HAD NO idea what was happening to him. He had a vague notion that he was in recovery at the hospital, except for some reason, he'd been trussed up like a Christmas tree ready to be stuffed in the rear hatch of a car to be sure branches weren't broken.

He opened his eyes and felt a surge of panic. Why couldn't he see anything? He hadn't been blinded, had he? He tried to lift a hand to his face, but a tight restraint kept him from raising his arm. A minute ago, whatever he was lying on had tilted upright enough that he'd tried to grab for purchase, but then it leveled off.

The reason he should be—would have sworn he *was*—in the hospital flashed in jerky movements as if filmed with a handheld camera that often wasn't pointing the way it should be.

Knock on the front door; Eaton muting the TV and going to the door to look through the peephole. Stanton was there, too. Rafe saw him stiffen and unsnap his holster. They weren't expecting anyone. But Eaton immediately relaxed and unlocked and then started to open the door.

"Hey." Clearly, he knew the visitor. "What are you doing here?"

A burst of gunfire. Stanton yelling, "Run," as bullets sprayed the living room. Rafe leaped to his feet, bounced off the wall in the hall and spun into a bedroom. Smashed a chair through the window and dove out, a lilac bush scratching him as he fell. One arm useless. He rolled, seeing a man framed by the window he'd just thrown himself out of. More gunfire. Bullets struck his torso, and his body repeatedly jerked. Nothing hurt yet, but it would. Why had he been so complacent, he wasn't carrying this evening? Were his bodyguards down? Must be.

Voices raised, sirens. He couldn't see anyone through the jagged-edged windowpane now. Couldn't help closing his eyes.

It was all vivid but chaotic.

Didn't help him understand where he was now or why.

Then everything around him began to vibrate.

THE TWO MEN seemed to be engaged in a low-voiced intense conversation from the minute they took their seats in front. But Bill did turn his attention to business because the engines fired up.

After stowing her suitcase out of the way, Gwen scanned the cabin as she hurried through some of what should have been preflight checks, and her gaze caught on the surprising sight of what appeared to be a fully loaded backpack with a sleeping bag tied on. She tugged to be sure it was adequately wedged in so it wouldn't become a missile if the flight turned out to be turbulent. *Is it Bill's?* she wondered idly, then put it out of her mind.

She leaned over the patient to make a quick evaluation of his condition before she flipped through his chart. To look at his dressings, she'd have to pull back blankets, but that meant first undoing straps that kept him immobilized. That could wait. He wasn't on oxygen, but she considered putting him on it. Better to be preventative than to react to trouble. What surprised her was that thick foam plugs had been inserted in his ears, and a black mask covered his eyes. She hoped somebody had explained what they were doing before depriving him of two major senses. There were reasons why it was sometimes a good idea, but... He might freak if he'd still been in a hazy postanesthetic state and now surfaced to find himself blind and deaf.

She glanced at the manila envelope with a sticker on the front identifying him as one Rafael Salazar. Hair very dark, maybe black, disheveled and spiky from whatever he'd been through. Skin darker than hers that stretched over sharp cheekbones. Dark stubble on a strong jaw. Probably a good-looking guy. It was hard to be sure under the circumstances and didn't matter, anyway.

Besides...criminal, she reminded herself, even as instinct had her smoothing his hair back from his forehead.

She made herself take her own seat and belted herself in. Borrowed helmet—check. Somewhere in her bag were her own earplugs, but she didn't always wear them, and that could wait.

Normally, part of her job was handling four radio frequencies, although today not quite as many would be required. The pilot had several, too. Right now, she had to wait for the intercom to come on to talk to him.

"Gwen?" Bill's voice came in her ears. "Barring any problem, I'll need you to let me handle radio communications once we've lifted off. Agent Kimball is insistent that we stay off the air as much as possible. The agency would just as soon no one knows who we're transporting or where he's being taken. Or even that we have a federal agent on board."

Her forehead crinkled. It wasn't as if she'd have chatted on the radio about her patient, and they were still required to connect with local controllers along the way in part to make sure there were no midair collisions. This flight had been scheduled to be routine. Why would anyone, hearing them confirm altitude, direction or ETA—destination, for that matter—suspect for a moment that they carried a federal agent and his prisoner? Did Agent Kimball think they'd be shot out of the sky if the wrong people learned who was aboard?

Ridiculous.

As for the radio, a former military pilot would probably be accustomed to handling complex communications, or he wouldn't sound so casual about it.

Still, the unusual request ratcheted up Gwen's unease. Company policy was that if any member of the team felt strongly that the flight wouldn't be safe—usually because of expected severe weather—and refused to go, the mission was canceled, and the helicopter stayed grounded. Period. In these circumstances, Gwen could demand an okay from someone higher up the chain of authority.

Feeling vaguely unsettled didn't justify that step, she decided. Honestly, if Agent Kimball had been friendly and more open with her, she wouldn't be as uneasy as she was.

"Sure, Bill," she said. "Let me know if you need me to jump on."

"Will do." He still sounded cheerful. The pilots she knew

best were happiest in the air or maneuvering to land at a tricky site.

She double-checked her seat belt and the patient's restraints, then felt the helicopter lift off. She remembered her terror on her first flights when she looked at the radio console, with a zillion buttons and switches. Like most newbies, she'd made mistakes. Today...she could switch most of them off. Why listen if she was supposed to keep her mouth shut?

Over the noise of the engines, she couldn't even hear Bill confirm departure with base dispatch, but she could see him at an oblique angle. He was talking into his mic, seeming relaxed.

As the ground below them receded, she felt some of her usual excitement. No, they weren't racing to the scene of an auto accident where cops were even now employing the Jaws of Life to pry someone out of a dangerously compressed space, or aiming to pick up a mountain climber who'd fallen and suffered unknown injuries, or collecting a kid who'd been shot while playing with a gun.

Her gaze rested again on the man who lay within hand's reach—the man who *had* been shot twice. By the cops trying to arrest him? Clearly, she was never going to know.

Oxygen? she asked herself again. It wouldn't hurt anything, and even if it wasn't otherwise needed, it combated nausea and motion sickness.

Studying him, she was troubled to see movement, as if he were fighting against the restraints. No matter what, he had to remain secured in case of unexpected turbulence, but she could talk to him.

She could see part of the back of Kimball's head and one ear, but he couldn't get a good look at what she was doing. So she leaned forward, eased the foam plug from the patient's ear and spoke as close to it as possible. As it was, she had to raise her voice to have any chance of being heard.

"How are you doing? I'm Gwen, taking care of you during a helicopter ride, in case you wondered why your whole body is vibrating."

His head turned, just the slightest amount. Her lips brushed his ear.

She stole another look at Kimball, then pushed the mask up to Rafael Salazar's forehead. His eyes opened briefly. He squeezed them shut, then opened them again and stared blankly upward. Finally, he managed to focus on her face.

Those eyes were a rich brown—*dark chocolate*, she thought. He hadn't regained complete clarity postsurgery but was close to it.

He stared for so long that she repeated her introduction and explanation of where they were. "Do you understand?" she asked.

He swallowed, worked his mouth and finally spoke a single word. "Yes." Pause. "Where?"

She spoke slowly, and only after another glance to be sure Kimball couldn't see her or, presumably, hear her, given the noise made by the engines. "I understand we're transporting you to Harborview Hospital in Seattle to make sure the surgery you underwent in Yakima is all you need."

"Surgery?"

"I'm told you were shot twice. Do you remember?"

"Yeah." Another swallow. "Yes."

"Good." She smiled instead of apologizing for her choice of words. Unlikely *he* thought being shot twice was good. "Let me know if you become nauseated, hurt too much, feel anything unexpected. Okay?"

"Gwen?" A voice came through her earpieces. Bill, she realized.

"Yes?"

"Everything okay?" he asked.

"Yep."

"Agent Kimball would prefer you don't make any attempt to communicate with the patient. He says Salazar is a dangerous man."

"Mr. Salazar seemed distressed, so I took out an earplug long enough to explain where he is and reassure him. That seemed to help."

The second voice didn't surprise her. "Unless he has a medical crisis, I'm asking you to keep your distance."

She felt steam building up. That was an order, not a request.

"Whatever you want to think, I don't work for you, Agent Kimball. The patient is in my charge until I hand him off to another medical professional."

She cut off his sputtering, at least temporarily, and met Salazar's eyes again. Something had changed. That gaze was sharp and alarmed, if she was reading it right. What had she said?

She opened her mouth…and he gave his head the tiniest shake, all the restraints permitted. But she understood: he didn't want her to continue challenging Kimball or to ask what might be the wrong questions.

Chapter Two

Had he heard her right? Agent *Kimball*? Rafe's brain tried to grind itself into motion despite the rust clogging it. What would Kimball be doing here? Rafe barely knew the man and didn't much like him. Unless he'd been transferred recently, he belonged in Chicago.

Must have heard this woman wrong, Rafe decided. Gwen... Allen? Something like that. She was taking care of him. Nurse? She didn't wear scrubs. Instead, her jumpsuit looked like what a navy pilot might wear. Rafe guessed it was made out of fire-retardant fabric, which made sense if they really were in a helicopter. Now that he could exam his surroundings, albeit in a limited way, he decided that's exactly where he was. A radio console with a forest of lights, switches and what have you, barely visible out of the corner of his eye, and a window taller than it was wide that let him see bright blue sky.

He'd thought the haze in his head was clearing, but if so, it was being replaced by a different kind of confusion. At the hospital, Zabrowsky's face had hovered over his for a few minutes. Rafe's supervising special agent must have been allowed into recovery in lieu of a next of kin. Rafe thought he'd mumbled a few questions that weren't answered, but he was quite sure nothing was said about shipping him across the state.

Was he more seriously wounded than the nurse in recovery had said? Possible, but where was Zabrowsky? How was a federal agent who should be in Chicago involved in the latest mess?

Which had started because Eaton had known whoever knocked on that door. The same someone who'd burst in firing a semiautomatic weapon, who'd chased Rafe into the bedroom and tried to gun him down. Unless the person who'd come by had been followed and had also been a victim?

None of this made sense. Rafe would give a lot to have been clearer in his head when Zabrowsky came to talk to him.

He studied the woman who was presumably a nurse or EMT. She appeared to be inspecting him with equal interest.

Her smooth hair, the color of maple syrup, was pulled back from her face and disappeared under a flight helmet. Eyes the rare gray of a dove's feathers, not so much penetrating as gentle. Fine-boned hands, slender build. He guessed tall but couldn't be sure. Her face drew him.

Would *she* answer any of his questions? He decided to try.

"Do you know how badly I'm hurt?"

Given the racket in here, she was probably lip-reading. She answered by bending again so that her mouth tickled his ear.

"Two gunshot wounds. If you'll wait a minute, I can read your chart."

"Yes."

He pondered her some more as she removed paperwork from a manila envelope and concentrated on every page. She didn't wear much if any makeup, he decided, although that might be the case only on the job. If she was a nurse, she might have to deal with squirting blood and the like, good reason not to bother with foundation or mascara. She didn't need it.

She shifted a little, setting aside a page, and he saw the patch on the upper arm of her Nomex suit. The letters EMS were part of a bird in flight. He guessed they were a rescue organization, the kind that plucked wounded or sick people from remote or difficult positions when ground transportation to a hospital would be too slow. He'd…encountered people from other such organizations before. Made him think of military medics. Same skill set, same personality type.

At last she raised her head, appeared to sneak a peek toward the front of the helicopter then leaned toward him.

"You took a bullet to your upper arm. That one will require physical therapy and conceivably additional surgery, because of the complexity of the rotator cuff where muscles and nerves are bundled together."

He tried for a nod but failed because his head, along with the rest of his body, was strapped down.

"Second bullet struck your thigh but missed the bone. You lost a lot of blood, though. You also have a cracked sternum and two broken ribs. I can't tell how those injuries came to be."

He could have enlightened her but chose not to. He might have been careless enough to leave his weapon in his bedroom, but he'd routinely worn a Kevlar vest, however relaxed he and his guards had become after over a month in the small ranch house in a working-class neighborhood in Yakima. Sounded like he'd be dead if he hadn't bothered with the vest.

He didn't remember noticing whether Eaton and Stanton had worn theirs. The air-conditioning only partially combated the summer heat, meaning vests weren't comfortable.

Why Yakima? Rafe wondered for probably the hundredth time. He'd barely heard of the town before getting deposited there. It had been settled on a river that joined the broad Columbia River not far downstream. These days, it was wine country, from what he understood, irrigated vineyards having supplanted other kinds of agriculture in the surrounding landscape. Wine grapes thrived in the hot, dry climate. That was the sum total of his knowledge of the town where he'd been prepared to stay for up to a year.

Gwen had flipped a couple more pages and now looked perturbed. Again, she leaned forward. "It sounds like you came through surgery with flying colors. Not sure what kind of follow-up they expect for you at Harborview, but it's a top-notch hospital, so you could have a worse destination."

Rafe only caught parts of what she said, given the engine noise. She seemed to be talking partly to herself, her puzzlement apparent.

He was becoming more aware of how much he hurt. Shouldn't he be in a hospital bed with a handy button within reach that he could push to boost the level of painkiller?

A memory niggled at him. He'd dated an ER nurse, Nina Caldero, who said she'd worked helicopter rescue in Washington State for a few years. He thought this was the outfit she'd mentioned, which meant EMS Flight was reputable. A sense of wrongness still had Rafe's skin prickling, but he couldn't imagine Gwen or a pilot with the company cooperating in anything nefarious.

Maybe because he'd been on edge for so long—over a year now—it had become second nature to expect trouble. Literally tied down, there wasn't a damn thing he could do about it if his twitchy feeling was on target and everything was about to blow up in his face. Again. He might as well give in. The vibration and racket penetrating even the earplugs made his eyelids heavy. Maybe this would all make more sense if he slept for an hour or so.

Gwen must have thought the same or believed he'd already fallen asleep because he felt her touch as she replaced the plug in his ear. He was grateful she didn't cover his eyes again.

WATCHING THE MAN who slept beside her, Gwen began to feel a little drowsy herself. Flights weren't usually anywhere near this long. From takeoff, she'd have normally been mentally running over what equipment she'd need when they landed, what she could expect. Everyone on board would share the tension; they had a job to do, and it could go sideways in a heartbeat.

Today, she could have kicked back and admired the view from the window if it weren't for Rafael Salazar and his guard. She had a feeling Kimball wouldn't like knowing she'd talked to Salazar and began speculating even harder about why he was being taken to the hospital in Seattle. She felt sure the surgeons who'd operated on him in Yakima were competent.

She pulled a book from her tote and read for a while but found it hard to concentrate given that she also glanced up often to check on her patient. During one of those checks, some extra sense made her look out the window. Wisps of white appeared—and behind them was a sight any Washingtonian would know instantly: Mount Rainier, an active volcano that was the highest mountain in the lower forty-eight states. Black rock and glaciers forming a steep slope that plunged into the dark green of northwestern forests felt almost close enough to touch.

In other words, terrifyingly close.

Gwen snapped shut a mouth that had dropped open. As

huge as the mountain was, she'd have expected a distant view of it as they crossed the Cascade Range toward Seattle. There was no reason whatsoever they should be this close.

She used the mic to talk to Bill.

"Did you get lost?"

He chuckled. "No, Kimball wanted to see the mountain, and I didn't see any harm. We're not that far off course. Heck of a view, isn't it?"

"I'd like it better if it weren't for the clouds."

Whiteout could be a problem at higher elevations of a mountain that was over fourteen thousand feet and rose almost from sea level, unlike the Rocky Mountains. It seemed to Gwen that Bill was flirting with trouble. Micro weather events were the norm here. The National Park Service had their own resources for rescues on the mountain, including the giant Chinook helicopters from the army base, Fort Lewis, that could fly as high as the summit, which meant EMS Flight had never had reason to be in the vicinity.

Did Bill have any experience with the conditions he might meet here?

It's July, she reminded herself. Not exactly summer in the park, as it was elsewhere; snow would still be covering some trails, flowers just appearing in the meadows. She'd hiked one stretch of the Wonderland Trail that circled Mount Rainier. Eventually, she hoped to complete all of it, albeit one section at a time.

The engines sounded steady. She kept watching out the window, seeing less and less mountain, more and more clouds.

The helicopter gave an odd shudder.

Bill's voice in her ears. "Just a gust. I'm dropping in elevation."

Gwen had lost any hint of drowsiness. She sat tensely,

expecting…she didn't know. The other shoe to drop in a day that was already peculiar.

"The fire light has come on," Bill suddenly snapped, a new sharpness in his voice.

She'd done the associated drills a hundred times. Her role right now was to look outside for smoke and identify where it was coming from. She all but did contortions to try to see where the trouble was, but the cloud cover had deepened, making it harder to pick out darker smoke.

"Nothing," she said. "Nothing."

"Damn it." Yes, there was mild tension in the pilot's voice, but mostly he sounded calm. A helicopter pilot with the experience he must have had to be hired by EMS Flight would remain calm and employ his every skill to, at worst, land the bird safely. "Going down," he added, confirming her suspicion. "Looking for a clear LZ."

LZ was the landing zone. Usually they'd be worrying about power wires, traffic and the competency of whatever firefighter, cop or ambulance crew had deemed a particular spot safe. Here, it would be too-steep slopes, enormous trees, tumbled boulders and lakes. Gwen wished intensely that she'd taken the seat beside Bill, where she could be of real help. That was a big part of her role, watching for unexpected trouble. What were the odds a DEA agent knew what a helicopter could handle and what would send it into a cataclysmic crash?

Instinctively, she tested the patient's restraints, then her own belt. She at least wore a helmet and a fire-retardant jumpsuit; Salazar was unlikely to have anything but scrubs on beneath the blankets that wrapped him. At least scrubs were cotton, better than fabrics that could melt into the skin.

If there was a fire, none of them were likely to survive.

Even emergency medical helicopters staffed by experienced teams occasionally went down. Weather, rugged terrain, mechanical failure or a pilot's mistake could contribute. Right now, she couldn't see anything out the window except the lowering cloud cover, and the rocks and ice too close to her window.

The tail of the helicopter with the smaller rotor whipped subtly side to side.

The unusual movement had awakened the patient, whose dark eyes looked past her to a window, then fixed on her face. She sat close enough to him to remove both earplugs.

"Problem?"

"We should be fine," she shouted into his ear, "but we may have to set down. A warning light came on."

Still meeting Salazar's gaze, she sat back. "Bill?"

"We're dropping below the clouds. I think I see a potential LZ. Pretty lake. We can go fishing while we're here."

She could match his insouciance. "Just what I'd like to do today."

She heard an odd noise—somehow choked. Bill? *Please don't let him be having a heart attack, or—*

Abruptly, there was a hard thud after which they rocked, and suddenly she had the sense they were zigzagging. She automatically checked to be sure the oxygen was turned off, but of course it hadn't been on in the first place. Her patient didn't need it.

Bill had to be struggling to maintain control. What had really gone wrong? She wanted to talk to him but knew better than to distract him. Gwen focused on the view; she could see a glint of water, trees, a rocky buttress. No ideal place to set down.

And then they spun around entirely. Her fingers dug into

the seat, as if she could hold herself in place. There was yelling, a screech of metal, and she knew they were down, bumping over rough ground. Her body was snapped forward, then back, and she knew vaguely that the top of the helicopter had been sheared off.

They came to a complete stop. The radio must have been damaged, because for a moment, the silence was absolute.

HER HANDS SHOOK as she unsnapped her seat belt and yelled to the front, "Bill? Kimball? Are you hurt?"

"I'm okay," the agent called back. "Pilot's unconscious."

"Get back here and help me unload the patient."

"What?" He must have unfastened his belt, too, because he'd twisted enough to look at her. "Why?"

"Fire. Jet fuel is incredibly volatile."

He let loose with some obscenities but, because the helicopter had become a convertible, was able to stand and step between seats. "We should get Bill first."

"No. Patient first. That's our protocol. He's completely helpless."

"You want *me* to help *him* first."

In the close quarters, she elbowed him out of the way so she could free the backboard. "Yes! Let's move. Get him to a distance."

"I don't see any fire."

"I smell fuel. Try not to do anything that might incite a spark."

He went still for a moment, then his body language abruptly took on the urgency that she shared. Within moments, they'd heaved the backboard with a large man out an unapproved and usually nonexistent way. Once they were on the ground, she broke into a trot despite the weight she bore, and he did the same. Gwen didn't let herself stop until they were a good hundred yards from a helicopter that might blow sky high at any time. She was actually grateful for Kimball's strength, until he dropped his end without bothering to bend all the way. The sudden descent even to soft loam had to be painful for an already injured man.

Gwen finally turned to look at what had been a shiny, beautifully maintained helicopter and couldn't hold back a gasp.

The rotors at the rear were half drilled into the soil, half deep in a gash cut in a huge old tree. The main rotors were... gone. The cabin consisted of shards of metal that still formed a cup shape.

Kimball swore again beside her, sounding as shocked as she was.

She started at a trot back for the helicopter, calling urgently over her shoulder, "I'll grab what supplies I can. You wouldn't know what to get. Check on Bill. If he's alive, we'll have to pull him out even if we risk damaging his neck and spine."

If they had time, the chopper carried another backboard and a C-collar.

Time was something she was very afraid they didn't have.

Kimball looked reluctant, and she didn't blame him, but he was running beside her.

She lost sight of him when she clambered back inside the broken helicopter. The smell was almost overpowering, but she still didn't see any flicker of flame.

Hurry, she thought. Trauma bag first, her own tote that held some snack bars and other useful bits. Suitcase...no, the backpack. It had fallen and was wedged into an awkward spot, but the sleeping bag was something they might need if rescue didn't come quickly. Had Bill gotten off an emergency call?

Hurry.

Drugs. Only by long habit did she find her keys quickly and was able to fumble open the cabinet and narc box for pain relievers and syringes. Thank God EMS didn't require two people and two keys to get this open. Small bottles and more plastic syringes fell to her feet. She stuffed what was in her hand into the trauma bag. They had to get out of here… Her eye fell on a white plastic bag that was the kind the hospital used for a patient's personal effects. Salazar would need more clothing if they were here long.

There was nothing soft in the bag. Alarmingly, her fingers recognized the shape of a handgun. How could that be if he had been arrested?

She looped the strings over her arm, hefted the pack over her back and clambered back out, careful of the jagged metal. Not a good time to cut her own flesh open.

The moment her feet were on the ground, she broke into a run. She felt as if she were moving through sludge and bent under more pounds than she could possibly be carrying. Was she breathing in a whiff of smoke? Oh, God— hurry, hurry.

Kimball was already beside Salazar. Her first thought was to be mad. He could have tried to help her. But then her heart sank. He'd have called for her, surely, if Bill was alive but unconscious.

She fell to her knees beside the two men.

"Bill?" she wheezed.

"Dead. I think his neck was broken."

The man on the backboard yelled out, "Fire!"

"What?"

She turned her head to see the first flicker of flame. "We're too late to—"

With a hideous *whump*, a firestorm erupted.

A funeral pyre, she thought in horror.

Chapter Three

The blast of heat reached them in seconds.

As transfixed as the others, she managed to say, "Back. Let's get farther away."

Kimball reached as if automatically for the backpack. "Patient first."

He frowned. "I can carry it at the same time."

"It's heavy. Let's move Salazar first. At worst, the bags will be hit by flying..." She petered out. Not coal. Bits of superheated metal? It didn't matter.

Once again, Kimball hoisted one end of the backboard and let her direct where they went. Water shone through the trees. She steered them that way. It seemed...safer, given the inferno behind them. They set down Salazar, and both ran back for the limited stuff she'd been able to pull out.

The uneasiness she'd felt all day made her kneel on the ground with her back to Kimball so she could slide the white hospital bag into her tote. Of course, he wore a weapon in a holster, but she could imagine how he'd react to learn that another gun was just kind of lying around.

In fact, she made sure he didn't see her remove the big black handgun from the bag and push it under the clothes she'd changed out of earlier.

Then she grabbed her two bags and stood. Both hurried

back the way they'd come to escape the searing heat. She already felt as if she had a sunburn.

Once they reached the still bound patient, aka captive, Gwen sank to the ground. Kimball set down the pack and knelt beside it, twisted at the waist so he could look back the way they'd come.

"Will the fire spread?" he asked tersely.

Breathless, she said, "I think the couple of trees that are closest will burn. At this altitude, mid-July is more like spring than summer. I hope the vegetation hasn't dried enough to allow the fire to spread. That's...why I wanted to get farther away, though." She could only be grateful that Bill had found a relatively open place to set down.

A pang of grief struck her as she remembered his friendly face.

"You're right. I see a patch of snow," Kimball said in surprise.

"Yes. Um...worse comes to worst, we can immerse ourselves in the lake."

He gave her a sardonic look, for which she didn't blame him. How could they possibly stay under long enough if a full-blown forest fire roared along the shore?

They both watched as fire first crawled then leaped up the tree that had been impaled by the rotor. The crackles and hisses gave her chills. Burning branches plummeted to the ground. Within minutes, however, the flames fell back, having reached barely halfway up the massive trunk.

"Thank God," she murmured.

Kimball let out an audible breath. "Amen."

Seeing the possessive hand he kept on the pack, she nodded at it. "That yours?"

His gaze flicked to her patient, who had probably been watching the fire as well as he could, given his limited range of motion, but who was now watching them. Salazar hadn't said a single word to the DEA agent, she realized, but Kimball hadn't spoken a word to him, either. No matter how adversarial their relationship, that seemed…strange.

In response to her question, Kimball said gruffly, "Yeah. I was planning a short vacation once I delivered Salazar." He actually gave a twisted smile. "Ironically enough, I planned to backpack here in the park. I've never been to the Pacific Northwest before."

What was he going to do, take on the Wonderland Trail? Who knew they'd have an interest in common? She became suddenly and acutely aware of the aches and pains she'd acquired during that rough landing. *Focus*, she told herself.

"Do you have your cell phone? We should both check to see if we have service."

He went very still. "If?"

Had it never occurred to him that they might be entirely isolated in the middle of a wilderness? The pack did look awfully new. Maybe heading into the backcountry was a new hobby for him. Or maybe his hiking had been in regions where tall mountains didn't block phone and even radio service.

Gwen decided to be polite, informing him that cell phones didn't work in much of the park. "I wish I thought Bill had been able to let authorities know we were going down."

"He did." Now he sounded calm, albeit condescending. "Of course he did."

She'd heard chaos, maybe voices, but nothing she could pin down as responding radio traffic.

"Okay," she said slowly, wondering why she doubted his word. There was surely no question he was the law enforcement agent he'd introduced himself as; Bill and the dispatcher at base would have checked his badge, maybe even made calls to verify his credentials. "Then I guess we just settle in and wait."

She still dug to the bottom of her tote to find her phone. Something flashed in Kimball's eyes at the sight of it. Annoyance that she would still bother checking?

Didn't matter; she had no bars. Maybe a flicker when she turned slightly... No. She'd imagined it.

"This isn't the most comfortable spot," she said. "Let me scout around a little."

Kimball didn't offer to do it for her, but in fairness to him, she hadn't mentioned her suspicion that she had cracked a couple of ribs during the rough fall to earth. Maybe if she had, he'd be more chivalrous. Probably he was afraid Salazar would suddenly throw off the restraints and, despite being recently postsurgery, spring up to take her hostage for his escape.

Right now, her pain felt...distant. Unimportant. She recognized the effect of adrenaline and shock.

Thinking she saw what might be a small open meadow through a nearby cluster of evergreens, she walked toward it. She realized she'd wrapped one arm protectively over her torso, and she was bent forward slightly like an old lady. Rescue couldn't come soon enough for her. She'd just stepped into the trees when she glanced back at the continuing hiss and crackle of the dying fire and heated metal, and instead saw Kimball straddling Rafael Salazar, his hands seemingly around his neck.

She shouted and ran back, her breath wheezing. By the time she reached the two men, Kimball knelt at one side of his prisoner and said, "Thank God! I think he was having a seizure! I was trying to get something in his mouth for him to bite on."

A thick chunk of bark fell from his hand, making his

claim credible. But she also saw red prints on both sides of Salazar's neck.

She, too, fell to her knees and laid a hand on her patient's chest. "Mr. Salazar? Are you okay?"

His hands clenched into tight fists at his side. His deep voice had become impossibly gritty. "Now...that you're... here."

Was that a plea she saw in those dark eyes? Did he want her to stay beside him, as if she were his only protection?

"I think we should free him from the backboard," she said. "There's no indication he had a neck or back injury. It would help if he could walk when—"

"No," Kimball said flatly. "I need to keep him under as much restraint as possible." He glanced at the sky streaked with dark smoke. "I expect help will arrive in no time."

His note of smugness disturbed her, contributing to the tingle she recognized as fear. This...wasn't right.

She looked worriedly back at Salazar, seeing his jaw muscles flex. She knew, *knew*, that he wanted to tell her something.

"Well, I for one would like to stretch out on the grass instead of a rocky shore," she said, as lightly as she could manage. "Why don't *you* go check out that meadow beyond the trees? I'm better qualified to be here if Salazar seizes again. It wouldn't take you three minutes."

"Not happening."

Kimball's eyes were brown, too, she realized, but much lighter. Maybe hazel. She couldn't decide.

He knew a lot more about Rafael Salazar than she did— maybe the guy had committed heinous acts as a cartel enforcer, say—but if so, why hadn't he spoken quietly to her so she understood his wariness. As it was, she might not fully understand why she distrusted Agent Kimball, but she did.

It seemed smart not to confront him, so she shrugged. "Oh, fine. If you'll turn your back, I think I'll change clothes."

"Why?" He surveyed her. "What's wrong with that getup?"

"The fabric is designed to protect against fire, not from the cold, and it feels chilly here to me. It'll get colder as the sun lowers." Actually, the sun was high in the sky right now, but it sounded like a good excuse.

"I suppose so." Apparently, Kimball hadn't noticed the bite in the air. She hadn't, either, until she needed to make a production of rethinking her wardrobe.

She'd apparently been convincing, because he didn't pay any attention while she poked around in her overstuffed tote and dug out a small pile of clothes: a pair of jeans, a T-shirt and the thin fleece jacket she hadn't anticipated needing until they landed in Seattle.

Maybe he really was a gentleman, because he did raise his eyebrow and then ostentatiously turned his back to her. She didn't wait to see if Salazar turned his gaze away, too. Whatever he saw, she felt confident he'd keep to himself.

Still, with two strange men so near, she got dressed in stages as she peeled off the Nomex suit, glad to finally button her jeans and pull on the jacket over the only long-sleeve T-shirt she'd packed. She hoped neither man noticed when she bent over the bag as she laid the now neatly folded flight suit on top of her other possessions in the tote—and eased out the handgun, checked that it was loaded and tucked it into her waistband.

It wasn't comfortable to realize that at this point, she couldn't trust either man. What if no one came for them, and they needed to lean on each other to trek out of what might well be a part of the park lacking roads or trails? She didn't like Kimball, but it was entirely possible that Salazar was playing her with the goal of convincing her to free him.

She had to pretend to explore without taking her eyes off the two of them for more than a minute at a time.

WHEN HE SAW her walking away again, Rafe would have sworn viciously if he didn't have his mouth clamped shut. He'd felt a moment of hope when he saw Gwen handling his gun so competently, then hiding it on her person. Now it appeared that Kimball had convinced her to see him as a threat.

Rafe had no more had a seizure than he had the flu. The fingers wrapped around his throat would have crushed it in short order. The agency rarely had defectors, but Bruce Kimball had to be dirty. And if that was the case, Rafe knew exactly who was paying him.

Out of the corner of his eye, Rafe saw that the woman had disappeared in the trees that weren't more than twenty feet away. The moment she did, Kimball rose abruptly to his feet, looming above him. His teeth showed in a near snarl. "You've been luckier than you deserve so far, but luck always runs out."

"And you're going to see to it." Rafe would have given anything to be able to wrench a single hand free in case Kimball decided to make this up close and personal again.

No such luck. He pulled his gun and aimed it at Rafe's face.

"I'd feel bad if I liked you, but nobody likes glory hogs. Did you really think you were going to bring down the Espinosa family? Sorry, Salazar. They're smarter and more ruthless than you are."

"And you don't feel a single qualm about helping deliver fentanyl to American households in lethal quantities."

A nerve twitched in his cheek. "Maybe I do, but the Espinosas caught me in a bad moment, and now they expect my help when they need it. A man's got to make choices."

Rafe didn't bother asking what Kimball had been doing in that "bad moment." Why bother? Rafe knew he'd be dead any minute. His almost legendary luck had indeed run out. In one of those strange twists, what bothered him most was the certainty that Kimball intended to kill Gwen Allen, too. What else could he do? Unless he had some slick explanation up his sleeve?

Would she be smart enough to at least pretend to accept that excuse for having to shoot and kill a fully restrained man?

Kimball cast a glance toward the trees. Rafe couldn't even roll into that scumbag's legs in hopes of knocking him off balance thanks to the damn backboard and more secure fastenings than a prison guard could have managed.

"What are you doing?" Gwen called sharply.

Rafe's heart stopped at the same moment Kimball jerked and half turned toward her.

Rafe could barely see her stepping into sight. Chin up, hands at her sides, challenging a federal agent trained to kill under necessity. *Damn it, what was she thinking?*

He yelled, "Run!"

Kimball kicked him and turned his gun toward her.

"You're going to shoot me?" she asked, as if in disbelief.

"Yeah. Too bad." He shrugged. "You weren't supposed to be here, but you had to push."

Kimball was so damn arrogant that his stance was utterly relaxed. Why not? He expected his audience to be dead in the next minute or two. Rafe had never hated anyone so much before.

Kimball steadied the gun as if he had all the time in the world.

A shot rang out. Rafe waited for death to smash into his head, but instead he heard a second shot, then another, the *crack*, *crack*, *crack* obscene in this magnificent country.

Bruce Kimball took a step forward, tripped over Rafe and crashed to the ground as if a logger had felled a magnificent old-growth Douglas fir that made the earth shake when it died.

Stunned, Rafe saw Gwen running forward, a pistol gripped in both hands in firing position.

SHE'D WATCHED ENOUGH cop shows to know it was smart to kick Kimball's weapon a distance away. Then her eyes met Rafe's. "He didn't shoot you?" she asked breathlessly.

"Didn't have a chance."

"Oh, God." Her voice trembled as she looked back at the fallen man. "Do you think…? Is he dead?"

"Yeah," Rafe said hoarsely. "I saw his face when he went down. But…you better check."

Her teeth chattered as she edged closer, leaned over, the gun still in her right hand, and laid two fingers on Kimball's neck.

Then she stumbled back and collapsed onto her butt. "I killed him. I killed a man."

"He didn't give you any choice," Rafe said as gently as he could. "It was you or him."

"You, too," she whispered.

"Definitely me."

Given that she was a person accustomed to making quick decisions in critical situations, she felt weirdly…blank. "What do I do now?"

"Put the gun down," he suggested.

"Oh. Oh, yes." She fumbled to set it on the ground. "Is, um, this yours?"

"I assume so. My boss defied hospital rules and gave it back to me when I was in recovery at the hospital."

She hadn't taken her eyes off the dead man. She was going to see that face, waking and dreaming, for a long time. It wasn't that she hadn't failed to save patients; she'd seen plenty of dead men, women and even children at accident and even disaster sites. But this was different.

I shot and killed a man.

A shudder ran through her.

"Gwen?" Rafe's voice pulled her back to the moment. "We need to move. Can you free me?" he asked.

Still feeling dazed, she looked at him. "I don't understand any of this."

"I…have a good idea. He just filled in a few of the blanks."

"Will you tell me?"

A bald eagle soared far above. With the vast wingspan and bright white head, it was unmistakable. They were common in the Pacific Northwest but always magnificent. She fixated on it, soaring free, because…she didn't want to focus on what had happened.

His voice and words pulled her back. "Yeah," he said. "If it's any consolation, he might have regretted having to kill you."

"Consolation?" she said incredulously. "He didn't sound all that regretful to me. In his worldview, it's my fault that I'm here." She shook her head. "He didn't want me on board. What I don't understand is why Bill—he was the pilot— had apparently agreed to the flight with an injured man and no medical personnel on board. I wanted to think he didn't know what he was doing."

"I'm guessing he didn't, not entirely."

"But…he must have agreed to this…detour." She waved a hand toward the mountain she could no longer see but knew still towered behind rock buttresses and thick ever-green trees.

"Figured pocketing a little money wasn't so bad. No-body hurt by it."

Her laugh hurt. She curled forward into a tight ball, arms wrapped around her knees.

"He didn't get you, did he?" Rafe sounded alarmed. "I don't see any blood—"

"No. No. I think I suffered some damage during the crash. Like a cracked rib or two."

Which hurt like hell.

She rested her head on her crossed arms and studied him before asking baldly, "Can I trust you?"

Chapter Four

Was she really so naive, she didn't realize how effortlessly he could lie to her? Rafe wondered. It was one of his specialties.

But here and now...he wouldn't. His natural protective side had kicked in anyway, but above and beyond that, this woman had saved his life at least twice already. He owed her. He'd do anything to get her out of this mess alive and well. "You've gotten involved in something worse than you know. Yes, you can trust me. I'm a DEA agent. I don't have my badge or wallet on me—"

"I...think I might have them." She pushed herself to her feet and circled wide around the body to reach that bulging tote bag. After rooting around in it, she produced a white plastic bag with a string closure that he recalled from previous hospitalizations. All that she removed from it was a wallet and a simple billfold. She opened that and had to be looking at his badge.

Finally she lifted her head again. "Now I *really* don't understand."

Even frantic to be released from the restraints, he understood her doubts. "I've been undercover for the past year. I'd gathered enough information to justify warrants and a cascade of arrests. I was put in a safe house in Yakima to wait for the trial, which could be a year or more away. I expected nothing but excruciating boredom. Somehow, we were betrayed. One of my guards knew the man he opened the door for. I didn't see him. I'm guessing he and the second agent who was there for security are dead. I don't know, except if either had survived, they'd have ID'd the shooter. I crashed out a window, heard sirens as I lost consciousness. The cracked sternum and broken ribs? That's what happens when you're wearing a Kevlar vest and are shot. You survive, but you aren't always happy about it."

"Oh, no," she whispered.

"Next thing I knew, I was in recovery after surgery at the hospital. Like I said, my boss gave me back my gun, badge and wallet, but they must have cut my clothes off. He said some things I didn't comprehend. After that, I was on the helicopter."

"Were you working with Agent Kimball? Or...*was* he an agent?"

"Unfortunately, yes, but based in Chicago. We were in the same office a few years back—Miami, I think—but I've never worked directly with him. I got a real bad feeling when I heard you say his name."

"You think he's the one your guard recognized."

"Makes sense."

He knew she was having trouble taking all these details in, but he worried about how much time this complicated explanation had eaten up.

"We need to get moving." He had an itch he never ignored, but he hadn't gotten through to her yet. "We're not safe sticking close to the helicopter. I think the pilot was supposed to land somewhere near here, drop Kimball and me off, and fly back. Not sure how he'd have explained that—"

She shook her head. "He was supposed to be flying an empty helicopter to Seattle to be loaned to the base I work out of. We're a lot busier than the team in Yakima, and we have a helicopter that needs serious maintenance. He could have dropped it off as planned, nobody the wiser."

Understanding dawned. "Until you got in the mix."

She explained jumping at the chance for a free ride to Seattle. "Except...there you were."

"I hate to hurry this, but I can't help wondering whether he was expecting a pickup."

"He might have planned to shoot you and then hike out. He did bring the backpack."

"Maybe, but his extracurricular employer might have wanted to see proof that the problem I represented was actually handled."

"We are really exposed." The whites of her eyes showed as her head turned. "We can't be exactly where Bill intended to set down. I mean, this isn't an ideal landing zone, but..."

Rafe followed her gaze to the dark smoke painting an obvious signal in the now mostly blue sky.

He couldn't tell if he'd convinced her at last or if pure instinct had her scooting toward him, her hands reaching for fastenings. Even the anticipation of being freed was almost more than he could stand. This involuntary immobility felt like being buried alive would, or maybe being mummified if you hadn't died yet. Rafe wasn't sure he'd ever be able to lie on his back again, bed covers tucked snugly around him, without feeling the kind of phantom pains amputees did in the missing limb.

Just being able to turn his head was an exquisite relief.

To move his shoulders. As she worked her way down, to lift his arms, which promptly cramped.

When he lunged to a sitting position, Gwen fell back, fear on her face.

GWEN SCUTTLED BACK a few feet on the cold ground.

Salazar lifted a hand. "I didn't mean to scare you! I'm sorry. I was just…desperate to move."

She saw only sincerity on his face. The face, she realized even through her fear, that was model handsome, complete with hollows beneath high, sharp cheekbones, a straight, bold nose and a strong jaw darkened by the beginnings of beard growth. It was too bad her willingness to believe and trust was at a low ebb.

Uh-huh, an inner voice commented. *Didn't you already make a decision?*

When she turned her head, her gaze fixing unerringly on the man lying face down on the gravelly lakeshore. Dead. Because *she'd* shot and killed him.

Her stomach turned queasily.

What if she'd made a terrible mistake?

He'd admitted he intended to kill her. *You weren't supposed to be here, but you had to push.*

Even so, all she knew was that she'd gotten in the middle of something ugly and maybe convoluted. There might not be a bad guy and a good guy. What if *both* guys were bad?

But Rafael Salazar was still her patient. He'd done or said nothing to rouse her suspicions. She certainly couldn't leave him here to wait for a helicopter sent to pick up Agent Kimball, who had definitely intended to kill him.

She let out a breath and wondered how long she'd been holding it. She felt light-headed. "No, I'm sorry. After everything that's happened, I guess I scare easily."

To her dismay, his smile made him even more hand-some. "Understandable. Uh... I think I can get the rest of these straps."

"No, I'll do it." She scooted closer again, then made quick work of freeing him. As he swiveled so that his lower legs lay stretched over the ground, she asked, "How do you feel?"

"Like I've been shot a few times, but I think I can walk."

After what she'd read in his chart, she thought he'd do well to shuffle. Even that would have been impossible if the bullet had struck a little higher and damaged his hip.

Before she could open her mouth, he said, "Except..." He waved at his feet, covered only by hospital socks.

"Oh, no! There weren't any shoes or boots in that bag. At least one of them might have gotten soaked in blood."

He grimaced. "That's...likely. I hate to ask you to rob from the dead, but will you bring me one of Kimball's boots to see if it would fit me?"

Cold—dead?—fingers tripped down her spine, but *practical* probably topped her list of personal qualities. She could do this. She half crawled the short distance, constantly aware of the heat from the helicopter, and studied the boots while trying not to see the rest of the body. No ties, like her hiking boots. These were what were usually called tactical boots. Good sole but flexible, and easy to slide in and out of. She'd seen plenty of cops wearing them. She pulled both off and carried them to Salazar, who said, "These can't be too far off my size."

After shoving his foot into the first, he said, "They're a little too big. If he has extra socks in that pack, the boots should be fine. Some borrowed clothes would be good, too."

Yes, if they had to go on the run in the high mountain wilderness, he'd do better if he wasn't wearing only thin scrubs. She gave thought to whoever had brought his gun and wallet. He couldn't have picked up a change of clothes while he was at it?

She realized she was straining for the distant sound of helicopter rotors. "We should hurry. We can get better organized once we're tucked away."

"You're right." He shoved his other foot in the boot and slowly, torturously got to his feet.

Gwen rose with him and discovered her arms were out to catch him if he fell. Astonishingly, he didn't, although he swayed initially. She'd guessed he was tall, but at six foot two or three, minimum, he towered over her.

"What do we need to take?" he asked in a rougher voice.

Still half expecting him to go down, she stayed close as she scanned their few possessions.

"Pack, this bag—let me see if I can tie it onto the pack." She suited action to words, securing the trauma bag so she wouldn't have to carry it separately. She looked around. "My tote, your gun—" Which she no longer held, she realized with a tiny burst of panic. No, there it was. She'd set it down after Salazar told her to.

"Kimball's gun, too." He sounded all cop now, no human emotions allowed. "I hope he has clothes in the pack, because I don't think we dare take time to strip him."

"Yes. Okay." Even out of the corner of her eye, she saw that both of Kimball's shirts were bloody. She hurried to pick up both guns, tucking one back in her waistband, putting the other at the top of the tote before she positioned the handles over a shoulder and then hefted the pack onto her back. The weight was reassuring, suggesting that it held both clothes and food.

Unless it was really full of bomb makings or who knew what?

Nice thought.

When Salazar reached out as if he intended to take the tote from her, she stepped away. "Do you go by Rafael?"

"Usually Rafe. I can carry—"

"No, you can't. In fact, you'd better lean on me."

She saw the internal war play out in his dark eyes, but finally he dipped his head.

"I'll keep a hand on your shoulder until I can be sure I'm steady on my feet."

"Good." Gwen didn't even ask which way he thought they ought to go. The sun was too high in the sky to provide any idea of east, west, north or south. A ridge steeper than she thought they could handle rose beyond the lake. Running parallel to it, another ridge, both rocky and treed, put them in...not quite a valley. It wasn't wide enough for that. It was a V. She could see why Bill had seen this as the only option for an LZ.

She wasn't enthusiastic about passing the helicopter because of the heat, and she didn't want to look at the blackened remnants that included a man's body. That left the opposite direction.

She stopped in the act of turning. Even sickened, she had to say this. "What if we put Kimball's body in the helicopter? Or...or right beside it? Would that fool someone into thinking everyone had died in the crash?"

"They probably don't know about you." The man beside her sounded unnervingly thoughtful, but after a moment he shook his head. "I don't think we could pull it off. Not with the gunshot wounds. Anyway, the metal is too hot for us to get near, and even if we were able to put the backboard in, there should be blackened bones. Fire doesn't entirely burn up a body, you know."

She sort of did, since she had a box filled with what was left of her grandmother at home. Even a crematorium, which was *trying* to burn what was left of a human body, couldn't completely succeed.

Grateful that Rafe hadn't jumped on her macabre idea, she felt weak for a minute but hoped he didn't notice.

Still careful not to look at the body sprawled only a few feet away, she led Rafe past it in retracing her earlier path. They needed to find somewhere to hide soon, preferably near enough they could see if a rescue helicopter appeared, and to give Rafe a chance to get into warmer clothes, if there were any, and for her to give him a pain shot.

Once she was back on the job, she was going to have some explaining to do about the quantity of narcotics she'd appropriated without a plan or a coworker to sign off on them. Rules were strict where handling them was concerned.

They were almost to the first line of trees. She looked up to see only grim determination on Rafe's face—and stiff, careful placement of each foot that told her how much pain he had to be suppressing.

Once they reached the trees, Gwen allowed herself a glance over her shoulder. She could no longer see the remains of the helicopter well from here, only the body and the backboard as well as…some litter, she guessed, not sure what it was. She hoped they hadn't left anything important lying around.

If nobody showed up in the next hour or two, she could maybe go back and look more carefully. Also, to strip the man she'd shot of any clothes that didn't have bullet holes in them and weren't stained with blood.

That would be a very last resort, she reassured herself, and felt comforted by the thick cover the copse of feathery evergreen trees provided.

HE'D DO THIS *because he had to*, Rafe thought grimly, but at the moment, he had no idea how. When Gwen had freed him from the restraints, he'd had a burst of euphoria that made him unrealistically optimistic. Now, agony struck with every step, and the pain when he tried to take in a deep breath didn't help. He became aware that he wouldn't have been able to breathe deeply, anyway. His torso was wrapped tightly. Cracked sternum, he reminded himself. Broken ribs. Without the wrap, he'd probably fall to his knees screaming.

He took the next step, only then realizing how tightly he was gripping Gwen's shoulder. As slender as she was, she hadn't so much as flinched, but he was probably bruising her. He loosened his fingers.

"Sorry."

"Hold on as hard as you have to. It'll be worse if you go down."

In so many ways. He squeezed his eyes shut for a minute, picturing what it would feel like to crash to the rocky, uneven ground.

He moved his right leg forward. That was slightly easier, which meant… Left leg. He hoped that was a grunt rather than a groan that came out of his mouth.

"I'm taking us up this side of the ridge, where it isn't too steep," she said, the stress in her voice telling him she knew what he was going through. "I'm hoping it'll seem… unlikely."

This grunt was meant to be agreement. She seemed to take it as such, because the next bit was a struggle. She wedged herself under his good arm, at points getting behind him and pushing.

Rafe's eyes burned from sweat. The too-large boots rubbed and would eventually cause blisters if they kept moving, but he didn't think he'd be able to keep going very long at all.

Yet somehow he did. The strong woman beside him led and supported and sometimes bore almost all his weight, which had to be sixty, eighty pounds more than her finer-boned frame carried. *Conditioning*, he told himself. She must frequently lift one end of a backboard that carried someone a lot larger than him and carry it a distance to the helicopter. He'd be dead if it weren't for her. Again.

Eventually she said, "Let's take a break," and she guided him to a boulder that had a reasonably flat top. Bending to sit was almost worse than walking, but once his butt was supported, he let his head fall forward, closed his eyes and did nothing but breathe through his pain.

She watched him anxiously—he knew she was—but didn't say a word. No perky "You're doing great!" Or "Not that much farther!" which would have been a lie.

What she finally did say was, "I'm going to give you a shot of narcotics."

Real narcotics? Had he misheard?

She went on, "I should have done it sooner, but I have to calculate dose and—"

They hadn't dared sit around.

With a definite groan, he straightened his upper body. "You thought to grab pain meds from a helicopter that was going to blow up any second."

"Last thing I did," she admitted as she rooted in her voluminous tote. "In the helicopter, I intended to ask you about your pain level when I saw the mountain and realized we were so far off course. And… I guess I knew subliminally that we weren't going to be rescued in the next half hour. If you had to move at all, you'd need the good stuff."

He raised his eyebrows.

"Morphine." She asked for his weight and calculated a dose. As he watched, she progressed to drawing a clear liquid from a bottle into a syringe.

Rafe didn't say anything, not wanting to distract her.

"I'm thinking… I won't give you as much as you might

get in one dose if you were lounging in a hospital bed. I don't dare take the chance of knocking you out. So you're going to keep hurting." She made a moue of distress.

"But able to stay on my feet. That's a good decision. Besides—" he eyed the syringe "—I don't want to get addicted."

"No. I have Tylenol in my bag, but that wouldn't help you much for at least a few days."

He only nodded. "Do you want my hip?"

"Well…yes."

He fumbled with the string around the waist, pulled the thin pants down and turned sideways, rolling onto his opposite hip.

The jab came without any warning. The relief that almost immediately rolled through him had him groaning again, his muscles going slack.

"Better?"

"You're an angel of mercy."

She chuckled as she tugged the pants back up but let him tie them at the waist. He felt good enough at this first glorious moment, he wouldn't have minded her fingers playing down there.

Damn. Was he grinning like a fool?

She capped the syringe and replaced it and the bottle in her tote bag. "I think we'd better have a snack. I have some water that's probably warm. We'll undoubtedly come across streams where we can refill the bottle."

What she put in his hand was a Payday candy bar. He ripped it open and took a bite. Salted peanuts and caramel. Did life get any better?

She had chosen an Almond Joy, and both ate in contented silence, taking sips in turn from her water bottle.

Rafe drew in a deep breath without the hit of pain. The

air was so clean; it tasted and smelled of evergreens and something more ephemeral. There were sounds: the rustle of branches high above in a faint breeze, what might be the ripple of water, a birdcall answered by another, but the immensity of the sky and the stunning beauty of the vista around them had the impact of an ancient cathedral.

"I've never been to the Northwest." He grimaced. "Except Yakima, and I barely looked out a window."

"Eastern Washington is spectacular in its own way. The Columbia River Gorge, with crumbling red basalt rim rocks, is magnificent. But the Cascade Range has the most beautiful country in the US, at least."

"I can't argue," he said, taking pleasure in the moment.

Until she stirred. "We haven't come that far. I think we should keep moving, if you're up to it."

What could he say but "Yeah" and let her help him to his feet?

Chapter Five

Before they started out, Gwen did her best to orient herself by pinpointing the base of the column of smoke. It was dismaying to see what a short distance she and Rafe had covered. Not surprising when his every stride had been torturously slow.

Unfortunately, they hadn't crash-landed among old-growth forest, where centuries-old woodland giants would have hidden them well. Plus, that would have given her a better idea of where they were. The trees here were on the small side and seemed to grow in clumps that left quite a bit of open rocky ground and small meadows bright with wildflowers in between. She'd hoped that, in climbing, they'd find something like an overhang that would at least shield them from above.

"How are you?" she asked.

On his feet, Rafe rolled his good shoulder in self-assessment and said, "Better."

Unfortunately, Gwen's rib cage was not feeling better. Maybe she should have given herself some narcotic relief, too, but that would have fuzzed her thinking and would also, as a decision, be hard to defend when she sat down with her supervisor. If worse came to worst—well, she'd think about it then.

Turning her head, she spotted what appeared to be a cliff with tumbled boulders beneath it. That could be a dead end—or give them a place to hide. So she steered Rafe that way.

Apparently, this was her day for denial, because she kept blocking thoughts about everything from her initial decision to get on that cursed helicopter despite her sensible doubts to the crash, the explosion, the—nope. Especially not going there.

Look where you're putting your feet, she instructed herself. *Keep an eye on Rafe's tense face and be aware of his body language. Listen for the distinctive sound of another helicopter. Stay in the moment.*

Everything else could wait for later, including her inconvenient sexual awareness.

Twice she had to detour around crunchy-topped, gleaming white snow fields to be sure they didn't have a clear line of footprints. If he noticed the long ways around, it wasn't apparent.

He was able to reach with one hand for branches to pull himself up a few feet, taking some of his weight off her shoulders. That was an improvement. Still, she had a feeling his thoughts weren't trying to scatter like a covey of quails the way hers were, but rather were grimly focused on the next moment. Maybe on-the-job experience had taught him an intense focus. Either way, she'd bet he was thinking about nothing but the next step.

Except then he spoke up in a gritty voice, surprising her.

"Do you know where we are in the park? I assume we *are* in the national park?"

"I think we're still in the park. We were awfully close to the mountain not that long before things went wrong. As for where…only sort of. I mean, the glimpse I had was out the left window, which would put us on the east side, except we could have been curving around the north side, depending on where Bill and Kimball had agreed to set down. Also, I have no idea how much time passed or how far we traveled after Bill claimed the alarm had gone off. And, well, the sun isn't any help yet."

"Hard to set a route, then."

Matter-of-fact, but with a growly undertone that spoke of pain.

"Unfortunately, yes. Depending on where we came down, we could be near a heavily used trail or even an entrance to the park." She hated to say this. "We could also be miles from help."

"Kimball wouldn't have wanted anyone to see the helicopter set down."

Yes, he was right. Had he and Bill plotted an especially remote part of the park?

Except…logic said if Kimball had intended to walk away with that pack on his back, he'd have planned for the original LZ to be within a reasonable distance of a trail. She didn't point that out. Speculation wouldn't get them very far.

Rafe didn't say any more for a long time. She didn't blame him, given that they were scrambling more than walking at the moment.

During a brief break to catch their breath, she decided a little optimism might help. "Once we look through the pack and see what resources we have, we might be better able to make an educated choice for our next move."

Surely this grunt wasn't meant to dismiss her near perkiness but was just the best he could do at the moment.

It felt as if they'd been on their way for an hour or more, but she suspected the time was a lot shorter than that. She saw what she'd been looking for, though—a boulder leaning against another that created something close to a shallow cave beneath. Soil and small pebbles made a nearly flat spot.

"This way," she said.

She nudged. He changed his path. When they arrived and she stopped him with a hand on his arm, he stared straight ahead like a robot that had been shut down.

Gwen dropped the tote and lowered the backpack to the ground, wishing it wasn't bright red, then touched Rafe's arm. "Let's sit down."

She could tell what an effort it took him to turn his head and assess their surroundings, but he nodded finally and said, "Good."

He didn't argue when she knelt, put his hand on her shoulder and said, "Slow and easy."

The last part of his descent was more of a fall, but he landed safely on his butt, leaned his head against the gritty rock to one side and exhaled a breath slowly.

Studying him worriedly, she touched his forehead. Was it too warm, or was her hand cold? She pressed it to her own cheek and couldn't tell. Knowing wouldn't help since the best she could do if he had a fever was Tylenol.

Well, she could look under his dressings for signs of infection, but she had no antibiotics to give him and, at the moment, didn't even have any more water for him to swallow a pill.

"Still no helicopter," he said hoarsely. "Maybe you were right."

"About the hiking-out thing?"

"Yeah."

Gwen told him her earlier thoughts.

"Too close to a trail, he'd have risked witnesses," he commented.

She nodded. "No matter what, I may have chosen the wrong direction."

"No." His big hand caught hers. "Smart."

"Okay." She closed her eyes and tipped her head sideways to rest on his shoulder. Her body felt compressed, even her bones scrunched. She'd carried too much weight, but now they could rest. There was no reason they couldn't stay here for a while. Maybe even overnight. They both might feel better tomorrow.

She gave herself what had to be five minutes before she straightened.

"Cross your fingers. Let's find you something better to wear."

He did cross his fingers, and she pulled a laugh out of somewhere.

She unfastened Velcro and explored. Rafe was bent over the pack as eagerly as she was.

RAFE WAS INCREDIBLY grateful when they found a couple changes of clothes in the pack, as well as three pairs of socks. He removed the boots and showed Gwen the red places on his feet close to forming blisters.

"Try two pairs of socks when we move on," she decided. "I wish we had some moleskin, but if you're still uncomfortable, I can figure out something else to cut up to protect those places."

Even one pair of socks warmed his feet. The fact that she knelt in front of him to put them on felt…good.

Apparently, Kimball really had intended to backpack, whether here at Rainier or elsewhere, because the pack disgorged a small stove with an extra fuel canister, a number of freeze-dried meals, purifying tablets for water, bags of dried fruit and nuts, and energy bars.

"This will keep us for a while," Gwen said with satisfaction. "I have some energy bars in my bag—I never go anywhere without any—and more candy bars."

"Sweet tooth?"

Her smile lit her face. "I'm not shy about admitting it. You?"

"I'd say no, except that Payday really hit the spot."

She chuckled, dug some more and laid out a miscellany of things: a lighter and matches, a folding knife with additional tools, a tarp and cord that could be used to rig a cover in case of rain, a compact pair of binoculars and a couple of magazines for Kimball's handgun.

"Did he know guns are banned in the park?"

Rafe raised an eyebrow at her, and she blanched. Frowning, he laid his hand on her arm. "I didn't mean it like that."

Suddenly, she started to shake. "I never thought I'd kill anybody."

She'd been so tough, he'd forgotten how disturbing today's events must have been for her. "You shot him in self-defense." He hoped his voice conveyed comfort. "Do you regret that choice?"

"No. No. It's just—" face pinched, Gwen hugged herself "—I couldn't let him kill us, but… I chose my profession to save lives," she said finally.

"I can see that." Damn. He wanted to put his arm around her but wasn't sure how she'd take that. "Gwen, look at me."

She did. In fact, she searched his eyes in a way that shook him, as if she saw deep into his darkest memories, the ones that turned up in an occasional nightmare.

"You did save my life," he reminded her. "Remember that. Isn't that your job?"

Her forehead creased as she visibly tried to reconcile the two concepts. "I just…never thought…"

"Why did you become a paramedic?"

"I became a nurse and then wanted to do more. I've always... I guess you could say I enjoy adrenaline. I mean, I don't do extreme sports or anything like that—"

"I'm relieved to hear it," he said dryly.

"But my rotation in the ER made other kinds of nursing seem dull. I got certified as an EMT and worked on an ambulance for a while, went back to the ER, then studied to become a paramedic."

"You still haven't said why. Were either of your parents in the medical field?"

She went so still that he suspected she'd quit breathing. He'd unwittingly touched on a sore place. Was this something she didn't talk about?

"Rafe," she said suddenly, her hand shooting out to grip his forearm hard. "Do you hear that?"

He did. Only his attention on her had kept him from noticing the distant sound of a plane flying low or a helicopter.

They both knew which it would be.

"Gun," he said, and she dug quickly in her tote and produced Kimball's Glock, the same model as his. Not surprising, since agents were encouraged to carry one of a couple of Glocks. Even with the pain in his shoulder, Rafe did a quick check to be sure it was ready to fire.

She produced the binoculars, too. Smart thinking. "Maybe...maybe somebody spotted the smoke, and it'll be a rescue helicopter."

She was whispering for no logical reason, but he understood why.

He took the binoculars, lifting them to his eyes and adjusting them until the vicinity of the crash, visible from here only by the smoke, snapped into sharp focus.

"There," Gwen said.

He saw it, too.

What emergency flight helicopters he'd seen were clearly

marked. Big numbers on the tail, logo of the organization operating it on the side, paint job white or a bright color. The goal was to be visible. This one was black with a white stripe. Law enforcement? But even when it got close enough and he could examine it carefully, he saw no logo, and the FAA required numbers on the tail were present but small enough he couldn't quite make them out.

He handed the binoculars to Gwen and let her study it. She worked in the area and must see helicopters belonging to any number of emergency responders, sightseers, and search and rescue groups.

She shook her head. "It has to be private."

They watched it drop low and circle the crash site. Even from this distance, the noise was near deafening. It appeared to settle on the ground for what had to be five minutes. Undoubtedly, someone had gotten out to identify the dead man and try to figure out what had happened. Then it rose again, tipping to one side to curve into the beginning of a circle as if it were turning back the way it had come. Except it flew in a complete circle, then another, each enlarged.

"Search grid," he murmured. "They know at least one person is missing."

Her fingers bit into his arm.

"Let's pull back under cover as much as we can manage," he added, grateful when she didn't argue. In fact, she used her head and pushed the too-bright red pack to the very back of their V-shaped hideout, poking her flower-print tote bag after it. Finally, he and she shuffled backward until they were crouched, Rafe holding the gun in his right hand but propping that arm up with his stronger left hand.

The helicopter got louder. It passed frighteningly close to them. Rafe didn't try to use the binoculars, afraid a flash of light off a lens would give away their location. It didn't slow, though, only continued in another wide circle, this time passing above and behind them.

Finally, they could no longer see it or, after a few more minutes, hear it.

Gwen whimpered. "That was—"

"Scary as hell," he agreed.

She'd been the one shaking earlier, but he felt a tremor in his own hands now. In one way, he'd expected this. In another, he hadn't understood how difficult escape would be with him in such bad shape and with them having absolutely no idea which direction to go to find even an occasionally traveled trail. And there had to be *some* roads in the park, too, didn't there?

"Do you...think it'll come back?"

Rafe mulled over how to answer. Clearly, the enforcement arm of the traffickers had landed, seen the dead DEA agent they'd suborned and been forced to assume that Rafe had overpowered Kimball, shot him and gone on the run. They had no way to know he had help. They might wonder if he'd been injured as badly in the first place as they had been led to believe.

Problem with that was, they'd set up a pretty elaborate operation with only one goal: killing Rafe, the federal agent who'd fooled them well enough to gather information on their operations to bring down significant parts of their organization. Their goal was to keep him from ever testifying. A judge and jury needed him there in front of them to verify and elaborate on the evidence he'd collected. What the men who'd been given the job of getting rid of him had found was the body of their dirty agent. The scene suggested Rafe was still alive and therefore a threat to some higher-ups in the cartel.

How could they go back to the bosses and admit he'd

gotten away? That kind of major screwup wouldn't be accepted with any understanding.

"I wish you'd never gotten involved in this," Rafe told Gwen honestly, "but I wouldn't have a chance without you."

"So, that's a yes," she said slowly.

He had to think back to her original question and nodded. "My best guess is that they hadn't come prepared to drop any men to hunt for me. I think the pilot has gone back to pick up some armed trackers."

"I thought we could spend the night here." She sounded sad.

Seeing her exhaustion and stress and shock, Rafe wished he could spare her. "We're too near the crash site," he said bluntly. "We need to get as far away as we can before they come back."

She wrinkled her nose at him, straightened her shoulders and said with determination, "Then let's not waste any time."

He couldn't possibly have gotten any luckier in a partner, Rafe thought again, then hoped she didn't see his wince.

Rafe wasn't much for introspection. He planned, he stayed fit in preparation for whatever would be thrown at him, he relied on his lightning-fast reaction time and, yeah, he knew one of his strengths was the subconscious calculations that he called gut feelings.

He compartmentalized, too, as most people in his line of work probably did. Had to shut bad experiences, tragedy, ugly scenes away. For the first time, it struck him that the consequence might be self-centeredness. He thought of himself as a compassionate man; he'd give his life for that of an innocent, no hesitation. But day to day...he calculated in terms of how events and people would help or hinder *him* on the job.

That's what he'd just done. Gwen Allen was a gutsy woman who improved his chances of escaping this disaster and making it to court to bring down a lot of bad guys.

But what would the fallout be for *her*—assuming both of them in fact survived? Keeping her alive had been a high priority for him, but was that enough?

Chapter Six

Gwen had set aside a map of Mount Rainier National Park found among Kimball's belongings. After laying out a change of clothes for Rafe, she said, "Let me know if you need me," and then turned her back to give him privacy to strip and get dressed. Over her shoulder, she added, "Oh! Or if you see any blood on your dressings."

While he was changing only a few feet away, she completely unfolded the map to scrutinize it. No, she wasn't delusional enough to think Kimball would have marked a big red X at the rendezvous point, although people did do things like that, didn't they? After all, he had no reason to believe anyone but him would get their hands on the map.

It wasn't completely pristine; there was enough wear and tear that she could tell the map had been opened a few times, and whoever had done it—Kimball—had struggled to refold it correctly so that it didn't tear or end up a wadded mess.

Rustles and scrapes came from behind her. Rafe's arm brushed against her. Gwen winced at some pained sounds, even as she pictured his powerful body unclothed. She'd seen enough of his muscles to know there had to be a lot more of them. She wanted to slap herself for even thinking like that. He was still her patient! She'd taken care of well-built guys before and not felt even an instant of attraction.

She let out a breath. Surely he'd let her help pull the shirt over his injured arm and shoulder.

Quit thinking about him seminaked, she ordered herself, bending to search the map.

Unfortunately, there were no helpful ink or pencil circles, Xs or margin notes to grab her attention. What was spread in front of her was just a topographical map published by National Geographic identical to one she owned, beautifully detailed, but not giving her a clue where their helicopter had come down. If only she had caught a better glimpse of the mountain before the clouds closed in!

She frowned. Since they'd gone on the run, she should have paid more attention to the foliage, the trees in particular. Pines were more common on the dryer east side, for example. Thinking about it now, she didn't remember noticing one, although her attention had been split too many ways.

She could identify different elevation zones because some species or types of trees lived only at lower elevations while others only appeared higher up. At the moment, she didn't believe they were at the subalpine elevation of 4,500 feet above sea level or higher, but they might not be much below that. In fact...

"Where are you from?" she asked Rafe.

There was a startled silence behind her. "We're going to exchange background info right now?"

She rolled her eyes. "No, I'm thinking about elevation. I've been puffing and panting more than usual, thinking my exercise regime doesn't cut it, but it's occurred to me that we might be at a high enough elevation that it would be normal for us to find it harder to breathe. Unless you're from somewhere like Denver..."

"No. I grew up in Southern California, and with the DEA, I've been transferred several times, but Miami, Houston and

San Diego are essentially at sea level. Probably Chicago, too. Damn. This means there's another reason we're moving so damned slow."

"Afraid so."

Too bad their current elevation didn't help in identifying their location.

She leaned over the map again. The distinctively parallel ridges rising to each side of that narrow valley had worried her. She shouldn't generalize from them—her view had been pretty limited—but there were a number of places in the park where the land folded that way. A lot of those areas tended to be devoid of roads or trails because the terrain was so difficult.

Rafe said grittily, "I could use a hand."

He'd managed to pull on the heavy-duty cargo pants but had gotten stuck halfway taking off the surgical scrub top.

"Oh, no!"

He was so tangled that she grabbed the pocket knife and cut it off him. It wasn't anything he'd want to wear again, anyway. Of course a wide, white wrap supported his ribs. Somehow, she hadn't been picturing it. Rafe had a beautifully muscular chest with warm copper-brown skin and a dark dusting of hair, and powerful arms and broad shoulders. It was even better than she'd imagined. She wanted to touch him, but the lack of fresh blood on the dressing around his upper arm and over his shoulder meant she didn't have an excuse.

Considering they were on the run for their lives and he was seriously injured, what was she *thinking*?

"Um, let's see." She picked up the T-shirt like she'd never seen one before, finally deciding to slip it over the arm on his bad side, then maneuver to get his head and other arm in it. She gently pulled it down, reluctant to hide that lovely male body, but reached for the Polartec fleece quarter-zip.

Only when he was fully dressed did she let herself meet his eyes. If there was a knowing glint in them, she wasn't acknowledging it.

"Boots," she declared, and helped him put them on.

He stamped each foot, then sighed. "Anything on the map?"

"Sad to say, no X marks the spot."

He leaned closer, and she pointed out some remote areas with the kind of ridges—or were they really mountains?—that might fit. There was a large area west of the Chinook Scenic Byway, for example, in which no roads or trails were displayed. From there, it wouldn't be that many miles to the highway—if they could get there at all. And they'd have to head east instead of the generally westward route she'd chosen. Those folds were more than ridges, she saw; they were definitely mountains over six thousand feet in elevation, many named.

The Chenius Mountain area, too, was devoid of trails. But really, by its very nature, the land surrounding a volcano this size consisted of pleats of land formed in some cases by glaciers, or at least the runoff of melting ice and snow. In other words, she had no more idea where they were than she'd had before she opened the map.

Rafe's dark gaze rested on her as she folded the map and put it away. She wasn't sure she wanted to know what he was thinking. Surely they'd eventually come upon a view of the mountain that would offer her guidance, but that was no help right now.

Look for the fastest path, she told herself, the one that would let them open up some distance, but still have thick groves of trees or rocky ground that might offer an overhang or the like to hide them. They'd have to avoid being in the open as much as they could, she realized; flower-strewn meadows made for more pleasant walking but were danger-ous for them. Searchers might be on foot, but when the heli-copter reappeared, it could hunt them from the air again, too.

"I guess right now, we just need to cover as much ground as we can while never being far from someplace we can duck to get out of sight."

"I agree," he said. "Except it would be ideal if we had a sight line when that helicopter comes back."

More reason to go up rather than scrambling along the side of the ridge. She could only hope it didn't get too steep.

Somehow he shoved himself to his feet, his good shoul-der braced against the side of a boulder to give him support.

Relieved he hadn't asked for another shot of morphine, Gwen loaded herself down again even as she realized she had no idea how to determine intervals between shots. She didn't wear a watch, although she might rethink that after this adventure.

One more thing she'd have to guess at.

Those dark eyes raked her. "Do you have any idea how much I hate seeing you loaded down like a pack animal while I'm strolling along empty-handed?"

"*I* don't have two gunshot wounds," she pointed out tartly. "I carry this much weight when I'm backpacking, which I do for *fun*, and regularly for short periods on the job."

He grunted, his favorite sound.

She laughed at him and saw the beginnings of a reluc-tant, sexy grin.

"I think…this way." She pointed.

MAYBE HALF AN hour along, Rafe's feet balked. Since the rest of him was in agreement, he managed to grind out, "Break."

"What?" Gwen turned, saw the expression on his face and looked around. "If it's not too rotten, we can sit on that fallen tree."

He plodded that far, sinking down with enormous relief. She followed suit and moaned.

After a minute, he became aware she was watching him sidelong.

"Something on your mind?" he asked.

"I keep remembering. You know?"

He did, but that was part of the difference between them. He sought answers that might be of use; she might be stuck on the two deaths they'd walked away from. He had no idea whether he should discourage that or encourage her to talk it out.

He settled for making an inquiring sound.

"Back in the helicopter," she said in a rush, "I heard something strange just before it started spinning. What if we crashed because Kimball knocked Bill unconscious or even killed him *before* we landed?"

Although Rafe hadn't thought about it, that seemed entirely possible to him. At some point Kimball would have realized that Gwen's inclusion meant Bill couldn't live, either.

"What would make him think *he* could land a helicopter?" she begged.

He hated seeing the turmoil in those beautiful eyes. "DEA agents aren't like Navy SEALs," he explained, "who claim to be able to operate anything from a submarine to a NASA rocket." The couple of SEALs he'd met had been full of themselves. "But depending on what kind of investigations we've been involved in, we develop skills. I'm good with boats." He'd even piloted an illegal submersible. "We do have helicopter pilots. Kimball might have been one."

"If so, he chose a terrible time to take over."

"He was plenty arrogant. That isn't necessarily what happened, though."

After an interval, she said quietly, "Poor Bill."

"He chose a slippery slope."

Gwen didn't say anything. A minute later, without another word, they rose and set out again.

As they walked, he heard birdcalls and an odd shrill whistle he couldn't identify but felt sure wasn't human, saw the flick of a squirrel tail. Even he recognized the *rat-a-tat-tat* as a woodpecker.

Their next stop was made when crossing a small creek carrying snowmelt down to the lakes and rivers at a lower elevation. Just above them, a small waterfall dropped no more than five feet. The water sparkled as it danced and tumbled over moss-covered rocks, ferns clustered to each side. Thirsty as they were, Gwen recommended against drinking it without treatment. They filled her bottle and the empty one from the pack and dropped in the purifier tablets Kimball had thoughtfully provided for safe drinking. According to her, there were several nasty pathogens in what appeared to be pristine high mountain water.

Rafe slipped when stepping over the rock-strewn stream, twisted his ankle but found that Kimball's boots were more or less waterproof. Good thing, because he'd have hated to squelch as well as struggle for his footing over a rough side slope. He took a few cautious steps before deciding he hadn't done any significant damage.

He'd about hit his limit again, but he kept his jaws clamped together so he couldn't admit it when he heard something that made the hair on the back of his neck rise.

"Oh, no," Gwen breathed.

Good thing helicopters were such noisy machines. He and Gwen had enough advance warning to plunge into a stretch of woodland that wasn't as thick as he'd have liked but should serve to hide them.

Once he'd knelt and she crouched amidst some rare understory vegetation with purple berries, further shielded by low, almost feathery branches of an evergreen, he calculated it might have been an hour and a half to two hours since the helicopter left.

Sure enough, the damn thing started by flying over the same territory it had earlier and then expanding what wasn't quite a systematic grid but was close. On its last pass, it nearly went right overhead again.

But finally, it turned back and presumably set down, although Rafe could no longer see the thing.

Damn it, he *needed* to see what he and Gwen were up against, so instead of staying put, he pushed to his feet again. "I'm going to try to find a viewpoint."

"Wait! I'll come, too."

He wanted to say no, but right now, she was stronger than he was, so he waited until she'd shrugged off the pack. They were too far away to worry about being heard but had to be careful not to pop out too precipitously into the open.

All he could tell for the next few minutes was that the helicopter was still there, although the pilot never shut down the engines. Rafe must have subconsciously kept in mind where the crash site was, because this time, he led the way until he saw a rock promontory ahead. It took some effort to lower himself to his belly and crawl forward. Gwen stayed behind him.

He'd put the binoculars around his neck earlier. If too many tall trees blocked their view, they were screwed, but Gwen's strategy of gaining elevation was the best they could have done.

He reached the edge of the rocky outcrop, braced himself with the elbow on his good side and raised the binoculars. There was the smoke, a dark trail diminished now but still obvious. Maybe no longer visible from any great distance. Yeah, he could see the whirling blades on the helicopter…and movement beside it. Two men—no, there was another pair. All wearing green camouflage and equipped with hefty packs.

No rifles to be seen, but he supposed they wanted to look like your average backpackers if they happened upon any climbers or hikers.

Even so, he hoped no park ranger met up with them and asked too many questions. He doubted they'd bothered with backcountry permits.

One man lifted a hand, and the helicopter rose again, banked and returned the direction it had come.

Rafe wondered if Bruce Kimball's body was now in the belly of the helicopter. Had to be. If legitimate search and rescue should find the crash site, questions about a dead man with bullet wounds could prove awkward.

Rafe watched the foursome until his eyes burned, then squirmed backward. He looked at Gwen.

"Four men," he said, "wearing camouflage and carrying dark green packs. They're being discreet but no doubt have some firepower tucked away."

Her eyes closed for a moment, and then she retreated all the way to where she'd left their pack. He followed, rising to his feet at the end.

The only positive he could think of was that the two of them were also armed, and she'd taken out Bruce Kimball with a deadly accurate shot. Later, he'd have to ask Gwen how and why she'd learned to shoot like that, especially given her dedication to saving lives rather than taking them.

On the negative side, the two of them currently moved

at the speed of a banana slug. They also weren't dressed to blend. He doubted either of them had paid attention to whether they were trampling vegetation when they set out. For all he knew, they'd all but laid down an airport runway.

"Let's move while we can," he suggested.

Once she'd hefted the damn pack on her back, Rafe bit off another groan as he pushed himself to his feet again. His body instantly revolted, muscles cramping into white-hot knots of agony. For a minute, he had to bend over at the hips, hands braced on his thighs, and do nothing but wait and try to breathe. Gwen hovered beside him, anxious. She reached for him, hesitated then took her hand back, obviously knowing there was nothing she could do.

Except give him more morphine, but he refused to ask for it. He had to push those intervals out as long as he could. For starters, he didn't know how much of the stuff she had. He didn't want to become too dependent, either, and he especially didn't want a drug scrambling his brain. Things were likely to get worse before they got better.

"I'm okay," he said roughly, straightening.

With an uneasy glimpse back the way they'd come, she started out again, bowed beneath the weight of the big pack. He shuffled after her.

THE PRIMAL INSTINCT that had steered Gwen toward higher ground despite the harder going kept flaring. She wanted to *see* behind and below them. They might initially have laid a trail a Scout could follow, which meant now sticking to rocky ground as much as possible would be smart.

Divorcing herself from her aching body, she brooded. This whole thing kept escalating. Four men were prepared to spend however much time was necessary to hunt down her and Rafe.

She'd thought that the moment when she realized Kimball was trying to strangle Rafe was the worst—until he'd turned his gun on her and she'd had to make such a horrible choice. Now she understood this might never end.

The whole elaborate scheme had been meant to make Rafe vanish from the face of the earth. That wouldn't have been hard to do in a wilderness where a tossed body would have been down to bones in no time, and those probably dragged off by animal activity.

She was the one who'd been the monkey wrench in the works. Next time…

Rafe would be dead if it weren't for me, she thought. *Although Bill would be alive.*

Only she no longer believed that. Could Kimball really have let Bill fly on to Seattle as planned and trusted he'd stay mum about his part in all this?

Gwen had to wonder what Rafe's boss at the DEA was doing right now, too. Even if he'd flown back to the office, wherever that was, he'd have learned at some point that Rafe was no longer convalescing in the hospital, that in fact he was missing.

Figuring out where he'd gone initially should, on the face of it, be a no-brainer. The hospital wouldn't have handed over a patient to just anybody. Kimball must have flashed credentials at the hospital as well as at the air rescue base. An ambulance crew had transported Rafe to the airfield and loaded him into the helicopter. Plenty of people knew what had happened to Rafe, up to the point when the helicopter took off.

Except, Kimball almost had to have used a badge with a fake name. He sure wouldn't have wanted to be on record. If that was so, why did Bill have his real name? She puzzled over that one, until she thought, *What if Bill recognized him?*

Military helicopter pilot, DEA agent—they might have encountered each other at some time in the past.

If that was the case, Bill wouldn't have survived to fly the helicopter to Seattle no matter what.

Well, the helicopter never did arrive in Seattle. A search should have been instigated on both ends. Unfortunately, the initial focus would have been the expected route, not the scenic detour Bill had been paid off to take.

Whatever the scenario, she saw an inevitable outcome.

If Kimball had used a false name earlier, as that seemed logical—could he have stolen some other agent's badge?—that would confuse any attempt to find out who was involved in kidnapping Rafe.

"Let's take another break," she said.

His expression didn't change, but he nodded.

Once they were seated, she handed him the water bottle and then dug in her tote for the bottle of Tylenol. When she gave him several pills, he swallowed them without question—for what good they'd do.

When her turn came to drink, she took some Tylenol, too.

"Do you think they'll split up?" she asked after a minute.

"Makes sense." He paused. "Maybe search in pairs."

What if they were able to stay in touch with SATCOM radios, too?

"You said you saw your boss at the hospital," she said abruptly.

He gave her a surprisingly sharp look from those brown eyes, given his exhaustion and pain. "Yes."

"Well, do you trust him?"

His silence lasted long enough to make her uneasy.

"Yeah. He's never given me reason not to." The slowness of his response told her this wasn't the first time he'd wondered. "He did give me back my weapon."

"In recovery at the hospital. That's…surely not usual."

"No. I was too out of it to think it through, but now I wonder…"

She wondered, too. About a lot. "If we had internet access we might be able to find out whether your bodyguards died."

"Unless the whole incident was buried."

"Why would authorities—" *Oh, heck*, she could think of reasons. The city of Yakima may never have known that a federal law enforcement agency had set up a safe house there. They wouldn't have appreciated not being informed, especially after a gun battle erupted in a peaceful neighborhood. Or… "If one of the other men is alive…"

"I think that's unlikely, but I can hope."

She watched as a bird—a bright blue Steller's jay—sidled along a branch, head tilting one way and then the other as *he* watched her. After a moment, she said wryly, "I can't decide if I wish I'd bought a ticket on that Greyhound bus or am glad I didn't."

Rafe's hand caught hers. "You know my vote."

The warmth and strength of his grip was more comforting than it ought to be. She clasped his hand in return, and neither moved for a long time.

Chapter Seven

"Can you go on?" Gwen asked.

A flash of anger showed in Rafe's eyes. "I should be asking you that. You're having to do all the work."

Feeling a little grumpy herself, she retorted, "Here we go again. Is this because I'm a woman?"

"No!" He glared at her. "It's because you're half my weight."

"That's an exaggeration."

"And you're injured, too."

She sighed. "I don't think my ribs are broken, or they'd hurt more than they do." Which was bad enough, but she wasn't telling him that. "They're maybe cracked or just bruised. Later, I'll have you help me wrap them."

His jaw tightened still more.

"Have you forgotten that you were *shot* multiple times last night? That you had surgery *early this morning*? Were still woozy enough not to know what was happening to you when you got tied hand, foot and the rest of your body and then were kidnapped from the hospital? And, hey, a few hours later, *we fell out of the sky*?" She was practically shouting.

He stared for a minute longer, then let his head sink forward.

Gwen took a chance and patted his broad back. "I understand."

Lifting his head, he growled, "You had to do that?"

"Express sympathy?"

"You should have just slapped me and marched away. Let me catch up if I could."

She studied him. "Is it really so bad to lean on someone else a little?"

"Sometimes I work with partners. Needing to trust someone else isn't the same as feeling useless. Useless gets you killed in my profession."

Uneasiness had begun creeping over her. "Can we walk and argue at the same time?"

"Did you hear something?"

"No. Just…"

"Yeah." He pushed himself up. "Put the damn tote bag over my good shoulder." His eyes narrowed to slits when she hesitated.

As exhausted as she was, not carrying the surprisingly heavy and awkward bag would be an enormous relief. Once they stopped for the night, she should go through it. There might be things she could ditch. She did as he asked, then shrugged into the pack and forced herself to straighten.

"We don't have to argue," he said, as this time they fell into step together.

"No. Just…" He'd hate this, but she wanted to say it, anyway. If only once. "What you've succeeded in doing, essentially rising from a hospital bed postsurgery, is next to miraculous. You know that, don't you? And…if I were out here alone, I'd be a lot more scared than I am."

No, she'd probably still be sitting shell-shocked and sniveling beside the body of the man she shot and killed. Because of Rafe, she'd had to pull herself together and remember who she was: a strong, capable woman who wasn't going to let some drug-trafficking scum kill her *or* her patient.

HE'D APOLOGIZED FOR his momentary breakdown and then spent what was probably the next half hour trying to figure out what had triggered it.

It was true he hated being helpless. Most people probably did, and anyone who served in the military or law enforcement more than most. Not being at the top of your game equated to vulnerability. And, yes, that was certainly true right now. If he hadn't been so seriously wounded, *he'd* be carrying the pack, and he and Gwen would be moving a lot faster. That she had to travel at the speed of a patient shuffling up and down the hospital corridor gripping an IV pole was his fault.

Hell, it was his fault she'd gotten mixed up in this in the first place.

Except that wasn't so. It was Bruce Kimball's. If he hadn't sold his soul to the devil, there never would have been an attack on the safe house. Rafe would still be resigned to the months of tedium to come. Gwen would have made her way to Seattle, and Rafe would never have met her. Bill the pilot wouldn't have been tempted, and he'd be alive.

And above and beyond all that, if an organization of morally bankrupt human beings weren't determined to profit by providing an incredibly dangerous substance to relative innocents, none of this would have happened.

A powerful, intensely addictive opioid, fentanyl could be produced cheaply and mixed into recreational drugs, in some cases increasing the high but too often killing the user, who wasn't even aware that an unknown, deadly substance was in their favorite products from the local dealer, or the pills labeled as painkillers or antianxiety meds or even muscle relaxants bought off the internet. If the quantity of fentanyl was too high, people died quickly. It was as simple as that. Fentanyl was currently considered to be the leading cause of death for Americans aged eighteen to forty-nine. It had zoomed to the top of the Drug Enforcement Administration's priorities.

The cartel Rafe had inserted himself into was based in Mexico, but the organization had tentacles spread throughout their chief market, the US.

Rafe had never hated the people he was investigating as much as he had the Espinosa family and their underlings. People smuggling cocaine knew it was illegal, that it was addictive, but it didn't have as much possibility of killing someone when they took their first snort. Every single person involved in manufacturing and trafficking fentanyl knew the risks that even one hit could kill. They didn't care.

By the end, Rafe had been desperate to answer every question he could, collect proof that would send the maximum number of these creeps to prison for long periods. He wanted to be done, to breathe clean air again, to allow himself to sleep deeply without a knife and gun under his pillow.

The idea of a year of stultifying boredom hadn't excited him, but that was the price he'd known he would have to pay. Settled into the safe house, at least initially, he'd been glad for some downtime.

Who knew this was the closest he'd get to a vacation? Struck by the irony, he lifted his gaze from his feet to take in the grandeur surrounding him, puffs of cloud crossing the brilliantly blue sky and the small yellow flowers growing from gritty soil between rocks. Then he absorbed the sight of the woman in front of him, her fat caramel-colored braid swaying over her slim back and her endless legs and a perfectly shaped rear that made his fingers twitch.

I'm damn lucky, he realized—which didn't shut down his fear that this gutsy woman might end up dying beside him.

He almost walked into her. Had she seen or heard something?

"The sun is dropping," she said. "At least the sun confirms we're northeast of Rainier. Probably in the park, but I can't be positive. There's a protected wilderness outside the park boundary. Anyway, we should look for someplace to stop for the night."

He tipped his head again. Yes, the sun was lower than it had been, but the sky was bright. This didn't look like sunset to him.

"If we can keep going even for another hour..."

She shook her head. "Night falls fast in the mountains. Then the temperature plummets just as fast, even at this time of year. Besides, we both need a serious rest. I keep stumbling and my knees want to crumple and—"

He squeezed her upper arm. "You're right. I've gotten so all I do is stare at my feet to be sure I don't misstep. A grizzly could come roaring at us, and I wouldn't notice."

Her smile brought life back to her face. "No grizzlies in this part of the state."

He grimaced in return. "One small blessing."

Transfixed by her laugh—by her *ability* to laugh—he had to be staring. Her eyes widened, and she backed up a step or two.

"Well, let's, um, check out those trees over there."

"Good idea," he managed to say, and tore his gaze from her.

AS EXHAUSTED AS she was, the sound of falling water wove into her consciousness like orchestra music appropriate to the beauty around them. Gwen clambered above a small patch of snow, Rafe right behind her, the noise growing in volume until alarm belatedly riveted her attention.

Twenty feet farther on, they came abruptly in sight of the furious foaming white of a stream bigger than any they'd yet seen tumbling down a stair step of cliffs. Given the force of the waterfall, even from this distance, the mist wet her face and clung to her eyelashes. Surrounding rocks gleamed with moisture and bright green moss that would make them treacherous.

They wouldn't be crossing here.

Gwen groaned and turned, bumping into Rafe.

He stared expressionlessly at the falls. "Pretty."

"I *hate* to backtrack." And that was putting it mildly. She was close to spent and guessed he'd passed that point a couple of hours ago.

Rafe grabbed her arm. "Look."

He didn't sound alarmed, but she still turned her head quickly. *Oh.* A deer accompanied by fawn drank from the stream. They hadn't noticed yet that they weren't alone.

At Gwen's first movement, the deer raised her head, and within moments, both had leaped into the trees.

She and Rafe retreated far enough that the rocks beneath their feet weren't slick, and the roar of the falls wasn't battering their ears.

She'd been taking in their surroundings, desperate for an alternative to making their way downstream far enough for a crossing to be feasible. "If you think you can get up there—" she pointed "—we'd be out of sight."

He looked. His mouth tightened, but he nodded. "Let's do it."

This was…well, a rock climber would have dismissed it as a mere scramble, but for two injured people as tired as they were, it felt more like scaling a straight-up-and-down cliff. A few handholds felt damp from spray blown this far. Her thigh muscles screamed. Once, her foot slipped out of the crack she'd thought secure, and the weight of the pack pulled her backward. Rafe leaned into her, using one strong hand and his bulk to keep her safe until her pulse settled down and she had overcome the rush of adrenaline to try again.

The stiff lower branches of small firs whipped her face but were also strong enough when she seized them to pull herself up.

All the while, a sixth sense she hadn't known she possessed kept her aware of the man behind her. She could *feel* his determination and the sheer will that kept him going. A few muttered curse words escaped him, and a few pained sounds that weren't uttered voluntarily.

I should have had him go ahead of me, she thought, but if she'd done that, she would have fallen far enough that she could have been seriously injured.

More seriously.

If *he* fell…

Gwen blocked that horrifying fear, instead worrying that they'd get up there and find no place adequate to set up even a minimal camp. No, she wouldn't second-guess herself now; from down below, she'd been sure she saw a ledge.

She groped for her next handhold until she satisfied herself that the rock outcrop wouldn't crumble. She heaved herself up another couple of feet. Six inches. A foot. She *had* to be almost there.

And then, suddenly, she was. She was able to crawl forward, brushing aside the dense, low branches of small evergreens. Above her, a bird took indignant flight. All she saw was a flash of yellow. Her pack snagged; she wriggled to free herself. *Keep going, keep going.*

She flopped face down, not sure she could move again. Unless Rafe— No, he stretched out beside her, eyes closed, pale lines of strain on his face.

Neither of them moved for a couple of minutes. Then she sighed, rolled and squirmed to get her arm out of one of the straps of the pack. A hand reached up to help.

"Thanks," she said. Once she was liberated from the pack, she managed to sit up and look around. A rock overhang seemed to promise protection from a helicopter flyover… if they could get to it. More clouds had been gathering, too, the threat of rain another thing she'd refused to let herself dwell on. Neither she nor Rafe had rain gear—or parkas if they should grow chilled once they were wet. This might be the perfect burrow.

She crawled forward, dragging the pack behind her, not caring about the beating her hands were taking. Yes, the ground was reasonably flat right in front of the overhang. They could compress some minor vegetation and be shielded behind the cluster of dark green trees.

"Perfect," she said, and stayed where she was on her hands and knees, swaying.

RAFE DIDN'T THINK he'd hurt like this when he was taking the bullets in the first place. Ten more feet, and he might not have made it.

He wasn't alone. Gwen had hit a wall, too, he saw.

"Hey," he said, "let me give you a hand."

His crawl was like a three-legged race since he knew he'd regret putting any weight on the damaged upper arm. Still, he got far enough to kneel beside her and wrap his good arm around her waist.

"Let yourself go," he murmured.

She collapsed in his hold, but only for a moment. Then

she twisted and plopped down on her butt. "Thank you. I was about ready to do a face-plant."

"That actually sounds good."

Resilient enough to laugh, she continued to amaze him.

"I should have given you another shot of morphine at one of our last stops. Why didn't you ask?"

He wasn't about to admit how close he'd come to begging. "Figured the further we could spread them out, the better."

"Actually, that's not really true. Staying on top of the pain helps with recovery."

"I also didn't want to mask any pain that would tell me I was doing more damage," he told her.

"Oh. That makes sense." Apparently making this her first priority, she found what she needed and drew up whatever quantity of the drug she'd calculated for his size. He shifted, unfastened his pants and shoved them down far enough for her to administer the shot in his butt cheek.

And, oh, damn, that felt good. It didn't make him a new man, but it gave him back some of his natural confidence that he could overcome just about any obstacle.

Once she'd capped the used needle and slipped it into a baggy, she said, "We can set up camp here for the night."

Rafe frowned at her as she reached for the pack again. "You look to me like you need to sit for a minute first."

"I guess there's no hurry. Wait!" She dug almost frantically in her tote, finally coming up with her phone.

Good thought. He all but hung over her shoulder.

No bars. She turned in a circle, lifted it over her head and finally said bitterly, "Things never work when you need them to."

Their lives might depend on them eventually regaining cell phone service, but he didn't have to say a word. She knew.

Less animated, she dropped the phone back into her tote and began searching again. "Let's have a snack before we start setting up."

Rafe couldn't remember how long it had been since they stopped long enough to each eat an energy bar. A single bar hadn't had enough calories for anyone working as hard as they had been, and especially not for someone his size. He pictured a juicy steak and baked potato heaped with sour cream and immediately regretted it when his stomach whined.

After digging deep in the bag, she produced another couple of candy bars. He suspected they'd be running low on those soon—these might even be the last—but he didn't ask. He took one, tore the wrapping and sank his teeth into it—he hadn't even looked to see what it was. It tasted damn good. That's all that mattered. Forget the steak.

"I hope we didn't break branches getting up here," he said after swallowing the last bite.

When she looked at him, he had an unsettling remembrance of thinking how soft the gray of her eyes was. Gentle, comforting. That wasn't true anymore. Maybe not surprising after what they'd gone through, they had darkened, almost seemed haunted. He tried to tell himself he was seeing a reflection of his own feelings about a brutally hard day but suspected that wasn't entirely true.

"Tarp," she said, as if to nudge herself, and opened the pack.

The additional crawling around was manageable for him now after the relief of the painkiller, and he liked the idea of something approaching comfort—and being able to stay put until morning. So he helped set up the tent, push the pad and the single sleeping bag inside it—something to think about later—and tie the green tarp over the too-bright red tent that might as well be a beacon should a helicopter fly right over them.

She set the stove aside and spread out the packets of freeze-dried meals. "Ten."

Rafe gazed at them. "Do you suppose he'd have enjoyed backpacking?"

"Maybe he did it all the time. Still..." She wrinkled her nose. "Weird plan."

"It was, but sure as hell his home office has him down as being on vacation. Heading into the backcountry gave him an excuse to have no cell phone service. In the original plan, the helicopter and my body would have just vanished. No reason to connect him, just one more hiker emerging from the park as far as possible from the crash site."

"Except that he'd flashed his credentials at the hospital and airfield."

"Those couldn't have been his."

"Bill knew his real name." She told him her speculation about the pair meeting in the past and said, "If that was so, it must have come as a shock to Kimball."

"That's one way to put it," Rafe said dryly.

"Do you suppose once he hiked to a trailhead, he was going to call someone for a lift?"

Instinct had Rafe shaking his head. "I doubt it. I'll bet he'd have put out his thumb. Some vacationers or other backpackers would have picked him up. A night at a hotel at SeaTac, and he could have flown out."

She sniffed. "*I* wouldn't have picked him up. Or I'd have kicked him out of my car ten miles down the road. Unless he managed a personality upgrade."

Rafe grinned. "Well, he wouldn't be threatening to shoot whoever gave him a ride."

"I don't know." She looked contemplative. "He jumped

straight to hostile the minute he set eyes on me. He didn't even know who I was, and he was bristling. It was like his default. You know?" She shook her head. "I'd have been less suspicious if he'd dialed it back a little and tried a semi-pleasant 'Hey, this area is restricted. Are you looking for somebody?'"

Rafe cast his mind back, trying to remember why he'd instinctively disliked a fellow agent he'd never had much to do with. It wasn't the first time someone rubbed him wrong, of course. The snap judgments he made about people were presumably based on a subconscious conclusion rather than conscious reasoning. Because he and Kimball hadn't been assigned to work together, he'd had no reason to dwell on that twinge of dislike.

Now, though, he said, "I think that's what I responded to, also. Put a bunch of federal agents together for the first time, and there's often some posturing. Who's the alpha here? But we don't fight to determine it. We work together, smooth out any rough spots, determine strengths and weaknesses, and depend on each other. Kimball had a bad attitude. I saw him bump another guy's shoulder hard in passing when really he was the one who should have stepped aside. I didn't like the way he looked at a particular female agent, either."

"So, your dislike was more rational than you knew."

"I guess so." The corner of his mouth quirked. "On the job, I sometimes have to go with my gut. There are times I need to walk back my opinion, but not often."

She sighed. "This time, you were right on target."

"Except being arrogant doesn't translate to being willing to violate the very principles you're supposed to be defending."

"No." She slipped on a fleece jacket and zipped it. "Do

you think it would be safe to take a quick nap before we make dinner?"

"I don't think anyone can sneak up on us here. We'll have to get cozy, though."

Her gaze shied from his. "Not like we have a lot of choice."

Was she still holding on to any doubt that he was who he claimed to be? He said carefully, "I'm afraid not."

The smile she offered him was more complicated than it appeared on the surface but was still so beautiful he quit breathing.

"I'd be delighted," she told him.

What?

Oh, getting cozy. Somehow, he doubted either of them would stay conscious long enough for the proximity to get awkward.

She let him make his awkward way into the tent first before following him. She wadded up extra clothing for pillows, and then they settled down side by side on top of the sleeping bag. Despite the talk of cuddling, their bodies barely brushed each other. He didn't like the distance between them. He wanted to roll onto his side and gather her into his arms, but he knew better. Any more intimacy than absolutely necessary had to be her decision.

Scaring her was the absolute last thing he wanted to do.

Chapter Eight

Gwen lay completely still until she was sure Rafe had fallen asleep. As his breathing deepened, genuine relaxation replaced what she'd recognized as pretend calm. A nerve in his cheek jerked a couple of times; his fingers twitched. He had to be dreaming.

Only then did she give herself permission to roll onto her side facing away from him, close her eyes and surrender to her own tiredness.

As it turned out, for all its aches and pains, her body was ready to let go, but her brain kept working. She didn't understand why she had been so determined not to be the first to fall asleep.

The answer just leaped into her mind: *I'd have been too vulnerable. Was I afraid he might hurt me?* she wondered in shock, but that wasn't right. Mostly...she didn't really *know* him, she realized. They'd gone through an awful lot today, but none of it allowed much in the way of conversation. So it was true that, in many respects, Rafe Salazar remained a stranger.

Not entirely, though. Despite suffering from extreme pain, he'd reached out over and over to save her from falls, to support her.

Yes, she reminded herself, but just because Kimball

turned out to be corrupt didn't mean Rafe wasn't conning her. He could really and truly have been under arrest; only whoever he and Kimball were both working for had determined to shut him up before he could be compelled to speak to law enforcement. Snatch him before he was fully conscious and be sure he never had a chance to open his mouth. The drug trade was notoriously violent. Mistakes—like getting arrested—she knew could be punishable by death.

Yet her instincts insisted that Rafe was one of the good guys. He could so easily have overpowered her, taken the pack, the food and the morphine, and gone on the run by himself.

Yes. Instead, he'd been…careful with her. Gentle. *She* mattered.

She had a sinking feeling that some of the tension came from her awareness of him as a man. And…maybe some reciprocal awareness on his part?

Face it, he was a beautiful man. She resisted the temptation to roll over to study him. She didn't have to; behind closed eyes, she saw him. Big, broad-shouldered, lean and muscled. With those cheekbones and penetrating dark eyes, he could have modeled, although she felt sure he would laugh at the idea.

So, okay, if she'd met him another way, she'd have been interested. As it was…

A flutter of panic explained some of her self-consciousness. It would be easy to fall for him, given their mutual dependence. If she was okay with a casual easy-come-easy-go relationship, that wouldn't be any big deal. But she never had been. Having the last guy she'd been involved with ditch her the way he did left scars on top of her natural caution. Anyway, if—when—she and Rafe came upon other people or were finally able to make a call and get rescued, they'd go their own ways. His life was really complicated, and from what he'd said, he didn't even work out of the Seattle office, assuming the DEA had one.

Better to be sensible now.

Smart conclusion.

And, face it, the mutual attraction thing could be entirely wishful thinking. He might be protecting her because he needed her to get him out of a wilderness he couldn't navigate on his own.

Fine, she thought.

Having figured out what made her skittish, she was armored now. With that settled, she sank into sleep with astonishing speed.

THE NEXT THING she knew, she woke up with a jolt. Had she heard something alarming? The helicopter, or—

A hand smoothed hair back from her forehead. Rafe, of course. *Oh, heavens!* Somehow she'd ended up with her head on his upper arm, his body spooning hers.

Subconscious? Weren't you listening?

Apparently not.

"Sorry," he murmured. "I need to get up."

He needed to— *Oh.* Now that she thought about it, she did, too.

Busy with her thoughts, she let Rafe maneuver out the unzipped opening, climb to his feet and head for a rock outcrop. Once he was mostly out of sight, she tensed her stomach muscles in preparation for standing up herself and grimaced. Now that she thought about it, *everything* hurt. Darn it. She stayed in decent physical shape! She did.

Apparently, her several-mile three-times-a-week jog really wasn't enough. And then there were her ribs.

Glad Rafe couldn't see her as she managed to scoot out

of the tent and get up without a hint of grace, Gwen went the opposite direction from him. Her thighs were *really* unhappy with her when she squatted.

Surely, she'd feel better in the morning. She sighed and made her way back to their encampment.

Dusk deepened the sky to violet tinged with a darker purple that was almost…gray. Clouds, she realized. It was good he'd woken up. A threat of rain looked more realistic, which made her glad they'd set up the tent.

She returned to find Rafe studying the tent with what she read as disfavor. She knew why. "Do you suppose that's his favorite color?"

Rafe grunted. "I'm thinking he chose it to grab attention. If he was lucky, he'd be seen half a dozen times by other hikers who could testify that he was by himself, just a lone, innocent backpacker."

Thank heavens for the green tarp. She'd succeeded in stretching it out above and in front of the tent, tying cords to branches and, in one case, a rock, giving them some room to sit in front without getting wet if it rained. Without asking her, Rafe now took the jackknife from a pocket in the pack and set to cutting branches that he laid over the tarp and sides of the tent.

"Looks like a deer blind," he said, closing the knife. "A lot of work for one night, but worth it if that damn helicopter flies overhead come morning."

"I've been thinking about that," she said.

In the dimming light, she could no longer make out his face clearly but could tell he'd narrowed his eyes. "Am I going to like this?"

"I don't know." She hesitated. "It's just…this was a really hard day."

"I can't argue." He rolled his one good shoulder and, with obvious effort, lowered himself to the ground again.

"Well... I'm wondering if it might be a good idea to stay here tomorrow and not set out again until the following morning. Right now, we're staggering around blind. I suspect that given an extra twenty-four hours, you'd do a lot of healing."

"I might, but then they could get ahead of us. That's not a comfortable idea."

HE'D HATED TO remind her of a brutal truth but knew he had to. That might be a small shudder she tried to hide.

After a minute, she said quietly, "You're right."

End of conversation. Gwen fired up the stove, and they agreed on an entrée from the array of freeze-dried meals Kimball had chosen. She set aside two of the packets. The guy was—had obviously been—a meat eater. Which made Rafe think.

"What kind of predators do we need to watch out for?" he asked.

"You mean, aside from the human ones?"

At her wry tone, he grimaced. "Just thought I should know about any other threats."

She stirred the concoction that smelled better than it looked. "The only two animals in the park that can be a danger to people are black bears, and usually only females with cubs near, and cougars, which we're unlikely to see. Once in a while, a cougar will attack a human, but it's not common. There are smaller predators, like bobcats, which are rare to spot, and, hey, there was an episode a few years back when a mountain goat over in the Olympic Mountains attacked a backpacker. Most often, when people are injured by wildlife in one of the parks, it's not the animal's fault.

It's because the humans have forgotten all common sense, if they ever had any. People will go so far as to set their kid on the back of a bear so they can get an exciting photo."

"I've heard stories like that. I'd say they get what they have coming, except it's their children who might suffer."

"Yes. There's a reason the park service has worked so hard to keep bears away from both roads and campgrounds in the parks. Yellowstone was most notorious for problems way back when. You wouldn't think you'd have to tell tourists that a moose is a really big animal with an impressive rack on his head, and you might want to give him space."

"Are there moose here at Rainier?"

"No, but there are elk and foxes, not to mention marmots and picas, as well as rabbits, deer mice and—" she pointed upward "—bats."

The darting motion against the dusk sky was familiar.

She dished up his share of the stew in a lightweight bowl and ate hers out of the pan. The ranger-type patter had cut down on the tension, at least on his side. This was the first time since Eaton opened the front door upon seeing a familiar face and gunfire raked the small rambler that Rafe had felt relaxed. He couldn't remember what time that happened. Yesterday, for sure. Twenty-four hours ago? He wouldn't have survived most of the ensuing day if not for Gwen. Watching surreptitiously, he decided she had relaxed, too. Tension was less apparent on her face. He'd say they had been lucky to find someplace as safe as this, but luck hadn't had anything to do with it. He could thank her for that, too.

"Coffee?" she asked. "We even have sugar and powdered creamer, if you take either."

He moved from side to side to scratch his back against the rough rock he leaned against. "All the pleasures of home. Coffee sounds good. Yes to both."

She chuckled. "You're not one of those tough guys who drinks his coffee black even if it tastes like battery acid?"

He let himself smile, too. "Not me."

She heated some water, washed the dinner dishes with soap and a sponge she'd found in the pack, then started over with water for the coffee. He should be helping, but one-handed, how useful would he be, anyway?

"You know how to handle a gun," he commented. "You're a good shot, too. How'd you learn?"

Watching the small pan as if her focused concentration would make the water boil faster, she said, "I...knew someone." She paused. "Oh, I guess it doesn't matter. A foster father. Kind of paranoid. You know, the kind who was sure the government would be coming for his guns. I guess he must not have expressed much of that thinking to social workers, or his foster care license might have been suspended, but anyway. He taught all of us kids how to handle a .22 rifle and both an old-fashioned Colt six-shooter and a semiautomatic. It was fun shooting cans off a fence rail. It probably goes without saying that I didn't hurry out to buy my own handgun once I was living alone. In fact, I haven't handled one since I was in that foster home. He really drilled us, though. I guess some things you don't forget."

"Like riding a bike." If a little more lethal.

She shrugged, then concentrated on pouring not-quite-boiling water into a metal cup and some other container she'd unearthed from the kitchen supplies. "I never thought I'd be thankful for the skill."

"No," he said gently. "Maybe once you're home, you should drop him a note." He added half a spoonful of creamer to the coffee, followed by part of a paper packet of sugar.

Her smile looked sad. "Maybe I should. I didn't make any effort to stay in touch, and I feel bad about that."

Rafe guessed that she'd as soon drop this whole subject, but it would probably be at least a couple of hours before they'd crawl into the tent again, this time for the night. They had to talk about something. She'd gotten him curious earlier anyway, when he'd asked what had motivated her to become a medical first responder. There'd been something in her expression...

Trying to sound easy, undemanding, he asked, "What happened to your parents?"

With a hint of belligerence, she retorted, "Why don't you tell me about *your* parents?"

"Fair enough." His background was more complicated than this answer would tell her, but he could answer the question without getting personal. "Believe it or not, they're both university professors. Philosophy for Dad—I learned early on to tune him out when he got off on his thing—and Mom is a linguist. Teaches several languages at the university level and is working on a grammar and vocabulary dictionary for an obscure African language on the verge of disappearing. This is following work on a Central American Indigenous language."

"Huh."

Rafe laughed. "They're smart people. Well-meaning parents, but heads in the clouds. Mom would be away for months at a time on one of her research trips. Dad has written several books. I could tell you the titles, but they wouldn't mean any more to you than they did to me."

"That...doesn't sound like an easy household to grow up in."

Not for the first time, Rafe had that feeling she was seeing deeper than he liked. She'd hit the nail on the head.

Crash Landing

"Your turn," he said roughly.

She watched him for another minute or two, then nodded. "Dad died when I was a kid, too young to remember him. One of those heart things that no one predicts. He was in his twenties, playing in a pickup basketball game, and just collapsed. Gone."

But she hadn't aimed to be a cardiologist, he thought.

"Mom..." Gwen had a gift for stillness, but now she shifted in a way that gave away her discomfort. "She and I were in a car accident. Head-on, drunk driver. The car was pushed through a guardrail and over something like a thirty-foot drop. This makes me really obvious, doesn't it? Mom was killed right away. I was...in bad shape. I thought I was going to die, too. I guess emergency response was reasonably quick. It felt like forever, but it probably always does when you're trapped like I was. I was eleven and in the front seat, too. The car was crumpled, and they couldn't get mom *or* me out, which was bad because she was *right there* and so obviously dead, and my legs were broken and I was bleeding bad. They used crowbars and whatever else they could lay their hands on, because later, they told me they didn't think I'd have survived a long wait."

He swore softly.

"They were calm, even when they probably weren't really, and caring. This guy got an IV line in me, gave me oxygen when he thought I needed it and stayed with me except when the others made him get out of the way. He just talked, even told a few jokes, and he held my hand."

She wasn't crying at the memory, just appeared pensive. "So. Like I said, I'm not subtle. I wanted to grow up to do what he did."

He should have expected something like this, but hadn't. He felt fierce anger and a tight knot of pain behind the different kind of pain in his breastbone, but knew he shouldn't let her know what a hit he'd taken on her behalf.

"So, did they give you the good stuff, too?"

Obviously startled, Gwen giggled. "Yes, they did. Whatever they put in that IV was amazing."

"Morphine?"

"Who knows?"

Rafe set down his cup. "Did you ever see that guy again?"

"Yes. He visited me a couple of times in the hospital and, way later, got permission for me to ride along in his ambulance a couple of times. I wished..." This shrug was a cloaking device.

"Wished?"

"He could have taken me as a foster kid. I knew better than to ask, and he didn't offer."

"If he was single, he probably wouldn't have been allowed to take in a girl."

"That's true." Her chin rose, and she wiped the memories and regrets from her expression. "There are a few candy bars left. Do you want one?"

"I don't think I can resist," he admitted. "The only thing is, we may not be able to share a tent if neither of us can brush our teeth."

Gwen laughed. "Who gets to stay out in the rain?"

He grinned. "I'm the patient. Gives me priority, right?"

"You wish." She laughed again. "We're really going to owe that creep Kimball, you know. As it happens, I noticed a handy-dandy little travel pack with toothpaste. And get this, it looks like it came with two toothbrushes! Sort of miniature ones, and maybe meant to be disposable, but they'll do us."

"Has he used either?" Rafe asked dubiously. He wouldn't

mind sharing spit with some people, but Bruce Kimball wasn't one of those.

"I doubt it. Doesn't look like anything has been touched since he packed it."

The silence that fell after that felt surprisingly easy. They'd said quite a bit for two people who had known each other for only twelve hours or so. He was glad for the fleece as the temperature dropped. Night sounds he wouldn't have otherwise noticed were soothing in their own way: a few hoots that had to be from an owl, or two of them chatting, small squeaks and rustles, the very distant murmur that he guessed was the muted roar of the waterfall. Once, there was a sharp squeal, quickly cut off, and Rafe reminded himself that owls were hunters.

Finally, he said, "We have a plan for tomorrow?"

Gwen sighed. "I wish."

He waited, and after a minute she went on.

"If possible, I'd like to reach the top of this ridge. It would help a lot to get a glimpse of the mountain."

That made sense.

"My goal has been to reach a trail, both for easier walking and in hopes we'll encounter other people. But I've had second thoughts."

He'd vaguely had the same hope, but now that the subject was out in the open, he had concerns, too.

"Would the people after us hesitate to gun down a couple of backpackers that happen by?" she asked.

Rafe suspected she knew the answer as well as he did.

"I doubt it," he said harshly. "Also, if we can move faster on a trail, so can they."

"So...maybe we could sort of make our way a few hundred yards from the trail. If we're lucky, we might spot a ranger. I'm pretty sure most of them are armed these days, and I assume they carry a radio with some distance."

Rafe didn't wonder aloud what the odds were of happening on a park ranger, partly because her plan was as good as any.

And *that* was assuming they kept ahead of their pursuers long enough to stumble upon a trail.

Chapter Nine

There had been an odd sense of intimacy while they talked, Gwen couldn't help thinking. She'd told Rafe things she hadn't talked about in a very long time, if ever. None of her relationships with men had progressed to the point where she wanted to tell them about the eon she'd spent trapped in the crumpled metal of the car along with her dead mother. Doing so made her feel...vulnerable.

Damn it, there was that word again.

Especially since, now that she thought of it, *he* hadn't shared anything comparable in *his* background. His parents were college professors. So, why wasn't he an academic, too? If there'd been a hint, it must have to do with the suggestion that neither parent was all that present for their son—or for their other children, if he had siblings.

That car accident had been what a psychologist would call a defining experience for her, and she guessed he'd had one of his own. But really, he didn't owe her answers. The bigger question was why *she'd* felt compelled to tell him something so important about herself.

Something he might have found mildly interesting, Gwen reminded herself. It wasn't a deep, dark secret. And they didn't have a real relationship.

Well, not the kind she'd been thinking about, anyway.

After their last depressing exchange, silence settled again until she stirred.

"Let me give you another shot, just enough to give you a chance to sleep, and then we should get ready for bed. An early departure might be a good idea."

"I agree." Was he frowning? "I can do without the morphine."

"No, you can't. Keep on top of the pain, remember? The better you sleep, the more relaxed your muscles, the more healing will happen."

He muttered under his breath but didn't argue while she found the supplies in her tote bag. As she drew up an accurate dose, he held the flashlight, shading the beam with his hand to limit how far out it could be seen from. While he had it on, they put toothpaste on the brushes, and she wet a washcloth and grabbed the bar of soap from Kimball's well-stocked pack. She had to have sweated more today than she usually did in a week.

Rafe eyed the washcloth and said, "Do I get kicked out of the tent if I don't follow your example?"

She made a face at him. "You're a patient. I'm assuming you started the day spotlessly clean."

"I'll bet you did, too."

"We'll see how you feel tomorrow." She waved the syringe. "Drop those drawers."

She enjoyed hearing him laugh, suspecting that the brief sting was worth the rush of euphoria and relief. He pulled the trousers back up, rising to his feet as she collected her toiletry supplies and sought privacy to do some minimal scrubbing. He presumably stepped a few feet away from their small camp to use the facilities, but she didn't hear a thing. When she returned to the tent, he had half sat on a rock and was wrestling off the boots.

"Oh! I can help—"

"Got 'em." He pulled off the socks, too, seemed to glance at her, and removed his pants and the Polartec quarter-zip, leaving him wearing only a pair of stretch boxers he'd appropriated—although he hadn't looked happy about it—and a T-shirt.

He was right, Gwen realized. He had only a single change of clothes in the pack, and she was in even worse shape. If only she'd been able to grab her suitcase! As it was, she could wear the Nomex suit one day instead of her current clothes, but it wasn't ideal for scrambling through the woods and over rocky ridges, to put it mildly. Given their extremely limited wardrobes, they needed to mostly strip at night. She would definitely do that stripping in the pitch dark, preferably once he'd already gone into the tent.

As if he wouldn't be able to tell how little she was wearing the minute she slipped into that sleeping bag with him.

Rafe suggested he get in the sleeping bag first, which was logical. They'd laid it out so their heads would be close to the tent flap in case of trouble. He held the flashlight, a bare glimmer escaping the top of the sleeping bag. Enough to guide her. Gwen wanted to claim she wasn't sleepy yet, but it wasn't true, even after the nap. Anyway, what would she do? Despite the matches Kimball had packed, they hadn't dared light a fire she could sit beside.

Just do it.

She crouched, mostly lay down and squirmed like a snake until she was far enough in. Of course, she bumped and slid against him the whole way. She tried very hard to pretend the solid wall that gave off such welcoming heat wasn't a man she'd known only a day.

Rafe only said, "You can use me as a pillow," and then, "No rain yet."

"No." Where else could she put her head? She should have bundled up some of their limited clothing again to form a facsimile of a cushion, at least for him.

She lay rigid until she felt light-headed and became aware she'd been holding her breath.

"Don't be afraid of me," he murmured, his mouth brushing her hair.

"I...don't think I am," she said after a minute. "It's just... I'm not used to hopping into bed with a guy I don't know that well." And that was putting it mildly.

Humor in his voice, he said, "We've had quite a first date, though, wouldn't you say?"

The laugh was just what she needed. "It's definitely the most eventful I've ever been on."

He chuckled, too, and she felt his chest vibrate even though she wasn't touching it. Was she?

"Want me to tell some jokes?"

"Jokes?" Then she got it. "Like the paramedic. Thank you, but no. Unless you have a really great one."

He told her a bawdy one that had her laughing despite herself. After that, when he said, "Can we get more comfortable?" and eased his arm beneath her head to wrap her in an embrace, she was relaxed enough to allow it. Even rest her head where she could hear his heartbeat and have some wistful thoughts she wouldn't let herself put into words.

Too concrete for something that wasn't happening.

IT WOULD BE nice if they could have shut down and *stayed* shut down until the dawn light beckoned them with a promise of a less painful day, but the truth was, Rafe thought he and Gwen both slept pretty well for three or four hours, but after that, he, for one, hurt and couldn't stay still, she had a nightmare and flailed an arm at his face, and, unable to help waking each other up, they tried half a dozen positions that didn't remain comfortable for more than an hour.

He took pleasure in holding her close for a few minutes at a time, wishing he had the right to cup her breast or slide his hand over her lithe, subtly curvaceous body. Those moments were torturous in their own way and didn't last long.

By morning, his mood was testy, and his first glimpse of Gwen's face suggested she was as tired and grumpy as he was. He submitted to another shot, at which his muscles untangled as if he'd had a deep-tissue massage. *Thank God.*

"You sure you don't want one, too?" he asked, nodding at the syringe she was dropping into a plastic bag seemingly made for the purpose.

She grimaced. "I wish."

A cup of coffee and a couple of handfuls of trail mix helped both of them.

"That wasn't as cozy as I hoped it would be," she said after a lengthy silence.

Rafe was startled into laughing and was glad to see the corners of her mouth twitch. "You're right. It was more like a high school wrestling match."

She giggled. "I don't think I've ever really slept with anyone."

That was interesting. He said, "I haven't often, and on those occasions, we shared at least a queen-size bed. Not the same thing."

"No." Gwen sighed. "It's infuriating when you want to toss and turn, but you're too trussed up to be able even to turn over."

He lifted an eyebrow. "And you wondered why I was so desperate for you to release me from that damn backboard."

"Oh. Yes." She actually looked apologetic. "I'm sorry."

Rafe smiled. "Don't be. We had a lot going on at the time."

"Yes." Her shoulders slumped. "I suppose we should pack up."

"Yeah," he said gruffly.

Without another word, she started on the cords holding up the tarp, then rolled it, the sleeping bag and pad, and broke down the tent. He was able to take the stove apart and pack up what little they'd left out.

He watched as she delved in her fat tote bag and started discarding things. He saw her hesitate before putting an electronic reader back, but she chose to abandon a swirled glass paperweight about the side of a baseball—a gift from her friend, she said, after glancing at him—along with a box of tampons he pretended not to notice, a bottle of hand lotion, a zip bag that he suspected held makeup and a bag with a couple of wrapped presents she'd been taking back to friends. She looked sad about those, but he didn't say anything, because she was right: the lighter their load, the faster they could move.

She ditched most of the contents of what she called a trauma bag. "If one of us gets hurt again…" she mumbled. "But what are the odds we'll need any of this stuff?" That included emergency airway supplies, something she called a pleural decompression kit, IV supplies and blood pressure cuffs. The bulk and weight saved was substantial. About all she held on to were packages of bandaging materials, which she shifted back into the pack.

While they were able to weed out a couple of things from Kimball's pack, most of what it held was necessary. As in lifesaving. Rafe hesitated over an extra magazine for Kimball's semiautomatic, briefly bouncing it in his hand, but made the decision to keep it.

Lifesaving.

As he attached the tent, sleeping bag and pad to the pack, Gwen asked how he felt today.

If he'd been honest, he'd have said, *Worse than yesterday.* Wasn't that always the case with injuries and abused muscles? Of course, he shrugged and said, "Better."

Gwen rolled her eyes. "Good for you. *I'm* sore."

"Walk it off."

She stuck her tongue out at him, which he fully deserved. Walking wasn't in their immediate future. Scrambling, climbing, bushwhacking was more like it.

And so it proved. They went up instead of back down, Rafe glad she went first so she couldn't see his gritted teeth or hear his mumbled curses as his thigh and hip especially cramped and zinged with electrical impulses and occasionally felt as if a knife was stabbing him. And this was *after* a dose of morphine. He'd been injured enough times to know he could have forced himself to go on no matter what, but he didn't want to contemplate how bad this trek would have been without the medical aid.

The terrain was incredibly difficult, heavily forested yet steep and rocky. Most of the time, they couldn't see more than ten paces away, but at least they had the comfort of knowing no one else could see them, either.

They obviously scared what wildlife they spotted. Birds went silent long before the humans reached them, then took startled wing at the last moment, often in bright flashes seen out of the corner of his eye. Rafe continued to hear running water, whether the same stream or different ones, he didn't know.

They didn't talk. The effort of climbing coupled with their various disabilities and the muscle soreness left from yesterday's exertions meant that he, at least, had to concentrate to take each painful step. To use a branch to heave himself upward. Not that he'd have gone far if he did fall; he'd just slam into a tree trunk. The thought made him wince. If he took a solid blow on his thigh or already excruciating rib cage…

Don't think about it.

When he saw daylight ahead, he clenched his jaw, unwilling to groan with relief. He kept up a facade of strength with everyone. Hell, maybe even to himself. By the time he'd been a teenager, he'd perfected the swagger, the confidence, the incredulity if anyone was foolish enough to challenge *him*.

The tree line ended suddenly, exposing rough-textured gray granite. By the time they'd scrambled the rest of the way to what he prayed was the ridgetop, he'd scraped and nicked his hands in several places.

In the back of his mind was the realization that he might have left a blood trail to follow, but really, what were the odds their pursuers would climb so exactly behind them? And, no, as he straightened cautiously, he saw that neither hand bled copiously. Just smears.

Gwen grabbed his arm. "Look!"

He took in a stunning vista. Way the hell down from them were at least a couple of lakes. And when he turned his head slightly, there was the mountain, enormous almost past understanding. Flying by it didn't count as a view. A few clouds drifted around the gleaming summit. It occurred to him that they were quite a long way from Mount Rainier here, but seeing the landscape formed by its historic eruptions made him a little queasy.

"Wouldn't want to be here if Rainier suddenly decided to blow its top," he remarked.

"No." Gwen paused. "All the Northwest volcanoes are monitored for seismic activity. Scientists learned from the

Mount Saint Helens's eruption and at least delude themselves they can give some warning."

"Uh-huh." He bet the most magnificent mountain he'd ever seen knew how to keep its secrets. "Can we sit?" he added.

"Oh! Yes, of course." She joined him in looking around, then pointed. "That looks good."

"Good" would have been a recliner made for a large man, one that allowed him to put his feet up, but his mouth twitched into a smile at the thought. Somebody was getting soft.

The rock was flat enough to let him plant his butt. Gwen sat close to him, keeping her arms at her sides as if she didn't want to brush him. That bothered him, given how snug that sleeping bag had been, but he had to respect her need to maintain some space.

Both allowed themselves a few quiet, contemplative minutes before she dug out the water bottle and bags of peanuts and raisins.

"It's…steep going forward," he said finally.

"Yes."

More open than was safe, too, although following the ridge would be worse.

"Do you recognize where we are?"

"I think I might. Let me get the map out." She set down her bag of peanuts and dug deeper in the pack. "Oh, and my phone, too! Maybe we're high enough…"

She got nothing. They both stared at the black screen.

"You didn't turn it off so the battery wouldn't run down?"

She looked stricken. "It never occurred to me. I hardly ever do."

It took him a minute to ask calmly, "When did you last charge it?"

"Um…early evening before we left. And—" she shifted a little "—the battery isn't what it used to be."

"I should have said something." Why hadn't he? He upgraded phones often to have maximum battery life even more than the features touted in commercials.

"Why didn't your boss give you yours back?" she asked, sounding timid.

"I didn't have it on me when I was shot. In the chaos, who knows what happened to it? The shooter might even have grabbed it, thinking he could get in and see who I'd been talking to."

Gwen nodded. She didn't want to meet his eyes, he thought. He refused to let her feel as if she'd screwed up, not when she'd been his lifesaver in so many ways.

"You thought you'd be home in a few hours when you got on that helicopter," he pointed out. "Unless you usually turn it off when you're in the air, you had no reason to give it a thought."

"Not then," she argued. "But after—" *After I shot and killed a man*, was what she meant.

Her fingers curled around the phone so tightly her knuckles showed white. Rafe pried it out of her hand and took that hand in his.

"Remember how busy we were? I was with you when you checked for bars. I should have thought of it, as well. I'm the guy who does this for a living, after all."

She gave a watery-sounding chuckle, even though there wasn't a tear to be seen. "Better you than me."

"I sit behind a desk sometimes."

The chuckle became a laugh, and he realized he was smiling, too. Either the morphine was speaking or the ever-present pain, but he felt incredibly reluctant to move. *Yeehaw*, he thought, remembering his gung-ho self from a decade ago. *Maybe I'm too old for this.*

Something to think about later.

She did say, "We had a portable charger in the helicopter. We always do. Only…" No need to finish that sentence. She could only grab so much so fast.

After a minute, Gwen tipped her head sideways to rest it on his upper arm for a moment, whether in understanding, solidarity or apology, he didn't know. He turned his head enough to brush a kiss against her forehead.

Then they both retreated as if they'd never shared that moment and resumed crunching on their lunch.

Until he felt a subliminal tingle right before Gwen stiffened, hearing as he did the distant sound of a helicopter.

"Oh, no!"

Could be a park ranger helicopter or a search and rescue one, he tried to tell himself, but his mouth twisted. When had he last been that optimistic?

No. They had to get out of sight and fast.

Chapter Ten

Why, oh, why had they had let themselves stop out in the open without first identifying a way to get out of sight quickly? That had been Gwen's cardinal rule so far.

Frantically, she spun to look around. The drop forward off the ridge was too precipitous for them. They had to go one way or the other...or back the way they'd come to get under the cover of the forest.

"Back!" Rafe said, grabbing the pack and slinging it over his shoulder before she could protest.

Maybe she'd been carrying the pack too long, because she felt unbalanced enough that she stumbled almost immediately and went to her knees.

Rafe yanked her up. She clutched the tote bag and scuttled after him over the rough ground.

The distinctive roar of a helicopter grew nearer. Given her experience, it should be a good sound, even heartwarming. They were on their way to save lives. Or on the ground, hearing backup coming. Her current fear made clear how drastically her perspective had changed.

They held hands as they skidded over the back edge of the ridge. The trees seemed impossibly far away. The climb hadn't been *that* long, had it? How could they possibly make it before the shadow of the bird covered them?

Rafe pulled her sideways. Her ankle tried to give way, but he wouldn't let her fall. Through the salt of sweat dripping into her eyes, Gwen saw what he aimed for. Not an overhang as perfect as they'd found the first day, but a jumble of slabs that might provide cover.

She still couldn't see the approaching helicopter, but it could be upon them any second, and someone in it would be using high-powered binoculars to search for movement or colors that didn't fit.

They'd draped the tarp over the pack, but it was subtly too bright, and they weren't currently surrounded by greenery, anyway.

The next time she stumbled, it was because Rafe had bent over and was pulling her between broken slabs.

"Get down!" he ordered. "Go, go!"

There was a narrow passage barely open to the sky above. He shoved her ahead of him, then pushed the pack after her. Somehow, he had lowered himself to a crouch that had to be unbearably painful, and he had his gun in his hands. The hard look on his face scared her as much as the circumstances.

The roar had become deafening. She squeezed against gritty rock, feeling the print of it on her cheek, trying to make it absorb her.

The shadow did literally fall over them, giving her chills.

But, oh God, oh God, it was continuing on. The terrible sound receded.

Rafe lowered his hands so his weapon pointed at the ground in front of his feet. "It might circle back," he said tensely.

"I never saw it. Did you?"

"A glimpse." With dark humor, he added, "Good thing Kimball didn't extend his passion for red to this fleece top."

"I never studied the map," she said, trying to sound as calm as Rafe did. This wasn't an ideal place to lay it out.

"No hurry," he said.

She kept leaning, not sure she'd still be on her feet if it weren't for the rock. Except that she felt sure if she started to topple, Rafe would step in to support her. The very thought made her ashamed. He was in worse shape than she was. He was her *patient*.

Only they'd moved irrevocably past that, hadn't they?

He swiveled to look right at her, his eyes even darker than usual, penetrating. "You're not going to like this." His voice was gritty. "It occurs to me that nobody but Bill and Kimball knew about you. I'm...not going to tell you to take off on your own right away. You could get into trouble, and I'd never know."

"You need me."

He bent his head in agreement. "But if they see me but not you, I want you to hide. Run. Whatever you can do." His jaw muscles flexed. "Seeing you die for me—"

"I feel the same about you!" she cried.

"But they'd leave you behind, not knowing what you've seen. They will never leave me."

"Rafe." She was afraid it came out as a whimper. He leaned toward her...just before they both heard the hum growing in volume.

He said a few vicious words and squeezed his eyes closed.

Gwen tried even harder to become one with the rock.

IF THEY MIRACULOUSLY found a trail, he'd make her leave him, Rafe decided. Who would know she was anything but another hiker trying to complete the Wonderland Trail, which circled all the way around Mount Rainier? She'd go for it if he convinced her that she could safely find help and send them back for him.

Nice, selfless thought, except he hadn't seen any suggestion of a trail as he scanned the vista, and he was pretty sure Gwen hadn't, either. Thinking about how close she'd come to falling yesterday, he knew he couldn't send her on alone. She didn't deserve any of what had happened to her in the past day and a half, and he was determined to protect her from anything more.

Yeah, except exhaustion, stress and the fun of being hunted by killers. Of perpetually feeling eyes on their backs and looking down from above.

Maybe the feet-on-the-ground hunters had gone in entirely different directions. Given the vast wilderness, it was possible, even likely. Rafe just couldn't count on it.

The fact that the helicopter had flown up one side of the ridge and back on the other gave him a bad feeling. He thought he'd have heard the roar, however muted, if it had been flying the kind of pattern they'd seen before. Had it come so close today out of sheer logic or because one of the pursuers had set eyes on them or just spotted a few broken branches or scuffs in the loamy soil beneath the trees?

"Okay," he said finally. "I think we can assume the search has shifted to another area. Let's move while we can."

He was very aware of her swallow followed by her squaring her shoulders. Gutsy as always.

"You're right. First, though, if we can get in a slightly more open spot, I want to take a look at the map again."

Rafe nodded, grabbed the straps of the pack and pulled it behind him as he edged out of their temporary refuge. Gwen came right behind, carrying the tote bag he'd started to equate with Mary Poppins's bag. Gwen had stuffed some damn wonderful things in it.

The minute there was room, she spread the map and pointed at the trio of lakes she thought they were looking down on. No trail came near, of course, but he didn't see any good alternative but to drop down to them, then make a torturous way south toward what the map had labeled as the Northern Loop Trail.

He didn't bother commenting. Gwen folded the map and stowed it at the top of the pack before closing it.

"You still carrying the gun?" Rafe asked.

She nodded.

"Safety on?"

"Yes." She turned her back to him and lifted the layers of tops she wore. "You can check it if you want."

He wanted to. The idea of her taking a tumble and the damn gun going off and potentially putting a bullet in her was enough to give him nightmares.

The safety was still in the off position, which didn't entirely satisfy him, but what could he say? Conceivably, they might find themselves under fire and need to respond without delay.

She hefted the pack again, something else Rafe didn't like, but he slung the now lighter tote bag over his shoulder and let her go ahead.

The next hours were grueling. Tree cover was sporadic, rocks crumbling, drop-offs potential killers. The sun climbed high in the sky, then began to descend. Rafe hadn't seen anyplace flat enough to set up the tent or even where they could lie side by side. They had to go on. Scrambling downward put more stress on his quads than going up had. His thigh had passed sheer agony and had almost become numb. A couple of times, he thumped it with a fist to be sure he still had any feeling in it.

They took a few breaks, which weren't much help. Looking at Gwen disturbed him. She'd lost enough weight to be visible, which shouldn't be possible in a day and a half. Her cheekbones stood out more prominently, and her eyes had sunken deeper in her face. He wanted to believe he was imagining things, but couldn't quite do so. She studied him the way he did her, but he didn't ask if he looked as bad as she did.

His gaze rested on her feet in the athletic shoes. *Good tread*, he thought, not for the first time, but no protection for her ankles if one twisted.

He clung to the idea of setting up camp on the shore of one of those pretty, probably rarely visited lakes, although at the moment, he couldn't see any of them.

Disaster struck between one heartbeat and the next. Ahead of him, Gwen crept along a narrow ledge he wasn't looking forward to traversing. Gravel crunched beneath her feet. Usually as sure-footed as a mountain goat, she stumbled, swayed and fought to regain her footing.

He lunged forward even as the weight of the pack helped pull her sideways. With a cry, she fell.

RAFE COULDN'T SEE HER. Anguish riding him, he rushed forward faster than he should have and knelt to look over the edge. She sprawled, unmoving, maybe thirty feet down. She hadn't tumbled as far as she could have, but she'd probably bounced off rock outcroppings, and she'd landed on what looked like the remnants of a rock fall. Her head pointed uphill, as if she'd struggled to right herself until the end. He saw no apparent soil, except here and there a few scrubby trees had dug roots deep.

She wasn't dead. She couldn't be.

He looked around frantically, needing to get to her. It was too steep to go directly down unroped, but he saw a zigzag path that might work. It required all his discipline to walk carefully. He wanted to run; he wanted to slide down to reach her side.

Every time he looked, he hoped she'd moved. A groan would have been music to his ears. But there was nothing.

He didn't even want to *think* about how long this was taking. Ten minutes? Fifteen?

What can you do for her when you do get there? an inner voice seemed to mock. *She* was the medic.

Rafe gritted his teeth. When she regained consciousness, she could tell him what to do for her.

He had to be especially careful the last few feet, given the precipice waiting if a hand-or toehold failed. But finally he made it, dropped the tote and squatted next to her.

"Gwen!" he called hoarsely. "Damn it, Gwen, talk to me!"

He rested his fingers on her neck, for a moment not feeling anything. With his own heart beating so damn hard and his hand shaking, would he be able to? Relying on sheer willpower, he calmed himself.

"Gwen." Not so calm. His voice was as gravelly as the ground beneath her.

But he felt the flutter of her pulse. She was alive. He'd thank God, except she could have broken her neck or back, have suffered a head injury that had her in a coma. He didn't dare remove the pack yet, but he was able to extract the sleeping bag. No matter what, she'd be in shock and unable to hold on to her own body warmth. What's more, the sun's downward path was becoming noticeable.

He tucked the down sleeping bag around her, then stroked hair away from her forehead, his fingertips rough against her smooth skin. He delved into her hair, his touch as delicate as he could manage, searching for any lumps.

Yeah, there was a goose egg not far back from her right

temple. Was he seeing swelling and discoloration starting on her temple and reaching down toward her eye, too?

"I need you to talk to me." He swallowed. "Tell me where you're hurt."

Nothing.

What if the helicopter returned now?

They'd be dead, that's what. Even so, he took the handgun from the small of his back and laid it on the ground within reach.

Focus.

He ran his hands down her legs, not finding any obvious breaks. Up her spine and to her neck, which scared him the most. Did she have a cervical collar in the supplies she'd brought? He didn't remember seeing anything like that.

At a soft moan, his gaze snapped to her face.

Her lips had parted.

"That's it, sweetheart," he murmured. "I know you must hurt, but you have to talk to me."

She mumbled something.

He bent his head closer. "What?"

"Don't...wanna."

"I know," he said softly. "Do you know where you are? Who I am?"

Her lips unmistakably formed his name.

"That's right. You fell. I...can't tell how badly you're hurt, except that you lost consciousness."

She seemed to be trying to dampen her lips. "Head hurts."

"Yeah. You have a hell of a lump." He slipped his fingers into her hair again and touched it lightly. "You scared me." *You're still scaring me.*

Her lashes fluttered; her face scrunched, and her eyes opened to slits as if she couldn't handle full daylight.

All Rafe could do was stroke her cheek and wait.

"…seen?"

Seen? He abruptly realized what she meant. Yeah, they were exposed to anyone from above on the ridge or, as he feared most, if the helicopter made another pass over. There was nothing to be done about that yet.

"We're exposed," he admitted, "but first things first. Can you tell me where you hurt besides your head?"

Her shoulders moved. She flexed each leg hesitantly, one at a time.

"I'd like to get this pack off you, but I'm not sure you should move yet."

"It…saved me."

The hell it had.

"The weight pulled you off the ledge."

She rolled her head to see him better.

"Don't move!"

"Neck…feels…okay."

He growled a couple of words he should have kept to himself.

"Hit…rocks, but the pack…protected me." Her speech was clearer all the time. "It…snagged. So I didn't fall as far. As fast."

She'd fallen in two segments. That's what she was saying. A strap on the pack catching on a small tree growing out of a crack, or maybe a sharp outthrust rock, really had saved her life.

Rafe sank onto his butt as if the adrenaline that had kept him crouching beside her had been expelled. Until this moment, he hadn't realized the stress his position had put on his wounded thigh.

"Okay." He sounded worse rather than better. "Let me do the work taking it off."

She obeyed, staying mostly still as he gently worked the

straps over her shoulders and down her arms. Finally setting the pack aside, he put his hands on her back, moving
them up and down, kneading the muscles between her neck
and shoulders. "Where does it hurt?"

"Everywhere," she said so quietly he hardly heard her,
"but mostly my head. I...think I'm okay. Just...a little battered."

"You were unconscious."

"If I sit up, I can take some Tylenol."

"You need the good stuff more than I do now," Rafe said
grimly.

"Not...a good idea after a concussion."

He wanted to argue but had read or heard that before.

"Let me help you."

When she moved, he took most of her weight. Once she
lay on her back, they paused, but since she hadn't gasped
in pain, he continued to support her as she sat up.

Keeping his arm behind her, he said, "You scared at least
ten years off my lifespan."

Was that a faint laugh? "Me too."

They sat quietly for a minute, but the still bright sunlight
and sense of exposure made his skin crawl.

He took out a bottle of water and found the Tylenol in
her tote bag, shaking out a couple onto his palm and offering them to her.

Gwen swallowed them, sighed and said, "We're mostly
at the bottom."

"You took a plummeting elevator."

"Not recommended."

"No." He hesitated. "I hate the idea of making you go on,
but we have to get as far as the trees."

"I know. I can do it."

The words were strong, but what he saw on her face

scared him in a different way. The swelling and discoloration were worsening, and her eyes, darker than they ought to be, seemed to have sunk deeper yet. Her skin wasn't a healthy shade, despite the tan.

But they couldn't stay here. The risk was too high. He had to push her when he hated the very idea. They had to get under cover. He'd carry her if he had to. He wanted to believe he could despite his injuries and silenced any doubting voice.

He urged a handful of dried fruit on her, since eating seemed to settle people in shock, and finally boosted her to her feet.

Her eyes dilated, then became glassy. He couldn't make her continue hiking. He might kill her. But after standing very still for a minute or two, she blinked hard a few times and straightened.

"I'll carry both bags." He made sure his voice had no give. "I want you to hold on to my arm."

She swallowed and finally dipped her undoubtedly throbbing head a tiny bit. Too soon, they set off, one slow step at a time, as Rafe wished he had an earbud that received intel from a teammate situated to be his extra eyes.

With him and Gwen both severely injured, the danger had just expanded exponentially.

Chapter Eleven

Reasonably alert at first, Gwen understood why Rafe guided her the way he did.

The slope remained quite steep, the footing either irregular over remnants of a volcanic flow or chutes filled with small rocks that slid from beneath the soles of her shoes. When he stopped and turned her almost back the way they'd come, letting her go long enough to move to the downside before gently propelling her forward again, she thought, *Switchback. Smart.*

No more elevator.

Awareness of what he intended along with realizing her body was one solid mass of bruises and strained muscles faded into nothing so concrete. Her head pounded as if a jackhammer was trying to break apart a road surface to clear it away before laying a new one. She wasn't quite sure how she stayed upright, then didn't care if she really was. Rafe's arm wrapped around her, and occasionally he lifted her with the strength of only that arm when he must have doubted whether she could pick up one foot or the other enough to step over an obstacle. Was she leaning on him?

Maybe.

Time blurred. She heard his deep, often gravelly voice but didn't even try to make out words. If she wanted anything in the world, it was to sink to the ground, but the iron bar of his arm kept her upright, and her feet kept moving without any conscious order from her.

They went on, and on. His voice grew more insistent, but she could concentrate on only the one thing. Her next step and the one after that.

When he wrapped her more fully in those strong arms to stop her, she didn't understand. She lifted dazed eyes to him.

"Talk to me."

Was that what he'd been saying all along?

"Sit?" she managed to say.

"We can do better than that. As soon as I get the pad and sleeping bag spread out, you can lie down. Here." Once again, he took command of her body until she found herself sitting on the loamy ground that she began to realize was a forest floor.

Never docile, she didn't know if she could so much as lift a hand. Rafe whipped out the pad and sleeping bag, spreading them right next to her, unlaced Gwen's athletic shoes and eased her over onto the softer layers and onto her back.

She moaned in relief, wriggling her toes, and stared straight upward. The trees rearing above were larger than any they'd yet seen. On many, the lowest branches were far above her head. A squirrel watched her with bright eyes before disappearing in a flash.

Gwen transferred her gaze to the man sitting beside her. *So beautiful*, she thought, despite the lines carved deeper into his cheeks and forehead. The worried way he watched her gave her the strength after all to lift a hand and let it flop onto his hard thigh, the only part of him she could reach.

"All right," she muttered.

"God." He bent his head, but he also seized hold of her hand and held on tight, almost painfully so.

She hoped he never let go.

GWEN DRIFTED OFF to sleep. Rafe didn't move for a long time, watching for every twitch and flicker of an eyelash, at first afraid she wasn't asleep at all, but unconscious. At last, she tried to turn onto her side, convincing him this was a natural sleep. He yanked clothes out of the pack indiscriminately, bundled them up and placed the makeshift pillow under her head.

Then he left her long enough to push his aching body into action to walk a perimeter to be sure no obvious dangers lurked, and that there wasn't anything convenient, like a cave, in case they had to bolt.

No such luck, but at least they couldn't be seen from above, neither from the helicopter nor someone searching with binoculars from the ridge above.

Once he'd returned to their small camp, he started setting up. He didn't want to do this in the fast-approaching darkness. It took him a lot longer than it would have Gwen to get the tent up, simple as it was, but he managed. The stove, he fumbled, but had it ready to heat two more meals from Kimball's stash once Gwen woke up.

His stomach rumbled enough that he did some snacking on nuts and dried fruit, but limited his intake. Who knew how much longer they'd have to stumble around in this primeval wilderness before they were able to contact anyone to call for rescue? They should start portioning out the food more carefully.

As Gwen continued to sleep, he took everything out of the pack and examined it, unfortunately not finding anything he hadn't already seen. He repacked more carefully, with an eye to squeezing in necessities from Gwen's tote bag. They'd have to discard more yet, but he wasn't going to root through her personal possessions without her, much less make that kind of decision.

She didn't stir until the sky had turned a deep purple.

The movement had him turning toward her. She scrunched her face up and mumbled, "Ugh."

Yeah, that about said it all. He couldn't help a silent laugh that cut off quickly as he waited to see how alert she'd be.

"Hey," he said, and she blinked bemusedly his way before starting to push herself up. He reached out to help her.

An owl hooted, and she swiveled her head to look around them. "How long have I been asleep?" She made another of those faces he'd think were cute if it weren't for the distortion caused by swelling. "How would you know?"

"I'm guessing four hours, given how close it is to full darkness. How do you feel?"

How she felt was that she needed privacy. He walked her to her chosen tree, stepped away, then gave her his arm when she reappeared, looking flustered.

After that, he encouraged her to eat a handful of the snack mix and swallow some water before taking more Tylenol.

"I guess if I said I feel fine, you'd know I was lying, huh?" she said unexpectedly.

"Yeah. You lost consciousness long enough to be a real worry."

"The headache is the biggest problem. Otherwise, I think mostly I have bruises."

"Like head to toe?"

"Not quite that bad."

He cocked an eyebrow at her to express his opinion of her upbeat evaluation of her own condition. She quit trying.

They agreed on another of the freeze-dried meals, and he

fired up the stove. Since he hadn't seen any running water or heard a stream all afternoon, it was a good thing they'd filled a couple of bottles with water and treated it midday. He decided to dispense with any scrubbing except for his teeth, and would encourage her to do the same. A cup of coffee tonight and another in the morning would do more for both of them than a sponge bath.

Their surroundings dimmed rapidly. She turned on the flashlight a couple of times as he dished up the meal and then made the coffee, but otherwise they sat side by side on the sleeping bag, indulging in long silences but also talking in odd spurts.

Not about today or tomorrow. Gwen didn't bring up the subject of Bill or Bruce Kimball or the map. She told him a few stories from her working life: about delivering a baby in the helicopter, about transporting two men who'd been in a shoot-out and who kept trying to break the restraints to resume their conflict.

"Best friends, one of the wives said. And they were trying to kill each other. What could be worth that?"

Rafe's first thought was that one might have caught his wife in bed with the friend. There'd be two betrayals there, but he personally would consider his wife's the greater.

If he ever married...

After a suitable silence, Gwen asked softly, "Did you grow up with a best friend?"

"Yeah," Rafe said gruffly. The memories and the pain only occasionally jabbed at him. Mostly, they'd dulled.

She didn't ask a question or even turn her head, as if expecting him to elaborate. She'd let it drop if he didn't say anything, Rafe felt sure. She'd been open enough, though, that he felt a twinge of guilt. And really, what difference did it make if he bled a little for her?

"Mateo and I were friends from second grade on, after his mom moved with him and his little sister to live in my school district." Rafe wondered now and again what had become of Ileana but hadn't let himself try to find out. It probably wasn't anything good.

"My parents didn't pay much attention to what I was doing or where I was. Mateo's mom didn't, either, because she worked two jobs. He was supposed to be watching over his sister, but when she got old enough, he decided she could take care of herself."

Gwen was looking at him now. Rafe could feel her regard more than he could make out her features.

"By the time we were fourteen, fifteen, we'd gotten sucked into a gang. At first it was a lot of strutting, wearing the right kind of kick-butt boots and bandannas. Feeling tough. As we got older, closer to graduating, we were expected to do some things." He stared ahead at the trunks of trees he could barely make out. "I started to get cold feet. I think he did, too, but he wanted to belong more than I did. I was afraid I'd be killed if I tried to walk away. He stood with the gang. We had a fight. I'd always believed we'd have each other's backs forever."

Slim, cold fingers slipped into his hand, shaped into a near fist. He squeezed her hand harder than he probably should have.

"When I made noises about walking away, eight or ten of the guys took turns beating me. I ended up in the hospital, lying to my parents about what had happened. At around the same time, our gang and another had been butting heads. I was still recuperating when a war erupted and Mateo was killed. He was found with drugs on him. I guess he got interrupted before he could deliver them."

"Was he using?" she asked softly.

He cleared his throat. "Yeah. By that time, he was. When I could, I went to see his mom. She knew I'd been part of it, and she screamed at me and then slammed the door in my face. I…waylaid Ileana after school one day, and she gave me a look I'll never forget." To this day, his throat clogged whenever he remembered.

Gwen's head tipped to rest momentarily against his upper arm. The generosity of her touch meant enough to make him uncomfortable. She could get to him. He wasn't sure he wanted that—or dared let himself soften to such an extent.

"My parents were sorry to hear about Mateo. It never occurred to them that I'd been taking the same road. As it was, I headed off to college, got summer jobs or internships that meant I was never home for more than a couple of a weeks at a time, and I dodged any chance of being seen by my former compatriots. Mom and Dad didn't understand my decision to go into law enforcement, and especially when I chose the DEA, but, uh…"

"That's what you intended from the minute you learned about your friend's death."

"Yeah." Hearing how rough his voice had become, he decided he'd said enough. In fact, he released her hand and rose to his feet.

"Time to get some sleep." If he sounded brusque, so be it. "How's your head feel?"

DESPITE THE FACT that she'd had a lengthy nap not that long ago, Gwen felt sure she could sleep again, no problem. She'd taken as much Tylenol as she dared, so there was no point complaining about the drilling still going on in her skull.

She and Rafe briefly discussed whether to set up the tent and agreed they didn't need it. Through the dense lace of the forest canopy, they could make out astonishingly bright stars against a velvety black sky.

Rafe said tersely, "Unless rain is a possibility, I'd prefer to be able to better hear and see what's approaching."

Thank you for the reminder.

Of course, she couldn't disagree. He was already easing into the sleeping bag when she suddenly said, "I didn't have a chance to give you your shot this afternoon. I can—"

"No. I did okay. My injuries aren't the kind that require continuing on a painkiller as powerful as morphine."

She stood above him, not moving. "I know that, but you weren't in any shape to leap up and go on the run in the mountains, either!"

"I'm not sure I could have that first day," he admitted, his voice a deep rumble that made her think of the purr of a big cat.

Why did he sound gentle? Did he think she needed soothing? If she hadn't proved her competence by now—

"Are you coming?" Nice segue into impatient.

Her response was wordless and grouchy, which she felt a little bad about. Only…she was entitled! Most of her body still hurt. The pad beneath the sleeping bag was maybe half an inch thick. She was grateful for it—really, she was—but she was starting to crave a fat memory foam mattress.

Living long enough for luxuries to be any kind of possibility had to be their priority, she reminded herself. Rafe hadn't whined, and neither would she.

"Yeah," she said, and lowered herself to her hands and knees to begin the backward squirm to fit herself into the limited space left after his big body filled most of it.

The awkwardness seemed to be missing tonight, though. Maybe she just felt too miserable to care about anything like that. And maybe it was the way he helped her, hands careful, until she settled with a sigh, her back to his front so that he spooned her. He held out his arm to provide a perfect resting place for her head, and the heat he seemed to emit all the time was seductive enough that she had to make an effort to hold some small distance between them.

Once she fell asleep...well, she wouldn't know, and neither would he. At least, until morning, when they were bound to be intertwined like ivy climbing a solid brick building.

She took responsibility for pulling up the zipper, necessitating some more wriggling, then relaxed.

"G'night," Rafe murmured, his breath stirring her hair. Unless she was imagining things, he hugged her.

"Good night," she whispered, and closed her eyes, pondering how few times in her life she'd ever slept wrapped in a man's arms, and why this felt so different. So...comforting.

She tried to think about the ultimately tragic story he'd told about his childhood and his best friend, but didn't get any further than picturing a young, possibly lanky Rafe with a bandanna tied around his head, his black hair longer. Maybe even brushing his shoulders? Tough guy, but not as much as he'd imagined.

What things had he been asked to do? How many had he persuaded himself to do before the values he'd been raised with had kicked in? Did he imagine that if he'd been with Mateo when the gang war broke out, he'd have been able to save his best friend?

Wasn't that what he'd been trying to do ever since?

Feeling fuzzy, Gwen sighed and let herself snuggle just the tiniest bit into the hard curve of Rafe's body. Then she slept.

RAFE HAD TO readjust Gwen a couple of times during the night. The first time, he woke up to discover his dream had prompted the erection he had pressed to her firm but still well-rounded behind. Or maybe it was the other way around. She made some grumbly noises but never really woke up as he eased himself to his back with her partially sprawled over his chest. It took some willpower to persuade his body to subside, given that he still had an armful of sexy, brave, compassionate woman. He must have managed, because he did fall asleep again, this time to a pale dawn and the discovery that Gwen had somehow squirmed her way entirely on top of him.

Her face was pressed into the crook between his neck and shoulder. Her toes flexed against his shins. With him able to feel every curve and dip between, his body had reacted with enthusiasm.

Rafe held himself very still, listening to her slow, even breathing. He didn't feel any need to move even though he'd been fully alert from the moment he opened his eyes. Why not enjoy the pleasure of a harmless arousal?

For all that he relaxed, his mind was always determined to puzzle over every hint of anyone's motivation, including his own. And what he realized was that, beyond the straightforward lust, he felt something more that he hardly recognized: contentment. A quiet sense of peace, as if all were right with his world.

His cynical side kicked in with no trouble. So much had gone wrong in the past three days, he couldn't count all the disasters on one hand. Maybe not even on two. Had she drugged him during the night, and he just hadn't noticed?

Rafe knew better, but he was disconcerted enough by the strange mood that he immediately tensed, shifted Gwen to the side and squirmed out of the sleeping bag.

Peace.

He'd half hoped she would keep sleeping but wasn't surprised after he'd gotten dressed to see that she had sat up and was pushing her tangled hair back from her face. Apparently, the elastic she'd used to keep it tamed in an increasingly disheveled braid had disappeared altogether. It might have looked sexy if not for the bruises on her face.

"It's early," she observed.

"Yeah, sorry to wake you." He'd been about to go use the facilities but paused. "How do you feel?"

Her eyes were clear, no longer dazed, the best sign he could have hoped for.

"Not bad." She grimaced. "My back hurts. And I still have a headache."

"You slept well."

"I guess I must have," she said in bemusement. "Unless I went sleepwalking."

Amused, he said, "Nope. I'd have noticed that."

She gave him a crooked smile that didn't succeed at being as upbeat as she may have meant it to be, given the deep lines between her brows and the furrows on her forehead.

After deciding priority one was bringing her Tylenol and water to wash it down, he did that much before disappearing for a few minutes.

He came back to find she'd washed down the pills but otherwise hadn't moved.

"We should make an early start. Just…give me a few minutes," Gwen said.

Not fooled, he squatted to her level and studied her more carefully. He didn't like this idea but had to offer it.

"We have enough food. What if we rest for the day?"

She fired back, "You mean, what if *I* rest for the day. We didn't sit around when you were in worse shape than I am."

"I didn't have a concussion," Rafe said bluntly. "You slept especially heavy last night. You picked at your food." He'd finished her portion last night. "Be honest. How does a big breakfast sound?"

She scrunched up her face, then winced. "Bacon and eggs?"

"What if I said yes?"

Her chin lifted. She wanted to tell him to bring it on, he could tell, but she finally sighed. "I'm queasy."

"That's what I thought." He frowned at her. "We're tucked away pretty well here."

"I don't remember much after I fell, but that side of the ridge was mostly rock. We had to have been in plain sight for at least a couple of hours, if not more. Especially as slow as I must have been once you picked me up and put me back together."

"That's…a worry," he agreed. He'd been preoccupied by her, too, and not as observant as he usually would be.

Staying put on the assumption they *hadn't* been seen was a gamble, but he also hated to put her at any more risk than she already was.

Chapter Twelve

"We have to keep moving." Gwen dug in stubbornly, but Rafe didn't argue too hard even though he also didn't appear happy. He had to know she was right; they didn't dare laze the day away, giving any pursuers time to catch up.

Or, as he'd pointed out once, even worse would be walking into an ambush because they'd allowed those cold-blooded creeps to get ahead of them.

After insisting he handle packing up, Rafe seemed to dawdle. Gwen defied him by drying the couple of dishes he'd already washed and dismantling the stove. She refused to admit to Rafe how lousy she really felt after the amazing stoicism he'd displayed the first day. She might have worried he could see right through her, except once he'd conceded the argument, he noticeably retreated. For a while, he seemed to pretend she wasn't there at all.

He did finally urge her to help consolidate what was left in the tote bag with the contents of the pack. "I'd rather you didn't have to carry anything."

In the end, she looked in dismay at her discard pile.

"The rules are that if you carry it in, you carry it out."

"Our situation is extreme."

"Yes, but…" Seeing his impatience, she gave up, but she

did insist on burying the bag to the best of their ability, considering their lack of a shovel.

She had a feeling Rafe cooperated only out of a reluctance to leave any trace of their presence behind.

Given that they had no compass, and she had no memory of which way they'd come, she had to depend on his sense of direction. Although, passing through a grove of large trees that they had to wind between made her wonder in a short while whether they might be going in a circle.

Pride kept her walking, with only one break in her composure. She had to lurch behind a tree to empty her stomach of the small amount of breakfast she'd managed to eat. Rafe's expression was so grim when she returned, she avoided meeting his eyes.

"I'm all right."

He didn't say a word.

Since he stepped back to let her go ahead this time, she felt his gaze boring into her back. Excellent incentive for keeping her shoulders squared and her throbbing head high.

They couldn't have been on their way an hour when he said, "Let's take a break."

Gwen didn't argue or even comment. She wondered if the Tylenol she'd taken earlier had been absorbed before she puked, but decided she didn't dare double up. Sitting down on a huge, ancient fallen tree, if only for a few minutes, was a massive relief.

Staring into the shadows of the forest, he said, "I'm depending on you to tell me when you need to stop. Even lie down and close your eyes for a while."

"I'm not sleepy."

"The more rest—"

She huffed out a breath. "I took a four-hour nap yesterday, then we went to bed as soon as the sun went down. I think it's safe to say I've had plenty of sleep!"

He scowled at her, which was the most expression she'd seen on his face since she woke up. She didn't think she'd behaved especially badly this morning. Was this fallout because he'd told her more last night about himself than he'd intended to? Or did *he* hurt more than he wanted to admit? Maybe now that *he* felt stronger, he would become impatient with their slow pace.

Heck, maybe he hadn't gotten any sleep at all, given that he couldn't so much as roll over with her wrapped around him like an invasive vine.

Would he tell her what was going on in his head if she asked?

A little brooding of her own coupled with the brief rest, and she decided there wasn't any reason not to discuss options.

"Maybe we should rethink the plan to stay together. What if *you* go on and leave me hunkered down here instead of the other way around?"

This scowl made him appear forbidding. "Don't be ridiculous! If anyone saw us yesterday, they now know about you. Do you really think I'd leave you?"

"How should I know? You're not being very…communicative."

"Maybe I think it's a good idea for us to try to be quiet."

Because she never shut up? Starting to get mad, Gwen opened her mouth but forgot what she'd intended to say when he abruptly cocked his head and lifted a hand in a stop gesture.

She didn't hear a thing, certainly not an approaching helicopter, but she froze, holding her breath.

With a suddenness she could never have predicted, Rafe

tackled her backward over the log. At almost the same instant he fell on top of her, a distinctive *crack* rang in her ears, and bark splintered just above them.

RAFE FOUGHT TO free himself of the pack. Damn this soft ground! He'd never hear footsteps. He didn't even know whether a sound or hint of movement had triggered his alarm in the first place.

Face inches from hers, he murmured, "Once I return fire, throw yourself into those ferns. I think it's a well around the tree that would give you some protection."

Eyes wide and dark, she bobbed her head. He hoped like hell he hadn't hurt her by flattening her, but there'd been no choice.

He pushed himself up enough to half crawl forward, leaving her free to move. Once he'd opened some distance from her, he lifted his Glock and took a few blind shots. A startled sound came to his ears.

Behind him, Gwen squirmed away.

A flurry of shots tore into the rotting log they'd taken cover behind as well as a tree above his head. Bark flew, some peppering his face. He flicked a glance back. Thank God Gwen had disappeared. He edged forward another few feet.

Would these bastards be wearing bulletproof vests? He'd guess they weren't. The things were hot and uncomfortable, and these kinds of enforcers were more likely to lift weights to achieve impressive muscles than run or hike to stay in shape.

A faint whisper of sound gave him a target even though the bright green camouflage blended too well. He fired even before he'd raised himself high enough to see the SOB not twenty-five feet away. Marking himself as a dead man

walking, the bastard's eyes were narrowed on the cluster of
ferns surrounding the giant cedar, but he had already started
swinging toward Rafe.

Not fast enough. Rafe pulled the trigger with the instinct
honed by endless hours at the range. Once, twice, three
times.

The man shouted, fired wildly as he staggered and then
crashed down with as much force as one of these trees would
have if a saw severed it from its roots.

A flicker of movement almost gave Rafe time to dive
for cover again, but the second man was already firing. A
sting told Rafe he'd at least been grazed by a bullet as he
dove sideways.

A series of shots coming from a different direction had
him rolling to look behind him. If the four men had joined
together—

But what he saw was Gwen, who'd popped into sight like
a genie from a bottle and was firing with the same assur-
ance she had when she brought down Kimball.

This second man's face went through the same stages as
Kimball's had, too: astonishment, agony…and a vacancy
Rafe had seen too many times in his career.

GWEN TRIED TO keep holding the gun steady but saw that
her hands shook as if she had a raging fever. Her teeth chattered, too.

Out of the corner of her eye, she saw Rafe rise to his feet
as lithely as if he'd never been hurt and rotate in a circle, his
own weapon still held in front of him in firing position. He
surveyed their surroundings with that hard expression she'd
seen so rarely. She suspected that, despite the dim green-
tinted light here in the dense forest, he saw more sharply
than she ever had, too. Finally, he approached the man he'd

shot, kicked his handgun away and stared down at him, then approached the man she'd shot and did the same.

Once she really looked at that body, she couldn't look away. Even from here, she saw the blood and a hole in his temple.

Slowly, her hands dropped. The next thing she knew, she was retching violently, nothing but thin bile coming up, but she couldn't seem to stop.

She'd killed again. How could she have done that?

How could she not?

Rafe prowled out of her sight. He was gone long enough that she assumed he was searching to be sure these two had no nearby backup. When he at last reappeared, he carried a camouflage print pack over one shoulder and a second one with his free hand.

He dropped them both and came to her, dropping to his knees in front of her. She hadn't realized she still held the gun in a tremulous grip until he gently relieved her of it.

"You're not hurt?" he said.

She shook her head, reminding her just how much her head ached. That didn't count.

"I... They followed us."

"Yeah." He cleared his throat. "Lucky we stopped. Otherwise, we'd have had no cover at all."

"No." They might have been gunned down from behind and died. Just like that. Just like... With her gaze compulsively drawn back to the face of the man she'd killed, she had dry heaves.

Rafe rubbed her back. When she raised her head, he smoothed her hair back from her forehead with a completely steady hand, in contrast to hers. *He often did that*, she thought, and imagined how wild and tangled her hair must be by now.

"C'mon." He reached out a hand. "Let me pull you up."

As he had guessed, the ferns had disguised a hole around the tree trunk. She'd essentially fallen into it and had fought to right herself fast enough to be able to provide backup. As shaky as she felt, she was grateful for the strength that swung her up as if she weighed nothing.

She probably *had* lost weight, she thought, her mind inexplicably drifting. *What a diet plan*, she thought.

Rafe settled her on the log again so that her back was to the dead men.

"Let's go through their packs quickly and see whether there's anything that will help us. Otherwise, later we can try to pinpoint where we left them."

"Their guns?"

"We'll take those."

Because he thought they might still need them? Or because he didn't want a backcountry hiker stumbling on them?

Did his motives matter?

She wasn't an awful lot of help, mostly watching as he transferred first a pair of wallets and then some food to their own pack.

"We could take a second sleeping bag," he offered, sounding oddly neutral, "although that would probably mean carrying a second pack, too."

"If you'd prefer that…"

"No. I thought you might."

She couldn't imagine nights not having the comfort of his arms around her. "No," she whispered.

His eyes caught hers for an unnerving moment. The creases in his forehead betrayed a perturbation she couldn't read. Did he think she might be cracking up?

Was she?

No.

She quit bothering to watch him sort. When he said, "Let's cover some distance before we stop for a bite to eat," she stood up before Rafe could help her. The idea of eating didn't entice her, but she'd have to try at some point, wouldn't she?

THOUGH THE PACK was now weighed down by four handguns—two full-size, two smaller backup weapons—as well as a few supplements to his wardrobe and to their diet, Rafe was barely conscious of it. He focused primarily on Gwen. Even as her drawn face and careful steps that were clumsy compared to her usual grace scared the hell out of him, he felt unfamiliar pride in her strength and the intense concentration that kept her moving forward despite what had to be a world of pain. Out of necessity he also listened for any sound coming from behind that wasn't natural. And, of course, for the hum of helicopter rotors.

He brooded about why he hadn't found a SAT radio. Why wouldn't they have carried one to stay in touch with the other pair and their base? Once the men on the ground spotted him and Gwen, you'd think they'd have called in backup. He'd located one cell phone, but it had been locked by fingerprint or some other method that made it as useless as Gwen's phone with the drained battery. Had it worked to reach whatever airbase the helicopter was flying out of?

It was also possible, he reflected, that none of these men was aware that cell phones didn't work in much of the park. Unless they'd hiked or climbed here, why would they? To most Americans, the idea that there were still wild parts of their own country where their precious mobile phones became useless baggage was unthinkable.

He'd noted on the map he and Gwen carried that they might be coming in reach of cell phone towers to the north, although plenty of mountainous terrain could still be interfering. Unless the helicopter showed up again in the near future, Rafe's intent was to get Gwen and himself to a trail where they might find hikers with working cell phones.

Between trees, he saw water glinting blue ahead. The lake nestled in a bowl in the land, but he suspected it was still at a significant elevation. The water was startlingly clear, the shores rocky.

Some serious work remained ahead of them to climb more ridges or to see if it was possible to follow one of the streams he remembered noting on the map that meandered to ultimately join the west fork of the White River. What Gwen had called the Northern Loop Trail crossed the west fork at one point.

Otherwise, the distance wasn't great to another pair of lakes to the south with a backcountry campground and even a park ranger patrol cabin marked on the map, but the scrambles over more ridges might be beyond Gwen's capability now. What Rafe knew was that they wouldn't make it today. This was as good a place to stop as any, although they needed to retreat back into the trees so as not to be seen from above.

Predictably, she said, "I can go on," but Rafe shook his head.

"One more day, we should make it to that patrol cabin. We don't have enough hours of daylight left today."

"I don't think there's always a ranger at those cabins."

His mouth tightened. "There's also a campground marked."

"The kind with something like three or four sites."

"I get that. But from that point, our odds improve of

meeting someone with a working phone, or a charger you can use."

"Yes. You're right." She looked around with unsettling vagueness. "Here?"

"Looks good enough to me."

He wished he had any idea *which* lake they'd found, but it was pretty. One shore was wooded enough, somebody would have to stumble over them to find them—unless, like the dead men, they'd been tracking him and Gwen.

He shied away from thinking about the two corpses they'd left to the mercy of the wildlife. The glassy look in Gwen's eyes either meant she, too, was picturing them or that her concussion was deeper than he'd believed.

As soon as he lowered the pack to the ground, he extracted the sleeping bag and pad and spread them out. A glance at the sky found a scattering of clouds, but whether they suggested rain tonight, he couldn't tell. For now, he just wanted Gwen to lie down.

Once again, he helped lower her to a sitting position. She watched as he knelt, untied her shoes and tugged them off.

Her smile was unexpected. "I can't remember any man who wasn't a shoe salesman taking my shoes off."

He grinned. "If I put them back on in the morning, just to be sure they fit, you know..."

Gwen wrinkled her nose. "Cinderella, I am not."

Rafe wasn't so sure. She was beautiful enough to play the part, although he felt damn sure she wouldn't have ducked her head and obeyed the cruel stepmother no matter what she dished out. Under these circumstances, they'd gotten to know each other in a way a couple might not in a normal relationship, even over the course of months.

He frowned. *This isn't a romantic relationship.* He hadn't had one of those in years. Sex, yes. Letting himself feel hope for the future? No. And he didn't even know why he was thinking about this.

He let that slide, though he wasn't a man who usually let a lie to himself pass.

GWEN WOULD HAVE liked to find a comfortable slab of rock overhanging the lake and lie there watching for minnows. She didn't even try, for too many reasons, starting with the lack of a conveniently placed slab. Placing herself out in the open would have been foolish beyond belief, too. What she *really* wanted, she realized, was for them to be on a backpacking trip for fun instead of being the prey still hunted by a ruthless offshoot of a drug cartel.

She wanted to have saved a life instead of taking two.

Except...she had. Rafe's.

She caught him watching her, as she so often did, and wished his expression wasn't so often unreadable.

He swore suddenly.

Oh, no. She heard it, too—distant but undoubtedly approaching.

"They can't see us even if they fly right overhead!" she cried.

"If they get close, it's because they have a damn good idea where we are," said Rafe, rough voice shaped by familiar grimness.

"You think the four men on the ground stayed in communication? Which means the two we haven't met might know where we are?"

"I do."

Head cocked as she listened, Gwen said, "It's coming fast."

"I want to see it. Where did we stash the binoculars?" He flung a few things out of the pack before locating them.

"I should come, too."

Rafe barely hesitated before nodding. "Bring your gun."

A couple of minutes later, they found a thicket of what Gwen said were huckleberries growing from a rotting stump that showed signs of having burned from a lightning strike or forest fire at some point in the past. Right at the edge of the tree line, they were able to see a stretch of sky above the lake. He'd set his handgun within easy reach, and now lifted the binoculars to his eyes.

The helicopter snapped into sharp focus minutes later as it buzzed a lower elevation than it did yesterday. It had to be skimming barely over the treetops. A small herd of what Rafe recognized as elk burst from cover onto the lakeshore and ran in great bounds before disappearing again. The damn thing was flying straight enough toward them that his gut tightened.

Through the binoculars, he could just see a couple of men crouched in the open side door, rifles raised. Fury struck Rafe. Enough was enough. He was going to bring the whole organization down, if it was the last thing he ever did.

"Do you hear that?" Gwen murmured as if she were afraid they could be overheard.

"What the hell?"

A second later, a much larger helicopter appeared on a trajectory meant to cut off the first one. This second one was painted an army green and displayed what Rafe thought had to be government insignia. Was that a Chinook? Not impossible, considering how near the joint army/air force base of Lewis-McChord was.

The helicopter that was their nemesis abruptly lifted, gained altitude and circled back the way it had come, topping the ridge moments later to take it out of sight. The army helicopter changed path, too, swinging in a wide semicircle in apparent pursuit. Or just aiming to drive an unauthorized intruder past the national park boundaries?

In anguish, Gwen exclaimed, "If only we had a flare!"

"Took the words right out of my mouth," he growled.

Chapter Thirteen

After watching the army helicopter disappear over the tree-tops and ridge, Gwen had clung very briefly to the hope that it might reappear, might even have been assigned to search for her and Rafe.

Or at least for Rafe.

When twenty or thirty minutes passed and it hadn't returned, she gave up on what had been an unrealistic hope. How would the army have gotten involved?

Upon their return to their camp, Rafe asked that question.

Gwen shrugged. "I've read that they do call in the Chinook helicopters for rescues near the summit where the smaller ones can't go. If it had transferred an injured climber to an ambulance at Paradise or Sunrise or gone all the way to a hospital, there's no reason it would have been out this way, though. It might have been on some kind of training flight and didn't like the looks of an unmarked helicopter flying without clearance in the national park. Or..." Okay, she still had a grain of optimism. "Is there any chance the DEA could have reached out for help searching for the missing helicopter and you?"

Seated now on the sleeping bag beside her, he grimaced. "I doubt it, but...maybe. A search was surely mounted, but probably focused on the planned route."

"That's true, except…you'd think *some*body, somewhere would have seen that plume of smoke."

"If the crash site was located, I think we have to assume Kimball's body had already been removed. If that's so, I'm not sure what regular search and rescue personnel would have made of the burned helicopter. They'd have found the pilot and presumably contacted EMS Flight. They must have known you were on board. Are we sure they knew *I* was?"

She frowned at that. As sketchy as the whole thing was, she couldn't guarantee EMS did. Bill had claimed to be talking to dispatch, so she hadn't answered her phone. What if he'd lied?

And would the hospital who'd sent Rafe as a patient over for transport to Seattle have reason to connect him with a missing helicopter? Would the EMTs who'd loaded him have ever given that part of their job another thought? They'd certainly have had no way to suspect they were part of something secretive.

She told him what she'd been thinking.

"I've had most of the same thoughts, except I didn't realize your base didn't specifically send you to take care of me." He shrugged. "We'll know more once I can talk to Zabrowsky." Rafe's mouth quirked. "If he's able to snap his fingers and demand the army pick me up, I'll be impressed."

Gwen smiled. The never-ending headache and debilitating exhaustion had temporarily stolen her ability to laugh. Given a few hours of rest, she felt sure she'd regain her determination and maybe even optimism. Look how far they'd come! Relatively speaking, they didn't have all that far to go. And, would anyone dare send that helicopter out again after they'd received what at least constituted a warning? They'd have to be desperate.

Which, unfortunately, they seemed to be.

After some discussion about the increasingly gray sky, Rafe set up the tent and covered it with the tarp. He cooked dinner, too, which Gwen hadn't been sure she'd be able to eat. Her appetite was returning, though, which was good news. Maybe by morning, the headache would be gone, too. She made a face. Sad to say, she wasn't *that* optimistic.

When the evening became chilly as the gray of the sky deepened, Rafe urged a parka on Gwen that he'd appropriated from one of the dead men. She wasn't quite squeamish enough to refuse the cozy warmth. He seemed comfortable with a fleece quarter-zip, but it was heavier than hers. Plus, Rafe's natural thermostat had a higher setting than hers did.

They sipped coffee, letting the quiet sink in. An owl's soft hoot was followed by small shrieks as a nocturnal hunter—possibly the same owl—found prey. Rafe made her feel surprisingly safe by his mere presence, and that disturbed her. This was surely one of their last nights together. She had let herself become more…attached than she should. Than was safe, Gwen thought, deliberately echoing the word she'd used a minute ago in her head.

She'd never been a fan of sticking her head in the sand. Better to look straight on at reality. So she asked, in an I'm-just-wondering voice, "What will happen to you once this is over?"

This silence felt quite different. Rafe went still, with the coffee cup halfway to his mouth. Finally, he said, "Unfortunately, I suspect I'll be stashed again in some kind of safe house. I think I told you the trial will likely be at least a year away. Hell, maybe longer than that. After all this, the agency will want to up the protection."

"A dank fortress?"

He smiled faintly.

She asked, "How can you trust the same kind of arrangement after you were betrayed?"

"Not sure I do." He resumed movement, swallowing what appeared to be the rest of the coffee in his cup and then setting it down before he turned his head to look at her. He didn't have a lot of the tells most people did, the kind that would give away his real thoughts, and the oncoming darkness didn't help.

"So?" she asked softly. Whispered, really.

He shook his head. "I may have no choice. Even if I could get away with it, I can't walk away. I want to bring these scumbags down like you wouldn't believe. For the victims of the drug trade in general, for the guys who were gunned down guarding me, for that pilot who didn't know what he was getting into and now for *you*."

Her heart did something odd that made her briefly light-headed. No, she couldn't let herself believe for a minute that he was suggesting...what it sounded as if he was suggesting.

"You've saved me as often as I've saved you" was the best retort she could offer.

To her shock, he took her hand even as he said huskily, "This isn't all about our body count, or who has picked up whom the most times."

"You're stuck on the fact that you think I didn't deserve to get sucked into this."

"Partly," he agreed in the deep voice that gave her goose bumps. "Some of it is just because of who you are."

Gwen wanted desperately to ask what he meant by that. He seemed to be inviting the question, which scared her. They would part ways tomorrow or the next day. Soon. Assuming they *were* able to make a phone call to the DEA. Despite what a short time they'd had together, she could care too much about Rafe Salazar. Maybe she already did, but she had to nip it in the bud, or she'd suffer for letting herself fall for him.

"That's nice of you to say," she told him blithely. She was proud of herself for being able to sound so casual.

It worked, too, because after a moment, he released her hand and withdrew into himself.

Her newly chilled fingers curled into a painful fist at her side.

DAMN. IF HE wasn't in love with this woman, he was coming close. No, that was ridiculous. He'd never even kissed her. This was just the kind of intense bond that came into being when you shared a level of danger with someone else. He'd felt it working lengthy operations with fellow agents when they'd all developed complete trust. A few times, one of those agents had been female, so he couldn't blame these disturbing emotions entirely on the fact that Gwen was a woman.

Don't make this into something it isn't, he told himself, but he couldn't push back the crushing sense of dread he felt when thinking about saying goodbye to her.

Either she didn't share these emotions, or she was smart enough to know they couldn't go anywhere. He had to accept that.

It might have been easier if, half an hour later, they didn't have to squeeze into the same sleeping bag and almost effortlessly twine their bodies together as if they'd done this every night for weeks or months rather than mere days.

She didn't say a word after a mumbled "Good night." He didn't know if she felt the kiss he pressed to her head. What he did know was that she didn't surrender to sleep anywhere near as soon as her physical condition suggested she should have. Rafe loved the soft feel of her breasts pressed against his side and chest, her arm crooked over his belly and her hand splayed over his heart. Once she really conked out, she'd lift her leg and lay it across his, too. That she hadn't was one way he knew she was probably brooding the same way he was.

He sure as hell couldn't sleep until he felt her utter relaxation.

It came, eventually, after a soft sigh. He turned his head enough to kiss her forehead, having the wry thought that they'd both have slept sooner if they'd let themselves make love first.

Have sex. Love…was off the table.

The words, *for now*, drifted through his head just before he let himself relax into sleep, too.

As always, his sleep was restless. He'd tuned his radar to pick up any untoward sounds, and given how little time he had spent in the mountains in this part of the world, too many of those sounds triggered brief waking moments. Gwen squirming had the same effect on him, as did what he suspected were a couple of nightmares. Both times, she let out a gasp and stiffened. The second time, she cried out. Whether she actually heard his comforting words or felt him kneading whatever tight muscles he could reach, Rafe didn't know, but she gave no sign of waking up and relaxed back to sleep.

Would she keep having nightmares? Yeah, he'd bet on it. These days of sustained tension and fear provided plenty of material. They might have reawakened nightmares from after the car accident and her mother's death, too.

He had his own share of them. He'd come to think of them as a slideshow. A different one would haunt him every night. They tended to circle around until they replayed. Again and again.

Grimacing at the darkness, he knew damn well he'd added a couple new ones. Being tied securely to a backboard, unable to so much as lift an arm when that greedy sellout, Bruce Kimball, held a gun on him and then, worse, turned it on Gwen—that rose to the top. Watching her fall, unable to reach her... That had been bad, too.

The soft patter of rainfall on the tarp awakened him once, not heavy enough to be a real concern, although if it kept raining tomorrow—today?—the going would be miserable for two people not equipped with rain gear.

He did manage to drop off again, although by morning, he'd swear he'd been lucky to catch half an hour of shut-eye at a time throughout the entire night.

With the pearly light of dawn, he eased himself out of the sleeping bag without quite waking Gwen, who merely grumbled and clutched at him as if someone were stealing her favorite teddy bear.

He hastily dressed even as he looked around. The foliage was damp but no longer dripping, and what he could see of the sky made him think the clouds had cleared. Rafe grunted at the thought that they were lucky. He couldn't label much that had happened recently as lucky.

Except, of course, Gwen.

Growling under his breath, he opened some distance from their campsite to relieve himself, then returned to set up the stove again and put on water to heat for oatmeal and coffee.

RAFE'S MOOD DIDN'T appear to have improved today, although Gwen could hardly blame him. She wondered whether he could possibly have recovered from his gunshot wounds as miraculously as it appeared—or as he made an enormous effort to make it appear.

His face was drawn, hollows noticeable beneath sharp

cheekbones. He kept scratching irritably at dark stubble on his jaw and neck that could now be called a beard. She made an effort to brush out the tangles in her hair—along with twigs, leaves and one small slug that she tossed away with a shudder—but the best she could do was pull it back out of her face and hope it didn't look as greasy and sweat-soaked as it had to be.

"What I'd give for a shower," she muttered, not intending to be heard, but Rafe, who was strapping the tent and sleeping bag to the backpack, raised his eyebrows at her.

"I'd put living another day ahead of the shower, but both sound good."

She laughed, which made her realize she felt better today. *Better* being a relative term. His mouth quirked briefly in response.

Astonishingly enough, their route today headed downhill. Probably too steeply, so she'd run her fingertip along what looked to be their best path, although really, who knew? Even a topographical map only told you so much.

The zigzag lines of the Northern Loop Trail about where they hoped to join it made Rafe frown.

She said, "That's nothing compared to what we've already accomplished."

He bent to study the map again before saying, "You're right. This'll be a breeze."

She almost smiled again at the wryness in his tone.

Downhill was harder than uphill for aching thigh muscles and creaking joints. Grateful that the rainfall hadn't extended into the morning, Gwen pushed herself as hard as she could and felt guilty that Rafe still carried the pack.

Within an hour, her headache worsened and throbbed in time with every step. Scrambling along the side of a drop-off too steep to permit them to directly descend unroped kept her from being able to sink into the kind of lethargy she had yesterday.

Was it only yesterday that she'd fallen over the cliff? Her memory felt fuzzy enough, she wasn't sure.

Rafe issued curt orders to stop for a break every so often, usually when he spotted a fallen log or rock that allowed them to sit for a few minutes.

Halfway through the day, he suggested they get out the stove and heat water for one of the freeze-dried meals, of which they had plenty, and she could only say dully, "If you want to." None of the nuts or trail mix they had left appealed very much to her.

While he set up and prepared their meals, she refilled their water bottles at the creek they'd reached but hadn't yet figured out how to cross. She dropped purifying tablets in the bottles after returning. When she sat down and accepted a dish, she ate because he insisted on it.

She began to fear that when they actually came to the trail, she'd think it was a mirage.

Both ended up wet, and not just their boots and lower legs, when they scrambled over the rocky bed of the stream tumbling down the steep slope. From the map, she knew they'd had no choice but to cross it somewhere. At least here, it didn't quite qualify as a waterfall.

Midafternoon, when Gwen saw a lake a few hundred feet below them, she wanted to cry. That almost had to be Lake Ethel, didn't it? Which meant...

They'd made it.

Almost made it.

What if they reached the campsite and patrol cabin, and no one was there? She had no idea how long ago the map had been published. Maybe the patrol cabin had been abandoned, burned down—who knew?

What if…?

They'd keep walking, that's what. Once they reached the trail, it should be maintained and therefore mostly smooth, nothing like the country they'd traversed to this point.

Easy peasy, Mom would have said, because *her* mother had said it, too. Except, of course, for having to watch out for the ruthless men still hunting them.

The remaining descent to the lake and the short hike to the neighbouring Lake James, where the campsite was, wasn't as easy as she'd have liked it to be, but Rafe stopped her with a hand on her shoulder.

"I see a couple of backpackers."

"What?" Gwen whirled and made herself dizzy. She'd have gone down if he hadn't grabbed for her.

"Okay?"

"I…" She blinked a few times. "Just…shouldn't move so quickly."

He handed her the binoculars she hadn't seen him remove from the pack.

She didn't have to adjust them very much to spot the two hefty brightly covered packs carried by unidentifiable hikers. Unidentifiable, because the tops of their heads could barely be seen over the packs, and they were walking away—northeast, to be exact—taking the switchback descent depicted on the map.

Gwen couldn't see running after them, crying, "Stop! Do you have a phone?"

"Where they are," Rafe observed, "there'll be others."

"Like seeing a mosquito?" she asked politely.

He flashed a grin that weakened her already shaky knees. "Right. Except I'd have said an elk. People are herd animals."

That smile almost erased the lines of tiredness and pain

she'd become accustomed to seeing on his lean face. She had to look away. Sky? Blue. One long white tail of vapor left by a jet probably rising from the Seattle airport. No helicopters.

"Let's go." Rafe urged her forward, and she complied.

Just finding the trail was astonishing. They turned right: southwest. She'd been right. The way was not level, but relatively speaking, this was like strolling on a sidewalk. She'd never again think of hiking on designated trails as roughing it.

The campsite was empty.

After a detour to the patrol cabin, ditto. They knocked on the door, opened it and peered in. It looked abandoned.

Rafe muttered something she suspected was stronger than the *damn, damn, damn* Gwen was thinking.

He rolled his head, making her realize that his shoulders, at least, must ache. "Wait here? Or go looking for other backpackers?"

"Go looking. At this time of year, there are bound to be other hikers on a trail talked up in every guidebook."

"You want a bite to eat first?"

"Uh-uh. I'm afraid if I sit down, I won't be able to get myself up again."

Honesty was not, in this case, the best policy. Worry carved grooves in his forehead. "That means you definitely *should* take a break or even stop for the night."

"We can do better than that if only we find someone with a working phone," she reminded him. "Shower. Bed."

"Helicopter ride."

She had to think about that. Would she start feeling nervous on the job every time the copter lifted off the pad? Surviving a second crash would be pushing her luck. But Gwen had been flying for her job too long. She had…faith.

The EMS Bell helicopter wouldn't have gone down as it did if Bill had been left in control.

"A dream come true," she told Rafe, who half smiled, half grimaced and waved a hand ahead.

"You first, Ms. I-Puked-in-Secret-Last-Night."

And she'd thought he hadn't noticed.

Chapter Fourteen

The first backpacker, a lone young guy, looked alarmed at the sight of them. Rafe didn't think they could possibly look *that* bad. He asked, "Do you have a phone?"

The guy shook his head hard and scuttled by them, walking sideways like a crab. "No phone, sorry. There's, ah, some other people back there." He gestured vaguely, then hurried away.

Rafe watched him break into a trot.

Gwen smiled weakly. "Apparently, we could be cast in a horror movie."

"Maybe we're zombies and don't know it."

He was awed that Gwen had found humor in having their hopes dashed. That flash of laughter was gone, though, and now she stood still with her eyes closed, doing nothing but waiting.

He really wanted to get her to a hospital.

Rafe took her hand and squeezed it. "Onward."

Her lashes fluttered and she met his eyes. "Sure."

He wished the trail was wide enough for them to walk abreast, but instead he nudged her ahead. Without a word or a complaint, she went.

He didn't love to discover they were once again climbing, but Gwen trudged on, Rafe sticking close behind in case she hit the wall.

It didn't happen. She was still on her feet, putting one in front of the other, when he heard voices. She did, too, her head coming up.

This time, they were met by a group of four, three men and a woman.

Instead of panic, he saw concern on the face of the guy in the lead.

"What happened to you two?"

Rafe moved up beside Gwen and wrapped an arm around her. She leaned into him slightly.

"We were on a helicopter that crashed in rough country a few days ago. The pilot was killed. We're the only survivors."

All four people stared at them in a kind of awe. "I read something about a medical helicopter disappearing," another of the men said.

"That was us," Rafe agreed. "Is there any chance you have a phone with enough bars to allow us to make a call?"

He, for one, held his breath waiting for the answer.

THE RINGS WERE one of the best things Rafe had ever heard. The snarled "Zabrowsky" might be number two.

"It's Rafe Salazar." He watched as the woman and one of the men convinced Gwen to sit down on a folding camp stool—who knew there was such a thing?—and sip water. The woman had produced a Butterfinger bar that she handed over.

"Salazar?" Rafe's boss sounded genuinely stunned. "Goddamn. I was afraid you were dead. You just...disappeared. If personnel at the hospital were right, you were on that damn helicopter that went down, except there was no trace of you when we did locate it."

Rafe turned his back on the group and lowered his voice. "I was still coming out of anesthesia—couldn't have been long after they let you in to see me—when I found myself being transported to an airfield and loaded onto a rescue helicopter. Supposedly, I was being taken to Seattle for better care at a major hospital. Really, Bruce Kimball had paid off the EMS pilot to rendezvous with someone else in Mount Rainier National Park."

"Kimball?"

"You know him?"

"Vaguely. Was he the one...?"

"Who shot up the safe house? I assume so. I didn't get a good look, but I know Eaton let the shooter in because he recognized him. Uh, I don't suppose he or Stanton survived?"

The clipped no didn't surprise him.

"I'm on a borrowed phone. The paramedic who saved my life is with me. I'm still hurting, but she's in worse shape now. We'd love a pickup."

Rafe turned, consulted with everyone else and finally conceded that they would be best to go back to the campsite and cabin, where a helicopter could land.

Zabrowsky apparently pulled up a map on his computer and agreed he'd get a bird in the air as quickly as possible.

"Sit tight," he said, and Rafe gave a rough laugh. That sounded a lot better than any of the alternatives.

He handed the phone to the backpacker and said, "Thank you. Our ride will be along. I can't tell you how glad we were to see you."

Their new friends escorted them back to the campsite and insisted on waiting with them. He hesitated briefly, but most often there was safety of a sort in numbers, and even if that damn unmarked helicopter swept overhead, if Rafe and Gwen ducked their heads, they might appear to be part of the group.

All kinds of goodies appeared from the packs, and he dug out the remaining freeze-dried meals. A hot late lunch and early dinner helped fill the time until Rafe heard the distant, ominous roar of an approaching helicopter—except this one came from the north.

Gwen had a shimmer of tears in her eyes, although she never let them fall. The relief was so profound that Rafe might have shed some tears himself if they'd been alone.

But under it all, a heavy weight had settled in his chest, somewhere under his breastbone. He didn't want to leave Gwen. Say a quick goodbye to her in a hospital ER, say, leaving her to be evaluated while he walked away.

But would he be given a choice?

It TURNED OUT worse than Gwen had expected. Within seconds of the helicopter landing on the roof of the hospital, medical personnel ran to it. Her protests were ignored when someone wrapped a collar around her neck, she was eased onto a backboard and lifted onto a wheeled gurney. Talking to an older man who had walked out with the hospital employees, a man she presumed to be his boss, Rafe had his back to her when the team around her pushed her at the speed of a trot toward the entrance to the hospital.

Gwen opened her mouth to call to him…but then closed it. Anguish squeezed her chest. She didn't want more thanks, and would a last, terrible look into his dark eyes really be better than this, a clean severing of their relationship?

No. He was probably glad to hand her off safely. She needed to be glad *he* had made it this far safely, too.

Given what a short time she'd known him, how could parting hurt this much?

All she could do was close her eyes and experience being the patient for the second time in her life. Like most medical professionals, she was terrible at it.

"I'm sure I did have a concussion," she repeated countless times. "But I'm feeling better. I'm not dizzy anymore." Which wasn't quite true, but she just wanted to go home. She identified how many fingers were being held up, stared into the blinding light shone into her eyes and endured the claustrophobia induced by an MRI.

Her doctor, an eager young resident who she recognized from EMS deliveries to this hospital, finally conceded.

"I'm tempted to insist you stay the night, but as long as you go straight home—and not on a bus—" He broke off again to level a stern look at her. "I trust there are no tall flights of stairs in your building."

She almost laughed. She and Rafe had scrambled up thousands of feet in elevation, then down and up again, and now a staircase was supposed to daunt her?

"Elevator," she said.

The doctor frowned at her. "All right. You need to see your own doctor soon. Immediately if your headache worsens, you become dizzy, pass out or you experience difficulty with your vision."

Gwen tuned him out while making sure her expression was pleasant and accepting.

Only as she sat in a wheelchair and allowed an orderly to push her toward the main entrance was she hit by the realization that she couldn't even call for an Uber or pay for a taxi or let herself into her apartment. There had to be a way to reclaim her possessions, specifically, her keys, wallet and phone.

"Wait!" she said.

Almost simultaneously, she heard her name being called from behind her.

"Ms. Allen? Glad I caught you."

It was the man she'd seen on the helipad with Rafe. Iron-gray hair cut short, and the furrows in his face had her placing him in his fifties.

"I'll take over," he announced, firmly edging the orderly aside. "I need to speak to Ms. Allen."

His force of personality won the brief tussle, and she found herself being wheeled back to the elevator.

Once the doors had closed behind them and the elevator was dropping to what had to be a basement level, he introduced himself as supervisory agent Ron Zabrowsky and said, "I'd appreciate it if we could talk for a minute. I know an interview is probably the last thing you want right now—"

"No, it's okay. Is… Has Rafe—Agent Salazar—been checked out by a doctor?"

"Yes, immediately. He's recovered extraordinarily well given his activities this past week. From what he's said, he wouldn't have gotten far without you."

"Strapped to the backboard, he couldn't fight back," she said.

"No."

Was she in trouble for having shot and killed a federal agent?

They exited the elevator at a level that appeared to be deserted. Gwen felt uneasy for the first time. What would this man do if she insisted on walking? Having him behind her, pushing her to an unknown destination, made the hair on the back of her neck prickle. What if *he* had been allied with Bruce Kimball? When she asked Rafe what he thought about his boss, he'd hesitated.

"Where are we going?" she asked.

"Right here." He stepped to the side to open a door, held it with his hip and pushed her inside.

The first thing she saw was the pack lying on a table, a pile of things that had been in it to one side. A doctor rose from a padded office chair, scaring Gwen even more for a fleeting moment.

Then she realized he was *not* a doctor. It was Rafe—tall, sexy and somehow intimidating in undoubtedly borrowed clean blue scrubs to replace his filthy, torn clothing. Why intimidating? She didn't know. It wasn't as if she ever backed down just because a man or woman had the letters MD on an identity badge. She continued to take in Rafe's appearance, from his gleaming hair to the tuft of equally black hair that showed in the V of the scrub top, which bared his powerful arms. Her gaze swept all the way to the familiar borrowed boots.

She blinked back tears. Had *he* insisted on having a chance to say goodbye?

Humor seemed like a better idea than diving into his arms and sobbing.

"You look better than I do."

A grin flickered as he came straight to her. "For some reason, they insisted on cleaning me up before they replaced my dressings." Then his jaw tightened. "I can't believe they're booting you out! You can't tell me you don't have a concussion!"

"No, I did have one, but I don't have any symptoms alarming enough for the doctor to keep me overnight. I was going to take a taxi home, except I suddenly remembered I can't because you have my stuff."

He grinned. "I was holding it hostage so you couldn't get away."

"Oh." She cast a glance over her shoulder to see that Rafe's boss had strolled to a conference table and settled himself close enough to watch them but gave them a measure of privacy.

She lowered her voice. "Do you know yet where you'll be sent?"

Zabrowsky cleared his throat, and she realized that privacy was illusory.

Rafe grimaced. "That's...not yet settled."

She turned a blistering stare on his boss. "It had better be more secure than the last safe house!"

Rafe's crooked smile calmed her. "I'm not liking the idea of any agency safe house right now."

Gwen sniffed. "I can see why, at least until you can be sure Kimball was the only DEA agent willing to sell out."

Both men winced.

"So?" If she sounded acid, she couldn't help it. "Will you be put up in a hotel under a false identity until somebody comes up with a better solution?"

"You know I can't tell you," he said with the gentle timbre to his voice that always undid her.

Gwen tried to smile. "I know." He'd tried all along to hide how much pain he was in. Feeling vulnerable in any way might have been a new experience for him. Would he hate knowing she still felt protective of him?

She took a deep breath. Of course her idea would be shot down right away, but she decided to throw it out there, anyway. "You'd be welcome to come home with me while the investigation is underway. Who would expect that? Even though I was seen with you, does anyone know who I am?"

Rafe froze. She glanced uneasily at Zabrowsky to see a strange expression on his face.

"My apartment isn't super secure," she said tentatively, "but it's not bad. In theory, no one can get in or use the elevator without an electronic fob. If you stay out of sight..."

"I could be endangering you."

"We've kind of got a mutual aid society going already, don't we? I wouldn't mind having someone do the cooking until I'm feeling a little better."

"You won't be able to go back to work for a while," he said slowly.

Gwen sighed. "No. Even aside from the head injury, I'll be grounded until my ribs fully heal. I will need to let my superior know why I didn't show up to work Monday."

Zabrowsky joined them, half sitting on the conference table. "Surely he or she knows you were on the helicopter that disappeared."

"I'm actually not sure. Dispatch in Yakima offered me a ride along with the pilot to deliver an empty helicopter to Seattle. It's possible even that was kind of under the table. You know, a favor for a coworker. How much anyone higher up the chain knows about the unauthorized patient or Kimball as passenger—and whether I was on the helicopter or not—I won't know until I talk to them. And... I suppose you may want me to limit what I say?"

"We'll talk about that," Zabrowsky agreed.

She frowned. "You did look at the crash site."

"Eventually," he agreed. "I was still in Yakima when I heard some buzz about the medical helicopter that had gone missing, and then several days later, the fact that it had been found way off course, having gone down in the national park. Since supposedly there hadn't been passengers because it was merely being transferred between bases,

I couldn't be positive it was connected to Rafe's disappearance. We'd already turned that town upside down and given it a hard shake."

She would bet he was popular with the Yakima PD.

"At the hospital, several people claimed a DEA agent, who'd showed his credentials, had cleared Rafe's transfer to the EMS base and thus to Seattle. Needless to say, the badge did not belong to Bruce Kimball. Somehow, he'd gotten his hands on a badge belonging to an agent who had just retired. So recently—" he grimaced "—it might have been verified if anyone had thought to call to make sure it was legit. As it was, nobody did."

Keeping her focus on the crash, Gwen questioned, "The, um, body was gone by the time search and rescue found the crash site?"

His eyebrows rose. "Agent Bruce Kimball's body?"

That man she'd shot and killed. "Yes."

"No sign of it. No backboard. No proof anyone but the pilot was on board. To the contrary. The surroundings had been completely cleaned up. From what I know secondhand, it was assumed the pilot had deviated from his flight plan for an unknown reason, had a medical crisis or got caught in some weather anomaly and went down before he could let anyone know he was in trouble."

"I think Kimball must have killed him. Did Rafe tell you that?"

Rafe laid a hand on her shoulder. "I did. I told him everything that happened and all our speculation." He lifted his gaze to Zabrowsky. "What do you think?"

The already deep furrows in Ron Zabrowsky's forehead became chasms. "About the idea of staying with Ms. Allen."

Rafe's fingers tightened on Gwen's shoulder. "Yeah."

She held her breath.

"I have reservations for obvious reasons, but…it might work as a very temporary measure. Discovering we had an internal betrayal—" He broke off.

She didn't ask herself whether this was a good idea or whether she was just setting herself up for real heartbreak. She only knew she wanted this. Days if not weeks more with Rafe. Time to talk when they weren't running for their lives.

If it became awkward, if they turned out to have nothing in common, then that might be just as well.

"Gwen." Rafe crouched in front of her wheelchair, his hands covering hers where they rested on the arms. His dark eyes were searching. "Are you sure?"

"Of course I'm sure." To her ears, she sounded a little shaky. She hoped he hadn't noticed.

He kept looking into her eyes for an unnerving length of time before he gave her hands a quick squeeze and rose to his feet.

"Ron?"

"It would solve some immediate problems. You can't go with her right away, though. We need her to be seen making her way home alone." Zabrowsky gave her an apologetic glance. "Not that it's likely anyone is watching, but we can't afford to be careless."

Rafe's jaw had tightened, but Gwen nodded. "No. That makes sense."

"Then let's plan how we can slip him in late tonight."

Her chest expanded as if with the first full breath she'd been able to take in longer than she could remember. This wasn't goodbye—not yet.

Chapter Fifteen

"The pull-out sofa is fine," Rafe said even though what he'd really like was to sleep with her in the queen-size bed he'd caught a glimpse of in the single bedroom during the brief tour she'd given him after his 2:00 a.m. arrival. "You must be beat."

"I slept for a few hours." A smile lit her face. "*After* the best shower I've ever taken. I'm bitter the hospital personnel didn't let me shower then and there. They know me! But no—they sent me home in *filthy* clothes with *gross* hair. I won't be surprised if someone didn't take a few photos to post or at least pass around. Or maybe to blackmail me with."

He'd have been outraged if he hadn't been able to tell she was kidding. Who'd dislike the courageous, kind, patient woman who'd saved his life repeatedly?

And damn. Not even her visible bruises could keep him from thinking about how beautiful she was.

To distract himself, he said, "Ah, I didn't think to ask whether you have friends, neighbors, whatever, who are used to dropping by."

Her surprise was evident. "Not really. I'm not big on parties, and this place isn't large enough for me to host one, anyway. Usually, I meet friends out somewhere. With my work schedule being so different, even my closest friends can't keep track. When people call, I'll meet them somewhere else, like your boss suggested. That's usual for me, anyway. No one will wonder."

"Good." He dropped the duffel bag in a corner of the small living room. He unzipped it and removed the small toiletry kit, a result of the quick shopping trip Zabrowsky had personally made this evening while leaving Rafe stashed in that windowless, locked room in the hospital basement. It was unsettling that Zabrowsky was so determined to keep Rafe's reappearance among the living a deep, dark secret. He didn't dare even trust an underling enough to send him on the errand. The pilot and copilot of the helicopter that picked him and Gwen up were under orders to keep their damn mouths shut. The quote was straight from Zabrowsky. Rafe knew from experience that consequences for an indiscretion would be extreme.

At the moment, Gwen looked as uncomfortable as he felt. Him moving in with her here didn't feel like an extension of their desperate trek through the wilds of the park. It wasn't that he'd never had a roommate. During undercover investigations, he'd slept plenty of times in close quarters with the men he had to fit in with. In his personal life, it had been years. Generally when he was involved with a woman, overnights weren't included. He liked his space and privacy.

Had liked them, until he'd discovered the pleasure of holding this woman, waking to find her wrapped around him.

That's what he wanted right now and wasn't going to get.

"You probably haven't had any sleep yet at all, have you?" she said quickly. "I'll get out of your way. If you're up before me in the morning, I've programmed the coffee maker. Otherwise, help yourself to anything you can find. There isn't much, but I'll put in a grocery order in the morning. You can add to the list."

"Thanks."

"Well, then…" She backed up, bumped into the edge of the kitchen island and forced a smile. "Good night."

He opened his mouth, but she'd retreated down the extremely short hall to her bathroom, leaving him alone. For all that he was beat, he wasn't so sure sleep would come easily tonight.

HE'D BEEN RIGHT. The pull-out mattress was fine, if nowhere near as comfortable as his bed in his apartment had been, or the one at the safe house, for that matter. It was incomparable luxury compared to the thin, too narrow foam pad he and Gwen had shared the past few nights, so he couldn't use it to excuse his restlessness.

He did drop off, wake up and sleep again. The third time he came awake, he saw a faint glow coming from the bedroom or bathroom. Rafe lay still and waited. The toilet didn't flush; the light didn't go out. Finally, he climbed out of bed and walked on silent feet toward the source of the light: a six-inch crack where she'd left her bedroom door open.

He glanced down at himself and decided he was decent enough in pajama pants and a T-shirt from a package of three that had been part of his new wardrobe. He wrapped lightly on the door with his knuckles.

A no-doubt startled silence was followed by, "Rafe? Come in."

He pushed open the door and stepped into her bedroom. Gwen sat up in bed, pillows piled behind her, a laptop on crossed legs beneath the covers. Gleaming strands of golden-brown hair had worked their way loose from her braid.

"I'm sorry. Did I wake you up?" she asked.

He shook his head and wandered closer. "Wasn't sleeping well."

"The sofa—"

"Is fine. Just...have a lot on my mind." *Especially you*, he didn't say.

She smiled weakly. "Me too. I guess I shouldn't have slept earlier. Um... I was reading what coverage appeared in the *Seattle Times* about the crash."

"Yeah, I did that earlier. It's scanty, and what's there has no resemblance to what really happened."

"No." She looked shy. "If you want to sit down..."

On the bed, she meant. There were no other options. A dresser, bedside stand and treadmill filled most available floor space. He sat near the foot.

"You having nightmares?" he asked.

"I...don't really know." The uncertainty looked genuine. "I keep jerking awake, so my dreams probably aren't all sunshine and roses." Her forehead creased as she studied him. "What about you? Or... I suppose you become inured."

"To some extent." He talked for a minute about the necessity of being able to separate the ugly things he saw and did on the job from the rest of his life. He didn't mention that the process wasn't nearly as tidy as it sounded. "Right now, I'm having trouble remembering what the rest of my life was like," he heard himself say.

Where did that come from?

Her eyes were warm. "You were undercover for a year, you said. That's...a long time."

He moved his shoulders uncomfortably. Talking about feelings, that was something he did even less often than he went home, which he no longer had. He'd stored his possessions before taking on the last investigation.

"Then over a month in the safe house," he reminded her.

She closed her laptop and set it aside without looking away from him. "You must have friends."

"Sure." Rafe grimaced. Did he? Given that his best friend from growing up was dead, the closest to longtime friends he had were from college, and they were spread across the country and contact consisted mostly of an occasional phone conversation. "In my job, friends come and go. We get transferred, disappear for varying lengths of time. We intend to stay in touch but rarely do. It's hard to make friends outside the agency when you can't talk about most of what you do."

"No, I suppose not." She kept studying him. "What do you do for, well, recreation?"

"I run, lift weights, play in baseball and basketball leagues our agency fields. Join a regular poker group, read, watch TV." He shrugged. "On my rare vacations, I enjoy diving."

Gwen wrinkled her nose. "Diving in the Puget Sound isn't the same experience as it would be in the Caribbean."

He laughed. "So I hear. You've tried it, then?"

"Yes. I wasn't enthused. I did snorkel once in Hawaii and loved that."

He interpreted that as her saying she'd be open to diving again in warm, clear waters in some imaginary future with him.

They kept talking, voices low, sharing bits and pieces of their lives from the trivial to the important. Given the nighttime quiet, the atmosphere felt intimate. Just the two of them. They'd had that a lot recently, but this was different. He couldn't quite put his finger on why.

"What time is it?" he asked at last.

"Hm? Oh." She reached for her phone, which was plugged in on the bedside stand. "Five thirty. You should go back to sleep."

"I was thinking a cup of coffee sounds good. I'll try to be quiet—"

Gwen shook her head. "I would have gotten up earlier if I hadn't been trying not to wake you. I'll probably need a nap later, but hey! I don't have anything better to do."

With a yawn, he stretched his arms over his head, aware of a pull in the injured arm but overall appreciating more mobility than he'd have expected so soon. "You're able to go out, at least." Zabrowsky wanted anybody watching to see her follow a normal routine on days when she wasn't working. "Now, me, I'm free to do nothing but lounge on the couch and stare mindlessly at the TV."

"You don't even have a laptop, do you?"

A fact that irritated him no end. "Nope. And I won't have one."

"Well, you're welcome to use mine. And…surely you were given a phone."

"I was, but Ron made it clear he didn't want me online to do more than read news updates."

"Oh. Well, um, I do have the treadmill."

Rafe laughed. "And I'll use it, but probably not for a few more days."

She scrunched her face up. "Me either. So… I think there are some waffles in the freezer."

Accepting the signal, he stood. "I'd better get dressed."

It was while getting dressed in the bathroom, anticipating more than he should the very kind of breakfast he often had when hurried, that Rafe had an epiphany. That conversation really had been different. Simple as that. He'd never let himself talk to anyone as he had to Gwen. The closest might have been when he started a relationship with a girl in college, but it wouldn't have even crossed his mind to tell her about Mateo, as an example.

No, he and Gwen had shared like two people who really wanted to know each other, from the fun parts to the deep, hurtful places. They weren't on the run anymore; they were in the comfort of her home. What they'd gone through with each other had answered many of the biggest questions, meaning he could be open in a way he had never been with a woman.

The very fact that he really did want to know about everything that had made Gwen Allen the woman she was, from the heartbreaking to the trivial, shook him to his foundation. There was no question that he'd be walking out of her life soon. He knew better than to fall for her, if that's what was happening.

He stared at himself in the mirror. *Hell.* Maybe it was too late.

Gwyn's employers weren't thrilled to have to remove her from the roster for a minimum of a month. After Zabrowsky confirmed in some mysterious way that nobody beyond the dispatcher at EMS Flight had had the slightest idea she'd gotten on that helicopter—and the dispatcher had been exceedingly grateful to be ordered to forget that he knew anything about it—she'd required a new excuse for her disappearance and injuries.

Apparently, federal agents were encouraged to be creative. Now she and an unnamed friend had gone backpacking without taking sensible precautions, like charging their phones. They'd gotten lost, after which Gwen stumbled over a cliff. The friend had helped her hobble out of the wilderness. Gwen made herself grovel while clenching her teeth and being officially reprimanded. She didn't appreciate any of it. The only plus side was that she didn't have to explain helping herself to narcotics or what she'd done with the missing doses.

Rafe's annoyance that her courageous conduct had been rewarded so shabbily helped her get over being mad. She even resented the implication that she and an apparently brainless friend would have been so careless as to forget to pack a charger for their phones.

He'd wrapped an arm around her while she grumbled.

"I don't blame you for being irritated," he said sympathetically, "but the story doesn't hang together if you'd carried a charger. Claiming no cell service might make someone wonder if you hadn't been in Mount Rainier National Park, and that's the last thing we want."

"Yeah, yeah." She sighed, letting herself lean into him for a moment, but not too long. The heat she occasionally saw in his eyes let her know that surrendering to temptation could have long-term consequences she was trying to avoid.

Like making love with a man she'd never be able to forget and might forever use as a standard other men couldn't match.

In the next couple of days, she learned he was a good roommate in most respects. He never complained about the confinement, although she felt his tension as if he exuded an electrical charge. He tried to work it out doing exercises— she was awestruck by the number of sit-ups he could do— and he hadn't been kidding about using the treadmill. He ran what had to be ten miles or more a day on it. They'd be talking in the kitchen, and he'd suddenly jump up and say, "I need a run," and vanish to her bedroom.

Which meant, of course, that she couldn't go to her bedroom, because then she'd have to feast on the sight of him in low-slung sweatpants and a tank top that exposed an imposing amount of muscle as he ran. Fast and hard until sweat dripped, until the intensity on his face almost frightened her.

He did that *right next to her bed.*

She couldn't help thinking of another excellent way for him to burn off some of that stress. She wanted to burn off her own that way, too, except for this fear that making love with him would be *too* good.

By the third day, she felt better enough to start going out occasionally, even though she felt guilty because Rafe was one hundred percent confined. Since she'd been assigned the task of appearing as if she were back from her vacation a little battered but otherwise normal, except for the frustration of not being able to work, she had to show her face. She met friends from work for coffee, stopped by base to say hi and listened to them talk with shock about the crash and the pilot's death.

"I mean, I've never flown with him," a trauma nurse who was a frequent partner of Gwen's said, "but…"

She didn't have to finish. The dead man could have been any of the pilots they knew well and appreciated with every flight. *They* could be on the next flight that went down, claiming all lives aboard.

Of course, Gwen couldn't admit that she'd met Bill, never mind seen his charred remains. Puked after seeing that. Shot and killed the man who'd been responsible.

She claimed headaches to avoid getting together with coworkers after that. Instead, she grocery-shopped and stopped at the pharmacy to keep up on birth control she hadn't needed in a very long time and didn't need right now, either, but it still seemed…smart. She bought a pair of expensive athletic shoes to replace the ones now tattered and stinky after the use she'd put them through. She picked up a newspaper daily at the box on the corner. Both she and Rafe read it voraciously.

And every time she left her apartment, she had the uncomfortable feeling that she was being watched. She never saw anyone seeming to pay attention to her, but she tried.

On the fifth day, Rafe received a phone call.

"Bodies?" he repeated, glanced at her and went to her bedroom. She heard the door close as she continued with dinner preparations.

When he reappeared, his expression was grim. "Zabrowsky says they found the bodies of the two men we shot." His jaw tightened.

Gwen guessed those bodies weren't in good shape by this time.

"They also found a SAT radio that might have flown out of a pocket when one of them went down. It was deep in some ferns and other underbrush."

Her hands, one holding a paring knife, stopped, unmoving, above the cutting board and a half-chopped bell pepper. "A radio."

"That means they probably did report on us when they saw us descending the ridge. They know a woman was with me, likely even gave a description of you."

Her breathing had become choppy, and she looked down to see that her hands trembled. Carefully, she set down the knife. "They still don't know my name," she pointed out.

"It gets worse," Rafe continued. "The dispatcher who okayed you on that flight admits now to a phone call that came in three or four days after the helicopter went down. Somebody claiming to be a cousin wanted to be sure a woman made it onto a flight that was supposed to be going directly to Seattle. Since you hadn't been in touch, the caller claimed to be worried. He evidently confirmed you boarded the helicopter but can't remember whether he used your name when he agreed."

"Oh, God. You're not safe here. You need to leave."

"If they'd found you, we'd know."

"What?" She stared at him. "Somebody could be watching me."

"Somebody is."

"You're kidding."

"Why would I kid?" He sounded genuinely bewildered.

"Because I've had this creepy feeling that I'm being watched!" she cried. "I told myself I was imagining things, that it was just a leftover from when we knew we *were* being hunted, but now you're telling me…?" Conflicted emotions choked off everything else she wanted to say.

"I'm sorry." Rafe came to her, turned her slowly and pulled her against him, his arms wrapping her snugly. "I should have said something. With this kind of informal arrangement, Ron just about had to keep an eye on us. He and I agreed on a female agent we've both worked with before and believe in. Figured a woman would be less conspicuous."

Dark-haired, medium-height, friendly smile. Gwen had seen the same woman several times and just assumed she was new in the neighborhood. When she described her, Rafe nodded. "That's Carolyn."

Gwen debated between shoving him away and continuing to lean on his strong body. Outrage versus the usual temptation, which won. She punched him in the shoulder, anyway. The uninjured one, of course.

Finally, head resting on his shoulder, she said, "You're confident she'll spot anyone else following me or lurking around the building."

"That's the idea."

The answer wasn't as complete as she'd have liked, but

how could he give her a guarantee? She'd agreed to a level of risk when she offered him sanctuary with her. *Live with it*, she told herself.

"Okay," she mumbled.

Being held might have been comfortable if she hadn't been so aware that they were in full body contact—her thighs and breasts pressed against his chest, her cheek on her shoulder. And, was he getting aroused? He didn't say anything, just stayed exceptionally still.

Gwen realized she was doing the same.

Abruptly, his arms dropped from around her, and he backed away. "If you don't need help with dinner, I'm going to use the treadmill."

"This is getting to you, isn't it?"

"This?" he echoed sharply.

"I mean—" Gwen gestured "—being trapped in such a small space. It must feel like a prison cell."

A rough sound escaped him. "It's not the space. You have to know that."

The hot light in his dark eyes transfixed her. "I…wondered," she whispered. "You…get to me, too, you know."

"I swore I'd keep my hands off you."

She knew suddenly how much better having even a single memory of a night with him would be than nothing.

Warmth flushed her cheeks and she swallowed. "I wish you wouldn't."

One long stride, and his mouth closed over hers.

As if they'd done this a thousand times, they kissed deeply, intensely, tongues stroking and tangling. He gripped her butt to lift her higher while his other hand cupped her jaw. Gwen quit thinking, quit worrying and only felt. She slung her arm around his neck and rose on tiptoe. She wanted to touch him everywhere, but right now, the best she could do was to slide her free hand under his T-shirt and stroke the hard muscles in his back while her fingertips traced his vertebrae.

She wanted everything.

He nipped her lower lip and raised his head. "Gwen?" he asked hoarsely. "Are you sure?"

She wouldn't have sworn she could talk at all, but she managed. "I'm sure."

He said something gritty she couldn't make out, swept her high in his arms and carried her out of the kitchen and toward the bed where she'd felt so alone since he came home with her.

Chapter Sixteen

His hands were shaking. He'd never wanted a woman as much as he did this one, and it had been scaring the hell out of him. He'd have no choice but to leave her. Right now, though, he could give her everything he could.

Instead of throwing her down on the bed, he let her slide down his body until she was back on her feet. The friction with her curves felt so damn good, he wanted to do it again. Instead, he looked down at her face, so vulnerable, her cheeks pink, her eyes dazed, dreamy. She wanted this, too. He eased her shirt over her head, careful not to hurt her, and unclipped her bra, letting it fall. Then he stared, drinking in the sight of her long, pale torso and high, full breasts with delectable rosy nipples.

"I have to—" He lifted her again so he could lick and kiss and suck one of her breasts, then the other.

She whimpered and said something he thought might be "Not fair."

He did most of the stripping, but she helped. He was just trying to decide how he could bend over far enough with this erection to untie his shoes when she knelt at his feet. Rafe watched helplessly as she tugged off first one, then the other and finally his socks. Still on her knees, she squeezed his calves with strong hands before trailing them over his thighs and higher, until his back bowed in a combination of ecstasy and agony that forced him to take control again.

Once he had her on her back in bed, he stroked and tasted and kissed her until he was shaking again. Her legs spread, her knees tightened on his hips, and he had a horrifying realization. For the first time in his life, he wasn't sure he could stop, but he had to.

He pulled back. "I don't have a condom."

"I bought some a few days ago. Just in case. But I'm on birth control, anyway."

He had never dared trust a woman to that extent. This time...he did. Gwen wouldn't lie, but no one method of birth control was entirely safe, and he wouldn't be around. He couldn't take a chance.

"Where are they?"

"Drawer."

He fumbled, tore open a box with one hand, ripped the small packet even faster and covered himself.

And then he buried himself inside her, never taking his eyes from hers.

She moved with him as if she knew what he needed— or as if she needed the same. With one keening cry, she came with shocking speed, tightening around him until he groaned out her name and spilled himself inside her. If he hadn't been wearing the condom— *Don't think it.*

Rafe came down heavily on her, barely able to make himself move and roll to one side. She rolled with him, her head finding the familiar resting place, their bodies fitting together as if they were one.

Both sated and stunned, Rafe wished he could absorb her. He'd be happy to stay just like that for the rest of his life.

And if anything had ever rattled him, it was that thought.

NEITHER SAID A word in the aftermath. They did finally have dinner, avoiding even a glance at the elephant in the room. Gwen worried aloud about the earlier phone call. Rafe reassured her when he didn't believe himself.

If those bastards had her name or had even learned she was a paramedic with EMS Flight who'd hitched a ride on the helicopter that carried him, they'd find her. She was right—he should insist that he be moved *now*, except that would leave her alone. Here, he had a chance of protecting her. How would he feel if he'd been settled in another damn rambler in Idaho or Minnesota or South Carolina only to be told Gwen was dead?

That...really wasn't a question. Rafe didn't think he could live with the knowledge she'd died for him. He had a bad feeling he was head over heels in love with her, although it was hard to be sure since he'd never experienced anything like this before.

He cleaned up after dinner while keeping an eye on her. She plopped down on the couch and turned on the TV, going to local news on a Seattle channel. Rafe didn't know if she'd always been a news junkie, but she certainly qualified now. What did she think the air-brushed newscasters could tell her that she didn't already know...or fear?

When he joined her, sinking down on the cushion right next to hers and laying his arm around her shoulders, she didn't even look at him. He hoped it was his imagination that she stiffened. Whatever topic the reporters currently covered had them laughing. He didn't pay any attention.

"Are you sorry?" he asked abruptly.

Gwen turned sharply to scrutinize him. "You mean, about...? Of course I'm not! I've been...attracted to you since you were still strapped down and I was told you were a criminal."

"Ah." He relaxed. "I thought you were beautiful from the minute you uncovered my eyes, too. An angel of mercy, despite the fact that I was desperate to see where I was."

She made a face at the humor in his voice. "I did a lot more important things for you than that."

Even that flicker of amusement left him. "Yeah, you did. You'll have nightmares about them for years."

"No. I didn't do anything that wasn't necessary. And I'm not like most people, you know. I see terrible things on the job. We might pick up an injured person from a five-car pileup on the freeway, but we also see all the people, adults and children who didn't survive long enough even to have a chance."

Rafe knew that but had let himself forget. He'd say her job was what made her tougher than average, quicker thinking, willing to face danger most people would shrink from— except that her determination to become a paramedic said something about who she'd been all along. If she had nightmares, they were probably still about being trapped in that car as a child with her mother's body inches away.

He drew her to him and kissed her, maybe roughly, he didn't know, just that he had to have her again right now. With a sound that was nearly a sob, Gwen flung herself at him and kissed him back with all the passion he felt. At one point, he became irritated enough at the canned voices coming from the TV to stab a button on the remote and shut the damn thing up. That was the closest to a conscious thought he had.

Otherwise, he struggled to get her clothes off and enough of his so that he could make love to her again. The bedroom was too far away. He laid her back on the couch, pushed into her and kept thrusting until her climax flung him into his own.

Then he got the rest of his clothes off and did it again.

It wasn't until an hour later, as she led him by one hand to bed, that he remembered he hadn't used a condom either time. Despite knowing she was on birth control, his carelessness would have panicked him normally. This time, he had a tantalizing vision of her swelling with his baby.

He made sure she couldn't see his face while he shut down a dream he couldn't allow himself. What he felt for her was too new. Those emotions were the equivalent of tiny green shoots emerging from the soil. Most new growth ended up frozen because of late cold snaps or fried in a mid-summer drought or trampled under uncaring feet.

Rafe couldn't let himself forget that he wouldn't be around this fall or next spring or probably even next fall. Imagining that whatever he felt for Gwen, or her for him, would survive a year and a half absence was too much of a stretch to be believable.

The kindest thing he could do would be to make it clear to her that this thing between them wasn't going anywhere. Because it wasn't.

But he might have a few more days, a few more nights, and he couldn't make himself hurt her now—or miss the chance to have mind-blowing sex as often as possible.

Call him selfish, but he'd never lied to Gwen. She knew as well as he did that they were existing in a tiny slice of time that could be snatched away from them any minute.

For all the passion she showed him, she didn't ask for reassurance that he cared about her. Even as that was a relief, it bothered him. They made love twice more that night but never discussed it.

He remembered her saying something about going out for a few casual errands the next day, but wrinkled her nose when he asked her plans and said, "Maybe tomorrow. Unless there's something you need, I'm happy here." Her smile teased and tempted. "It's not like we're bored."

"No." He hadn't been bored a minute since he'd set eyes on her. There'd been days when he'd felt like a big cat pacing the perimeter of his cage in search of a weakness, but boredom hadn't been the reason for that. Nope. It was all about Gwen.

Right now, all he wanted was to extend the days with her as long as possible.

Ron called that evening. "I can't find any hint that Bruce Kimball wasn't working alone, at least out of the Chicago office. I spoke to his supervising special agent, who admitted there have been some issues with him. Mostly personality clashes, attitude. He was close to being terminated. Knowing that might have motivated him to take a big paycheck, although you'd think he'd have been smart enough to know the odds weren't good a cartel would let him live once he'd served his purpose."

"No."

"Given what I've learned—and what I haven't learned— I'm going to have you moved to a new safe house. Expect to hear from me in the next day or two."

"Will do."

Ron ended the call. Feeling almost numb, Rafe sat on the edge of Gwen's bed. Tell her how soon he was going? Or wait until he had no choice?

His conscience twinging, all he could think was *Hell*.

SOMETHING CHANGED AFTER the phone call Rafe took in her bedroom that evening. When Gwen asked about it, he only shook his head, his expression impassive in that way he had when he was in special agent mode.

She couldn't help immediately speculating. Had he

learned that other agents had been compromised, too, and was sick with disappointment or anger? Had the Espinosa family shifted practices or personnel in a way that would make Rafe's testimony less powerful to a jury? Or had the call been from someone else altogether, perhaps giving him personal news?

The reminder was timely. Despite their closeness, she didn't know much about his personal life. He enjoyed playing poker and baseball. His parents, he'd talked about. What happened with his friend Mateo, which she thought he'd offered up because she'd told him about the car accident that had killed her mother and changed the trajectory of Gwen's life. Otherwise, surely a man who looked like Rafe and had his charisma and wicked smile usually had a girlfriend. Probably not a live-in one currently, not after his year plus spent undercover, but there could still be someone for whom he cared deeply.

Gwen rolled her eyes. Way to feel sorry for herself. He kept warning her in his not-so-subtle way that what they enjoyed was temporary. In other words, he wasn't untildeath-do-us-part in love with *her*.

Too bad she did love him. Her little secret.

The next morning, she asked if he needed anything when she went out.

Sitting at the table with a cup of coffee in front of him, he frowned. "Nothing I can't live without."

"To rephrase, is there anything you *want*?"

His grin came close to making her knees buckle, except...it didn't seem to reach his eyes. Disturbed, she still didn't protest when he tugged her forward, slipped a hand behind her neck and urged her to bend over enough for him to kiss her.

"You," he whispered. "I want you."

But apparently didn't need her.

She emerged from the kiss, smiled at him and said, "I may buy all kinds of goodies while I'm out. You'll be sorry."

"I'll live with it."

Gwen grabbed her handbag, dropped her phone in it, made sure she had her keys and said, "Bye."

Too bad there was nowhere she especially wanted to go or anyone she needed to see.

Behave normally, she'd been ordered. Now that the bruises on her face had faded from sight and the lump on her head was gone, her only remaining physical symptom was soreness from her bruised rib cage. Give her another week, and she'd probably be able to persuade a doctor to clear her to go back to work.

What then?

Rafe would be gone. She knew that with painful certainty, one she both forced herself to confront and pushed back at. Why torture herself?

She let herself out of the apartment, took the elevator down and strolled out. She hadn't gone a block when she caught a glimpse of an attractive dark-haired woman sitting at a bus stop apparently intent on her phone. Carolyn.

Carolyn didn't so much as glance toward Gwen, who ignored her, too. As far as she could tell, the agent didn't follow her, or if she did, she had a gift for subterfuge.

Gwen went to her favorite neighborhood grocery store, not huge and really expensive because of the superior quality of their produce and breads. This was the only place she ever bought cherry tomatoes because they'd be really ripe and tasty. Maybe she'd make a favorite recipe tonight with cherry tomatoes and dumplings.

She browsed, bought more than she needed and had

enough to carry after she checked out to give her an excuse to skip any other errands.

Half a block from her building, just passing an alley, she saw something strange. A foot stuck out from behind a dumpster. Probably one of the houseless people who called this neighborhood home, she thought, although this was the middle of the day. And…the athletic shoe on the foot was bright white with a logo she recognized. Those shoes weren't cheap.

Carolyn had been wearing those shoes.

Gwen's step stalled. She should check, be sure it wasn't Carolyn or anyone else who needed help. But the leap of her pulse said, *You can't help.* She had to pretend not to notice, keep an eye around herself and hurry home while trying very hard not to *look* as if she were hurrying.

And…call Rafe?

She started to fumble in her bag, but she'd be home in a matter of minutes. In fact, the steps into the building were just ahead. She bounded up them, smiled vaguely at another tenant who had been coming out and held the door for her, and stole a look back the direction she'd come.

Two men had their gazes on her and were walking fast.

Gwen dashed in, pushed the button for the elevator and leaped in when it proved to be on the ground floor. The doors shut, giving her a momentary illusion of safety, but the elevator seemed to take forever to rise to her floor.

Once she was in her apartment, she and Rafe could hold anyone off, couldn't they? She should have called to warn him—maybe she still should?—but the elevator glided to a stop and the doors parted.

She ran and was fumbling to get her key in the lock when she heard the metal door at the head of the staircase slam

open not twenty feet from her. Running footsteps thud-
ded toward her as the apartment door gave way, and she
screamed, "Rafe!"

HE FELT RESTLESS, but not in a way running mindlessly on
the treadmill would help. In fact, had he stepped foot on it
since the first time he and Gwen had made love?

He shook his head hard. He never liked it when Gwen
went out by herself, for all practical purposes setting herself up as bait, although she didn't seem to realize that was
what Ron had in mind.

Part of what Ron had in mind, anyway.

Today his uneasiness grew even though she hadn't been
gone all that long. Nothing like when she'd met friends for
coffee. For all he knew, she'd taken the bus to the university bookstore to browse and would be gone for a couple of
hours. She hadn't said.

But half an hour after she went out the door, he began
to pace. Every so often, he'd crack the blinds at the front
of the small living room to let him see the street and some
of the sidewalk. He'd try to make himself sit but was too
antsy to be still for long, and the next thing he knew, he'd
be up and walking again.

Ten feet that way, twenty-five if he went through the
kitchen and down the very short hall, too. Then back. Peek
through the blinds. Repeat.

Instead of leaving his gun sitting on an end table, he
slipped it in his waistband at the back for quick access. Did
Gwen carry Kimball's, which Ron had not asked her to return? Rafe realized he didn't know. Maybe just as well if it
wasn't deep in that capacious handbag of hers. She'd proven
herself a good shot, but even the best of police marksmen

didn't dare open fire on a busy sidewalk with passing cars and buses. She didn't have their experience.

This time when he scanned the sidewalk, he saw two men walking fast in this direction. Nothing that would catch most people's attention—they could be hurrying to catch a bus or late getting back to their desks at work—but he didn't like the look of them. The thermometer was supposed to top ninety degrees today, hot by northwestern standards, but one wore a jacket and the other a denim overshirt.

He didn't see Gwen, but he'd swear their speed increased. Then they moved out of sight—as if they'd turned into this or a neighboring building.

He heard the elevator and tensed. Let it be Gwen. Feet that had to be running in the hall. Rafe had just reached the door when it opened and Gwen threw herself forward, yelling, "Rafe!"

Seconds later, a man brandishing a handgun shoved her in.

Rafe pulled his gun even as a bullet splintered the glass on a piece of framed art on the wall. He immediately noted from the thickness of their upper bodies that they wore Kevlar vests.

Gwen screamed and staggered, the second man having gripped her ponytail and using it to whip her to one side.

Rafe dove behind the easy chair as a bullet burned his arm. From behind the minimal cover, he fired without his usual icy calm. He wouldn't take a chance of hitting Gwen, but if he didn't take these two down, both he and Gwen would die.

The chair jumped from a fusillade of bullets. Only a decade and a half of practice and experience allowed him to aim carefully instead of firing wildly. He didn't like head-shots, but throats...

The first attacker went down, gun skittering across the floor toward Rafe. The second man, a brawny blue-eyed blond, wrenched Gwen in front of him, her head pulled painfully back, and pressed the barrel of his handgun at her temple.

"Drop the gun! I'll kill her! You know I will."

Rafe calculated. If he dropped his Glock, would he have time to get his hands on the other gun that lay temptingly close to him? Would the piece of scum turn his sights on Rafe the minute he moved or shoot Gwen and throw her aside as if she were a distraction done serving his purpose?

"I'll put it down," he called. "Let her go."

The creep laughed. Gwen made a gurgling sound.

Rafe gathered himself, laid his Glock on the floor and gently pushed it away. At the very moment he launched himself forward for the other weapon, the man holding Gwen started swinging his gun toward Rafe.

Chapter Seventeen

Gwen grabbed her assailant's arm and shoved it up.

Bullets flew over Rafe's nearly supine body. He snatched up the gun he'd gone for, raised it and risked a couple of shots at the arm and shoulder, away from Gwen.

Her captor reeled and kept shooting wildly as he went down, bringing Gwen with him. Rafe leaped forward to free her from the grip on her hair, except she hammered a fist down on the fool's wounded arm. He screamed, letting go of both her ponytail and his gun. Rafe took barely five seconds to flip him face down on the blood-slick oak floor.

"Call 911!" he ordered, drilling his knee into the man's back. "Check the other guy."

She sensibly did that first. "He's dead," she said, almost calmly, and a moment later, he heard her talking to a dispatcher.

Zabrowsky would not be happy about this debacle, except his witness was alive, and there wouldn't have to be an explanation as to why an innocent local woman had been killed.

Rafe felt sick at how close it had been.

Gwen turned as she ended the call and said, "I have to go down and let them in."

"You're not hurt?" he asked hoarsely.

She was shaking but shook her head. "You are. You're bleeding."

"Nothing significant." How had he sounded so calm? After surveying her, he said, "You have blood on you, too. You have time to change shirts."

Without a word, she turned and disappeared into her bedroom. She returned looking almost pristine, except for the shock and stress on her face and a ponytail that was wildly askew.

Rafe had rarely felt a desire to kill unnecessarily, but right this minute, the relentless effort to hunt him and Gwen down, the ruthlessness of it, weighed on his shoulders, and he stared down at the profile of the first of their attackers, who'd survived.

"Nobody would know if I broke your neck," he said, almost conversationally.

The bastard was smart enough not to beg for mercy. Not that he'd be getting any. He would undoubtedly go away for a good long while.

"You're not worth it," Rafe said decidedly.

Within minutes, the apartment was overrun by emergency personnel. A medic treated Rafe, determining the bullet was a through and through, and although she bandaged his arm, she encouraged him to have a doctor look at it, too.

With a sense of unreality, he looked around. He'd seen dozens of similar scenes. No, that was an understatement. Bullet holes decorated the walls and had torn the chair Gwen most often sat in to shreds and broken pieces of wood. Everyone stepped around the broken glass from the framed art that now hung drunkenly on the wall. The contents in grocery bags she must have dropped were smashed flat. Something red leaked from one of them. He glanced up; yeah, there were even a few bullet holes in the ceiling. Thank God this was the top floor of the apartment building.

She stood in the kitchen out of the way, pressed to the lower cabinets, her expression stricken. Did she have insurance that would cover this mess? How would the landlord react? Would she be able to give an explanation resembling anything close to the real story about what happened?

No, of course not. Zabrowsky would work his wizardry, expect silence from the responding cops, and Gwen would be stuck as the victim of a vicious home invasion assault.

And Rafe? He was powerless and knew it.

FIRST, THE INJURED assailant was removed, and finally, after the appearance of a pair of detectives who asked questions Rafe and Gwen had already answered but did again, the body was zipped into a bag and also hauled away.

Sometime during the chaos, Rafe had disappeared long enough to make a phone call. She didn't like the expression on his face when he reappeared. She'd have called it desperation if she hadn't known better.

He wouldn't be allowed to stay here any longer; she did know that.

The door had no sooner shut behind the detectives, leaving her alone with Rafe, than he said, "Give me your bank account number. I'll make sure you're reimbursed, even if I have to do it myself."

As if they'd ever let him trot off to a bank or even access his own account from a safe house. But she nodded numbly, called up her own account on her phone and scribbled the numbers on a piece of paper that he pocketed.

"This is it, then?" she asked, holding on to her pride with both hands.

"I'm afraid so." He looked around. "You've paid a high price for getting sucked into my problems."

"I don't regret it." She didn't move. Her eyes might be burning, but she refused to let a tear fall until he was gone. "If somebody is coming soon, you'd better make sure you have everything together."

"Gwen…"

She tried to smile. "If you're going to tell me you're madly in love with me and will be back in a year or so—"

Of course, he was shaking his head before she got that far. "You know I can't say that. I won't forget you, but I'm looking at a minimum of a year, maybe as much as two years, before the trial is behind me. I might as well be going to prison in the meantime. You need to move on with your life. I can't promise anything."

That last sentence seemed to be torn from him, as if— No, she wouldn't delude herself.

"I'll be fine. Back to work before I know it."

To give herself something to do, she grabbed a black plastic bag from beneath the kitchen sink and started by sweeping up the glass. Rafe picked up shreds and broken pieces of her chair to add them to the bag.

They'd mostly straightened what was left in her small living room when a knock came on the door. Rafe looked through the peephole, a safety feature that was one of the reasons she'd rented this apartment—and had been so much help today—and let a man and woman in. If she'd seen them on the street, she'd have guessed they were FBI agents from their clothes and their sharply observant expressions. But nope, they were DEA instead. Apparently, feds all looked alike.

One kept an eye on Gwen as he asked Rafe, "You ready?"

"Yeah." He sounded hoarse, turned to face her.

She just shook her head. "We've said everything. You... take care, Rafe. Try to avoid any more bullet holes, okay?"

He almost smiled, then was gone.

Gwen locked the door behind them, and finally let herself collapse.

SHE DIDN'T GO back to EMS Flight. The higher-ups were jerks about her injury and need for weeks off, and then were shocked to hear she'd been the victim of a home invasion. Gwen didn't like the attitude and resigned. Medical helicopter rescue organizations all across the country were desperate for paramedics as well trained and experienced as she was. She wouldn't have any trouble finding a new job.

Once she did her best to repair her apartment and dealt with the landlord, she made the decision to move away from the area. Here, she caught glimpses of Rainier from city streets, and it dominated the skyline every time she went up in a helicopter. She loved Seattle and the Northwest, and she'd be leaving behind a lot of friends, but...she needed a change. To go someplace she wouldn't be constantly reminded of Rafe.

She tried to convince herself it wasn't him so much as the crash, followed by the traumatic days fleeing through incredibly rough country to escape armed pursuers—all culminating in the horrifying attack in her own apartment. But she knew better. It was all about him.

He hadn't even been in her life two full weeks, but she'd fallen in love with him. They'd...meshed, maybe in part because they'd both learned to guard themselves from the sight of desperate survivors of violence, accidental and otherwise. Of course, she arrived in the aftermath, while he might have been part of a whole bunch of shoot-outs, for all she knew. Or, worse, he'd had to see men or women tortured and been unable to do a thing to stop it because he'd been undercover and had to stay in the role if he was ever to bring down the monsters he investigated.

Maybe he wasn't capable of loving a woman, or maybe she just wasn't the right one; she didn't know. Only that she had to believe him when he told her to forget him and move on. Well, he hadn't said the "forget him" part, but he'd meant it.

She couldn't go back to her life as if nothing had happened. A complete change was what she needed.

Gwen applied for several jobs in parts of the country she thought she might like and finally accepted one with CAL-STAR in Central California. She was able to live within visiting distance of San Francisco, a city with a flavor of its own that she quickly grew to love, but had a halfway affordable apartment in Stockton. She made friends, if not as close as the ones she'd left behind, had an alert on her phone for any news about the Espinosa family and read articles about the never-ending battle against drug trafficking in general, the profitability of fentanyl and connections to the Mexican cartels, and major DEA operations. Nothing ever popped up closely enough related to the operation Rafe had described, admittedly in skimpy detail, for her to believe it had to do with him.

Months later, when she let herself think about him, she imagined him trapped indoors all this time, able to do nothing but run on a treadmill, maybe lift weights, read, watch TV, chat with fellow agents who shuttled in and out to protect him. It had to be driving him mad. Of course, some of those agents were women—she thought about Carolyn, but nobody had ever told her whether Carolyn had lived or died—so maybe he had a sexual partner. Or would he let himself, when the other agents who were around would know all about it?

Probably not.

She convinced herself it was good she didn't have a photo of him and couldn't find one online. Sooner or later, she'd forget what he looked like. Anyway, she'd mostly quit thinking about him, although the anniversary of him walking out of her life was hard. She was grateful that she had to work and that she was busy. Also that no one died that day, or she'd have had to feel guilty about being glad her services were needed.

I'll meet someone, she tried desperately to convince herself. She mixed with cops, firefighters, doctors and other emergency personnel. There had to be a man among them who'd measure up to Rafe Salazar and who would also be attracted to her. No, not just attracted—who would fall in love with her. Who wouldn't be able to sleep with her but then shrug and say, *Move on with your life.*

Except he'd also said, *I won't forget you.* And, *I can't promise you anything.* Both of which made her wonder if he had felt more for her than he'd admitted, if there was any chance at all—

Of course there wasn't.

The intercom blared to life, calling her unit to Interstate 5 and a head-on collision with at least three fatalities and several critical survivors. Probably other helicopters would be needed, too.

RAFE HAD THOUGHT himself to be patient. Damn it, he'd *known* what he was getting into when he'd agreed to go deep undercover with one of the most notorious illegal drug manufacturing and trafficking organizations in North America. After the assault on the safe house and the death of two fellow agents—good guys—and then the ruthless disregard for Gwen's life as he was hunted, Rafe had been even more determined.

That was a year ago. A year during which he couldn't say he was actually living. *Existing* was a more accurate word. Updates on progress were rare. He got to wondering whether he'd been forgotten, whether warrants were being issued at all or whether no one wanted to admit to him that his testimony wouldn't be enough and he'd now thrown away *two years* of his life.

Except for the days—weeks—with Gwen. Those, he fixated on like a shipwrecked man might the broken piece of his boat that kept him afloat. It was downright pathetic.

He was stunned when things actually started to move, and he had to concentrate on reviewing material and reviving his memories of the hellish year he'd served as a useful underling while pretending to ignore assassinations taking place right in front of him and terrorization of whole towns where the cartel operated.

Turned out, getting excited didn't mean the first and biggest trial was actually starting. Arrests did finally take place, including a DEA operation that scooped up the head of the family who'd been in hiding, a man Rafe particularly despised. Rafe would be very glad to testify that he'd seen Papa Espinosa himself hold a gun to a Mexican police officer's temple and pull the trigger, after which he'd curled his lip and walked away while others hustled to toss the body into the back of an SUV and take it away.

Jury selection commenced and dragged on.

Fifteen months after he'd said goodbye to Gwen, Ron Zabrowsky brought him a couple of new suits and hustled him to a hotel in Houston, where he'd stay for the duration of the trial. It might drag on for weeks, and, yeah, there were at least two more in which his testimony would be required, but he saw the light at the end of the tunnel. And he knew that he'd come to the right decision for him.

The day the final trial ended, triumphantly or not, he was turning in his resignation.

GWEN WALKED AWAY from the helicopter carrying debris from their latest mission. Not the body—that waited for the morgue van. A sixty-four-year-old man had been nailed in a crosswalk by a speeding car that tossed him twenty feet or more to land on his head on the pavement. The driver didn't stop. An unusually observant teenager had noted at least part of the license plate number, which had the cops hopeful they'd be able to make an arrest in this particular hit-and-run. CALSTAR had been called because the incident had happened in a small town without a medical facility. An ambulance would have been too slow getting the victim to a trauma center.

But despite offering first-line trauma care themselves, he hadn't made it. From the moment she'd knelt at his side, she'd known he wouldn't live.

Thank God this was the end of her shift and she had a couple of days off coming to her. She felt as tired and discouraged as she had in a long time. A chill February wind tore hair from her braid and made her long for a hot shower.

"Call me shallow," her partner and friend who walked beside her said, "but that is one nice-looking man."

Gwen hardly noticed nice-looking men anymore, but she said, "Yeah? Where?" Her words dried up. That couldn't be—

The tall, dark and handsome man leaning against the door leading into their quarters straightened as he saw them approaching. Gwen quit walking. Didn't even notice that

Nancy stopped, looked from one to the other and tactfully kept going.

"Rafe?" Gwen whispered.

He started toward her. "Yeah. It's me." He sounded as hoarse as he had when he said goodbye. "It's been a long time…"

"It has." She was surprised she could speak at all beyond his name. She didn't know what to feel.

"And I told you to forget me."

"No, that's one thing you didn't say. You said I should move on with my life." She gestured vaguely at the airfield and the bright red helicopter behind her. "I have."

"We hadn't known each other that long."

Her head bobbed.

He stopped right in front of her, head bent so he could look into her eyes with all the intensity she'd never forgotten. "If I'd said anything else, it wouldn't have been fair to you."

Wow. Suddenly, she wanted to scream at him. A year and a half of misery, and that was *fair*? But she also understood. His year and a half couldn't have been any better than hers, even if he hadn't been pining for her.

"I get it." Then she blinked, realizing. "The trial is over? Did you win?"

He grinned, doing impossible things to her heart. "Multiple trials. Once the head of the family was convicted of a dozen charges, including first-degree murder, his two sons, a cousin and five men who were also high-ranked went down like bowling pins."

"Then the entire cartel is done for?"

Now his smile twisted. "The leadership, but someone else will step into their place. And there are other cartels, other drug traffickers. It's a triumph, a warning to the rest of them, but we never achieve real victory in this fight."

"Oh, Rafe." Loaded down as she was with several bags, she could only reach out with one hand. "I'm sorry. Glad for you, too. I mean, you did more than anyone could have expected, but you sacrificed a lot for it, too."

He lifted one of the bags from her shoulder and gripped her hand. "I sacrificed any chance of a relationship with you."

She'd taken a step before what he said sunk in and she stopped again, swinging around to look at him. "That's what you were doing?"

"What would you call it?"

"I suppose I thought…"

"Thought?" he prodded, voice getting sharper.

Oh, just say it. "That you were just as glad to have an excuse to leave without having some kind of big scene."

Now his eyebrows shot up. "You don't consider having your apartment shot up, the guy you were sleeping with shot and him getting hauled away by a couple of federal agents while leaving you holding the bag a *scene*?"

A laugh she'd never expected bubbled up in her. "Now that you mention it…"

He offered her a friendly grin that looked only slightly forced and said, "I'm told you're going off shift. Can we find someplace to talk?"

"Of course." She might as well be on a roller coaster, because suddenly tears blurred her vision. Despite the various bags and her being less than clean, she threw herself at him. "Oh, Rafe! I didn't think I'd ever see you again."

He pulled her close with his free arm. "God, Gwen. I missed you. If you're involved with someone, I understand, but—" He didn't finish, because she was sniveling against his shoulder.

She forced herself to lift her head. "I'm not. I…couldn't."

His dark eyes searched hers. "Even though you'd given up on me?"

"I guess I couldn't quite."

He bent and rested his forehead against hers, and for a moment, neither moved. Then he said gruffly, "Can we get out of here?"

Gwen wiped her tears on his denim shirt. "Absolutely."

Naturally, she took him home to an apartment that was barely bigger than the one she'd had in Seattle. He followed her in a shiny sedan she suspected was a rental, and was able to use a visitor slot in her parking garage.

The moment they got there, she begged off and took a quick shower. When she came out, he'd made coffee and offered her a cup.

Seeing something on her face, he said, "Bad day?"

"Until I saw you."

Sitting on a stool at the breakfast bar, he separated his legs and drew her to stand between them. "Tell me about it?"

Gwen did, seeing the understanding in his eyes. When she was done, she asked, "How long do you have? Zabrowsky doesn't have the nerve to call the time in a safe house a vacation, does he?"

Rafe laughed at that. "Even he's not that brazen." He hesitated. "After leaving the courthouse the last day, I quit my job. My schedule is entirely open."

Weirdly, she didn't feel the need to ask him why he'd done that. *Or maybe not so weirdly*, she thought, after what he'd said about the hopelessness of stopping the drug trafficking. But he led her to the couch in her living room, and they sat as they had so many other times, her curled up next to him, and he talked. When he was done, he tipped his head so he could see her face.

"I guess I just have to ask." Without moving a muscle,

he still appeared to be bracing himself. "Are you open to picking up where we left off in Seattle?"

She suddenly wasn't sure she could draw a breath. "That's what you want?"

"It's what I want." He hesitated, his expression becoming wary. "It happened fast, but I fell hard for you. I've never felt close to the same about any other woman."

Gwen wanted to burst into sobs, which was a completely counterintuitive response. After sucking in a breath—yes, she could still do it—she said, "Yes. Please. I fell for you, too. You had to have known."

He swallowed. "I hoped. *God.*" He pulled her onto his lap and kissed her. They didn't talk after that for a long while.

By the time they got dressed again and she called to order some Thai food to be delivered, she asked what he intended to do professionally and offered to move anywhere he could get a job.

"I can work anywhere," she said.

Rafe's smile crinkled the skin at the corners of his eyes. "I figured. I think I'll stay in law enforcement, but something local." He shrugged. "I could get on with San Francisco PD, but I think I'd like a smaller town."

It didn't take them long to agree that they'd take a good look around and do some serious thinking before they decided. And that in the meantime, taking up where they left off was exactly what they'd do. Only this time, fear had no claim over them.

The last thing she said on the verge of sleep was "I can't believe this."

As he pulled her into a wonderfully familiar embrace, he murmured in a low, deep voice, "I'm here for good."

* * * * *

HUNTED HOTSHOT HERO

LISA CHILDS

With great appreciation and respect for all the hotshot
firefighters—the real heroes!

Prologue

The hotshot holiday party ended without the bang everyone had been expecting and dreading, no one more so than
Rory VanDam. Ever since that reporter dredged up the plane
crash that had happened five years ago.

No. Ever since the plane crash.

No. Even before that.

Rory had been waiting for the big bang or the next crash.
While he'd been waiting the longest, the other hotshots had
begun to expect bad things to happen, too, and not just because of their jobs. Being a hotshot firefighter was more
dangerous than being a regular firefighter because they
battled the worst blazes—the wildfires that consumed acres
and acres of land and everything in their paths. But it wasn't
the job that put them in danger lately, it was all the bad
things that had been happening to the hotshots. Explosions.
Murder attempts. Sabotage.

But tonight, the holiday party ended with an arrest but
no gunshots, no fight, not even a fire. The party was over
now and the hotshots, who had traveled to their headquar-
ters in Northern Lakes, Michigan, to attend it, were tucked
up in the bunks at the firehouse unless they had other places
to stay. And, since falling in love and getting into relationships, many of them had other places now. So maybe it

wasn't just bad things that happened to hotshots. But for Rory, to fall in love or have someone fall in love with him would be a very bad thing. He couldn't risk a relationship with anyone ever again.

So, with nowhere else to stay, he was lying on his back on one of the bunks, staring up at the ceiling. Despite that arrest tonight, Rory was still uneasy, waiting for the next bad thing to happen.

The immediate danger was only over for Trent Miles tonight. The person who had been threatening Trent in Detroit, where Trent worked out of a local firehouse when not on assignment with the hotshots, followed him up to Northern Lakes. While the young man had run Trent and his girlfriend off the road the day before, he hadn't harmed anyone tonight. Trent's girlfriend, a Detroit detective, quietly arrested her and Trent's would-be killer. Except for that whole running them off the road thing, Rory was relieved that the killer was the only one who'd followed Trent up to Northern Lakes and not the man's sister again.

Trent's sister, Brittney, was beautiful, with her long curly dark hair and big topaz-colored eyes. But Brittney Townsend was also an ambitious young reporter who would sell out her own soul for a story. Or at least her own brother.

Not that Rory could judge anyone for selling out their soul, not when he'd already done it himself. But it still affected him, leaving him feeling hollow and empty inside and alone even in a bar full of other people like he'd been earlier tonight for the party. His coworkers. His friends. At least he hoped they considered him a friend and not the saboteur.

Who the hell was behind all the damn dangerous "accidents" the hotshots had been having? Broken equipment. Like the lift bucket coming loose with Trick McRooney in it and all of the cut brake lines on trucks that had sent or nearly sent hotshots to the hospital. And the loose gas line on the stove in the firehouse kitchen that had caused the explosion that had taken out Ethan's beard and revealed his real identity as the Canterbury heir.

Rory touched his jaw where stubble was starting to come in again. And his uneasiness grew. His disguise was being clean-shaven and short-haired; something he hadn't been for a while until his hotshot training and his new identity.

His new life. But this new life was proving to be every bit as dangerous as his last one. And he couldn't help but think that this life was going to end, too.

As he lay there, he heard the rumble of an engine and then another and another. The firehouse was on Main Street, but there was never much traffic in Northern Lakes at this hour and especially during the winter. And these engines weren't just passing by, they were running inside the building.

The fire trucks.

Who started up the truck engines?

They hadn't been called out to a fire because the alarm hadn't gone off. It would have woken up everyone in the bunk room if it had. And as far as he knew, he was the only one awake because all around him, other hotshots snored.

Trent Miles stayed behind in Northern Lakes after his girlfriend left. A couple of the younger guys, Bruce Abbott and Howie Lane, stayed because they'd been drinking at the party. And a couple of the older guys, Donovan Cunningham and Carl Kozak, stayed, probably for the same reason.

Michaela was here, too. The female hotshot worked as a firefighter in St. Paul, which wasn't far away, but while she hadn't been drinking, the party ended too late for her to want to make the drive home.

Not everybody staying was a hotshot. Stanley, the kid who kept the firehouse clean, was sleeping here tonight with the firehouse dog, Annie. Stanley's foster brother, Cody Mallehan, and his fiancée, Serena Beaumont, had recently gotten licensed as a foster home and had taken in a kid who was allergic to Annie. And Stanley didn't like to be separated from the big sheepdog/mastiff mix that had saved his life.

His life wasn't the only one she'd saved, though. She'd rescued many other hotshots and their significant others over the past year since Stanley had adopted her to be the firehouse dog. Maybe she was about to make another rescue because she whined and crawled off the bunk below Rory where she'd been sleeping with Stanley. Then she jumped up, put her paws on the side of Rory's bed, and she whined again, obviously as confused and concerned as he was about those running trucks.

"You hear 'em, too," Rory said, and he jumped down from his bunk. While the diesel trucks didn't emit as much carbon monoxide as gas engines, if all of them were running, like he suspected they were from the sound, the level could get high enough to kill.

The air was already getting thick. He coughed and sputtered, trying to find his voice to wake the others. "Hey…" he rasped out the words. "Hey…"

Annie barked, but it wasn't as loudly as she usually barked. Rory needed her to bark as loud as she had the first time she'd seen Ethan without his beard. He needed her to wake the others, or they might not be able to wake up ever again if the carbon monoxide level rose any more.

And he needed to get the hell downstairs and shut off those trucks. He would pull the alarm in the hall, too, before going downstairs. That would certainly wake up everyone easier than he and Annie could.

But once he stepped through the door to the hall, something struck him hard across the back of the head and neck, knocking him down to his knees before he fell flat on his face. His last thought as consciousness slipped away was: Would he be able to wake up again or was his most recent life ending right now?

Chapter One

He was having that dream. The one where he was falling through the air, his arms flailing as he kept reaching and reaching, but just nothingness slipped through his fingers. Nothing.

That was all he had now, all that he was now. He had a new name to replace the one he never wanted to hear again. But he'd lost much more than his old name.

And he was about to lose even more.

Before jumping out of the sputtering plane, he'd strapped on a chute, and the weight of it was pulling at his shoulders. It was supposed to open. He had been trained as a smoke jumper. He knew how to do this. But whoever had sabotaged the plane might have rigged the chute, as well. He wasn't the only one who'd jumped out, though.

At least one other chute had opened. He could see it in the distance. Just as he could see the plane, continuing on its doomed flight, spiraling toward the ground as the engine cut out entirely. He was spiraling, too.

Free-falling…

For a second, despite all of his training, he forgot what he was supposed to do. And he'd been trained by the best in the elite firefighting business: Mack McRooney.

But he forgot more than his training. He forgot who he

was now: a hotshot. Mack's voice echoed inside his head. "Breathe. In and out. Relax. And pull the cord."

Mack, with his bald head and booming voice, demanded total obedience. And this student obeyed. He reached for the rip cord, pulling it, and he waited for the jerk on his shoulders, for his body to go up instead of down.

But there was no jerk; it didn't come. The chute hadn't opened, hadn't rescued him. He kept hurtling toward the mountains, to all the pine trees and jagged ridges. And he braced himself for the impact.

For death.

Jolting awake, he jumped and gasped, trying to breathe. But something had been shoved in his mouth and down his throat. Panic gripped him.

They had found him again.

And this time they would, no doubt, make certain that he died.

YOU ARE BEING WATCHED, and if you don't drop this story, you will die.

Brittney Townsend's fingers shook slightly as she held the note she'd just pulled from beneath the windshield wiper of her van. When she'd seen the slip of paper, she figured it was a ticket or a flyer for a restaurant or a food truck. She had not even considered that it would be this: a threat.

After weeks of alternating between feeling paranoid and flattered, she should be relieved that her suspicions were confirmed. She'd had this strange feeling someone was watching her.

It had been easy enough to spot the ones who openly stared at her, some of them because they must have recognized her as the reporter who'd broken the big story, who had discovered that Jonathan Michael Canterbury IV was still alive. Or maybe they'd been staring because they had recognized her from the other stories she did. For the fluff pieces her local Detroit station had hired her to do, like report on gallery openings and concerts and new shops and restaurants.

She hated doing stories like that and figured she got saddled with them because she was young and, as her producer told her, cute. And the way he said it...

She had considered reporting him to HR, but everyone else loved him. So she let the comments go. For now. He was probably harmless enough, and she doubted that he was the one watching her. She also doubted that it was any of the people who'd spoken to her after recognizing her. None of them had given her that uneasy feeling that she kept having.

That creepy sense of foreboding, like whoever was watching her wasn't doing so out of admiration but something else...

Obsession. Anger. Revenge?

Her brother had recently had someone go after him for revenge, because Trent hadn't been able to save that person's loved one from an apartment fire. But Trent was a firefighter. His job was definitely a lot higher stakes than hers.

Except for the one big story she'd done about the hotshots. And that plane crash.

She glanced around now, peering into the shadows of the parking garage. It was late, so the only light was the soft glow from the small overheard fixtures scattered throughout the concrete structure. Was whoever had stuck the note under the windshield wiper out there? Watching her from the cover of the shadows?

Goose bumps lifted on her arms despite the heavy wool coat she wore. She reached for the door handle she'd already unlocked and jumped up onto the driver's seat of the van.

She suspected that someone had been watching her when she left the station a short while ago. Because it was late, she was the last one leaving the building for the parking garage. But she'd heard shoes scraping behind her on the sidewalk.

She glanced over her shoulder, but in the darkness, she wasn't able to see anyone. But she knew they were there, just as she'd known all those other times she had that uneasy feeling.

Someone was definitely following her. But her stalker wasn't a new fan like she wanted to believe, someone impressed with her reporting, someone who recognized her talent. No. This was someone threatening her.

You are being watched, and if you don't drop this story, you will die.

She really didn't have to wonder what story. Because she knew.

This threat wasn't for her to stop working on any of those fluff pieces. Nobody cared that she covered a gallery showing or the opening of a new restaurant; sometimes not even the owners cared because people didn't watch the news on TV. The read it on social media instead.

No. There was only one story of any interest that she had ever covered. The plane crash from five years ago, which had presumably taken the life of Jonathan Michael Canterbury IV and confirmed his family curse, that all of the Canterbury male heirs died much sooner than they should.

But Canterbury hadn't died. Other men had, though, except for one: Rory VanDam. Like Canterbury, he'd survived for a couple of months in the mountains before the two of them had been rescued. Because both men had refused to give her an interview, she wasn't sure how long each had been on their own before finding one other and then being rescued together. The wreckage of the plane and the pilot and a couple of other men, who'd just completed hotshot training and been on board, too, had never been found.

Nobody knew for sure why and how the plane had crashed. Or what had happened to the others. Canterbury claimed he didn't know for certain, but he'd suspected that it was because of him, because someone had been trying to kill him even before that crash.

But what if he was wrong?

The man who'd been trying to kill him, his brother-in-law, denied any involvement in the plane crash. Of course, he could have been lying, as people so often did. But why admit to everything else but deny involvement in the crash? It didn't make sense. If he wasn't the reason the plane had gone down, why had it crashed?

And what if Canterbury hadn't been the intended target after all?

Those were questions that Brittney had been asking herself ever since she discovered Canterbury alive and working with her brother as a hotshot out of Northern Lakes. She wanted to make sure that whatever had happened with that crash didn't happen again, with her brother as one of the hotshots who didn't survive.

Desperate to keep Trent safe, she'd tried asking other people about what had happened to that plane. Like the Federal Aviation Administration, who should have been able to locate the black box of the wreckage. She'd also tried talking to the director of the hotshot training center that the plane had left before the crash.

And she kept trying to talk to Jonathan Canterbury, who was still calling himself Ethan Sommerly. But he refused to give her a follow-up interview. She glanced at the note. Writing that didn't seem like something Ethan would do even if he wasn't best friends with her brother. He was more direct than this. He would just tell her, as he'd been doing every time she asked him, that he had no intention of ever talking about the crash again.

That left Rory VanDam. She'd seen him in passing when she'd been in Northern Lakes covering that story. The thought of him had her heart skipping a beat, but that was just in anticipation of getting more information out of him. Not because of how startlingly good-looking he was, with short blond hair and very pale blue eyes. She hadn't seen much of him, though, because he kept slipping away before she was able to ask him any questions. And both Ethan and her brother had refused to give her a contact number for Rory. Her brother was barely speaking to her after that story.

A twinge struck her heart with regret and with fear. She'd nearly lost him over the holidays when that person who'd wanted revenge against him had been trying to kill him. No, he'd been trying to kill someone close to Trent.

She still hadn't gotten the full story out of Trent yet, she only knew that person had been arrested. Detective Heather Bolton had made certain of that. She'd saved Brittney's brother's life and had stolen his heart in the process.

A tug at her lips curved them up into a slight smile even as a wistful sigh slipped through them. She wasn't jealous. Not really.

It wasn't as if she wanted a relationship for herself. Not right now. Maybe not ever. Despite everybody thinking she'd been too young when her dad died for her to be able to remember him, she did. She remembered that loss and pain not just for her but for her mom and her brother, too.

And every time her hotshot brother went out to fight a fire, she worried that she was going to lose him next. She nearly had, not to a fire but to someone holding a grudge against him.

Like he was holding one against her.

Would he ever forgive her for investigating his hotshot team? For exposing his best friend's secret and real identity and for, inadvertently, putting him in danger because of her exposé?

Hopefully Trent was out of danger now. But she didn't know for certain. Even though the detective had caught the person after him, Trent had stayed up in Northern Lakes.

Too many bad things had been happening there and not just because of her exposé. The Huron hotshots had been having a run of bad luck for a while now.

That was the reason she'd gone to Northern Lakes and had stumbled upon Canterbury, because she'd known something was going on with her brother's hotshot team, and she'd wanted to investigate all those unlikely "accidents." Too many of Trent's team members had been getting hurt or worse. One member of the team had died, and so many others had nearly died, as well.

Had something else happened?

Was that why Trent had stayed up there? And by doing so, had he put himself in danger yet again? But apparently she was in danger, too.

She glanced around that parking garage again, peering into the shadows. She couldn't tell if that person was out there yet, watching her. Or maybe they figured that leaving the note would scare her off.

If so, whoever had left it didn't know her well at all. Leaving that note only piqued her interest more as well as pissed her off.

Feeling a sudden urge to reach out to one of the people who knew her best, she pulled her cell phone from her purse. Before this whole mess with his hotshot team, she'd thought her brother knew her and would have known that she never intended for anyone to get hurt, least of all him. But she couldn't call her mom and stepdad, who probably knew her and her heart better than her brother did, because she didn't want to worry them. So she called Trent.

"Hey."

The quick reply startled her, making her nearly drop the phone. Trent had been declining her calls for so long that she hadn't expected him to actually answer.

"Brittney?" Trent asked, his voice a little louder with concern. "Are you there?"

She drew in a shaky breath and nodded. "Yeah, yeah. I just didn't expect you to pick up." Especially at this hour. Not that eleven was late for Trent when he so often pulled overnight shifts.

He chuckled. "Then why did you call?"

She froze for a moment. Why had she called? Was she going to tell him about the note? If she did, he would no doubt tell her to back off even though he knew that she wouldn't. Then he would worry about her and try to intervene, playing his usual part of overprotective big brother. And he might get hurt trying to protect her, which was her whole reason for wanting to discover the truth, so that he wouldn't get hurt like the other hotshots who'd been lost in that plane crash.

"Uh…"

"You're at a loss for words?" Trent asked. "That's so unlike my little sister."

"Stop teasing her," another voice chimed in on Trent's end. Heather's husky voice.

"You're back in Detroit?" she asked.

"Yes."

"Why did you stay in Northern Lakes for so long?" With the way he and Heather seemed to feel about each other, she was surprised he'd stayed away from the female detective for five minutes let alone two weeks.

"Ah, and now my little sister is back, too," he said. "Firing her usual questions at me."

Brittney felt another twinge then, of nostalgia, remembering how young she'd been when she'd started questioning everything and everyone around her. Trent had always been the most patient with her back then, even more so than their dad and her mom. He'd always been the best big brother.

But she hadn't always been the best younger sister. "I'm sorry," she said, her voice cracking a bit with the emotion overwhelming her, thinking of how close she'd come to losing him over the danger he'd been in. The danger he could be in again...

"Brittney?" Trent said her name as a question filled with genuine concern.

She forced a little chuckle. "What? Not used to me apologizing?" She had actually apologized a few times, over that story she'd done on his friend, but he hadn't been listening to her then.

Maybe that was because he'd known that she wasn't sorry at all about doing the story and would have covered it again. She was genuinely sorry about putting Ethan and Trent in danger, though.

And she definitely didn't want to do that again. But what if they already were in danger, either because of whatever had been happening with the team or something related to that crash?

And her story... That wasn't going away. It seemed to literally be following her around because, as she peered through her windshield, into the shadows of the parking garage, she noticed a little flicker of light.

The flame of a lighter?

The flash of a cell screen?

Or a camera?

Was someone not just watching her but taking pictures, too? For what or for whom?

She was tempted to grab her camera from her bag and take pictures of her own. Maybe she would be able to develop them with light enough to see who was out there, hiding in the shadows, watching her.

She always carried her camera with her because she preferred taking her own photographs. Hell, she would prefer to be a print reporter instead of a network one, but she'd taken the first job she'd been offered.

"Brittney?" Trent called her name loudly from her cell speaker, like he was trying to get her attention.

She nearly smiled again at the thought of all the times she'd tried to get his while they were growing up and most recently while he'd been ignoring her. Just like she intended to ignore that note.

And because she did, she couldn't tell Trent about it. She didn't want him in danger again and certainly not because of her. But if she didn't pursue the story, something could still happen to him and his other team members. She had to find the source of the threat and stop him or her; that was the only way she and the hotshots would be safe for sure.

Or as safe as hotshots could ever be given the hazards of their career.

"Sorry," she murmured again. Then she drew in a breath and forced a smile that, while he couldn't see it, he might hear in her voice. "So you're home?"

"Yes," he said.

And she could hear the smile in his voice.

"I'm home," he said.

But his home had burned down a month ago. So his home...

Was probably wherever Heather's was. His home was Heather now.

"Good," she said. She was happy for him, even as she felt that little bubble of wistfulness rise up from her heart again, as if she was yearning for what he had.

For love...

But she had no time for that now or ever. All she wanted was the truth despite the risk. But she didn't want it just for the sake of a story or her career.

She wanted the truth so that she was no longer being followed and threatened. After starting her van, she drove slowly out of the parking structure, and as she headed home, she continually checked the rear-view mirror to see if she was being followed again or still. There were other headlights behind her, so that person was probably back there, watching and waiting to see what she would do.

If she'd heed that threat...

She couldn't do it, not if backing away let someone get away with murder. And if that plane hadn't crashed by accident, that was exactly what had happened five years ago. Murders and attempted murder, if either Canterbury or Rory VanDam had been the real target. And if they had been, that meant they were still in danger and could put anyone close to them, like her brother or the other hotshots, in danger, as well.

SUPERINTENDENT BRADEN ZIMMER should have been relieved that Rory was all right, that after two very long weeks he had finally awakened from his coma. But...

Braden's body shook a little as he leaned against the wall

of the corridor outside Rory's hospital room. He wasn't sure it was Rory who'd woken up, at least not the Rory VanDam that Braden knew. The head injury was so severe, the mild-mannered man that Braden had known for the past five years had fought the medical staff that had been trying to save his life. He thought they were trying to kill him.

But maybe that was understandable after what had happened at the firehouse. Someone had started up all the engines and then struck Rory over the head when he'd stepped out of the bunk room.

Had Rory been the intended target? Or would whoever had walked into the hall have been struck? And hit so hard that he could have died. That he might still have brain damage from what had happened.

Annie, that untrained, overgrown pup of a firehouse dog, had once again saved lives when her panicked barks woke up the other hotshots who'd been sleeping at the firehouse. If she hadn't woken up everyone...

They could have died, and Rory probably would have if he'd not gotten the medical attention he'd needed as quickly as he had. He might have bled to death or the swelling on his brain that had caused the coma might have killed him. As it was, he still wasn't himself. Not yet.

Maybe not ever.

Braden had to do more to protect his team from...one of his team?

The sabotage had started out harmlessly enough in the beginning. A piece of equipment or a vehicle was damaged, but it had been escalating in frequency and in severity to the point that someone was going to die if the saboteur was not stopped soon.

Chapter Two

The week since he'd awakened in the hospital ICU ward with a breathing tube down his throat he had spent trying to reclaim his memories. So much of the past had slipped away while he was in the coma.

Or maybe he had lost those memories when he'd been struck so hard.

Maybe that blow had knocked the memories out of his mind so that they returned to him only in his dreams. But having them come back to him that way confused him more because he didn't know what was real anymore.

If he was real anymore...

Hell, at the moment, he struggled even to remember his name.

Rory.

That was what everybody who'd come to visit him called him. Rory VanDam was the name on the hospital bracelet wrapped around his wrist. The chart he'd taken from the foot of his bed had called him the same thing while also chronicling all of his old scars and injuries. But a lot of those scars weren't from injuries *Rory VanDam* had received. Except for the blow to his head.

Had that been intended for him? Or would any other hotshot have been struck as hard had one of them stepped out of the bunk room when he had?

Rory, or whoever the hell he was, needed to figure that out, just as he had so many other things he needed to figure out. Like if it was even safe for him, or for his hotshot team, to stay here anymore. But he couldn't figure out anything from this hospital bed. He'd already spent too much time lying in it, the two weeks that he'd been unconscious except for those disturbing dreams.

Memories…

He had spent the entire past week stuck in the hospital because the doctors insisted on monitoring him, making sure that he was medically all right. He wasn't. His head certainly wasn't and neither was his heart. His blood pressure kept going up, probably as those memories had returned.

But he knew that if he intended to make any new memories, he needed to get the hell out of the hospital and figure out who had attacked him in the firehouse. And if they would try again for him or for one of his team members. Or had it been one of his team members who had attacked him?

The tubes were out of him now. The one down his throat and the IV in his arm were gone. So there was nothing but the blood pressure cuff tethering him to the bed. He slipped that off and swung his legs over the side of the bed. While he had some kind of socks on his feet, his legs were bare, as was his ass when he stood up and his gown flopped open in the back.

Where the hell were his clothes?

His legs shook a little beneath his weight as he stumbled across the room toward a cabinet. He jerked it open as the door opened behind him.

"Sheesh, man, have some modesty," a deep voice remarked.

"Hey, if you got it, flaunt it," he replied before turning around to face the man standing inside the door.

Ethan Sommerly's dark brows rose with surprise.

Rory usually didn't throw back smart-ass comments like the rest of the hotshots did. Usually he ignored any smart-ass comments directed at him. He'd learned, the hard way, that it was smarter to keep his head down and stay uninvolved. That way nobody got to really know him, and he didn't get to really know, or trust, anyone.

But that blow to the head had either knocked the sense out of him or maybe knocked his sense back into him. He really didn't know which.

"Everybody said you were acting a little off, a little less like your usual self," Ethan said, "but I didn't see it until now."

"Probably because you haven't been around," Rory replied, ignoring the little twinge of hurt that today was the first time he'd seen Ethan since the hotshot holiday party.

Pretty much every one of the twenty-member team of hotshots had checked in with him over the past week. Trent Miles had come that first day he'd regained consciousness; then he'd left for Detroit and Detective Bolton. But Ethan hadn't come around to visit.

But then the real Ethan couldn't come around anywhere anymore. He had died in that plane crash five years ago. Or so everybody assumed, since no other survivors and the wreckage had never been found.

But what if Rory and "Ethan" hadn't been the only ones who'd survived?

What if...

"You must have gotten whacked in the head harder than I thought," Ethan said, his tone a little defensive. "Because I've been around."

Rory narrowed his eyes to scrutinize his old friend. Ethan usually told the truth about most things, except for his identity that he'd kept secret for five years. Secret from everyone but Rory, who'd always known since the crash who Ethan really was. But Rory had kept Ethan's secret for the same reason he kept his own, because they would have been in danger had the truth ever come out.

That had certainly been proven when Brittney Townsend revealed Ethan's real identity as Jonathan Michael Canterbury IV. The minute everyone had known the infamous Canterbury heir, as the media had dubbed him years ago, was alive, someone had been trying to kill him.

"When were you around?" Rory asked him. And how could he have forgotten?

Ethan's face got a little pink above his beard, which had grown back but was neatly trimmed now unlike how bushy he used to wear it, as a disguise. The man shrugged. "It's probably been a week or so..."

"You were here when I was unconscious," Rory said. Even as his heart lifted a little with that knowledge, he added, "How the hell could I know that?"

Ethan shrugged again and chuckled. "I don't know. They say people in comas can still hear you talking to them."

"*They* don't know what the hell *they're* talking about," Rory said. "Because I didn't hear you. The last thing I heard, before waking up here with the tube shoved down my throat, was the sound of the engines running and Annie barking—"

"So she did save everybody again like Stanley has been swearing she did?"

His heart lifted even more. "If everybody really got out without getting hurt like Braden swore they did." That was the first thing Rory asked when he'd remembered Braden was his boss after he finally remembered who the hell he was supposed to be.

Ethan nodded. "Nobody else got hurt. Braden doesn't lie. Now, Stanley I wasn't so sure about…"

Did Ethan think that the teenager could be the saboteur? Since Braden had shared with everyone that he'd received a note warning him that someone among them wasn't who they'd claimed they were, everybody had been looking at everybody else with suspicion. But that anonymous note had referred to a member of the team and probably to either him or Ethan, not Stanley. And no matter how many memories he might have lost, Rory knew *he* wasn't the saboteur. He didn't think Ethan was, either. But Stanley?

He seemed like a sweet kid who loved his dog.

"I didn't make it across the hall to the alarm to pull it," Rory said. "So Annie must have woken up everyone else before the fumes got too bad. Stanley's right, then, she saved everybody who was there."

"But you."

"I'm alive," Rory said.

"The doctors weren't sure you were going to wake up again," Ethan said, his voice even gruffer than usual. "And after a week passed, your odds of recovering kept getting worse."

"Is that when you gave up on me?" Rory asked. "But that doesn't really make sense, because you, better than anyone else, should know that I'm pretty good at beating the odds."

Not only had they managed to parachute off the plane before it crashed, they'd also managed to find each other within a couple of days and had survived the next two months in the cold of the mountains before they were finally rescued.

Ethan rubbed his big hand across his beard, along the edge of his square jaw. "We both are good at beating the odds."

Rory nodded heartily in agreement, and pain radiated from the back of his head to his temples. Maybe he wasn't as recovered as he thought he was. But he ignored the pain and remarked, "You beat a curse."

"What did you beat, Rory? You've never told me what it was," Ethan remarked.

He sighed again, a heavier one full of all the pain from his past. "I beat a curse, too, of a sort..."

It hadn't been a family legacy of bad luck like Jonathan Michael Canterbury IV had beaten. It was more like the curse of someone who had sworn a vendetta onto him. Revenge for what he'd done all those years ago. But even knowing what he knew now, he would do it all over again. *The right thing.*

But he hadn't shared any of the details with Ethan because, as he'd told him when they'd been stranded in those mountains and had reiterated again a few months ago, the less he knew about Rory the better. The safer he was.

Ethan pointed toward Rory's head. "I don't think you've beaten it for good."

Had the blow to his head been about that or...

"You don't think it was the saboteur who started all those trucks and hit me over the head?" Rory asked. It had to have been. Nobody else knew he was alive.

Unless...

Had Brittney Townsend's exposé about the Canterbury heir got someone else checking out the plane crash more closely? Someone who now wondered if Rory was really someone else?

Ethan shrugged his broad shoulders. "I don't know. The

saboteur hasn't been responsible for everything that has happened to the hotshots."

"No, they haven't been," Rory agreed. "Your past came back to haunt you."

"Is that what's actually happened here?" Ethan asked. "Has your past come back to haunt you?"

Rory VanDam's past only went back five years, to the moment, with the help of a US Marshal, Rory VanDam had been created. But the other man...

The one Rory barely remembered, the one he didn't want to remember, *he* had a past. And that was where it needed to stay, for so many reasons.

But instead of answering honestly, he just shrugged.

"The trooper has been trying to interview you," Ethan said, as if warning Rory.

"Gingrich?" His head pounded harder as a memory niggled at him, something about Gingrich...something sinister...

Ethan's dark eyes widened with concern. "You really have forgotten things. Gingrich is in prison now," Ethan reminded him. "He took a plea deal for trying to kill Luke Garrison and Willow and for his involvement in Dirk's murder."

Rory shuddered as he remembered Dirk's gruesome death. That was even worse than...

He shoved that memory back, unwilling to relive that once again, and focused on his friend. Drawing in a deep breath, he asked, "So what trooper wants to see me?"

"Trooper Wells," Ethan said. "She's been wanting to talk to you."

Rory had done his best to avoid having any conversations with any of the state troopers who had investigated what had been happening with the hotshots. He hadn't wanted to give anything away, any clue to his own past and his real identity. Though right now he wasn't even sure what that was...

"But at least it's just her wanting to talk to you and not that damn reporter," Ethan grumbled.

"Brittney," Rory said with a slight sigh.

Ethan grinned. "You haven't forgotten her."

Brittney Townsend, with her gorgeous eyes, deep dimples and curly dark hair, would be impossible to forget but more so for her indomitable spirit and determination than her attractiveness even.

"No," Rory admitted, "and I haven't forgotten that I need to avoid her."

For so many reasons...

THE ANSWERS WEREN'T wherever the hell that plane had crashed. The answers to Brittney Townsend's questions were in Northern Lakes, the small town out of which the Huron Hotshots operated. And where Brittney was driving to right now.

Ethan, aka Canterbury, had already told her that he thought his brother-in-law had caused the plane to crash. But if that was the case, why was someone threatening Brittney now to drop the story? Ethan's sister's husband was already in jail, heading to prison for a very long time. He had no way of leaving those notes or following Brittney and no access to funds to hire someone else to do his dirty work now like he had before.

So if it wasn't about Ethan, then...

Rory VanDam had to have the answers she was seeking. He had to know something more about the plane crash and about the victims of it. Had one of them been the intended target? Or had he been?

Unlike the last time she'd tried to interview him, she

was not going to take no for an answer. No was definitely not the answer she was seeking. Nor was the second note she received after pressing Mack McRooney, the trainer for the US Forest Service hotshots, for information about the plane crash this past week. Well, she hadn't really pressed, she'd just left more messages for him. And then she'd received one herself:

You were warned. Now you'll suffer the consequences.

This note hadn't been typewritten on a piece of paper and shoved under her windshield wiper. This one had appeared on her cell phone as a text message with the contact's information blocked.

So the person had her number and knew about her questioning the US Forest Service. When Mack didn't return her calls, she'd tried talking to everyone who'd picked up the phone at the US Forest Service. Nobody had given her any answers, though. But somehow the person leaving her the notes had found out she was still asking questions. The hotshots worked for the US Forest Service.

Maybe one of them didn't want her asking questions about the crash. Ethan had no reason to threaten her—his secret was already out. But what about Rory? Was he hiding something about the crash? Or about himself?

She'd only met him a couple of times when she'd come to Northern Lakes to find out what was going on with her brother and his hotshot team. The twenty members were quite diverse in looks and personality. There were the younger crew members who were excited about their dangerous career, and there were older ones who were more blasé about it but were still incredibly fit because of the demands of the job.

Then there was the elite of the elite. Like her brother.

And his friend Ethan. They were next-level fit and strong and muscular.

The new guy, who'd taken the place of the deceased team member, Dirk Brown, was like Ethan and Trent. But Trick McRooney had been raised by the man who trained most of the hotshot firefighters to be as accomplished as they were.

She'd tried talking to Mack, too, since that plane had left his training center right before the crash. But he had yet to return any of the calls she'd left for him where he lived and worked in the state of Washington.

Maybe his son, Trick McRooney, or his daughter, the superintendent's arson-investigating wife, Sam McRooney-Zimmer, would be able to convince their father to talk to Brittney about that crash and about Rory VanDam.

Rory wasn't as big and muscular as Trent, Ethan and Trick. He wasn't as loud and silly as Brittney's brother and so many other members of the team. But there was something about him, something even more compelling than the others.

At least to Brittney.

Maybe it was just because he was so different than the others. He was muscular, too, but in more of a lean and chiseled way than the bulky muscular builds of the others. He was also quiet and watchful, with features as chiseled as his muscles. And with short blond hair and very pale, icy blue eyes, he looked like some kind of Nordic prince. Like royalty...

But it wasn't so much his good looks that were compelling to Brittney but what simmered beneath the surface. Secrets. She knew they were there, and that maybe he was so quiet because he was determined to keep them locked inside him.

How far would he go to keep his secrets?

Sending threatening messages? Carrying out those threats?

Instead of being scared off, as the notes had intended, Brittney was even more fired up to learn the truth. And not just for her sake.

Trent worked closely with Rory. If the man was someone that her brother shouldn't trust or who would put him and the other hotshots in danger, they all deserved to know the truth about him.

And about that plane crash.

What the hell had really happened to that plane that someone was so desperate to make her stop pursuing her story about it that they had threatened her twice?

The closer she got to Northern Lakes, the more her anticipation grew. Not of seeing Rory VanDam.

She wasn't even certain he was still in Northern Lakes after the holiday party. She hadn't dared ask Trent about him because, just like the notes, if he knew about them or her intentions to interrogate Rory, he would try to stop her. To protect her?

Or to protect his fellow hotshots?

She still didn't believe he'd forgiven her for the last story she'd done on them. But while she felt badly about that, she couldn't let whoever was threatening her get away with it. The only way to stop the person was to find out who they were. Hopefully Trent would understand that this wasn't about furthering her career, she was doing it for her safety and for his and the rest of his team's.

Last time she'd come up to Northern Lakes, she'd intended to find out why bad things had been happening to the entire team, but the majority of her story had been about Ethan or, rather, Jonathan Michael Canterbury IV.

While she'd been hounding Ethan and following him and his family around Northern Lakes, Brittney had made a good friend and was looking forward to seeing her again. Tammy Ingles owned the salon in Northern Lakes. She was hip and sassy and genuine. With Brittney's career being so competitive, she hadn't made many genuine friends since becoming a reporter, and the ones she'd had from school and college had drifted away as they got married and started families. Or maybe she'd drifted away because she'd been working so hard, trying to move up to serious news from covering those fluff pieces, trying to be as successful as the rest of her family.

The only friend she'd had for long and that she really trusted was her mom. And now Tammy. They talked often on the phone through FaceTime and texts. But she hadn't told her about that weird sensation she'd been having of someone following her. And she hadn't told her about the note and the text, either. She knew that Tammy and Ethan had promised each other no more secrets. So whatever Brittney told Tammy, she would tell Ethan. And he would probably tell Brittney's brother.

But Tammy wasn't just open and honest with Ethan. She would tell Brittney everything she knew about that plane crash and what had been going on with the hotshots. And if she knew, she would tell Brittney where Rory was.

Even if he wasn't in Northern Lakes right now, Brittney would track him down wherever else he was. Hopefully, though, he was still in Northern Lakes. The roads began to curve more as they wound around all the inland lakes in this northeast region of the Great Lakes state. She was getting closer.

The weather was also getting colder. Snow still covered the road despite what had been proving to be a mild winter. At least in Detroit.

The weather wasn't the only thing that was going to be

cold here—with the exception of Tammy, everybody else would probably be as chilly and unwelcoming toward her as they'd been the last time she'd visited Northern Lakes. But Brittney found herself smiling anyway. She was almost there.

Then something struck the windshield. Loudly. Like a gunshot blast. The glass spider-webbed, weaving together to stay intact, but obscuring her vision.

She couldn't see the road. Couldn't see the curve.

She stomped on the brakes and gripped the steering wheel tightly. But it was too late to stop the vehicle, as her van left the road and fell onto its side and then its roof, metal crunching as it rolled and rolled. And Brittney couldn't see where she was going.

If she was up or down...

And she had no idea if she was going to survive the crash, or if, just as that text had warned her, she was about to suffer the consequences of ignoring the threat. If she would die just as it had forewarned if she didn't drop her investigation. If she kept trying to find out the truth.

WAS SHE DEAD?

The shooter stared through the scope of the long-range rifle.

Brittney Townsend had been warned. She'd just been too stupid to heed the warning. So another one had been sent. But she'd gotten in her van anyway and headed north. And without her even noticing, the shooter, who'd been following her on and off over the past few weeks, had followed her again before passing her.

Once off the freeway, the shooter had found the perfect spot, on the road between the freeway and Northern Lakes, to set up this ambush. Just as they'd set up something similar before.

Those other "ambushes" had proved successful.

Or so the shooter hoped. They kept studying the scene through the scope, finger posed yet on the trigger. Would they need to fire again?

Was Brittney Townsend going to get out of that wreckage? Could she extricate herself from the crumpled metal?

Or was she, just as the note had warned her, dead?

Sirens began to whine in the distance. Had someone seen the crash? Or had the reporter, herself, called for help?

The shooter lowered the weapon and turned back toward their SUV. They had to get out of here now before anyone saw them. Before they were able to confirm if the reporter was dead.

And would it even matter if she was? Some stupid reporter wasn't the real problem. The problem was the past. It could not come back around, and it definitely could not be reopened all over again. Or too many secrets might finally be discovered and destroy the shooter.

The shooter couldn't let that happen, had to do whatever possible to keep the past in the past. So more people might have to die than one ambitious young reporter.

Chapter Three

After Ethan left his hospital room, with the promise that he would return and drop off Rory's truck, Rory found some clothes bundled up in a bag in the deep bottom drawer of the bedside table. They must have been what someone had brought him because he hadn't been wearing them that night. Those clothes had probably been cut off him in the ER.

Or by the paramedics who'd treated him at the firehouse. Two of the Northern Lakes paramedics worked with him. Dawson Hess and Owen James.

Someone must have raided his locker for the jeans, boxers, socks and deep green US Forest Service sweatshirt they'd found for him. Because the clothes were his. Well-worn and comfortable, so much more comfortable than that hospital gown he tossed onto the bed. He'd just done up the button of his jeans and pulled his sweatshirt over his head when the door to his room creaked opened.

Hoping it was the nurse coming back with the release papers she'd promised him, he turned with a smile only to let it slip away when he saw the trooper walk into his room. Trooper Wells. While he'd struggled a bit to remember her when Ethan had warned him about her earlier, the memories returned of her looking at him the way she looked at him now, with her green eyes narrowed with suspicion.

A lot of people had looked at him that way when he'd been growing up. Mostly because of the company he'd kept and his family than because of anything he'd ever done himself. For the past five years nobody had looked at him that way until recently. Until the bad things had started happening to the hotshots.

"Where do you think you're going?" the trooper asked him as if he'd been breaking out of jail.

After being in this room, tethered to that bed, for three weeks, Rory had begun to feel a little like he was being restrained in prison.

"The doctor told me that I can leave," he said.

"I haven't told you that yet," the trooper said.

"I didn't know you were holding me here," he said. "And on what charges? Is getting hit over the head some crime I don't know about?" Because he sure as hell knew about a lot of them, probably more than she knew.

"I need to talk to you about what happened that night," she said. "And you've been avoiding me."

He gestured back at the bed where his hospital gown lay crumpled on the tangled sheets. "I was right here this whole time."

"With a gatekeeper who kept insisting you weren't well enough to answer my questions," Trooper Wells said, her voice sharp with resentment.

"Well, for the two weeks I was in a coma, I'm thinking it would have been a little hard for me to hear you." Since he hadn't heard Ethan talking to him, or maybe he had and that was why he'd kept dreaming about the crash.

Or maybe there was something about the crash, something that he needed to remember. Some detail that had kept coming back to him in his dreams...

Only now he couldn't remember his dreams that well. They were fuzzy and unfocused since he'd regained consciousness. He pushed those blurry remnants from his mind and focused on the trooper.

"And if I couldn't hear you, I wouldn't be able to answer you," he continued. "Though even now that I can hear you, I won't be able to help you. I didn't see anything. I just stepped out of the bunk room doorway into the hall and got hit. I didn't see what hit me, much less who did it." It had all happened so damn fast.

"Why did you leave the bunk room?" she asked.

He tensed. Had Braden not shared with her about someone starting the trucks? He knew at one point Trooper Gingrich had been a suspect in the sabotage. And as Trooper Wells's training officer, Gingrich had worked so closely with her that nobody was certain that they should trust her. That she might have actually been working with Gingrich when he'd gone after Luke and Willow Garrison.

Even if she hadn't been, Rory didn't trust her. He didn't trust anyone. Not anymore.

He'd trusted Ethan for the past five years because they'd both had secrets they'd wanted to keep. But now that Ethan's had been revealed...

Rory couldn't totally trust even him any longer. Hopefully he'd kept his word about dropping off Rory's truck in the hospital parking lot.

"Mr. VanDam," Wells prodded him. "Why did you leave the bunk room?"

He lifted his hand and pressed it against the back of his head while he grimaced. "Ahh, I don't really know. With this concussion I've lost so many memories."

Unfortunately, too many of them had returned. Maybe it would have been better if they'd stayed gone.

"You remember walking out of the bunk room," she pointed out. "You remember getting hit."

He shrugged. "Maybe it's my memory, or maybe that's just because of what people told me."

Braden had had to remind him when he'd first regained consciousness and been in such a panic, over the tubes down his throat and over his jumbled mind.

"So other people have been talking to you since you've regained consciousness?" she asked, her mouth twisting into a grimace.

He shrugged again and pressed his lips into a tight line. He was not about to give up any of the team members' names. He might have already put them through more than they deserved to endure. He could be the reason they'd been in danger.

"What is wrong with all of you?" she asked. "I know, thanks to Brittney Townsend's story, that a lot of things have been happening to your hotshot team. However, none of you have reported any of those incidents to the police. I don't think that has anything to do with some stereotypical rivalry between police and fire departments."

There was a reason that rivalry had become a stereotype. Rory had seen it play out, again and again, in his previous life and career. But he couldn't admit to that because that man, the one he'd been back then, needed to stay dead, or he would die all over again and this time for real.

He sighed and admitted, "No. It has to do with your old boss. With Marty Gingrich and his obsession with my boss and hurting him, and he wasn't above using other people to do that, to get to Braden." He'd slept with Braden's first wife and had an affair with another hotshot's wife, too.

Trooper Wells's face flushed nearly as red as the tendril of hair that spilled out from beneath her tan hat. "I had nothing to do with what *he* was doing."

Rory understood all too well how frustrating it was to be judged by the company you kept rather than who you really were as a person. But because he didn't really know her, he had no idea who she really was. She could be just as complicit and cutthroat as her former boss.

"I'm sorry, Trooper Wells," he said with some sincerity. "But I'm not going to be able to help you. There's still too much I don't remember."

"Then maybe you better not leave the hospital," she suggested.

It wasn't just the hospital he intended to leave, and maybe she knew that, too. "I'm sure they need the bed."

As it was, the door hadn't shut tightly behind the trooper, so he could hear voices raised with urgency and excitement. "The paramedics are on their way in with the patient. ETA five minutes."

Not a lot happened in Northern Lakes to keep the hospital very busy unless it happened to a hotshot.

"What's going on…?" he murmured, panic pressing on his heart. Had someone else been injured? Another member of his team?

Trooper Wells's radio began to squawk in her ear, loud enough that Rory could catch tidbits. *Possible gunshots heard. Crash.*

Something bad had definitely happened. He could only hope that it wasn't to another hotshot. He stepped around the trooper and jerked open the door to the hall.

The hospital was small enough that his room wasn't far from the ER. He had only to go to the end of the corridor. The doors to that restricted area opened as a nurse, probably the one he'd overheard talking, rushed through them. And he ducked between them just as they were beginning to close again.

"VanDam!" Wells called out to him.

He glanced over his shoulder, just as the doors closed on her, shutting her out. He turned back, following the nurse who hurried toward where the ambulance would pull into the bay at the rear of the ER.

The nurse wasn't Luke Garrison's wife. Willow was off on maternity leave, taking care of the beautiful, healthy baby she and Luke had. This was another nurse. Older. And vaguely familiar, probably from all the times Rory and his team had been in and out of the hospital.

They'd been getting injuries treated from things they'd thought were accidents. And also from things they'd known weren't. Like having their brake lines cut, nearly being run down and shot at...

Like the patient on their way to the ER now.

A crash...

Gunshots...

Had someone been shot?

Who?

As he joined the nurse in the bay, she glanced at him. But she didn't tell him to leave the restricted area. Just as he'd vaguely recognized her, she must have recognized him as a hotshot.

Oh, God...

So it probably was one of his team coming in the ambulance. Who?

The paramedic rig, lights flashing and sirens wailing, appeared on the road before careening into the lot. The tires squealed and brakes screeched as the ambulance rolled up to the ER entrance.

Rory drew in a breath, but it was shallow, his lungs compressed from the heavy weight of dread and guilt lying on them. He couldn't draw a deep breath. He couldn't slow his speeding pulse, either.

The rig stopped, and the back doors swung open. Owen James jumped out. The former Marine was a member of the Northern Lakes fire department and Rory's hotshot team.

"Owen, who is it?" Rory shouted to the blond-haired paramedic as the hospital staff rushed out to the rig.

Between them and Owen, they pulled a stretcher from the back. Owen didn't answer him. He was totally focused on his patient, firing off stats to ER residents and nurses.

Having been around paramedics a lot, Rory recognized the stats. The low blood pressure and pulse. The low oxygen level.

This person was potentially in trouble. Rory stepped closer, peering over the nurses to see who had been hurt. A woman lay on the stretcher.

She was neither of the female hotshots. She wasn't a hotshot at all. But Rory recognized her. The curly dark hair, the caramel-colored skin that her eyes would have matched if they'd been open.

But they were closed, her thick lashes lying over the dark circles beneath her eyes. She was unconscious. But even unconscious a certain vitality radiated from Brittney Townsend. She was so bright and brilliant, like a star whose light should never dim. Only get brighter.

"Oh, God, no…" Rory murmured.

While the reporter unsettled him and he'd hoped not to see her again because of her determination to get to the truth, he had never wished her any harm. In fact, he'd wished just the opposite…

BRITTNEY SQUINTED AND closed her eyes against the lights that were so bright they threatened to blind her. And the pounding, it was so loud and intense that she flinched with pain.

Who was pounding? And where was it coming from?

Inside her head or out?

Earlier there had been the sound of a motor running.

Maybe her van's.

Maybe some kind of machinery.

There had also been voices yelling out to each other over that noise. Then someone had shouted her name, his gruff voice full of concern. "Ms. Townsend? Brittney?"

She'd tried to open her eyes. She'd tried to reply to him, but it had taken too much effort. Just as the last thing she'd done, grabbing her cell, calling for help, had taken too much effort.

Had she even managed to complete the call? With the way the van had been rolling, the metal crunching, hadn't she lost the phone?

She couldn't be sure now if she had called 911 or if her cell phone or vehicle had detected the crash and placed the call for her. Had she passed out? And why?

Was she hurt? Was that why the light affected her eyes so much? Was the pounding inside her head?

Her mom had gotten migraines from time to time, and until now Brittney hadn't understood how much pain Maureen Townsend must have endured. Probably because her mom had just powered through it as she had everything else in her life. The honorable judge Maureen Townsend was tough. Brittney tried hard to be as tough, as ambitious, as smart as her mother.

A little fluttery feeling passed through Brittney's chest, making her breathe faster, shallower, at the thought, at the realization that she would probably never measure up to the high standards her mother had set for life. Brittney worried that she would never make her as proud as Trent already had. And Trent wasn't even Maureen's son—he'd just come to live with them after his mother had died a few years after his and Brittney's father had already died during a deployment.

Tears stung her eyes, and she blinked, trying to chase them away and fight them back. She was tough, too. She'd had to be.

She drew in another breath and willed the tears away. As her vision cleared, her eyes focused on the man standing over her bed, his pale blue eyes intent on her face and filled with concern.

For her?

Or for himself?

Was he worried about her being hurt or being alive? And if it was the latter, would he try to do something about it, even right here, in what must have been the hospital?

Brittney opened her mouth to scream for help, but before she could get out more than a squeak, his big hand covered her face, cutting off her scream. And her breath…?

TRENT'S CELL LIT up with the name Owen James. And nerves tightened the muscles in his stomach. Sammy, the black cat lying on Trent's bare stomach, stood up, arched his back and sunk his claws into Trent's abs. "Owww…"

Sammy jumped off the bed and ran out of the bedroom. And for some reason Trent felt like running, too. He'd pulled a late shift at the firehouse here in Detroit—otherwise he would have been up already. For some reason, seeing this call come in, he wished he was more fully awake.

But maybe he was just overreacting. His fellow hotshots

were friends. Just because one of them was calling him now didn't mean that something bad had happened. Except lately.

Every time one of them called, it was because something bad had happened. He drew in a deep breath, to brace himself, and accepted the call. "Hey, Owen, what's up?" he asked.

Silence greeted him. No. Not exactly silence. Other voices murmured in the background of wherever Owen was. Had the paramedic butt-dialed him?

"Owen," he called out, raising his voice. Maybe his friend couldn't hear him over the noise around him, wherever he was. "Are you there?"

The paramedic released a shaky breath that rattled Trent's cell speaker. "Yeah, I…uh… I…"

"What is it?" Trent asked. No. "Who is it? Who got hurt?" Because he heard just enough of the background voices to catch a medical term here and there, he figured out Owen was at the hospital. As a patient or a paramedic? "Are you okay?"

"Yeah, I'm sorry," Owen said. "She doesn't want me to tell you, but I think you should know. And I probably shouldn't tell you because of privacy laws and such…"

"She?" Heather had gone to work a few hours ago, but the area she covered as a Detroit detective was nowhere near Northern Lakes. And Trent was so close to the female hotshots, Hank and Michaela, that he doubted either of them would have asked Owen to keep anything from him. Then he groaned with another realization. "Brittney."

Damn.

He'd wanted her to leave his hotshot team alone, to stop hounding Ethan for that follow-up interview, to not shed any more light on the situation with the saboteur than she already had when she'd reported on their string of unfortunate events. He didn't want Braden losing his job as superintendent, and that was bound to happen if any other hotshot got hurt.

But a hotshot hadn't been hurt. His sister had. "What happened?" Trent asked, fear gripping his heart. "Is she all right?"

"Yeah, yeah, she's in the ER getting checked out, but I think she'll be fine. I didn't detect any broken bones. Probably just a concussion."

"*Just* a concussion?" he asked, his voice cracking. "Rory spent two weeks in a coma from just a concussion!"

"She was pretty conscious."

"Pretty conscious?" Trent asked.

"She was going in and out a bit, but seriously, she looks fine," Owen said. "So you don't need to freak out."

But there was something in Owen's voice, something he was leaving unsaid.

"What happened?" Trent asked.

"She got in an accident," Owen said. "Her van went off the road and rolled over. The roads are still snow covered up here. Icy—"

"That's bullshit."

Owen said, "You were up here just a few weeks ago and went off the road—"

"Because someone pushed me off the road," he said. And into a lake.

"There's no evidence that anyone had tried to force her off the road. There's no damage to the front or rear of her van, except for broken windows, and that probably happened when it rolled," Owen said, and he almost sounded as if he was trying to convince himself as much as he was Trent. "She must have just been driving too fast for conditions."

Even though Owen couldn't see him, Trent shook his

head in denial of the paramedic's claim. Trent had taught his little sister to drive, and she'd learned how in Detroit. Since she was fifteen years old, Brittney had had no problem maneuvering rush hour traffic or snow-covered roads.

There was no way in hell that her crash was an accident. Any more than his crash had been when his truck had been forced off the road and into a lake. He was lucky he and Heather hadn't died in the crash or frozen to death in the lake. His stomach flipped at the thought of Brittney going through something like that alone.

But she wasn't alone. Most of his hotshot team was still in Northern Lakes because they'd been worried about Rory and what had happened at the firehouse with all the engines being started up. Trent had stayed there as long as he could, but he'd missed Heather so damn much. At least he'd had a week with her before having to go back.

He jumped up from the bed that they'd spent a lot of time in over the past week. "I'm on my way up," Trent said.

"That's good," Owen said, his voice even gruffer.

"What is it?" Trent asked. "What aren't you telling me?"

"I don't know for sure. Like I said, nothing at the scene indicated that it wasn't just an accident…"

Trent cursed. "I knew it! You don't believe it was any more than I do. What is it?"

"Somebody said something about hearing gunshots," Owen admitted.

Panic gripped Trent's heart so tightly that he gasped.

"But like I said, there was nothing to indicate that. The tires were intact. Nothing had been shot out. If anybody was shooting, it was probably just some hunter. Maybe the sound of the gunfire startled her."

"She wasn't shot?" Trent asked, his heart beating so damn fast.

"No. No," Owen assured him. "She doesn't even have any lacerations."

He released a shaky breath. But he still wasn't entirely relieved. Something was going on with his sister, something he should have known about.

When she'd called him the other day, he'd heard it in her voice. It had been a little brighter than usual, like she was trying to cover up something. He'd just figured it was because she thought he was still mad at her over that damn story she'd done on the team.

"Can you keep an eye on her until I get there?" Trent asked. "Make sure nothing happens to her and that she's—" his voice cracked "—safe?"

"Rory is in with her right now," Owen said.

Trent snorted. "Yeah, right," he said. "He works harder to avoid her than Ethan does."

And if Rory hadn't already been in the hospital himself, Trent might have suspected he was the reason for Brittney winding up there. If anyone wanted to get rid of the reporter, it was probably Rory. The man was even more intensely private and antisocial than Ethan was.

When he wasn't working as a hotshot, he was a ranger on a mostly uninhabited island in the middle of one of the great lakes. Only campers and hikers ever visited the island, which was a national forest, and none of them ever stayed for long. Only Rory had, and that had been his ranger assignment for the past five years.

Ever since the plane crash.

Was Brittney right? Was there more to that story than had already been revealed? And was her pursuit of that story the reason Brittney had wound up in the ER?

Chapter Four

He shouldn't have touched her. He'd known that the moment he'd pressed his hand over her soft lips. But when she'd opened her mouth, he'd known she was going to scream.

And that damn trooper was hanging around somewhere.

Ready to finish his interview and probably start one with Brittney. And if Brittney screamed while he was leaning over her bed, the trooper was going to think whatever Brittney must have been thinking...

That he was going to hurt her.

"Shh," he said, peering around the curtained-off area of the ER where her gurney had been rolled. He couldn't see any feet beneath the curtains, at least none close enough that anyone could be listening to them. But because the walls were just curtains, everybody in the emergency room would hear her if she screamed.

And they would wonder what he was doing to her.

They weren't the only ones. He wondered himself what had compelled him to come check on her. Owen told him she'd been in a vehicle accident. But from what Rory had overheard from Trooper Wells's radio, it sounded like this crash might have been very much like the other *accidents* the team had been having. And not an accident at all.

Gunshots.

"Calm down," he cautioned her. "If you have a concussion, you're only going to hurt yourself screaming." And because she had been unconscious since she'd arrived at the hospital, he suspected she did have one. But at least she was breathing on her own. And she'd already regained consciousness.

"I'm not going to hurt you," he assured her. That must have been what she'd thought, or why else had she looked like she was about to scream?

Her beautiful topaz eyes narrowed in a glare.

"I'm not," he insisted, and he pulled his hand away, his palm tingling from the contact with her lips. She was so damn beautiful, which was something he was an idiot to even notice much less react to, like he was reacting with a quickening pulse and that damn tingling skin.

And he wasn't an idiot just because she was a reporter and his team member's younger sister...

He was an idiot because he should have known better than being attracted to another woman who would wind up destroying him. And she would...

It was no doubt why she was here.

"Trent left a week ago," Rory told her. At least that was what Braden had told him, that Trent hadn't left until after Rory had regained consciousness. But even after he'd woken up from his coma, Rory hadn't been exactly clear about who was whom. Hell, he hadn't even been certain about his own identity. "So if you've driven up to see him..."

"I drove up here to see you," she said.

His pulse quickened even more, and it wasn't just with attraction now but with apprehension. "Me? Why? Do you know about the..."

He didn't know what to call it. It hadn't been an "accident." Nobody had *accidentally* whacked him over the head hard enough to put him in a coma for two weeks.

Brittney's forehead furrowed beneath corkscrew curls of her chocolate-brown hair. "About the plane crash? Of course I know about it. I reported on it."

He shook his head. "No, I was—"

"There you are," a female voice said, the tone accusatory, and Trooper Wells jerked aside one of the curtains around Brittney's gurney. The woman was looking at Rory, though, before she turned toward the bed and added, "And there you are. I've been looking for both of you."

"Why?" Rory asked. "I already told you that I don't know anything about what happened in the firehouse—"

"What happened in the firehouse?" Brittney asked, and she struggled to sit up from the stretcher. But her delicate features twisted into a grimace of pain.

"Sit back," he said, and he touched her shoulders, trying to ease her onto her pillows again without hurting her. Then he peered around the trooper, out into the ER. "Where the hell is the doctor? Why isn't anyone treating you?"

The head nurse, Cheryl, must have been hanging around within eavesdropping distance because she popped up behind the trooper. "The doctor saw her and ordered an MRI, and we've just been waiting for an opening to use it. It's available now." She edged around Wells then to approach the gurney. "So I need to bring her downstairs to Imaging for it." She unbraked the bed and began to roll it toward Rory and the trooper.

The trooper stepped back but Rory hesitated for a moment. Seeing Brittney arrive in the back of the paramedic rig had affected him, had brought on all kinds of feelings he didn't know he had about her. Concern. Attraction.

Along with those unwelcome feelings had come the unwelcome memories of what happened to people who got too close to him. He didn't want to make any more memories like that.

Never again.

So with a slight shudder, he moved aside, but when the gurney started past him, Brittney reached out and grabbed his arm, stopping it and him.

"Don't leave me," she said, her voice cracking a bit with a vulnerability he wouldn't have expected her capable of feeling.

"I'm sure Trent will be here soon," he assured in case she was scared of being alone.

She shook her head and flinched at the movement. "I don't want Trent. I want you."

Despite knowing that she didn't mean it how it sounded, he felt a jolt like electricity and shock and something else, something he hadn't felt in a long time. A connection.

But she didn't want him. She just wanted his story. And the smartest thing he could do was get the hell out of there before she, or anyone else, could catch up with him again.

BRITTNEY HADN'T MISSED that look of panic on Rory's face when she'd said that she'd wanted him. But she hadn't meant that the way it had probably sounded. She hadn't, and yet when she'd said it, she'd felt this strange yearning for a connection, to not be so alone.

She'd been so focused on her career that she hadn't noticed how lonely she'd been, or maybe she'd noticed but just hadn't wanted to acknowledge it. Kind of like how she didn't want to acknowledge how damn good-looking Rory VanDam was in that conquering Viking kind of way, with his pale blond hair and pale blue eyes. But he had a shadow on his jaw for once, a dark shadow.

While she was closed in the MRI chamber, she focused on his image in her mind. She should have been focusing on her questions instead, about him and the plane crash and about what had happened on the road that had sent her van tumbling over and over.

But her mind shied away from that, from that fear she'd felt in the moment. When she'd heard...

What had she heard before the windshield metamorphosized into a spiderweb? A gunshot? Had someone shot at her? No. Nobody had known she was heading up north. She hadn't told anyone, not even at the station when she'd requested a few days off. But maybe her producer had figured out that she was determined to follow up on the plane crash story. Or someone had followed her...like they'd been following her.

The MRI didn't take long, and she was wheeled back up to the ER, to that cordoned-off area where she'd awakened to Rory leaning over her. Had he really been concerned about her or about what she might have learned?

And the trooper...

Why had she been looking for Rory? To talk about what had happened at the firehouse?

What the hell had happened?

The questions pounded inside Brittney's head like the pain. She probably had a concussion. With the way the van had rolled and the metal had crunched, she wouldn't be surprised if that was what the doctor told her once the results of the MRI came back.

The nurse pulled open the curtain to where a man sat in a chair that had been beside her bed. It wasn't her brother. Even if someone had called Trent, he wouldn't have been able to drive up within the time frame that she must have arrived at the hospital.

The nurse rolled her bed into place, next to that chair where the man was sitting, and asked Brittney, "Do you need anything?"

"Just answers," she murmured.

"The results should be back soon," the older woman assured her with a smile.

Those weren't the answers she needed, though. She just smiled at the woman and nodded.

The nurse was probably busy because she hurried away, stopping only to pull the curtains closed.

Brittney just glanced at those before rolling her head back toward the man sitting beside her bed. "You didn't leave..." she murmured, surprised that Rory had stayed like she'd asked.

He shrugged. "Trooper Wells probably wouldn't have let me. I feel like she's holding me here under house, er, hospital arrest."

"For what?" she asked. "For whatever happened at the firehouse?"

His lips curved into a slight grin. "Do you never not ask questions?"

"You set yourself up for those questions," she pointed out. But it wouldn't have mattered if he'd said nothing at all, she still would have had questions for him.

He sighed and nodded. "Yeah, I guess I did, but I've already been interrogated once today."

"So why did you stay?" she asked.

He sighed again, more heavily, and shrugged. "I really don't know..."

"No guess?" she teased.

"Because you asked me to," he said, as if he was reluctant to make the admission.

Something shifted inside her, making her heart feel

funny. Maybe she had an injury from the seat belt. The damn airbag hadn't gone off. But the seat belt had snapped tightly around her, holding her in her place while the vehicle rolled. She touched her chest then and drew in a shaky breath.

"You're not okay," he said. "Do you need pain medication? An IV? Why haven't they given you anything yet?" He jumped up from the chair then, but before he could stalk off, she caught his arm again.

"They're waiting for the results of the MRI," she said. "And I'm not in pain." To prove her point, she tried to sit up, but she flinched as her head pounded harder and her stomach ached.

"Liar," he said, but his deep voice was soft and the look in his eyes...

She couldn't be sure but it almost looked like admiration. She wasn't used to seeing that from any of the hotshots. Usually they looked at her with irritation. Especially him.

"Okay, maybe it hurts a little," she admitted.

"I'll get Cheryl or a medical resident," he said, and he started to tug his arm free of her grasp.

But she held tighter to him. "No. I don't need anything. It's not that bad."

He shook his head. "I still don't believe you. You trying to prove how tough you are?"

She flinched again, but the pain wasn't because of her concussion. It was because Rory was probably right. She kept trying to prove herself. No. She just wanted to be taken seriously. To be successful. But that wasn't the reason she was so determined to find out everything she could about that plane crash and about the hotshots; she just wanted to keep her brother safe, or at least as safe as he could be with his career.

"That's not it," she insisted. "I don't want to take anything that might knock me out again." She needed to stay awake and stay alert, so that threat wasn't carried out like it very nearly had been. The windshield hadn't shattered like that by accident. Something, and someone, had caused it.

Rory nodded. "I get that. I spent two weeks in a coma."

She gasped and tightened her grasp on his arm. "What happened?" And why the hell hadn't she heard about it?

"That's what I would like to know," another voice chimed in, and Brittney glanced up to see that Trooper Wells had returned, pulling back the curtain to peer in at them.

Rory's long, lean body subtly tensed next to her. Even though Brittney held only his arm, she could feel that tension in him and inside herself, as well. It was clear that the trooper was not done with them. But the hotshot shrugged and sighed. "I told you, Trooper Wells, I didn't see anything. And I barely remember anything."

"About that night or about anything else?" The trooper asked the question that was burning inside Brittney.

He shrugged again. "I have no idea what I forgot."

"Your boss said you barely recognized him or even knew your own name," the trooper remarked.

Rory glanced down at Brittney and then back at the officer. "Do you think this is a good idea? Talking about this in front of a reporter?"

The trooper's face flushed. But she lifted her chin as if powering through the embarrassment. Brittney recognized the gesture and the sentiment. She'd done it herself several times while she'd been covering something live and something had gone wrong.

But until this afternoon, until someone had tried to kill her, nothing had ever gone as wrong for her as this had.

She hadn't taken anything, but she felt strange, light-headed. Maybe with fear more than pain. She tightened her grasp on Rory's arm, deriving a strange comfort in his closeness. For the first time in a long while, she didn't feel so alone.

"I thought you two were more than acquaintances," the trooper remarked with a pointed look at Brittney's hand holding on to him.

Brittney would have jerked her hand away if she wasn't afraid that Rory would take off and leave her. And after what had happened with her van, she really didn't want to be alone. "He's a friend of my brother's," Brittney said. But she really didn't know Rory VanDam. She suspected nobody did. Yet, for some reason, she felt safer with him here with her.

"Who's your brother?" the trooper asked.

Figuring she could find out easily enough, Brittney replied, "Trent Miles."

The trooper's green eyes widened. "He just had an accident himself here recently. His truck went off the road and into a lake."

"That wasn't an accident," Brittney said.

"Was yours?" the trooper asked.

Brittney quickly nodded, grimacing as a sharp pain reverberated throughout her skull. "Yeah, snow-covered roads... all that..."

"Are you sure? There was a report of someone hearing gunfire in the area."

Brittney shrugged. "I don't know about that." And until she could figure that out for certain, she wanted to be the only one investigating her "accident." She knew that Trent and his team had reason not to trust their local police, after one of the troopers had tried to kill a hotshot.

"You didn't hear gunshots?" the trooper asked.

Brittney probably should have told her the truth, but she didn't know how close this trooper had been to the one who'd tried killing her brother's hotshot team member. Close enough to have helped him?

Clearly Rory didn't trust the woman because he had avoided her questions, but he had also avoided answering Brittney's. Until Brittney was certain she could trust the trooper, she had no intention of telling her about anything that was happening with her. About the gunshots.

About the threats.

"I don't know," she said. "I don't remember."

"But you know the roads are snowy? Is that why you went off in the ditch and rolled your vehicle?"

Brittney shrugged again. "I don't know. I really don't remember." It had all happened so fast. She'd always believed she would be better equipped to handle a situation like that. But that blast and the subsequent shattering of her windshield had startled and blinded her. And she hadn't reacted the way she'd wanted to, with the strength and calm that her mom or Trent would have.

She wasn't used to being in danger, not like the hotshots were used to it. And she didn't want to get used to it, so she had to figure out fast who was behind the threats she'd received.

The trooper stared at her, her green eyes hard. "I can't help you if you don't tell me the truth."

"I can't tell you the truth until I know what it is myself," Brittney pointed out. And that was as honest as she intended to be with the trooper.

"You better let the authorities figure that out," the officer advised. "And don't investigate on your own."

While the trooper seemed young, probably even a year

or so younger than Brittney, she was wise. Or maybe she'd simply heard about her.

Wells turned toward Rory again. "That goes for you and your hotshot team, too. Whatever is going on with all of you, you need to leave it to the police to handle. You might know what you're doing when it comes to fighting fires, but you don't know when it comes to fighting bad guys."

Rory's lips curved into a slight, almost mocking grin, and he chuckled. "Really, Trooper Wells. And being up here in Northern Lakes, you know a lot about fighting bad guys?"

There was something in his tone, something that made Brittney pull her hand back from his arm. He sounded like he knew much more about fighting bad guys than any firefighter should know.

Because he'd fought them? Or because he'd been one?

Chapter Five

"Where are you going?" Owen asked as Rory walked past him, heading toward the exit.

He wished he'd been able to slip past the paramedic undetected, but Owen had been hovering somewhere inside the ER since Brittney had been brought in. Just like Rory had been hovering, but now that he knew she was all right, he was free to leave.

He should have left before now, but he'd wanted to make sure that she wasn't in any immediate danger. So when the doctor had ducked behind the curtain and asked him and the trooper to leave, Rory had hovered, like Owen, but close enough that he could hear the results of her MRI.

No broken bones.

And just a slight concussion.

The pressure that had been on his chest since seeing her lying on that gurney finally eased. She was fine. Physically. For now...

But if someone had fired at her vehicle, if someone had caused her to go off the road, she was still in danger until that person was caught. And what if she was in danger because of him? Because she was so damn determined to find out everything about the plane crash?

The person who'd caused it wasn't going to want their secret getting out, that it wasn't an accident. Just like Rory getting hit over the head hadn't been an accident. And maybe her going off the road hadn't been one, either, which meant that he might be, inadvertently, responsible for her being in danger.

"Rory?" Owen prodded him, his brow creasing with concern as he studied his face.

Everybody had been looking at him that way since he'd regained consciousness from the coma. With such concern and...confusion.

It was as if they didn't recognize him anymore.

Maybe that was because Rory had not recognized or remembered many of them or even himself when he'd woken up after two weeks of bad dreams and oblivion. But he remembered enough now to know that he was in danger and not just because of that whack on the head.

"I got released," Rory said. "And Ethan dropped off my truck earlier." Or at least he'd asked him to do it and Ethan had promised that he would, that he'd have Tammy follow him to the hospital to drop it off before they left for a much-deserved getaway.

Owen peered around him. "Ethan's here?"

Rory shook his head, and his stomach flipped with the pain radiating from the back of his skull. God, he hoped Brittney's head wasn't hurting like his. And if it was, she was damn tough. "No, Ethan and Tammy were taking off, going someplace warm for a couple of weeks."

Owen nodded. "Oh, that's right. I keep forgetting that he quit the ranger job to stick around Northern Lakes."

"Around Tammy," Rory said. "And it's not like he needs

the money." The guy was the Canterbury heir no matter how hard his brother-in-law had tried to take him out.

As hard as someone had tried to take out Rory. And Brittney?

Had she been telling Trooper Wells the truth about the crash? Or was there more to it than she'd admitted?

He suspected there was, and that concerned him, way more than it should. But if she was in danger because of him...

"Somebody needs to stick close to Brittney until Trent makes it up here," Owen said. The radio in his hand squawked. "And I have to go out on a call."

Rory tensed. "Who's hurt?"

"Nobody's hurt," Owen said. "It's a transport from the hospital back to the nursing home for someone who is all right now."

Rory's tension eased. "That's good."

"Yes, and I put it off as long as I can, but Trent is still about an hour away," Owen said. "Can you stick around until he gets here?"

"Why me?" Rory asked, his pulse quickening with the thought of sticking close to Brittney Townsend. But that might be dangerous for both of them...

Owen glanced around. "I don't see anybody else here."

"But somebody else would show up if you'd called them," Rory said. "Or if Trent had called them."

"But you were here at the hospital when she got hurt."

Rory narrowed his eyes and studied his friend's face. "What are you saying?"

Owen held up his hands. "I'm not saying anything. But I think we both know that we shouldn't take any chances right now. You should know that better than anyone else after what you've been through."

Rory sucked in a breath. "What…what do you mean?"

"You were in a coma for two weeks, man," Owen said. "Because someone put you there."

He shuddered. Who had done that? A stranger? Or someone he knew and should have been able to trust?

"That's why we have to be extra careful."

"We have to," Rory agreed. "But her…"

"She's Trent's sister," Owen reminded him.

Rory groaned. "You know how I feel about her."

"I thought I did, but now I'm wondering if you know how you feel about her," Owen replied. "Or did you forget that like you've forgotten some other things?"

"What do you mean?" How badly had he slipped up in those first days after regaining consciousness?

"You've been sticking close to her since I brought her here in the rig, which surprised the hell out of me since you were so pissed off the last time she came up to Northern Lakes. You were trying so hard to avoid her then that you spent most of the time she was here hiding out in the woods."

"I like the woods," Rory said. "That's why I'm a forest ranger."

"You remember that," Owen said. "But you seem to have forgotten how much you dislike the reporter."

"I don't dislike her," Rory said.

"I see that," Owen said with a wide grin.

"I just don't trust her." She was determined to further her career with a story that might have already put her in danger and would certainly put him in danger if the truth came out. But then he already was in danger and apparently so was she…

"You don't have to trust her to keep an eye on her until Trent gets here," Owen said. "And I need you to do that because I have to go."

As if on cue, the driver from the rig called out to him. "Owen! Mrs. G. wants to get back to the home before *Judge Judy* starts."

Owen smirked. "She wants to get back to Mr. Stehouwer."

The names vaguely rang a bell with Rory. The older couple had been in a fire at the boarding house that hotshot Cody Mallehan's fiancée had owned. They'd been her boarders until the Northern Lakes arsonist had burned down her house.

Everyone had survived, though. But it was just one more reminder of how precarious life was, probably why Mrs. Gulliver didn't want to spend any more time than necessary away from her Mr. Stehouwer. While being alone was the safest option for him and people around him, Rory missed being around other people, being close to them. He hadn't realized how much until Brittney had grabbed his arm and said she'd needed him.

And if she was in danger because of him, he had an obligation to protect her that went beyond even his duty to his fellow hotshots. Rory sighed. "Damn it. Go."

Owen slapped his shoulder. "Thanks. I appreciate it and Trent will, too."

Rory wasn't so sure about that. As pissed off as Trent had been at his sister, he was still protective of her, protective enough that he hadn't wanted her left alone. But if Trent knew what Rory really thought about his sister, he probably wouldn't trust him to watch over her. She didn't just unsettle him with her questions but also with her attractiveness.

And her touch…

Rory didn't entirely trust himself to watch over her and not want more of a connection with her. But he drew in a breath, to brace himself, and turned back toward where he'd left her behind that curtained-off area.

But the curtains had been pulled back. And her gurney was empty.

His pulse quickened with fear. Where the hell had she gone? He started forward, but someone grabbed his arm. And from the way his skin tingled, even through his heavy sweatshirt, he knew who it was.

She chuckled. "You're not much of a babysitter," she remarked.

Obviously she'd eavesdropped on his conversation with Owen. "No, I'm not," he agreed wholeheartedly. And she didn't even know the half of it. She could never know the half of it or she might wind up like the last woman he'd been attracted to.

Dead. He had to make sure that didn't happen, that he kept her out of danger somehow. He couldn't carry any more guilt than he already did.

"Good thing for you that I don't need a babysitter," Brittney said. "But I do need a ride."

Rory narrowed his eyes.

"Ethan dropped off yours," she said, revealing just how much of his conversation with Owen that she'd overheard.

"I'm not driving you back to Detroit," Rory said.

"I don't want to go back to Detroit."

"You should," he said. "You should go back." If not for her sake then for his. Because if she stuck around Northern Lakes, Rory had no doubt that this wasn't going to end well. For either of them.

BRITTNEY SUSPECTED THAT Trooper Wells had underestimated her. She wasn't the first one who'd made that mistake. And she probably wouldn't be the last.

The person who'd left her that note and sent her the text

hadn't underestimated her, though. They knew that if she kept investigating she was going to discover the truth.

On her own.

But she wasn't alone right now. Albeit grudgingly, Rory VanDam was giving her the ride she'd requested. To the body shop that the state police used as an impound lot in Northern Lakes. Brittney already knew which one it was from when Ethan Sommerly's truck had been blown up.

Hers hadn't blown up, but it didn't look much better than Ethan's burned-out truck had looked.

Rory's breath whistled out between his teeth as he pulled his truck up to the fence behind which the mass of crumpled metal sat. He looked from the wreckage to her. "Are you sure you're all right? Did the doctor actually release you?"

"You really don't trust me," she remarked. She'd over-heard most of his conversation with Owen. "You think I would do anything for a story." Only a console separated her passenger seat from his driver's seat, and she was tempted to lean across it, to tease him, about just how far he thought she would go. But she was already all too aware of how close he was to her, and something inside her, that she'd ignored for a long time, was reacting to that closeness.

"Wouldn't you?" he asked. "Isn't that why we're here?"

"I would do anything for the truth," she said. And she hoped like hell she wasn't risking her life for it. But if she stood around and did nothing, that didn't mean the danger would go away. The only way she could control the danger was to find out who presented the danger.

While she'd had a few doubts about Rory when she first got that note, Owen had verified that Rory had been in the hospital when her "accident" happened. That was why he'd trusted Rory, over other hotshots, to protect her. She wanted to trust him, too; she needed someone she could turn to…

But she didn't want to put him in danger, either, although it seemed like it was already too late for that.

"When did you get hit over the head?" she asked.

His mouth curved into a slight grin. "Why? Do I need an alibi for something?" Then his grin slid away, and he focused on her face. "This isn't the first thing that's happened to you, is it?"

"Just tell me when you got hit and went into that coma," she persisted. He didn't need his coma for an alibi, though. She just wanted to know if the same person might have hurt him who'd been threatening her.

"The night of the hotshot holiday party."

She sucked in a breath and nodded. "That's why Trent didn't come back to Detroit with Heather."

He shrugged. "He stayed before that happened. He was here that night that…"

"You got struck over the head," she finished for him. "Something else happened that night, didn't it?" And was the person who'd left the note on her van the same one who'd hit him? Or was someone else after him? Or just after any hotshot they were able to hurt?

He grinned that slight grin. "My getting whacked wasn't enough for you?"

He was teasing her, trying to be funny, but she couldn't laugh, not at him getting hurt so badly. Instead, she was tempted to reach across the console and touch him, to run her fingers over his head to find his wound. And…what? Kiss it better?

A sudden urge burned inside her to lean closer, to brush her lips across his. Maybe her concussion was worse than she'd thought. "You were in the hospital for weeks, then?" So obviously his concussion had been much worse than the one she'd gotten in the crash. Maybe that was why he wasn't avoiding her like he previously had.

"You didn't check my medical records while you were in the hospital?" he asked. And he probably wasn't teasing now.

"I would have tried," she said, "but Trooper Wells might've caught me with the way she kept popping up like she was lurking around…" She peered out the windows, looking for a state patrol vehicle. The concrete and metal body shop building and the fenced-in yard behind it were on the western outskirts of town, farther from Lake Huron. Trees surrounded the area, blocking it from the highway and even the driveway that led back to it.

"She didn't follow us," he said.

Maybe she hadn't, but Brittney suspected someone else might have. She had that uneasy feeling again, goose bumps rising on her skin with the sudden chill that rushed over her. And she shivered.

"It's not her you're worried about," Rory said.

She glanced back at him to find him staring intently at her, his pale blue eyes narrowed with suspicion.

"What's going on, Brittney?" he asked her.

"Which one of us is the reporter?" she fired back at him with a smile.

His mouth twitched, as if he was fighting against the urge to smile back at her. His blue eyes sparkled.

Her pulse quickened, and not because of some unknown person watching her but because he was. And he was so much better looking than she'd even remembered. She'd been curious about him before, for the sake of her story, but now she was just curious about him. About how his lips would feel against hers…

How he would kiss her…

How he would touch her…

She blinked, trying to break that connection and focus again on what mattered. On finding out why they were both in danger. "I'll answer one of your questions if you'll answer one of mine," she offered.

If he'd been fighting it, the smile won, curving his lips up at the corners. He chuckled and shook his head.

"Chicken," she taunted him with a smile of her own.

He nodded now. "I am definitely afraid of you, Ms. Townsend."

"Why do I scare you?" she asked. Was he feeling what she was? This sudden attraction? This strange connection?

Was it because they'd both recently survived attempts on their lives? Or maybe whoever had caused their accidents hadn't meant to kill them...

Just what?

Scare them away?

"I'm scared," he said, "because I'm not stupid." Then he sighed. "No. I take that back. If I was smart, I would have taken off and left you alone in the hospital."

"Why didn't you?" she asked.

"It's tough to get an Uber in Northern Lakes at this time of year," he replied.

"And you were worried about me hitching a ride?" she asked. "Or were you worried about my brother? Is that why you agreed to babysit me until he gets here?"

"I thought you didn't need a babysitter," he reminded her.

"I don't," she said. Then she glanced around again and muttered, "Maybe a bodyguard..."

"What's going on, Brittney?" He repeated his earlier question.

She dodged it this time by opening the passenger door and jumping out. But when she approached the fence, she noticed that a chain, secured with a heavy padlock, held the gate together. She turned toward the building, but no lights shone inside, although it was kind of hard to tell with the only glass being in one panel of each of several garage doors.

"It's after five," Rory said. "It must close then."

The sky was already turning gray with a pink rim just below the thick clouds.

She cursed. "I need to get in there. My overnight bag is inside the van." That wasn't all. Her purse was in there, too. She rattled the gate, trying to push the sides of it far enough apart to squeeze between, but she couldn't even get her arm through the narrow opening. She cursed again.

"Even if you could get into the fence, I'm not sure we could get inside the vehicle."

She pointed toward where part of the metal had been peeled back like the top of a tin can. "They got me out that way," she said. "I can get back in that way." She rattled the gate again, but the chain was too thick to give her any more room to squeeze through. So she moved farther down the fence and jammed the toe of her boot into part of the chain links while she locked her fingers into another part. Using her arms, she tried pulling herself up.

Rory chuckled.

"Give me a boost!" she ordered him.

"Yes, ma'am."

Then big hands wrapped around her waist, pushing her up. As she went higher, his hands went lower, over the curve of her hips, along the outside of her thighs and finally, where she'd intended him to boost her, her boots. Her whole body tingled in reaction. She swung her leg over the top of the fence and turned to stare back down at him.

"That wasn't what I meant by a boost." But she wasn't really complaining. Her skin had heated up everywhere he'd touched her. And as the sun set, the temperature was dropping along with it. The wind kicking up tangled her hair across her face, blinding her.

But then Rory was there, close, as he climbed up the fence to her. He swung his leg over, too, and jumped down, landing lithely on his feet in the yard on the other side, with all the grace of a gymnast landing a somersault.

Brittney hadn't been a very good gymnast. She wasn't all that flexible. She struggled to swing her other leg over the top. But when she did, she lost her foothold with her other boot and dangled from way too close to the top and too far from the ground.

"I'll catch you," Rory said.

"I'm not like a cat or a baby being tossed out the window of a burning house," she said. "I'll flatten you."

"Ouch," he said. "You must think I'm pretty weak."

"Don't say I didn't warn you," she murmured. Despite her words, she tried to hang on and find footholds for the toes of her boots. But her fingers slipped from the chain links and she dropped, not to the ground, but into some strong arms.

It wasn't like catching a baby, though. He didn't cradle her easily in both arms. He caught one of her legs and just half her body, while the other half of her dangled forward, nearly hitting the ground. Then they both hit the ground as he stumbled back and fell. But she was sprawled across him, not the dirt, while he lay flat on his back.

"I warned you," she reminded him as her breasts pressed into his hard chest. His heart pounded fast and hard beneath hers, which probably matched its frantic pace.

"I guess I am pretty weak," he said in between pants for air.

She must have knocked it out of him. She wriggled around, trying to get off him. But his hands caught her hips, gripping them like he had when she'd been trying to get up the fence.

"Give me a sec," he said gruffly.

"Are you hurt? Broken bones?" she asked.

"No. Just that damn concussion."

"Did you hit your head on the ground?" she asked, and she stretched up his long body that was so very tense beneath hers and ran her fingers along his jaw to the back of his head. His spiky-looking hair was surprisingly soft, but then she felt what must have been a ridged line of stitches or staples. Her stomach lurched over how badly he'd been hurt, and how lucky he'd been to survive such a violent blow. "You really were hit hard. That was definitely no damn accident."

"And neither was yours," he remarked.

"How do you know?" She hadn't admitted to hearing those gunshots, but she was damn sure that she had.

He reached out, running his hand underneath her van. And he pulled out a bullet. "It must have fallen out of the wreckage."

She let out a shaky breath.

"You're not surprised," he said. "You did hear the gunshots. What the hell is going on, Brittney? And this time I want an answer out of you."

"I'll give you one," she said. "Just not here."

Because she had that feeling again, that sick, not sixth, sense that she was being watched. Her stomach churned with the fear gripping her. If that person was out there and armed again, she wasn't the only one in danger now. Rory was, too.

He'd already survived what must have been an attempt on his life. Would he survive another?

BRADEN ZIMMER SOMETIMES got this strange feeling, a forewarning, when a fire was about to start. That feeling had helped his wife catch the Northern Lakes arsonist the year before. Sam McRooney-Zimmer had caught Braden, too, when he'd fallen so deeply in love with the arson investigator. Sam had taken a little more convincing to give him and Northern Lakes a chance.

But since there, fortunately, weren't a lot of arson fires in Northern Lakes, Sam traveled frequently, and she was out of town now. Instead of hanging out in his empty house, Braden usually spent more time at the firehouse.

If only he'd been here the night after the holiday party…

But Sam had been home that night.

Despite all her help and her brother's help, Braden still couldn't figure out who the saboteur was. Or why.

Why do all these things to the hotshots, especially if he or she was one of them? Why hurt one of their own like Rory had been hurt? So damn badly.

He'd been released from the hospital, so Braden expected him to come back to the firehouse, which was another reason he was here. And that feeling…

It wasn't the one he got about fires. It wasn't a forewarning, it was certainty and dread, twisting his stomach into knots. Because he didn't need a sixth sense to know that something bad was bound to happen again. Until the saboteur was caught, bad things would keep happening.

His office door creaked open and Trick, his brother-in-law, poked his red-haired head through the opening. "Did you hear about that reporter?"

Braden tensed, and that dread in his stomach got heavier. "What reporter?"

"Trent's sister. Brittney Townsend."

Braden groaned. "What about her?"

"She's back in Northern Lakes."

He groaned again. "Do you think she heard about Rory getting hurt? Is she here about the saboteur?"

Trick shrugged. "I don't know."

"Is she here now? At the firehouse?"

Trick shook his head again. "She was in the hospital last Owen knew. He brought her there in his rig. She was in a crash."

Braden sucked in a breath. "Does Trent know?"

Trick nodded. "Yeah, Owen called him. He's on his way up. He wanted Owen to keep an eye on her but he had to go out on call."

"Then why aren't *you* watching her?"

"Rory is. He was just supposed to watch her at the hospital until Trent got there. But I checked in on them and they were both gone."

Braden groaned.

"It's not like Rory is going to tell her anything about the sabotage," Trick said. "He wants less to do with her than the rest of us do."

Braden dropped back into his chair, but he wasn't really relieved that Rory wouldn't talk to her. "Maybe we should talk to her."

"About what? Her crash? The roads are still pretty slippery. Even though Trent told Owen it wasn't an accident, I figure it probably was."

"Probably." Braden shook his head. "After everything that has happened, I struggle to accept that anything is an accident anymore."

Trick released a ragged sigh. "Me, too."

"We should talk to her," Braden said. "About what happened to her and maybe even about what's been happening around here."

"But Braden, that could cost you your job," Trick warned him.

He shrugged. "I'd rather lose my job than lose one of the team. Again."

"Dirk's death wasn't your fault. That had nothing to do with the team."

But that didn't make Braden feel any better about the loss of a good man. And he'd nearly lost another one when Rory had been assaulted.

With an axe handle.

A firefighter's axe.

That didn't mean that it had to have been a firefighter who'd attacked Rory, though. Stanley often forgot to lock the doors. Really anyone could have gotten inside that night. And once inside, it would have been easy enough to find the keys for the rigs. But Braden still had that sick feeling in his stomach, that dread that the saboteur was one of his team.

Chapter Six

Rory had wondered before if that blow to his head had knocked the common sense out of him or back into him. He had his answer now as he followed Brittney Townsend through the door she'd just unlocked to a room at the Lakeside Inn in Northern Lakes. He'd lost all his common sense and all sense of self-preservation, as well. Or he would have dropped her off and run away.

No. He would have left her at the hospital until Trent got there. But she hadn't wanted to wait for her brother or to even let him know where she was.

But no matter what was going on between Brittney and Trent, Rory shouldn't be here. He should be somewhere else, anywhere else where nobody could find him. Hell, he should have stayed missing five years ago instead of coming out of the mountains with Ethan, but if they hadn't banded together during those two months, neither of them would have survived. They'd struggled during the long hours it had taken them to find each other.

And now he kind of felt the same way about Brittney as he had when he'd found Ethan on that mountain. Like they were both in danger and wouldn't make it if they separated. That, together, they were stronger and safer. But Brittney wasn't Ethan. He wasn't sure he should trust her, or if she would take chances that would put them both in more danger than they already were.

"This is a bad idea," he said, hesitating on the threshold to her room.

She reached out and grasped his arm like she had in the hospital when she hadn't wanted him to leave her. And this time, instead of holding him in place, she tugged him inside the room and closed the door behind him. Then she locked both the handle and the dead bolt and leaned back against the wood of the door.

"You're not going to keep out a bullet like that," he said. And another of those old memories surfaced even as he fought to force it back down, to drown it out for good. "You need to call Trooper Wells."

"Do you trust her?" she asked.

He sighed.

"So why do you think that I should?"

"It's the hotshots who can't trust her," Rory said. "You should be able to."

"My brother is a hotshot," she said. "So why would I be able to trust her if my brother can't? If she has something against him, she might use me to get to him."

"I don't think she's had as much to do with Trent as she has other hotshots, the ones who live up here," he said.

"What about you?" she asked.

He shook his head. "The most interaction I had with her was today." Because he didn't technically live in Northern Lakes.

"You didn't seem to enjoy that very much," she pointed out. "Are you sure you want me to call her here?"

"I'll leave." He took a step toward the door, but she hadn't moved away from it.

Now he wondered if she had locked and leaned against the door to keep out whoever she thought was after her or if she'd done it to keep him inside with her. Was it that she didn't want to be alone again? Was she more scared than she would admit? Or was she feeling the same thing he was? This strange draw to her...

"I'm not going to call Trooper Wells," she said. "You don't have to run off."

"You should run," he said. And he meant it. "After finding that bullet, you know that was no accident." Just like so many of the things that had happened to the hotshots had been no accident, either.

"How can I leave?" she asked. "You saw my van. I'm not driving out of here in that wreck."

"You can take a bus," he suggested. "Or have Trent take you back to Detroit when he gets here. You'll be safe there." He hoped.

She shook her head.

He hesitated to ask the question he'd already asked her twice, the question she'd promised she would answer once they left the impound lot at the body shop. But once they'd extricated her suitcase from the back and her purse from beneath a seat, he'd realized that he might be better off not knowing the answer to this question.

Because if he knew, he might not be able to walk away like he should. No. He should run. Every instinct he had was screaming at him to do that, to run.

But to run away, he had to get closer to her. And when he stepped closer, the ground seemed to shift beneath him like it had when she'd dropped from that fence into his arms. He'd fallen for her then.

No. He'd fallen *with* her.

He could not fall *for* her. Or for anyone else. Not ever again.

BRITTNEY WAITED FOR him to ask that question again. She needed him to ask it, or even just to say something, because the way he was staring at her unnerved her. But it wasn't like that sensation she felt whenever someone else watched her.

She wasn't chilled by Rory's stare. Instead, heat rushed through her, and her pulse quickened. Then he closed his eyes, as if staring at her unnerved him, as well. Could he feel this, too? This attraction that was beginning to overwhelm her with its intensity.

His long, lean body tensed, and he asked, "What's going on, Brittney? Why did someone shoot at you? What the hell has been happening?"

For some strange reason she trusted him and not just because he'd been in the hospital when someone had shot at her van. Because he was obviously in danger, too, and he understood what she was feeling…all the fear and frustration and maybe even the determination to find out who the hell was after them.

"Someone's been following me," she told him. "At first I thought it was just my imagination, or maybe someone who'd recognized me." She shuddered now. "Or even my creepy producer."

His eyes opened, filled with concern. "Your creepy producer?"

She shrugged. "I can handle him. And there's no way he would have shot at me or even followed me up here to Northern Lakes." She creased her brow. "No. They might have already been here because the shot came from the direction I was going, not from behind me."

"Who knew you were coming up here?" he asked.

"Nobody."

"Not even Trent?"

"Especially not Trent," she said. "He's barely been talking to me since I did that story about Ethan."

"About Jonathan Canterbury…" he murmured.

"Did you know?" she asked. "Did you always know who he really was?"

He shook his head, but she didn't know if that was in reply to her question or in denial of answering it. "Ethan's refused to do a follow-up interview with you," he said. "And I refused to do one at all."

"I'm well aware of that," she said. "So when I got this note…" Her handbag was slung across her body, so she reached inside and pulled out the piece of paper and showed it to him.

"'You are being watched, and if you don't drop this story, you will die,'" he read the note aloud, his voice gruffer with each word. "What story?"

"It has to be the one about the plane crash," she said. "Because when I tried talking to Mack McRooney about it, this text came through…" She pulled out her cell, but the screen was black. The battery must have died after the crash, just like she might have died in the crash. She'd been damn lucky. "The text said something like, 'you were warned, now you'll suffer the consequences.'"

He shuddered. "And then you were shot at. Damn, Brittney. You need to report this."

"To whom?" she asked. "Trooper Wells? Why should I trust her when you don't?" And why did she feel like he was the only one she could trust? She didn't know him well or really at all. But since waking up to find him with her in the hospital, concerned about her, she had connected with him on a whole other level.

He sighed. "I don't trust anyone, Brittney. Not anymore."

"Why not?" she asked.

He touched the back of his head, where she'd felt those stitches. And she understood why. "Well, you can trust me," she insisted. "When you were getting hit over the head, I was in Detroit. And you were already in the hospital when I found that note on my windshield."

"When did you find that note?" he asked.

"Two weeks ago," she replied.

"And when did you get that text?"

"Earlier today."

His breath hissed out between his clenched teeth. And he shook his head. "Damn, Brittney. Instead of listening to these threats, or at least reporting them, you headed up here. Why?"

"Because I know the only way to make sure this person stops following me and threatening me is to find out who they are and stop them," she said.

"I hope you don't think it's me," he said.

She had briefly considered it but not now, not when she'd seen how concerned he'd been about her in the hospital and now. He was a good man. Like her brother. And she wanted to keep him safe, too. "Like Owen said, you're one of the few with an ironclad alibi," she said. "You're probably the only person I really can trust."

"That doesn't make it safe to be around me," he muttered the words.

But she'd caught them. "What do you mean? These threats are about you? About the plane crash?" That was her suspicion, especially after the text had come after she'd tried talking to the hotshot trainer. But there had been things that had happened to the hotshots since that plane crash. Many things.

He shook his head. "No. I don't know. I'm talking about that night at the firehouse."

"What happened that night?" she asked.

"Trent didn't tell you?"

She shook her head.

"He was probably worried about you reporting about it, about the hotshots again," he said. "So I shouldn't say anything because maybe that's it, maybe that's the story someone wants you to drop."

"If you don't tell me, I'll find someone who will," she said.

He smiled faintly. "I don't think any of the other hotshots are going to tell you about it, either."

She smiled widely. "Tammy will."

"Damn it."

Obviously Ethan must have shared that Tammy and she were friends. "Does that surprise you?" she asked.

He shook his head. "You saved her life. She owes you."

"Is that why you kept Ethan—Canterbury's secret?" she asked. "Because he saved your life?"

"You ask so many questions," he murmured. "Occupational hazard?"

"I just have so many questions," she said. "I always have."

"So that's why you became a reporter?"

"You ask a lot of questions, too, Mr. VanDam," she pointed out.

He shrugged. "I usually don't," he said. "But I'm interest— no, I'm curious."

She was amused that he'd stopped himself from saying interested. So to tease him, she batted her eyelashes and stepped a little closer to him. "About me?"

"About why someone would threaten you and force you off the road," he said.

"I'm curious about that, too," she said. "It has to be related to the plane crash."

"You ran that story months ago," he said. "And you already covered it. So why would anyone be trying to back you off from what you've already done?"

"Because they know what I know, that there's more to that story," she said. "That there's more to the plane crash."

He shook his head. "It was Ethan's brother-in-law. He was behind everything."

"He swears he wasn't," she reminded him.

"Yeah, because people died in that plane crash," he said. "So of course he's not going to admit to that."

"He's already in prison," she said. "And will be for a long time. So what difference does it make? And how would he be following me and leaving me these threats?"

"He hired people to go after Ethan," Rory said. "Maybe he hired someone to go after you."

She shook her head. "That doesn't make sense, and you know it. You're the one who wants me to leave that plane crash story alone."

"I have an alibi. I was in a coma," he reminded her.

She didn't really believe it but she felt compelled to throw his words back at him. "Maybe *you* hired someone."

He snorted. "With what money and how? I'm not a Canterbury."

"Are you a VanDam?" she asked. "Or did you take somebody else's name like Ethan did?" That hadn't really occurred to her before, but if Ethan had pulled it off, maybe he could have, as well.

He expelled a ragged sigh. "You need to stop, Brittney."

"Why? Am I on to something?"

"You must be *on* something," he said, "if you think there's any more to the story you already covered about Ethan. You must be working on something else that put you in danger."

She snorted. "Gallery and restaurant openings? I doubt that anybody wants me to drop those."

"Maybe the competition to those businesses," he said. "Or maybe the competition for your job."

She nearly snorted again. She didn't even want her job, but she once had. She'd once been desperate enough to take any position that would get her screen time, that might get her noticed by a bigger program or network like her mentor, her idol, Avery Kincaid. Avery had worked at the station Brittney worked at; Brittney had been her intern. Then Avery had covered a story about the hotshots when an arsonist had targeted them and Northern Lakes. Avery had gotten her big break after that article and a relationship with a hotshot. All Brittney had gotten from her story about the hotshots was resentment and the attention of someone who had sent her those threats. Who? And why?

Maybe it was about that, about what had been happening to the hotshots. Obviously someone was after them or Rory wouldn't have been hit over the head.

He clearly wasn't going to talk to her about the plane crash. At least not yet. So she circled back around to another question he had yet to answer. "What happened that night you got hit over the head?"

He shook his head.

"Tammy will tell me," she reminded him.

"Since she and Ethan left town for a romantic getaway, I think you'll have to wait until she gets back," he said.

And she groaned. "That's right." Tammy had texted her a screenshot of a plane ticket that Ethan had bought her for Christmas. "They're going on a cruise."

So she wouldn't get to see Tammy this trip. And if she didn't find out who was after her, she might not be alive to make another trip north.

"Damn it, Rory, please," she murmured, and tears of frustration and probably exhaustion stung her eyes. But she blinked them back.

He stepped closer to her now, so less than a foot separated

their bodies. "I got hit when I stepped out of the bunk room to find out why someone had started up all the fire engines."

"Was there an alarm? Why would someone start up all the fire trucks?"

He shrugged. "I don't know. A prank."

"Hitting you over the head wasn't a prank," she said. And she reached up to run her finger over that spot on the back of his head, over his spiky, soft hair and the stitches beneath it. "It must have been bad."

"I really don't remember much about it," he said. "I had no idea what happened. And Trent never said anything to you?"

She bit her lip and shook her head. "He doesn't trust me anymore. Not after I did that story."

"Were you and him that close before the story?" he asked. "He never mentioned you before you showed up in Northern Lakes. And then he didn't even admit you were his sister until after you helped saved Tammy's life."

Had he been ashamed of her even before that story? Or hadn't he wanted her to make a nuisance of herself like she had at the firehouse in Detroit? As she probably had the entire time they'd been growing up, when she'd trailed him everywhere, firing questions at him.

She closed her eyes against a sudden rush of tears.

"God, I'm sorry," Rory said. "That was so damn insensitive. I'm sure he had his reasons. He probably didn't want any of the guys hitting on you."

She shook her head. "I'm sure that's not it."

"None of his coworkers in Detroit have hit on you?" he asked.

Thinking of the catcalls and whistles whenever she'd stopped by the firehouse, a smile tugged at her lips and she opened her eyes. Most of them only made those noises to irritate Trent, but there were a couple of them who had made serious attempts to get her to go out with them. "But that's Detroit."

"What does that mean?" he asked. "You're only hot in Detroit?" he asked.

Feeling that pull, that attraction between them, Brittney gave in to the urge to flirt. "What do you think?" she asked. "Am I hot in Northern Lakes?"

"So damn hot that there won't be any snow left on the ground or ice on the lakes," he said. "Yeah, that must be why Trent didn't mention you. He didn't want any of the hotshots hitting on you."

"You wouldn't hit on me," she said. "You would be more likely just to hit me to get away from me."

"I would never hit you," he said. "And I know I should get far away from you, but for some reason I just can't." He stepped closer now and slid his arms around her waist. His chest touched hers, his thighs brushed against hers, and his body was so hard, so muscular.

She sucked in a breath as that attraction turned to desire. To *need*.

"Rory..." Her hand, almost of its own volition, reached for the back of his head again, to pull it down to hers.

But he resisted, his body going all tense.

"See," she said, releasing a shaky breath. "You wouldn't hit on—"

He pressed his hand over her mouth again, like he had in the hospital. Then he leaned close and whispered, "Listen."

And she heard the heavy footsteps in the hall, too. Then the door handle rattled behind her. Someone was out there, trying to get in.

So she'd been right. Someone had been watching her at

the impound lot. And they must have followed them back here, to the hotel. To do what?

Finish what he'd tried to do when he'd shot at her van? Kill her? And was Rory going to get hurt along with her? She'd wanted to stick close to him for protection, but she hadn't realized that she was putting him in danger, too. She didn't want him getting hurt any more than she wanted her brother getting hurt. She couldn't lose anyone else she cared about.

DAMN IT, BRITTNEY.

Why wasn't she answering her cell?

Was it payback for all the times that Trent had ignored her calls? Her texts? Her?

He wished now that he could go back. That he could take every call, answer every text.

The only spot he'd still draw the line was with her questions. He didn't want to answer those because he had a feeling that asking them was what had put her in danger.

Because she hadn't gone off that damn road on her own. The roads weren't even as bad as they'd been that day weeks ago when his truck had been forced off the road.

Brittney wouldn't have crashed like that, not without some help. And she wouldn't have disappeared out of the hospital without some, too.

Rory.

Owen had left her there with him.

"What are you worried about?" Owen had asked when he'd called to yell at him after discovering that they were both gone. "Rory couldn't have had anything to do with her accident. He was in the hospital."

"She didn't have an accident, and neither did he," Trent

had told the paramedic. "And because they're both in danger, they're in even more danger when they're together."

And Owen had cursed in acknowledgement that Trent was right. He'd offered to look for them, too.

They hadn't been at the firehouse. Or at the impound lot where her van sat all crumpled up like a wad of paper that had missed the wastebasket.

She could have died. And knowing that, that she was still in danger, Trent had headed next for the hotel. Thanks to her mom and stepdad, Brittney had money. So she'd probably check into the Lakeside Inn.

But the front desk refused to tell him if she had. And so he'd sneaked upstairs to check out the rooms.

As he started down the hall on the third floor, he heard something. Not her voice, like he'd been listening for at every door.

But a soft creak. Before he could turn around, something struck him, knocking him to the ground. He could only hope it wouldn't knock him out like Rory had been knocked out for weeks.

Chapter Seven

Rory had hoped that the bullet might have dropped out of some other pile of wreckage in that impound yard. But he'd seen right away that the windshield had spider-webbed out from a hole in the middle of it. She could have been killed. From that bullet. Or from the crash.

It definitely hadn't been an accident. Then there was the note and the text. The threats.

Was it really about the plane crash? Was that why someone had struck him over the head that night?

Had someone else already figured out the truth that Brittney was so determined to uncover?

So determined that it could cost her her life? He wanted to make sure that didn't happen, especially if it was because of him. So he'd driven her back to the hotel and followed her inside, and then he'd been the one in danger.

With the way she'd looked at him…

The way she'd touched him…

He'd wanted to kiss her so damn badly that there had been a buzzing noise inside his head. So he was surprised that he'd heard the heavy footsteps.

But then there had been no mistaking the turning of that doorknob.

Someone was out in the hall. And, since the old hotel had

doors with no peepholes, he'd headed out the window onto the fire escape. He'd only gone down one floor, in through another window and out into the hall. Then, worried about leaving her alone up there, he'd run up the steps, slowing his pace only to quiet his approach.

He'd drawn in a breath before pushing open the stairwell door to the hall. A big man, his back to Rory, stood near another door, listening.

He was definitely looking for someone, and Rory had a pretty good idea who.

Knowing that the man had been armed out there on the road, when he'd fired those shots at Brittney, Rory didn't take any chances. He snuck up and tackled the man, knocking him to the floor. Then, desperate to knock him out before he could draw his weapon, Rory swung his fist toward the man's face.

His knuckles connected with flesh and bone before his eyes focused and he saw whose face he was striking. Trent's.

His hotshot team member shoved him back, knocking him against the wall. Fortunately his shoulders struck first, but the back of his head followed, hitting the thick wainscoting of the hallway, too. Rory grunted as pain radiated throughout his skull. And he flinched and closed his eyes for a moment.

"What the hell!" Trent yelled.

"What the hell, exactly," Brittney said.

Rory opened his eyes and reminded her, "You were supposed to stay in the room."

Before going out the window, he'd told her to do that, and he'd been so damn tempted to kiss her then. But he'd been more worried about her life than how her lips would taste. And as distracted as he'd been, he hadn't realized she hadn't agreed to stay put.

She stood over them now, a lamp grasped in her hands. "And let you get shot or worse?"

"Shot?" Trent asked the question, his eyes wide with shock. They were the same light brown as his sister's, but now his gaze moved from Rory back to Brittney. "Are you all right?"

"I'm fine," she said.

Rory shoved himself up until he was standing, but when he did, the ground seemed to tilt like it had when she'd fallen off the fence onto him. And he staggered. He might have fallen again if Brittney hadn't rushed forward to slide her arm around him.

She pointed the lamp, which she held with just one hand now, at her brother. "What did you do to him?"

"To him?" Trent repeated, and he stroked his jaw. "He hit me."

"What were you doing sneaking around the hotel, trying to get into rooms?" Brittney asked.

She must have assumed what Rory had, that Trent had been the one trying the doors. Rory hoped he'd been, and since he'd kind of caught him in the act, chances were good that it had been him.

But what if it hadn't been...?

He slid his arm around her and peered down the hall in both directions. No doors had opened. Probably because it was still the offseason in Northern Lakes. Too cold for regular fishing and water sports and too warm for ice fishing and snowmobiling. Or was someone behind one of those doors, watching them?

"You should get back into the room," he advised her. She'd left that door open behind her.

"Why?" She looked around then. "Do you think someone else is out here?"

"It was just me," Trent assured them. "The front desk wouldn't give me your room number. And you wouldn't pick up your damn phone or text me back—"

"Frustrating, isn't it?" she interjected with a glare at her brother.

Trent ignored her and continued, "So I kept calling you and listening at the doors…"

"To see if you could hear her phone," Rory finished for him, and his apprehension eased. Since it had just been Trent, she should be safe in the hotel.

Unless whoever was watching her had followed them back to it.

He was torn. Trent was here now. So he had no reason to stay. Except…

What if she was in danger because of her story on that damn plane crash? Because if that was the case, it was all his fault. So he had a duty to protect her, and maybe she was right, that the best form of protection was to find out who was behind the threats and stop them.

So even though he knew he should take off and get far, far away from her, he let her guide him back into her room, as if he needed her support.

As if he needed her.

And he'd learned long ago that it was too dangerous to need anyone. It was better to rely only on himself, except for those two months in the mountains with Ethan. After the things that had happened to him, the blow to his head and her crash, he felt kind of like he was parachuting out of a plane again and that he needed Brittney to survive.

BRITTNEY WAS FURIOUS with her brother. For so many reasons.

So when he came back into the room with the bucket of ice she'd sent him to get, she glared at him again as she took it from him. Then she wrapped some of the ice into a towel and pressed it against the wound on Rory's head where blood had begun to seep through the stitches. She'd guided him to a chair once she'd gotten him into the room. He'd seemed a little unsteady after hitting the wall, and she wondered if he should return to the hospital.

Concerned and irritated, she asked, "What the hell were you thinking?"

The two men looked at each other, as if uncertain which of them was supposed to answer her. She'd tried asking Rory already, but he'd gone out the window so fast she hadn't been able to say anything or stop him.

But she'd been so damn worried.

When he'd rushed onto the fire escape to find out who was in the hall, he could have confronted a stranger with a gun. But Trent wasn't a stranger. Or he hadn't been until lately, since she'd come up to Northern Lakes. No, even before that he'd been keeping things from her. That was why she'd come up to Northern Lakes, to find out what was going on with him…because she'd known it had something to do with his hotshot team.

While she'd known about them, they hadn't known about her. Why?

"I was talking to you," she told her brother.

"And I already told you, I was worried about you, especially when you didn't answer my calls or texts," he explained.

She snorted. "So now you want to play my protective big brother after weeks of ignoring me? And even before that, you denied my existence."

"What are you talking about?"

"Here in Northern Lakes, with your hotshots, nobody knew I was your sister or that you even had a sister."

Trent turned toward Rory, glaring at him. Obviously he knew who had ratted him out to her.

She stepped in front of Rory, not wanting Trent to hurt his friend for just telling her the truth. "Don't blame him. He's not the one who denied knowing me. What was it? Three times before a cock crowed?"

"It wasn't like that—"

"Not exactly," she conceded. "But it sounds like it was close."

"I didn't deny it, but…"

"You didn't claim me, either," she said. "Why? Are you ashamed of me?"

He flinched.

And she felt a pang strike her heart. "Oh, you are."

"Brittney, it's not you, it's your job—"

"My job is who I am, just like yours is who you are," she said.

Trent snorted. "You can't compare fighting fires to reporting on the stories that you have."

Heat rushed to her face with embarrassment, especially with Rory listening to this whole exchange. But then a surge of self-righteous indignation chased away the shame. "I haven't always covered the most compelling stories," she admitted. Not until she'd found the missing Canterbury heir. "But I am good at what I do, and I'm going to prove it to you and everyone else."

Obviously she was on to something significant, or someone wouldn't have threatened her like they had. But the story wasn't as important as discovering who was behind the threats and stopping them. Then she would prove to Trent that she was good at what she did and she could take care of herself and even protect him and his hotshots, as well. As long as she made sure Rory didn't get hurt in the process.

"You're going to get yourself killed," Trent said.

She snorted now. "You could have died that night that Rory got hurt. You were in the bunk room, too. You could have been the one who got hit over the head and put in a coma. And *you* never said anything to me about it."

"I was fine," Trent said. "Nothing happened to me."

But it had to Rory, and knowing now that he'd been hurt affected her for some reason, some reason she wasn't willing to even acknowledge. Yet. "It could have happened to you, if not getting hit then the fumes from the trucks could have hurt you. I still should have known about it."

"I didn't want you reporting on it," he said. "If there's any more scandal around the hotshot team, Braden will probably lose his job."

She sucked in a breath and nodded. Apparently he cared more about his relationship with his hotshot superintendent than with his sister. "So that's how it is."

"After you did that story on Ethan, how can you expect me to trust you?" he asked.

Tears stung her eyes, but she closed her eyes to hold them in. "I need you to leave right now."

"Britt—"

"Go," she said. "Or I'll call hotel security—"

"The only hotel security here is Rory," Trent said with a chuckle.

She opened her eyes to glare at her brother. "Even with a concussion, he knocked you on your ass." But she didn't want him fighting her brother again, not for her or for any reason. "I'll be safer with him than with you right now." Because Rory understood the danger just like she did, and Trent had already been through too much recently. She didn't want him involved in this, and she didn't want to drive a wedge between him and other members of his hot-shot team.

"I would never hurt you, Brittney," Trent said. "You know that."

She shook her head. "You already have, Trent. Just leave, or I'll call Trooper Wells to throw you out."

"Something's going on with you," Trent said. "And I want to know what it is."

She shook her head again. "Nope. You can't ignore me for weeks and weeks like you have and then suddenly try to play my big brother again like—"

"I am your big brother."

"Right now you're trespassing in my hotel room," she said. "And I will call the police—"

Trent sighed heavily. "Damn it, Brittney."

"Just go."

She wasn't sure that he would. But he knew her well enough to know how stubborn she was. Even more stubborn than he was, so he sighed again and turned and walked out the door. She waited until it closed behind her to let out the breath she'd been holding. While she was relieved that her brother had left, that meant that she was alone again with Rory.

And the last time they'd been alone, she had nearly kissed him. Maybe Trent skulking around the hallway had saved her from making a big mistake. But now that she'd made her brother leave, she was worried that she might make that mistake yet. Or one that was even worse…

FEELING AS EDGY as if he was battling a blaze with no equipment, Ethan paced the airport terminal, walking up and down the wide aisle between the gates. He had been looking forward to this trip until Rory got hurt.

But now everything had changed.

Except his feelings for Tammy. He didn't want to disappoint her. She'd been looking forward to this cruise. But she stepped into his path, and he nearly collided with her.

"You're not this upset about a delayed flight," she said. "What's going on?"

He shrugged. "I don't know." But it felt like something was wrong, and it wasn't just that the saboteur had struck again. It was who they'd struck…

Rory.

Ethan had been through so much with that man, but there was so much he still didn't know about him.

"You've been quiet and tense ever since you dropped Rory's truck at the hospital for him."

He hadn't said much during their two-and-a-half-hour trip from Northern Lakes to Detroit, where they were supposed to catch this flight. If the plane ever arrived.

His stomach pitched as he thought of another plane that had never arrived at its destination. The plane he and Rory had been on, the plane that Rory…

"Ethan?" she repeated his name with a question in her voice and concern in her beautiful hazel eyes. "Are you okay?"

Trying to reassure her, he forced a grin. "I'm always quiet, remember?"

She shook her head. "No. You might have been quiet before, but you haven't been since…"

Since they'd become lovers.

And since Trent's sister had revealed Ethan's secret, he no longer had anything to hide. Except for what he knew about Rory.

"Since you," he said. "You make me want to share everything with you." But he couldn't share this, and not just for Rory's sake, but for hers. The way Rory had told him that it was better that he not know…

"So tell me the truth," she said. "Do you really want to go on this trip?"

"I do," he said. "So badly, especially after seeing those bikinis you packed…"

"But?" she prodded. She knew him so well, so well that she answered her own question. "You're worried about Rory."

"I'm worried about the whole team," he admitted. But specifically Rory.

If it was the saboteur who'd whacked Rory over the head so hard he'd put him in a coma, then that person was getting more and more dangerous. Which meant that everyone was in greater danger than they'd been before.

"And you feel like you're deserting them when they need you most," she finished for him, articulating that sick feeling he'd had in his gut since driving away from Northern Lakes.

That sick feeling that something was going to happen to the people he loved like family.

Chapter Eight

Rory shouldn't have stuck around at the hospital. He should have hopped in his truck and driven off without checking on Brittney Townsend, without ever talking to the ambitious reporter. He understood her ambition a little better now, after being a witness to the tense conversation between the siblings.

And while Trent hadn't slammed the door on his way out of the room, it felt like he had because the room was eerily silent after he left. So eerily silent that Rory felt awkward clearing his throat.

He felt awkward about more than that, though. Like that almost kiss...that kiss that he wanted to happen now. But that was crazy. They both had too damn much going on, were in too much danger, to entertain an attraction of any kind. But he was attracted to her. Too attracted.

He adjusted the makeshift ice pack against the back of his head. The concussion had definitely messed him up. That had to be why he was still here, why he hadn't gotten as far away from the reporter as he could get, why he'd started to believe that she was right, that it was best for them to stick together like he and Ethan had stuck together.

The person who'd put the threat on her vehicle could have been the same person who'd struck him over the head that night. Or maybe they'd hired someone. Like Ethan's brother-in-law and so many others in Rory's life had proved, a lot of people would do anything for money.

The towel was wet, the ice melting inside it. With a sigh, he pulled it away from his now damp hair and head.

"Are you okay?" she asked him, and she reached out with a slightly shaking hand and took the towel from him.

"Are you?" he asked with concern.

She nodded. "Yes, but I hate fighting with Trent."

"I'm sorry that you did," he said. "I shouldn't have told you what I did earlier—"

"It was the truth," she said. "And I deserved to know."

"Not when it upset you," he said. "And I am sorry about that." He didn't want her hurting emotionally or physically, and because of that, he had to make himself leave. So he stood up with the intent of heading toward the door. But the room spun for a moment, his head so light that spots danced in front of his eyes.

She grabbed him like she had in the hall, sliding her arm around him, using her body to steady his.

Except the heat and softness of her body unsettled him more. He wanted her for more than support. He wanted her.

He dragged in a breath. "I'm fine."

"You should go back to the hospital," she said. "Hitting the wall like you did might have done more damage than reopening your stitches."

"I'm fine," he repeated. "I just need to get some rest." After three weeks of being in that hospital bed, two of those weeks in a coma, he shouldn't need any more sleep for a while. But being active for the first time in three weeks had taken more energy than he'd thought.

Too much energy to fight this attraction to Brittney. So

he had to leave. Fast. Before he did something incredibly stupid...like kiss her.

"I need to leave," he said more to himself than to her. He had to remind his body that it had to move away from her, not closer. He stepped away from her, and her arm dropped back to her side. His legs heavy with reluctance, he headed toward the door. When his hand closed around the knob, he started to turn it, intent on making his escape.

Though he wasn't sure if he wanted to escape from her or from the temptation of her.

"Wait," she said. "Don't leave."

She hadn't touched him, like she had at the hospital when she'd grabbed his arm more than once. But she didn't have to touch him to stop him.

Just her words did that.

Or maybe it was his own desire to stay that stopped him from leaving her. He could give himself an excuse. That he had to stay to protect her, and he fully intended to protect her...after he got some rest. And he had no doubt that Trent was lurking around outside somewhere. Probably back in the hall, intent on making sure nothing happened to his sister. She didn't need Rory.

She might actually be safer if he left, unless she was right, like that instinct inside him that had had him searching for the other parachuter five years ago. That sticking together was their best chance of survival...

But he wasn't going to be any use to her or himself if he didn't get some rest. So he drew in a breath and forced himself to finish turning that knob. But he couldn't quite bring himself to open that door and walk away.

BRITTNEY CURLED HER fingers into her palms, so that she wouldn't reach for him, so that she wouldn't pull Rory back from that door. While someone had threatened her and apparently tried to shoot her, Rory could have been killed in the firehouse. He was in just as much if not more danger than she was.

"Don't leave," she repeated with concern for him and with something more, that desire for him that made her want to kiss him so damn badly.

His long lean body tensed even more than it had when she'd slid her arm around him to steady him. "It would be a very bad idea for me to stay."

He wasn't wrong about that. If he stayed, Brittney was pretty sure she would give in to that desire to kiss him and maybe in to her desire for more. And he was the last guy she should get closer to, because of that feeling she had, about how much danger he was in.

She wasn't going to fall for someone and lose him like her mom had lost her dad. Sure, she'd found love again with Brittney's stepdad. But Brittney remembered the pain her mom had tried to hide from her. Late at night when nightmares had woken her up, she'd heard crying.

Her mother crying.

And she had been so afraid to hear a strong woman like her mom sobbing with such pain and such heartbreak. Brittney wasn't as strong as her mom was. She couldn't love and risk the loss.

Not that she was at risk of falling for Rory VanDam. She didn't really know anything about him, except that he kept, albeit reluctantly, coming to her rescue. At the hospital he'd made sure she was all right, and he'd taken her to the impound lot. And he'd just taken on her brother in the hallway. But he hadn't known it was her brother.

It could have been the man with the gun. Hell, the man with the gun could be out there now. She sucked in a breath at the frightening thought of that. But surely whoever had fired at her wouldn't take a shot at Rory. Unless Rory was as involved in all of this, because of the plane crash, as she'd previously suspected he was. Maybe his getting hit over the head and the threats she'd received were related because someone didn't want him to tell her what had really happened.

"Where are you going to go?" she asked him. "Back to the firehouse?"

He moved as if a sudden chill had passed through him, his body shuddering slightly.

"You know you're not safe there," she said.

"Because of your brother?" he asked, and he turned back toward her then, touching the back of his head.

She shook her head. "As big an ass as my brother can be, he wouldn't have intentionally hurt you. I believe him, that he didn't know it was you when you jumped him in the hall. And he just instinctively shoved you off."

"I wasn't talking about then," Rory remarked.

And she bristled defensively. "There's no way it was him who struck you at the firehouse. Trent's hotshot team members mean everything to him. He would rather hurt me than hurt any of you."

"He would never purposely hurt you," Rory said. "He loves you."

She sighed. "I know. But just because you love someone, it doesn't mean you like them. And I don't think my brother likes me or respects me very much."

"Is that why you're so determined to report on something big, to earn his respect?"

Her face heated with embarrassment as she remembered what he'd overheard, her conversation with Trent. Replaying it in her head, it all sounded so pitiful now. "I want to report on something big because the truth should always come out."

"Why?"

"Because people deserve to know what's really going on." Instead of hearing her mother cry at night, when she thought Brittney was sleeping, she should have just told her what was going on. How much she'd missed Brittney's dad...

"Not if it puts them in danger," Rory said.

And now she knew, without a doubt, that her suspicions had been right. There was more to the story about the plane crash and about Rory VanDam than he wanted anyone to know.

"It's not the truth that hurts people," she said. "It's the people who are trying to keep the truth from coming out, who are trying to keep secrets, that are the threat. But once the truth is out, there's nothing for those people to try to protect anymore. Getting the truth out is the only way to eliminate the danger."

He expelled a ragged sigh and turned back to her, his pale blue eyes intense. "People don't kill just to protect their secrets," he said. "They kill for revenge. For passion..." As he said that, his gaze lowered to her mouth.

Her pulse quickened. The passion was there, burning so hotly between them. She stepped closer, irresistibly drawn to him and wanting to connect in a way she'd never connected with anyone else. And not just sexually.

This attraction between them seemed deeper than desire. But the desire was there. Too strong for her to not act on it, to not rise up on tiptoe and skim her lips along his jaw. "Tell me your secrets," she urged him in a whisper.

And he grinned, his eyes sparkling now with amusement as he stared at her. "You are..." His breath shuddered out, and then he lowered his head so that his mouth brushed across hers.

It was just the briefest of kisses, just his lips sliding across hers. Once. Twice. But she was suddenly aware of every nerve ending in her body, feeling as if she'd been jolted by something like an electrical current.

But he pulled away and stepped back and said, "You are right about one thing. It's not the truth that hurts people. It's people who hurt people." Then he opened the door and stepped out, pulling it closed behind him.

Leaving her alone with that thought and with her body tingling everywhere from just that brief kiss. Was he leaving because he was afraid that he was going to hurt her? Or that she was going to hurt him?

Or did he know who was behind everything?

The threats, the gunshots, someone hitting him so violently over the head?

But if he knew, why wouldn't he report that person? Even if he didn't trust Trooper Wells, surely there had to be someone he could trust.

Another police officer. Or at least his superintendent at the firehouse.

It would never be her. Since her own brother didn't trust her, she doubted that Rory VanDam ever would. He would never willingly tell her his secrets.

TRENT DIDN'T TRUST this strange alliance between his fellow hotshot and his sister. What the hell were they even doing together? Owen had said he'd had to leave for a call, so he'd asked Rory to keep an eye on her.

But the already injured hotshot had done more than that. He'd brought her here and stayed with her.

Trent didn't care how pissed his sister was at him, he wasn't leaving her alone. But she wasn't alone.

From the shadows of an alley across the street, Trent studied the hotel. Not many of the windows were lit up besides that one. The one that had to be hers, or had Rory booked the room?

After what had happened at the firehouse, he probably wouldn't go back there. And there was no way he could be medically cleared to resume his duties as the ranger on that small island.

But if it was Rory's room, why had he invited Brittney to stay with him? The last time she'd come to town nobody had worked as hard to avoid her as Rory had. Not even Ethan, whose whole life Brittney had blown up. After that, Trent would have expected Rory to avoid her even harder. And yet...

Rory was with her. And he'd done his damn well best to protect her. Trent raised his hand to his jaw, which was beginning to swell from where the guy had struck him. Hard.

Then instead of being mad at Rory, Brittney had gotten mad at him. Like a brother trying to find his younger sister was a crime or something.

The only crimes that had been happening lately had been the work of other people. Billy.

That poor kid who'd gone after Trent and Heather. But Billy was behind bars. He hadn't tried to hurt Brittney to get back at him.

But someone had.

She hadn't driven her vehicle off the road on her own or she and Rory wouldn't have been so damn edgy about hearing him in the hallway.

Something was going on, and Trent wasn't going to learn

about it when everyone else did, when Brittney did her damn story about it.

He was going to learn about it now because Brittney might not get the chance to do that story if someone wanted to harm her.

He lowered his gaze from that window then to the street around the Lakeside Inn. It was the offseason right now, so there weren't many vehicles parked near the building. It had been pretty empty, almost eerily so, like the hotel from *The Shining.*

He shuddered at the thought of that horror film. And the horror he would feel if anything happened to his sister or to Rory.

And that was when he noticed the shadow behind the wheel of one of those vehicles, a long black SUV. He was surprised he could see that much through the heavily tinted windows, but he was pretty damn sure someone was there.

And that he was watching the hotel for the same reason that Trent was.

Because of Brittney...

Chapter Nine

Rory was amazed that he'd been able to walk away from Brittney after that kiss. For one, his legs were shaky, and he couldn't blame it on his concussion. His head hadn't hit the wall all that hard, but it must have knocked some sense into him because he had walked away from her. Even though he'd wanted to stay so damn badly.

He'd wanted to be with her in every way. To protect her and to get even closer to her. For the past five years he'd done his best to keep his distance from people, even from his team, and he hadn't realized until today in the hospital with her just how damn lonely he was. How much he craved to be close to someone…

But Brittney Townsend?

Could he trust her?

He needed time to think about what she'd said as well as the thoughts that had gone through his own head. And he couldn't think when he was close to her. Well, he couldn't think about anything but wanting to be closer to her, to be inside her. Maybe a little distance would clear his head.

But once he stepped out of the lobby doors onto the dimly lit sidewalk, Rory had that strange feeling that Brittney had talked about earlier at the impound lot. That sensation that he was being watched.

But was *he* being watched? Or was *she* the one someone was waiting for out in the shadows? Those threats she'd received might not have had anything to do with him or even with the plane crash. But it might involve the hotshots...

Like whoever the hell had struck him over the head...

He glanced uneasily back at the lobby, making sure that she hadn't followed him out. She hadn't wanted him to leave, but she had to know it wasn't a good idea for him to stay with her. He wasn't exactly great protection for her, especially if that damn plane crash was the reason that someone was threatening her.

No. They'd done more than threaten when they'd fired those shots at her vehicle, when they'd caused her to go off the road and her van to roll over and over. She'd been trapped inside that wreckage until Owen and his crew had used the Jaws of Life to extricate her from the van. Whoever had fired that bullet at her vehicle could have finished her off then, before help had arrived.

So maybe they'd only intended to frighten her away. If that was the case, they didn't know Brittney. All that had been accomplished, with the threats and that gunshot, was her resolve to find out the truth being strengthened. She was even more determined to get the story than she'd been before. She seemed to really believe that it would stop whoever was threatening her from hurting her. But he knew, all too well, how the truth coming out could cause more damage.

Was this really all about the plane crash?

And if it was, then it was his fault.

So he'd been smart to leave her. He would be smart to leave Northern Lakes, too. Maybe even Michigan.

"Rory..."

He barely heard the whisper. Where had it come from? He glanced back at the lobby again to see if Brittney had followed him out. She hadn't, which was good because Rory had a feeling that the person calling his name was trying to lure him into danger.

"Rory…" the whisper echoed back, as if it was coming from between buildings. It was definitely too deep to be Brittney's.

But it sounded vaguely familiar. And Rory realized who it probably was.

"Trent?" he called back. Of course Brittney's protective older brother would have stuck close to her. Despite her un-willingness to share anything with him, he obviously knew she was in danger.

"Shh…" Trent whispered back from somewhere behind Rory.

He turned and saw the gap between buildings, the alley where Trent was waiting for him. He gestured out of the shadows, waving Rory over toward him.

Why? To pay him back for jumping him in the hallway?

To warn him to stay away from his sister?

Trent had probably never figured he'd have to warn Rory away from her. Neither had Rory. But Brittney had made sense about them sticking together in order to protect each other while working together to find out who was after them. Was it the same person? If it was, catching that per-son would definitely keep them safe and make sure they and the rest of the team stayed that way. Or, while they tried to catch him or her, that person got rid of both of them instead. It was a risk either way, and maybe not just to their lives.

Rory expelled a slight sigh of frustration and resigna-tion, then he walked toward the alley. "Hey," he began. "I'm sorry. I really didn't know that was—"

Big hands reached out of the shadows and yanked him between the buildings. He clenched his fists. Despite just apologizing to his team member, he was ready to fight him again. If he had to.

"Shh…" Trent said again.

"What the hell is going on?" Rory asked.

"I think there's someone sitting in that SUV over there."

Rory glanced around them. There weren't many vehicles parked on the street, but there were a couple of SUVs. "Which one?"

"The black one with the tinted windows."

The description brought one of his jumbled memories into sharper focus. The last time he'd ridden in one of them…

He shook his head, at the memory and at Trent. "How can you see anyone inside?"

"The windshield looks darker on the driver's side, like there's someone behind the wheel," Trent said, and he pointed a finger toward the vehicle.

So there was probably only a driver inside, not a passenger, unless the passenger was already out and maybe inside the hotel.

He let out a soft curse. "We should go back inside, make sure Brittney is okay." She was right—they were safer together.

Trent sucked in a breath. "What the hell is going on with my sister, Rory?"

"I don't understand what you mean." And he didn't know for certain. Was Trent talking about his sister's crash or about what he'd interrupted when he'd messed with the door earlier?

But Trent couldn't know what he'd interrupted. Rory wasn't even certain Brittney had intended to kiss him then. But he had damn sure wanted her to, and when she had just now…

Rory had had to force himself to stop at just that brush of

his mouth across hers, even though he'd wanted to deepen the kiss. Hell, he'd wanted to do a lot more than kiss her.

But she was off-limits and not just because she was Trent's sister. She was off-limits to him because Rory couldn't let anyone else get hurt because of him.

"You know what I mean," Trent insisted. "Or at least you know more than I do or you wouldn't have jumped me in the hall. You were expecting trouble."

"These days every hotshot should be expecting trouble," Rory pointed out.

"Damn saboteur," Trent murmured. "You don't think that's who's going after Brittney…"

Rory tensed. He hadn't considered it. He wasn't even sure that was who had gone after him. But he actually hoped it had been. He preferred to think they were both in danger because of the saboteur and not because of…

He turned back to focus on that long black SUV, and that sensation raced over him again like a cold wind. Someone was inside. Someone was watching them.

Or watching for Brittney? She'd said she'd felt that way before, like someone was watching her back home in Detroit and at the impound lot. The person must have followed them back here.

How the hell had Rory missed that long black vehicle following them? How had he missed it at the impound lot if it had been parked somewhere in the area? Because the person was a professional…either assassin or…

"You should go back into the hotel," Rory told Trent. "Make sure Brittney is okay."

Just in case that driver hadn't always been alone, just in case someone else had already gone inside the hotel to try to find her like Trent had.

"Damn it, Rory, what's going on?" Trent demanded to know.

"I don't know." He couldn't be sure. But maybe if he got closer to that vehicle, if he could see who was inside it, he would know if Brittney was in danger because of him, because of the man he used to be. The man he had never wanted to be again.

GUILT HUNG HEAVILY on Brittney, pulling her shoulders down as she hurried downstairs to the lobby. She shouldn't have let Rory leave. He was still suffering from his concussion, which her brother had probably only made worse when he'd knocked him into that wall.

Rory had bled quite a bit on the towel. She hadn't noticed it until after he'd left. She'd thought the reason the thick terry cloth was wet was from the ice melting. But it was more than water...

It was blood. Rory's blood had stained the fluffy white towel a deep crimson.

He needed to go back to the hospital for a CT scan and maybe more stitches if he was still bleeding. If the towel hadn't staunched the worst of it...

She shouldn't have let him go, not in that condition when he was so hurt and vulnerable. And yet he'd taken down her brother who was a big guy. Trent had always intimidated the hell out of the boyfriends she'd had in the past. Not that she'd had many.

She'd always been more focused on her family and her career. She'd never realized that she might have to sacrifice one for the other. When she'd done the story about the hotshots, she hadn't realized what it might cost her.

Her brother.

And maybe her own life...

And Rory's.

He'd handled Trent with ease. Even hurt, Rory was strong

and fast. Not fast enough to avoid a bullet, though. But maybe fast enough that he was probably gone by now.

But when she started across the lobby, she could see his truck parked on the other side of the street, the US Forest Service logo on the door.

He hadn't left yet. Where was he?

Had he fallen? Was he lying facedown on the sidewalk?

She hurried through the lobby, past the night clerk who didn't even glance up from his phone. If something had happened to Rory, the young clerk would not have even noticed.

Brittney pushed open the glass door and stepped onto the sidewalk, which was illuminated from the light from the hotel. Nobody lay there. There wasn't even any blood.

Had he fallen on the other side of the street?

She couldn't see beyond the two lanes to the sidewalk on the other side. The businesses over there had closed for the night and the streetlamp was farther down the block, casting no light onto the sidewalk over there.

Her heart pounding fast with fear for him, she started across the street. And then suddenly light came on. Two headlights, the beams so bright that they blinded her.

And an engine revved.

It wasn't Rory's truck. That was still dark. But another vehicle, one just as big or bigger because the headlights were so high. It pulled away from the curb, tires squealing, and steered straight at her.

"Brittney!" someone yelled her name.

But she couldn't move for a moment, frozen in the beam of those lights. Frozen with shock and fear.

THAT REPORTER WASN'T going to stop. That was clear enough now that the warnings weren't working. She wasn't backing off. She'd kept making calls, asking questions, and the more interest she showed the more someone else, like the authorities, might get interested.

She wasn't going away. And if she wasn't going to go away on her own, the driver had to make her go away.

Forever.

The SUV had been parked just far enough down the street to be away from the lights of the hotel and the streetlamps but close enough to watch the entrance. Two men had come out before the woman.

And both of them had slipped away into the shadows.

But as the SUV bore down on the woman, the men were suddenly there in the street with her. She was the only one who had needed to die. But the driver had no compulsion against taking out a couple of more.

Chapter Ten

Rory's heart seemed to stop for a moment as he stared at Brittney standing in the beam of those harshly bright lights, frozen, as the SUV bore down on her. While Trent yelled her name, Rory started running toward her, as fast as he could. He jumped in front of those lights and caught her around the waist. Then he propelled her out of the way, rolling across the asphalt with his arms locked around her just as the SUV passed them.

The SUV was so damn close that Rory's clothes rustled and Brittney's hair blew across his face. With as big as the vehicle was, it probably would have killed her. And maybe him and Trent, too.

Maybe Rory was dead. But if he was dead, his heart probably wouldn't have been beating as hard. And he wouldn't be able to feel the asphalt of the road beneath his back and the softness of Brittney's body lying stretched out on top of his.

"Are you all right?" he asked between pants for breath. His lungs burned with the need for air.

The breath that she must have been holding whooshed out in a ragged sigh, warming the skin of his neck where her face was tucked between his chin and his collarbone. Then she lifted her head, her hair brushing across his cheek, and stared down at him. "Are you all right?"

He closed his eyes for a moment, silently evaluating whether anything hurt more than it should. His head ached, like it had since he'd woken up from his coma, and now his shoulder and hip ached, too, but not so much that anything was broken.

A groan emanated from the darkness, and Rory opened his eyes with surprise. That hadn't been his groan.

"Trent!" Brittney called out with concern as she scrambled up from Rory and the ground. "Oh, my God!"

Rory rolled to his side and looked across the asphalt to where Trent lay a short distance from him. "Damn!" He shoved himself up, nearly dropping back down as his head got too light and his vision blurred. He drew in a breath, steadied himself and rushed over to where Brittney knelt beside her brother's prone body. "Trent, are you all right?"

"We need to call an ambulance," Brittney said. "But I left my cell upstairs."

"Mine's dead," Rory said, and he started toward the lobby. "I'll have the clerk call—"

"No!" Trent shouted. "I'm okay. Just knocked the damn wind out of me."

"It knocked you down," Brittney said. "You might have broken bones." She glanced over her shoulder at Rory. "You, too."

"I don't have anything broken," Rory assured her. He wasn't as certain of Trent's condition. He stepped closer and peered down at his hotshot teammate. "Maybe you shouldn't move—"

"I'm fine," Trent insisted, and he shoved himself up from the ground. "I'm just getting damn sick of nearly getting run down."

"Then you shouldn't have run into the street!" Brittney exclaimed. "Either of you!"

Trent shuddered. "You were just standing there, and it started straight for you…" He shuddered again. "I thought you were going to die. You wouldn't move."

She moved now, throwing her arms around her brother. She hugged him tightly for a moment. And Trent held her just as tightly, and over her head, he mouthed words to Rory.

He narrowed his eyes, trying to tell…

"Thank you," Trent said aloud. "Thank you for saving my sister."

Rory shook his head. "I didn't…"

"You did," Trent insisted. "I couldn't get there as fast as you did. I couldn't save her."

While Brittney had escaped injury this time, Rory suspected there would be another time. And what would happen if he wasn't around to save her? Would she survive?

Or was she only in danger because of him? Would she be safer if he left town, like he'd intended when he'd awakened in that hospital bed?

But even if he left, Brittney wouldn't be safe because he knew there was no way she was going to stop pursuing her story. Whatever story the person threatening her wanted her to drop…about the plane crash or about the saboteur or something totally unrelated…

Some story that she'd done in Detroit. And if that was the case, then Rory hadn't put her in danger, but maybe he could help protect her from it. And if it was the saboteur, Rory had no idea how to handle it. This person had pulled dirty trick after dirty trick on the team and yet nobody had figured out who it was.

Could Brittney? Or would trying to find out get her killed?

BRITTNEY WAS SHAKING so badly that Trent and Rory escorted her back into the lobby of the hotel. She wasn't shaking because she was cold, even though the temperature had dropped a lot when the sun had.

But even standing near where gas logs glowed in the lobby fireplace, Brittney couldn't stop shaking, at least on the inside. On the outside, she was trying to act tough. She was trying to be as strong and brave as her big brother had always been ever since they were kids. They'd both lost their dad, but Trent had lost his mom, too, a few years later. And he would have wound up in foster care if not for Brittney's mother and stepfather taking him into their home. They were wonderful, generous people, but they'd probably done it more to appease Brittney's fears than anything else.

Trent had been in the vehicle when his mother was killed, and Brittney had been terrified that she would lose him like they'd lost their dad and him his mom. That terror rushed over her now, threatening to overwhelm her. This was why she'd come up to Northern Lakes the first time, to find out what was going on with the hotshot team, to make sure her brother was safe. But now she was the one who'd put him in danger.

"We need to call the police," Trent said. "To report some-one nearly running you down."

"Call who?" Rory asked the question. "Trooper Wells?"

Trent cursed. "I'll call Heather."

"Your detective girlfriend has no jurisdiction in North-ern Lakes," Rory said.

"But she brought back that kid who followed you up here, who ran you off the road," Brittney pointed out.

Trent sighed. "She brought him back for the crimes he committed in Detroit. And she had to get special authori-zation to do that."

Brittney really didn't want Heather involved, anyway. Because Heather was good enough to get the truth out of her about the notes and the gunshot. But as good as she was, she and Trent had nearly died too many times just recently. Brittney couldn't count on their luck holding out. She couldn't risk losing her brother.

Then she turned around and realized she'd lost someone else. Only she and Trent stood in front of the fire. "Where did Rory go?" she asked with alarm.

Trent turned around then, too. "He's leaving…"

Vehicle lights flashed on again as, across the street from the hotel, Rory started his truck and pulled away from the curb. She couldn't let him leave, not when he was probably hurt. She started toward the lobby doors, but Trent stepped in front of her and caught her shoulders.

"You're not going anywhere," Trent said. "Until you tell me what's going on."

"I have to check on Rory," she said. "You hurt him upstairs, and just now…" She shuddered, thinking what could have happened to him. What could have happened to them both…

Maybe she should let him leave, though. She'd thought he was the reason she was in danger because of whatever he'd kept from her about the plane crash, but now she realized it might be the reverse. But who had struck him over the head?

"Rory's tough," Trent said. "He's survived a plane crash and a coma. I think he's indestructible."

Brittney wasn't so sure about that. Eventually his luck was going to run out. If it hadn't already…

"What if that person who nearly hit us goes after him and he's alone?" she asked.

"I think that person was after you," Trent said. "That vehicle didn't move until you stepped out of the lobby."

She shivered.

"Damn it, Brittney, you need to tell me what's going on," Trent insisted.

"Just like you told me what was going on with you a few weeks ago when your house burned down with the body of a murdered woman inside it?"

"I had received that Christmas card with the threat inside," Trent said. "Warning me that I was going to find out how it felt to lose someone close to me. At that time, the person closest to me was you."

Now it was Heather. Brittney felt a little jab of jealousy over that. Not that Heather had replaced her but that her brother was as strong as her mom, strong enough to love somebody that they could lose.

She also felt a little jab of envy that he'd received a card for his threat, and all she'd gotten was that sheet of paper stuck under her windshield wiper. The thought struck her as funny, but she couldn't share it with him despite being tempted. Gallows humor was how she and Trent had dealt with their losses. And she knew it was how his hotshot team dealt with loss and fear.

The humor fled, her fear for Rory's well-being chasing it away. "Where do you think Rory is going?" she asked. Hopefully back to the hospital, but she doubted that.

"Probably the firehouse."

"The firehouse, of course."

"You're not going there until you and I talk," Trent said, his hands tightening on her shoulders.

"Just like how you didn't want me involved in your drama, I don't want you involved in mine," Brittney said.

"You're trying to protect me?"

She gestured toward the street. "You could have gotten run down just now."

Lights flashed in the street as a police SUV rolled up outside.

"Did you call them?" she asked Trent. He was the only one who had his cell on him. Hers was on a charger upstairs, and Rory had claimed his was dead. Unless...

He'd lied, and he'd called after he'd left the scene.

"I called them," the clerk spoke up from behind the desk. "I saw what happened."

Brittney turned toward him, shocked that he wasn't still engrossed in whatever he'd been watching on his phone. "You called? That wasn't necessary."

Or appreciated.

"That dude deliberately tried to run you down," the kid remarked.

"You saw who it was? You saw the driver?" Brittney asked, her pulse quickening.

He shook his head. "No. The windows were too dark. But it definitely didn't look like an accident."

Brittney was pretty damn sure it wasn't, just like her crash earlier hadn't been an accident, either. Somebody wasn't just trying to scare her off now. They were trying to kill her.

TRENT HAD ALWAYS known his younger sister was stubborn. But he hadn't realized how stubborn until now. The state trooper who'd shown up at the hotel to take the report hadn't gotten much more out of her than shrugging and head shaking.

If Trooper Wells had shown up, she probably wouldn't have gotten anything else from her. Since he wasn't able to...

As much as Brittney liked asking questions, she disliked

answering them even more. And he had so many damn questions for her.

But she'd insisted she was tired and needed her rest.

"You're not getting rid of me," Trent had informed her as he'd booked the adjoining room to hers. And he'd made her open the door between them because he knew her too well.

She was probably going to sneak out the minute she thought he was sleeping. So he wasn't going to sleep.

Not now.

Probably not until he knew she was safe. So he sat up against his headboard, peering through the crack in the door between their rooms. He had a good view of her door to the hall. She wasn't getting past him. Just as she very nearly hadn't gotten past the person who'd tried running her down.

Who the hell could be after Brittney?

His stomach churned with the thought that had occurred to him, the thought he hated to even entertain. It could be a member of his team…if that was who the saboteur actually was. But it almost had to be because he couldn't see how anyone else would have been able to get close enough to sabotage their equipment without being noticed.

He'd always felt like his team was his family. But his real family might be in danger because of one of them. At least he knew it wasn't Ethan or Rory.

But who else could he trust?

He called the one person he trusted the most in the world right now.

"Hey, babe," Heather answered, her voice husky either with sleep or the desire that shot through him at just the thought of her. "How's your sister?"

He sighed.

"Your text said she was okay enough to leave the hospital," she reminded him. "Didn't you find her?"

He wasn't sure if he had. The Brittney who'd turned on him in the hall, yelling at him for shoving Rory into the wall, who'd berated him for not claiming her as family on her first trip to Northern Lakes, that Brittney didn't seem at all like the adoring little sister he knew.

That he'd probably taken for granted for too damn long. He could have lost her. Not just once but twice in one day.

"Trent, sweetheart?" Heather called out to him. "Is everything okay?"

He drew in a deep breath before replying. "For the moment…"

But he had a feeling that moment wouldn't last.

"But?" Heather prodded. "What happened?"

"I cheated on you," he said.

She laughed, and he smiled, loving how much she trusted him, how secure she was in his love and devotion to her. Just as he trusted her and felt so damn safe with her. "How's that?"

"I nearly got run over with someone else," he said.

She sucked in a breath. "Damn. Are you all right?"

"Yes."

"And the other person?"

"People," he said. "Brittney and Rory."

"They're okay?"

"Brittney is," he said. "Rory took off so fast that I'm not sure…"

"I didn't even know he was out of the hospital yet."

He'd told her about Rory's concussion, how he hadn't left Northern Lakes until he knew his fellow hotshot was out of the coma and on the mend.

"He just got released, and Owen had him watching Brittney until I got up here."

"The guy just woke up from a coma," Heather said. "How much protection could he be?"

"He saved her life tonight," Trent said. And he stroked his fingers along his jaw. "He took me down when he caught me lurking around her hotel room, too."

"You were lurking?" she asked. And he could hear the smile in her voice.

"Damn clerk wouldn't tell me which room she was in or call it for me," Trent said.

"But you found her," she said.

"Yeah."

"So why is Rory protecting her?"

"Owen figured Rory was the only one he could trust since he was in the hospital when her van went off the road."

"So he's assuming the worst about that crash, too?" she asked.

"Because I told him that there is no way Brittney would have gone off the road unless it was the same way we did…"

"Because someone forced us off."

"And tonight, with her nearly getting run down in the street outside the hotel…" Emotion choked off his voice for a moment, making him hoarse as he remembered the horrifying moment that Brittney had frozen in the beam of those bright lights.

"And you don't think that was an accident, either?"

"It's what she told the trooper who came for the report," Trent said.

"But you think she was lying."

"She's definitely hiding something," he said. "She won't answer any of my questions. She won't tell me what's going on."

Instead of commiserating with him, Heather chuckled again. "Payback's a bitch, huh?"

He sighed. "That probably is why she's not sharing anything with me. She's still mad that I didn't share anything with her. But I was just trying to protect her."

"And maybe she's doing the same for you," Heather pointed out.

He tensed with the realization. His baby sister was trying to protect him. "But what is she protecting me from?" he asked.

"I'll see what I can find out from her television station here," Heather offered. "I'll talk to her producers and co-workers, see if they have any idea what's going on and who might be after her...unless you want me to come up there?"

"I don't even know if she's staying here," he said. "So no. Focus on Detroit, on finding out what you can there. And I'll see what I can get out of her."

"You be careful," she said.

He smiled. "Of my sister?"

"She is fierce," Heather reminded him. "She's strong and smart."

He knew that in his head. But in his heart, she was that sweet little girl who'd followed him around, firing endless questions at him, confident that he had all the answers. She'd worshiped him then. Now she had to know that he had no more answers than she did.

Actually she had more than him because she knew what was going on, no matter how vehemently she kept denying that she did. Or if she didn't know for certain, she at least had a better idea than he did.

Because he could think of only one reason. His hotshot team. Why else would she have come up to Northern Lakes? Whatever she was investigating was here...

The plane crash? Or the sabotage?

He had to get her to back off for her sake now. For her safety.

"And, Trent," Heather said, her voice even huskier than usual as it emanated from his speaker. "No more cheating on me. You know defying death is our thing."

"Yes," he said, and he smiled. "Tell Sammy not to steal my spot next to you in bed."

"Nobody can steal your spot," Heather assured him. "And I'll talk to the people at the station right away and let you know what I find out."

"Thank you. I love you."

"Love you, too."

Love was their thing now, but their relationship had started as a ruse to flush out a killer. Or at least they'd thought whoever had sent Trent that card was a killer.

But there had been more dangers in his life than he'd even realized then. So pushing Brittney away had been the right thing, to keep her safe.

He'd known what to do then. He had no idea how to protect her now. Because he had a bad feeling that the biggest danger she faced was herself and her dogged determination to find out the truth no matter the cost.

Even if it was her life...

Chapter Eleven

When Rory had first been cleared to leave the hospital, he had had no intention of staying in Northern Lakes. He'd just intended to stop at the firehouse and grab whatever he'd left in his locker before leaving for good. Or at least for the island where he was the ranger on duty.

Would he be safe there?

Was he really even the one in danger?

Would it have mattered who'd stepped into the hall that night the engines had started? Would whoever had walked out of the bunk room been hit as hard as he'd been?

No. He couldn't be sure that he specifically was in danger or if his entire team was, with maybe the exception of one person...

If the saboteur was one of them...

He hated to think that, though.

Just as he hated to think of Brittney in danger. And she definitely was. All night that image of her standing in those high beams had flashed through his mind like those lights had flashed on—suddenly, sharply, sinisterly. If he hadn't been there, would Trent have gotten to her in time?

Or would they both have gotten hurt or worse?

He'd known Trent had stayed with her after that, and he would have made damn sure that nothing else happened to her. So he'd probably been more protection for her than Rory would have been after that last near miss.

He'd been so exhausted last night that when he'd sat down on a bunk to talk to Stanley, who'd been snuggled up with Annie in another bunk, he must have fallen asleep.

But those dreams…

That nightmare had kept waking him up. And he must have woken up Annie, too, because at some point the massive sheepdog/mastiff mutt had crawled into bed with him. He didn't know if she had needed comfort, or if she'd been comforting him.

Or protecting him?

If only Annie could talk…

She could probably tell them who the saboteur was. She must have seen whoever had struck Rory that night.

He stared at her now from where he was pretty much jammed between the wall and mattress since she was hogging the narrow bunk. "So who was it, girl?" he asked. "Who hit me?"

She whimpered and moved her head closer to his. Then she rolled out her big tongue and swiped it across the side of his face.

He chuckled. "Your kisses do not make it all better," he told her.

But he had an idea whose kisses might make him feel better. Brittney's.

Was she okay? She'd seemed so last night, and after what had happened, how close a call she'd had not once but twice, Trent would not have left her unprotected. He might have been irritated with her for reporting about the team and Ethan, but he loved her.

She obviously loved and idolized her big brother, too. But

she was also proud and determined to take care of herself while getting the truth she was looking for.

Was that his truth?

He knew what had happened to that plane. And why.

And it had nothing to do with Ethan and the Canterbury curse, or even the greedy brother-in-law.

No. That plane had gone down because of him. And guilt had weighed so heavily on him ever since it had happened. But that wasn't the only thing he felt guilty about…

Amelia. Not that she deserved his sympathy after what she'd done. But he'd hurt her.

Annie whimpered again and bumped her massive head against his. The dog was incredibly empathetic, which was probably why Stanley had bonded with her so much. The kid had aged out of foster care with nowhere else to go when Cody Mallehan had convinced their boss to hire the teenager to help out at the firehouse. Stanley had had a rough life, but he seemed happy now.

Rory looked around Annie to the other bunk, but it was empty, the bed already neatly made. "I thought you were the kid's shadow," he told Annie.

She whimpered again and swiped her tongue across his cheek.

"Hey, no more kisses," he said with a chuckle.

"Clearly you're not much of a kisser," a female voice remarked.

"Annie? You can talk?" he asked, joking because there was no mistaking to whom the voice belonged.

Brittney.

Annie jumped up from the bunk and barked, as surprised by the reporter's sudden appearance as he'd been.

"Down, girl," Brittney said. "I'm not trying to steal your man. I can see that what you two have is true love."

Rory chuckled, but Annie's barking probably drowned it out. He had to raise his voice to tell Brittney, "I don't know about that. She didn't save me from whoever hit me over the head."

"Shh," Brittney told the dog. "The two people in this room with you both have concussions."

Rory realized that maybe for the first time since he'd awakened from the coma that his head didn't hurt that much. It was just a dull ache now, like the aftereffects of a migraine or a hangover.

He might have preferred the hangover, though he barely ever drank. He had to make sure that he didn't lose control or get confused and talk too much.

Reveal too much.

Brittney had tilted her head to study the door. Her topaz eyes were narrowed with speculation. "Did she bark like this before you got hit in the head?" she asked.

"Not loud enough to wake everybody up," Rory said. "That's why I went out into the hall. To pull the alarm and to shut off the damn trucks."

Brittney nodded.

"What?" Rory asked uneasily.

"Annie knew whoever hit you over the head," Brittney surmised.

No. Speculated. That could be all that it was. She had no proof that one of his hotshot team members had tried to hurt him. Or kill him?

He didn't want to think that someone he knew could want him dead. Again.

But he shouldn't have been surprised. He was just so damn sick of having no one he could trust. No one who really cared about him.

But to want him dead, that was more than disinterest or distaste. That was hate. Or greed.

Because anyone could succumb to greed, he knew that all too well.

Had someone been hired again to try to kill him? Someone he knew. Someone he should have been able to trust...

He slid his hand around the back of his head, to where the skin had been pulled together with stitches and staples, leaving a thick ridge of flesh beneath his hair.

"How are you?" she asked. "That's why I left my hotel room last night. After I saw how much blood was on that towel that I wrapped the ice in..." She stopped and swallowed, as if she'd been choking on something.

Emotion?

For him?

She swallowed again and continued. "I wanted to make sure that you were okay."

"That's why you were out there? In the street?" he asked. And he rolled off the bunk then to stand in front of her. Annie stayed between them, though, as if trying to protect him from Brittney.

But Brittney was a stranger to the dog.

She must have been right, that Annie knew whoever had hit him.

"I'm the reason you came outside last night?" he asked again.

She nodded. "I wanted to make you go back to the hospital to get checked out."

His stomach pitched at the thought of her getting hurt because of him. He reached out to touch her cheek, sliding his fingertips along her jaw. She was so beautiful. And he wanted so damn badly to kiss her again, to really kiss her this time.

But he couldn't afford that kind of distraction now and neither could she.

"We both nearly went back to the hospital…" he murmured, thinking of how they'd rolled across the asphalt. "And Trent?" He glanced around her then. "Where is he? Is he really all right?"

Her lips curved into a slight smirk. "He's going to be pissed when he wakes up and finds me gone," she said. "He booked the adjoining room and tried staying awake all night. He lasted until about an hour ago."

Rory fought the smile curving his lips and shook his head. "It's not safe for you to go out on your own, not after what happened yesterday."

"What happened yesterday?" Braden asked.

Rory jumped and dropped his hand from Brittney's face. She whirled around to the doorway where his boss was leaning against the jamb.

Braden's dark eyes studied them both, and his forehead was slightly furrowed beneath a lock of dark brown hair. Clearly he wondered what was going on between Rory and Brittney.

Rory wondered himself.

Was she just flirting with him to get him talking? To get the story she was so determined to get that two threats and two attempts on her life hadn't scared her off?

In fact, those threats had just made her more determined to find out what was going on because she thought the truth would protect her, that it would lead to the arrest of the person threatening her. But the truth didn't always lead to justice.

Rory could have corrected that misapprehension. The truth hadn't saved him, it had nearly killed him. But knowing his truth would put her in danger, too. If it hadn't already…

"What happened yesterday?" Braden asked the question. "Owen said you were in an accident. And then something happened at the hotel."

"You heard about that?" Rory asked.

"The police were there," Braden said. "I heard the call over the scanner."

"The police were there?" Rory asked Brittney now.

She nodded. "The desk clerk called them. I didn't think the kid was even paying attention to the lobby, let alone out—"

"What happened?" Braden repeated. "From how you're evading my question, I take it that these things weren't really accidents?"

Brittney shook her head. "Not any more than the things that have been happening to your hotshot team have been accidents."

Braden's face flushed slightly. "Is that why you're here? To report some more nonsense?"

She sighed a heavy sigh as if she was disappointed in the hotshot superintendent.

Rory was a little disappointed, as well. Braden had kept a lot of things from them for a while. The note he'd received that had warned him that someone on the team wasn't who they said they were.

Had that note been referring to Ethan really being Jonathan Michael Canterbury IV? Or had it been referring to Rory? Not many people should have realized that he wasn't who he said he was…

Just him and maybe Ethan. But even Ethan didn't really know for certain.

And there was someone else…

Trick appeared in the doorway behind their boss and his brother-in-law. Trick wasn't just the brother of Braden's wife, but he was also the son of the man who'd trained most of them. Mack McRooney knew the truth. But Mack was the kind of guy who knew what secrets needed to be kept. And why.

So Rory doubted that Mack's son or daughter knew anything about him beyond that their father had trained him five years ago along with Ethan Sommerly and Jonathan Canterbury. The real Ethan hadn't survived that crash. He wasn't the only one who'd died in it, though.

Rory felt that jab of regret for the lives lost. Too many...

He couldn't let Brittney become another casualty.

ONE MINUTE BRITTNEY was standing with Rory in the bunk room, wondering if he was about to kiss her again. Then his boss showed up with another giant of a man following closely behind him. Within minutes of their sudden appearance, she'd been escorted to the superintendent's office.

And the red-haired man leaned against the door, as if blocking her inside with him and the superintendent. His body was so big that she could barely see the door around him. There was no way she was getting out with him there.

"I thought you guys were going to escort me off the premises," Brittney said.

"We probably should have," the red-haired man said with a pointed look at his boss.

Braden Zimmer smiled. "How did you get onto the premises, Ms. Townsend?"

"Call me Brittney," she said. "We're all friends here."

The red-haired man snorted. He had to be Trick McRooney. Braden's brother-in-law. Mack's son. She actually needed to be his friend, so that he could convince his father to talk to her. She suspected that Mack had to know something more about the plane that had just left his training facility in Washington state before it crashed.

Braden smiled. "Okay, Brittney, how'd you get in?"

"The door was unlocked."

Braden groaned.

"The kid with the curly blond hair had just walked out."

"So you let yourself in," Trick said.

She nodded.

"Why?" Braden asked. "Who or what were you looking for?"

Heat rushed to her face. Rory. She'd been looking for Rory, but not for the reasons Braden might have thought when he'd come into the bunk room and found them standing so close together with Rory's hand touching her face.

She'd wanted to kiss him so damn badly then. She still did. But that wasn't why she'd sought him out.

"I was concerned about Rory," she said.

"Why?" Trick asked. "You don't know him. He's barely spoken to you."

She smiled. "That was last time I was here. This time… he's different." He wasn't avoiding her as hard as he had last time. In fact, he'd saved her life last night in the street.

But only she and Trent knew that. The clerk hadn't realized that Trent wasn't the one who'd pushed her out of the way of that speeding SUV, so he hadn't mentioned a third person to the trooper who'd taken their statements. And neither had she nor Trent.

Rory had already been through too much that day. That month…

And five years ago…

He had survived a plane crash. One that Trick's dad had to know more about.

"I've been trying to get ahold of your father," she told Trick.

He just arched a red eyebrow. "You want to train to become a smoke jumper or hotshot?"

"Maybe I should," she said. "I might get more respect..." At least from her brother.

"But that wasn't your real reason for contacting Mack," Braden stated. He knew.

"No. I want to ask him more questions about that plane crash that happened, the one Ethan and Rory survived."

"Why?" Braden asked. "You know everything about it already."

"I'm not so sure about that," she said. She also wasn't so sure that she knew everything there was to know about Rory VanDam. Could Mack tell her more?

Would he?

Or should she just try harder to get the man himself to speak to her?

"So that's why you're really here?" Trick asked the question. "To get me to talk my dad into talking to you?" He was smirking at her.

And she knew the likelihood of him ever doing that for her was pretty damn low. "That and to talk to Rory," she admitted.

"And he's talking to you?" Braden asked. "About the crash?" He exchanged a quick glance with Trick.

Did they think there was more about the crash to discover? Or was it Rory they were worried about? She was worried about him, too.

"What the hell is happening in your firehouse?" Brittney

wanted to know. "How does one of your own almost get killed here instead of fighting a wildfire?"

Braden sucked in a breath and shared another glance with Trick. "I wish to hell I knew."

"You have no idea who's been behind all these things happening to your team?" she asked.

Braden shook his head. "They wouldn't be happening if I did."

A little chill passed through her. Was he saying that because he would have turned the suspect over to the police or because he would have dealt with him or her himself?

"What about that story?" Braden asked her. "Are you working on it?"

"About the sabotage?" she asked. "I've tried, but I haven't gotten any of the hotshots to really talk to me about it." Not even her own brother.

But if these guys thought she was working on it, the saboteur might, as well. Was that who had actually left her the notes? Who'd taken a shot at her van?

And last night...

Was it a hotshot behind everything? Was it another hotshot who had struck Rory so hard that he might have died? Brittney needed to find out for her sake and safety, as well as for the sake and safety of the entire hotshot team, including her brother and Rory.

Or someone could die...

BRADEN'S UNEASINESS INTENSIFIED during his impromptu meeting with the reporter.

After letting her out of the office, Trick closed the door behind her and leaned back against it again. "She's still working on the sabotage story."

"I know." And that might have been what had put her in

danger if Trent was right and she hadn't just had an accident when her van went off the road.

And what about last night?

Someone trying to run her down?

"Maybe you should follow her," Braden suggested.

"You don't think Trent is following her?" Trick asked. "He rushed up here to make sure she's okay. I doubt he's letting her out of his sight."

"That means he's probably in danger, too, then."

"We're all in danger until the saboteur is caught," Trick pointed out.

Braden's stomach churned with that dread. "I know." He released a heavy sigh. "Maybe it's a good thing she's working on this story. Maybe she'll figure out what we haven't been able to…"

"Who the saboteur is," Trick said. But then he wrinkled his forehead and scrunched up his nose. "That's not the only story she's working on, though."

"The plane crash." Braden shrugged. "That was all about Ethan."

"Ethan wasn't the only one in that crash," Trick said. "Rory was, too." He straightened away from the door. "Maybe I should give Mack a call."

Mack's kids rarely referred to him as Dad. He'd been much more than their father, he'd been their mother, too, after theirs had taken off. He'd also been their mentor and their best friend.

Braden nodded. "I'm going to call Trent," he said. "Make sure he's around and keeping an eye on his sister. I don't want anyone else getting hurt."

But he knew all too well that the chance of nobody getting hurt was extremely low. He could only hope they didn't get hurt badly. Or worse…

Chapter Twelve

Rory hadn't stopped Braden and Trick from whisking Brittney away from him. He knew that neither of them would hurt her. She was safe with them.

And yet he'd followed them. He'd waited outside the office, listening to as much of the conversation as he'd been able to hear through the door and probably Trick's body. Trick was close to the door, so Rory had heard everything he'd said.

Brittney had tried contacting Trick's dad about the plane crash. God, she was smart. So smart that she was probably going to figure out the truth. And that would undoubtedly get them both killed.

Unless...

He had some insurance. Insurance he'd been holding on to in case this day ever came. He just wasn't sure how to use it because he'd never known who he could trust with it.

Or if he should trust anyone at all.

Could he believe Brittney that she was really looking to stop whoever was threatening her? Or was she just looking for a story? Trying to further her career as if that would earn her brother's respect...

Where the hell was Trent?

He should have woken up by now and discovered that she was gone.

Before the conversation finished in the office, Rory slipped away. He hurried upstairs to the locker room, intent on cleaning out his and leaving town.

But every time he had that intention, something came up. Like Brittney. She was in danger, like he and Ethan had been alone in the mountains. But together they'd protected each other, they'd kept each other alive. Could he and Brittney do that for each other?

She stood in the doorway, watching him. "Where are you going?" she asked.

"I need to get back to work," he said.

"There's no wildfire," she replied. "No reason for the hotshot team to go out."

"That's just part of my job," he said. "I'm a forest ranger."

"You're recovering from a head injury," she said. "You shouldn't be out in the woods on your own."

"An island," he said. "But it is heavily wooded."

"Does anyone else live there?" she asked.

"There are a few cabins on it. But mostly it's national forest land."

"You shouldn't be alone," she said.

"There are plenty of animals on the island," he said. And there they were all of the four-legged variety, not the two like where he'd grown up.

"An animal can't call for help if you need it," she said.

"I probably won't need it since there are no other humans on the island this time of year," he said, and he touched the back of his head and that ridge.

"You should get your stitches looked at," she said. "Make sure the wound didn't open back up last night. You bled quite a bit on that towel."

"Sorry," he said. "Hopefully the hotel won't charge you for it."

"Hopefully they won't evict me," she said, "after the clerk called in that incident with the SUV."

"The trooper didn't come to talk to me," he said.

"Trent and I didn't give him your name."

"Him? It wasn't Trooper Wells?"

She shook her head. "She probably would have realized you'd been there, too."

So it was probably only a matter of time before the trooper came to question him again. "I really need to get out of here," he said.

"Why? You want to avoid the police?"

"I want to avoid being asked things I can't answer," he said.

"Can't or won't?"

His lips twitched with amusement over her persistence. "I can't say who was driving that SUV. The windows were too darkly tinted. And I didn't see a license plate. So can't."

"I wasn't talking about that."

"I didn't see who hit me the night of the holiday party, either," he said.

"If only Annie could talk…"

He smiled then. "We've all wished that."

"She could tell you who the saboteur is." She tilted her head then and murmured, "But I wonder if she would…"

"What do you mean?"

"Maybe she would protect him."

"What are you talking about?"

"Stanley," she said.

Rory shook his head. "Nope. No way. And don't you dare interrogate that kid. He was once suspected of being the Northern Lakes arsonist and it nearly killed him." He'd been hit over the head, too.

"Then tell me who you suspect," she prodded him.

"I don't." And that was the problem. He had no idea who the saboteur was. Which was another reason he needed to get away from the firehouse. He could hardly believe that he'd managed to sleep there the night before. But it had been just him and Stanley and Annie in the bunk room.

And he'd been so damn tired.

Still was. But that was her fault. He'd kept thinking of her last night, and not just that horrific moment when she'd frozen in the path of that SUV. But the moment before that, when they'd kissed. It had been such a light kiss and so brief, and yet so damn powerful, too.

"Where's Trent?" he asked.

She shrugged. "Probably still sleeping."

"He should be awake by now." Rory needed him awake and alert enough to watch over his sister so that Rory could get the hell away from her. She'd already messed with his head more than the concussion had.

Or maybe the concussion was the reason she was getting to him so much, making him want her so badly.

"Trent's not going to tell me who he suspects, either," she said.

"That's not why I asked where he was," Rory said. "And I really don't suspect anyone, least of all Stanley." He was a good kid. Everybody on their twenty-member team seemed like good people. But he knew better than to trust that anyone was really who they seemed to be.

Even Brittney. Maybe most especially Brittney.

THE WAY RORY had looked at her just before he closed his locker door had unnerved Brittney. It was like he wasn't sure what he was looking at. Or whom...

Once he closed the door, he grabbed up his duffel bag and stepped around her, heading toward the exit.

"Where are you going?" she asked, and she stepped in front of him, blocking him from leaving like Trick had blocked her. Rory couldn't be serious about going back to some deserted island, not when he was still recovering from a head wound.

"I'll make sure you get safely back to Trent," he said. "And then I'm leaving."

Something about the way he said it, with such finality, made Brittney wonder if she would ever see him again if he left. Not that she should expect to...

She had only been to Northern Lakes once before, and after what had happened to her since her arrival this time, she would be crazy to want to return.

Crazy to want to see Rory again, too. No. She wanted to do more than see him. She really, really wanted to kiss him and to really kiss him this time, not just brush their lips across each other's. But she wasn't about to do that here, in the firehouse, where anyone could walk in on them like Braden had earlier in the bunk room.

And the way he was looking at her now, with such tension and almost suspicion, Rory didn't look at all attracted to her now. If he'd ever been...

Maybe she'd only imagined that it was mutual. But even if it was, she had no time for this attraction she felt for him. She needed to focus on her story...whichever one the person threatening her didn't want her to do.

Was it about the plane crash?

Or the saboteur?

"I should go back to Braden's office," she said. "And see if he'll give me a list of every member of the team." She knew her brother wouldn't give her one. But Braden...

He hadn't seemed as upset about her reporting about the

saboteur as he'd once been. He might even welcome her help in figuring out who it was.

Or he would if he wanted to keep anyone else on his team from getting hurt like Rory had been hurt. But some of the other hotshots who'd been hurt hadn't been because of the saboteur. The dead man's wife had killed him. And a state trooper had tried killing another…

Then there was Trent, who had someone come after him for revenge.

"What about you?" she asked Rory, voicing her thought aloud.

"I won't give you a list," he said.

"What about your past?" she asked. "Anything or anyone in it that might be coming back to haunt you like it came back to haunt my brother?"

His long, lean body tensed even more than it had already been, and all the color drained from his face, leaving him deathly pale, like he had seen a ghost.

"What is it?" she asked. "Your head? What's going on?" And did she need to call a doctor for him?

Or Owen?

Where the hell was the paramedic?

Rory released a shaky breath. "I'm fine. I'm just…talked out, Brittney. If you want that list of team members, ask Braden."

"So you're not going to make sure I get safely back to Trent?" she asked. She was just teasing him. Really.

But she also wondered…did he care about her? Or would he just try to protect anyone he thought was in danger?

Probably. That was undoubtedly the reason he'd become a hotshot, to protect people from fires.

She wanted to ask him about that and about so many other things. But she could feel the opportunity slipping away from her. She wasn't even sure what island he was talking about let alone how to get to it.

Was there a ferry to it?

Since it was largely uninhabitable, probably not.

"We have to leave now for me to take you back to Trent," he said. "Because I can't stick around any longer."

"Why not?" she asked.

His forehead furrowed as if he was confused. "How can you ask me that after everything that's happened?"

"How can you just run away after everything that's happened?" she asked. "That's not going to stop things from happening, you know? The saboteur keeps doing things, and he or she isn't even making them look like accidents anymore."

"It'll stop things from happening to *me*," he said.

Shocked, she sucked in a breath. "And you only care about yourself?"

He hadn't come across that way to her. He'd seemed like he was genuinely concerned about her safety and about his team. Or else why the hell had he run out in front of that SUV last night? He could have let Trent get to her first.

But Trent hadn't.

Rory was the one who'd saved her. Who'd risked his life to do so. So he certainly didn't care only about himself.

Maybe he didn't care about himself at all. Or he would have gone back to the hospital last night. Maybe that was why he was deathly pale. Maybe he needed to go back there now.

"Before you rush off to the middle of nowhere, you should get a medical checkup," she suggested. "You were bleeding again last night."

He shook his head. "I'm okay. And I'll be even better once I'm out of here."

"Away from me and my questions?" she asked, her pride stinging. And maybe something even more vulnerable than her pride.

Her heart.

"Brittney, you need to look out for yourself," he said.

"Don't worry. I'm not your responsibility," she assured him. "You don't have to walk me back to the hotel. I can take care of myself."

"That's not what I meant," he said, his voice gruff with frustration. "I'm just… I can't stay…"

She stepped aside, out of his path, and repeated, "Don't worry about me. Just go. Run away."

Because no matter what he'd done last night, that was what he was doing now. Running away instead of facing the situation and trying to solve the mystery of the saboteur and whoever the hell was after her.

Were they one in the same?

She intended to find out, but she was disappointed that he had no interest in discovering the truth. She'd been such a fool to be attracted to him at all. And now she was damn glad she hadn't kissed him as deeply and passionately as she'd wanted to. Hell, she'd wanted to do more than that, but she was glad she hadn't, especially when he walked right past her and out the locker room door.

BRITTNEY TOWNSEND HADN'T been easy to scare away from the story she was after. And now she wasn't easy to kill. She should have died in the wreckage of that van of hers when it had rolled over and over, trapping her inside it.

Miraculously she'd survived that.

But last night…

It hadn't been a miracle that she'd gotten out of the path of the SUV just in time.

That had been interference of another kind. It certainly hadn't been divine intervention. It had been a man. Brittney's white knight wouldn't be able to save her again, though.

Because the next time he was going to die with her, like he should have the night before. The killer wasn't going to make the mistake of trying to use a vehicle again, especially one that had probably been described to the police.

So that vehicle was hidden for now...

Leaving the driver with nothing to drive at the moment. But that hadn't stopped them from following the reporter when she'd left her hotel earlier that morning.

She was at the firehouse now. Probably asking more of her damn questions.

The killer raised their weapon, peering through the scope into some of the windows. Who was in the three-story concrete building with her?

Her white knight?

The gun barrel focused on the door she'd entered. It would probably be the one she exited.

And when she did, she was going to die.

And if she wasn't alone, whoever was with her would die, too. But the killer would have to wait until they were far enough out of the building so that neither could take cover and avoid being hit, like they'd avoided it last night. This time they had to die.

Chapter Thirteen

Damn her!

Damn her so damn much…

Fury coursed through Rory, making his pulse pound as his blood pumped hotly through his veins as he ran down the firehouse stairs to the main level. But he wasn't mad at her. Not really.

He was mad that she'd spoken the truth.

He was running away again, just like he had more than five years ago. And then after running away, he'd hid out here in Northern Lakes and on Bear Isle.

But if he hadn't hidden like he had, he would probably already be dead. And hiding out hadn't just kept him from getting hurt, it had kept the people around him from getting hurt.

Or so he'd thought…

Maybe the saboteur was after the team because of him. Because of that damn note someone had sent Braden…

Someone on your team isn't who you think they are…

Sure, that could have been referring to Ethan, but who, besides Rory and Ethan, had known who he really was?

Nobody had recognized Jonathan Canterbury after those months they'd spent in the mountains before they'd been rescued. He had truly looked like Ethan Sommerly, the hotshot who'd trained with them in Washington state.

That man was gone now. And so was another man…

Rory felt that pang in his heart, that guilt and regret. It was all his fault. And instead of bringing their killers to justice, he'd hid to save his own life. And maybe he'd put other people in danger.

Brittney.

Was it his fault that someone was after her? Was she right, that the only way to stop the bad guy was to find out the truth once and for all?

That wouldn't necessarily protect him from the vendetta against him. From the hit sworn out on him…

But maybe the truth would protect her, like he had to protect her. He stopped at the door to the outside, his palm against the metal. And he closed his eyes and sighed.

A nose rubbed against his other hand, the one wrapped around the straps of the duffel bag. Annie whimpered.

"What's up, girl?" he asked.

She must have been waiting by the door for Stanley to return. The kid had probably gone back to Cody's, and he couldn't bring the dog with him there since the child Cody and Serena was fostering was allergic to her.

"I'm sure he'll be back soon," he assured the dog.

"What about you?" Brittney asked as she stepped off the last step of the stairwell. "Are you running away for good or just until I'm gone?"

"I need to get back to the island," he insisted.

"Why?"

He wanted to go back for that insurance. He hadn't been able to figure out exactly how it would help him, though, or he would have used it long ago. And because he didn't know for certain if it was of any use, he replied, "Because I work there."

"Doing what?"

"Monitoring wildlife, the woods, stopping poachers and trespassers. And enjoying the quiet…"

"You really want to go back there for that?" she asked.

He touched the back of his head. "Seems like a good treatment for a concussion. Silence."

But he really needed to retrieve that other thing, the thing that might be able to protect Brittney at least, if not him. But that was only if the person threatening her to back off wanted her to leave the plane crash story alone. If it was actually the saboteur after her, Rory had no idea what to do about him or her. Or he would have done that long ago.

Like he probably should have used his insurance long ago. But he'd never been able to figure out how to use it because he hadn't known whom he could trust with it…because the insurance itself had proved to him that he could trust no one.

"Why haven't you left already?" she asked, and she pointed at the door he had yet to open.

"Why are you leaving?" he asked. "Aren't you going to ask Braden for that list?"

"We both know he's not going to give it to me," she said.

Rory wasn't so certain. Braden was desperate to find the saboteur, which was why he'd hired his brother-in-law as one of the team, thinking Trick could be more objective than he could. But then Trick had fallen for Henrietta…

And for Northern Lakes. He wasn't going back to his life as a floater for other teams. He was here to stay. Or so Rory hoped, for Trick's and Henrietta's sakes.

"It's not like you to give up that easily," Rory remarked.

She narrowed those topaz eyes and stared at him. "You don't really know me."

"I know you're determined." Too determined. It was probably going to get her killed.

She smiled. "I can't deny that."

"Then why are you leaving?"

She held up her cell. "Tammy texted me. She and Ethan decided not to go on that cruise."

"Did she say why?" Rory asked. Ethan had been looking forward to that trip. Hopefully he hadn't canceled it because of him.

"I'm going to find out now," Brittney said. "I hope Trent didn't ask him to cancel, so he could be my babysitter. I don't need one."

"I'll go with you," Rory said, and he reached for the door handle again. He cared about Ethan, about Trent, about his whole damn team. And he cared about Brittney, too. Too much to leave her unprotected.

"I just said I don't need a babysitter," she reminded him.

"I'm not babysitting."

Annie whined.

"She wants to go, too," Brittney said. "She hasn't been barking at me now."

"She tends to get used to strangers pretty quickly," he said. "Except for Ethan. It took her a while to get used to him without his beard. I really shouldn't let her out. She tends to run off."

"Hmm… Wonder where she gets that from?"

Rory resisted the urge to smile. "I'm not running," he said.

"You did. Last night. To save me," she said. "I shouldn't have said what I did upstairs about you only caring about yourself. You jumped in front of an SUV for me."

And he would do it all over again. He didn't want anyone getting hurt, especially if it was because of him and especially her.

"You're not wrong about me," he admitted. "I have been a selfish jerk." He'd had to be, or he wouldn't have survived as long as he had.

But maybe survival wasn't enough, not when you had to give up so damn much for it.

"And I am going back to Bear Isle," he said. To get that insurance...

Maybe with her help, he could figure out who to trust with it. But should he trust her? Should he get her any more involved than she already was?

"I thought you were walking with me to Tammy's salon," she said. "That you wanted to talk to Ethan."

"I'll walk you over there," Rory said. "But I don't need to talk to Ethan." He knew what he needed to do.

He pulled open the door just far enough to try to keep Annie from squeezing out. But the dog was fast despite her size. And despite her size, she managed to squeeze through the opening and out.

"Annie!" he called to her, and he jerked the door open the rest of the way. And when he did, gunshots rang out, bullets pinging off the concrete building and the metal door. He dropped, pulling Brittney down with him.

She'd been in the doorway, too. Had she gotten hit?

"Brittney?" he whispered into her hair, which was soft beneath his cheek. "Are you all right?"

"Shh..." she whispered back at him. "The shooter might still be out there."

Rory was pretty damn certain that he or she was. And so was Annie. "Stay in here," Rory advised her. "Lock the door behind me and go get Braden and Trick." He pushed her farther inside so he could get out the door. Then he pulled it shut behind him.

More gunshots rang out, echoed by Annie's barks. She was going after the shooter. Trying to save everyone like she kept saving them...

But who would save Annie from a bullet?

BRITTNEY SCREAMED, "BRADEN! TRICK!"

They were already running down the stairs, heading toward her. "Who's shooting?" Braden asked.

"Where is it coming from?" Trick asked.

She pointed toward the door. "Rory went after him or after Annie..." She didn't know which, just that once again he'd run toward danger instead of away from it. And he had nothing with him to protect him.

Not a gun. No armor. He'd just rushed off with no thought of his own safety.

Tears stung her eyes as fear for him overwhelmed her. And remorse...

If something happened to him, she would regret so many things. Most of all that she hadn't kissed him like she'd wanted, with all the passion she felt for him. She hadn't really showed him how much she appreciated that he'd risked his life for hers last night, either.

And now...he was risking his again.

SOME NOISE, FAR-OFF but familiar, pulled Trent from his dream. Or maybe the sound had been part of his dream.

Or the memory he had of gunfire...

Of someone shooting at him and Heather...

Heather dropping through the fire-and water-damaged floor of his burned house. And him not knowing if she'd been shot...

Was someone getting shot now?

The sound faded away then. It must have just been his dream. Or memory.

But then the sharp wail of sirens jerked Trent fully awake. He should have been awake all along.

He'd never intended to fall asleep.

"Brittney!"

His heart pounding, he jumped up from his bed and headed toward the connecting door. It was closed. She must have closed it. When he touched the knob, it didn't turn. She'd locked it on her side. To keep him out or to keep him from seeing that she'd taken off?

Hell, she might have even checked out. But he doubted that. She wasn't leaving Northern Lakes without her story. But what was it going to cost her?

Those sirens…

He was sure she was wherever the police were heading. He pulled open the door to his room and rushed out into the hall. He didn't wait for the elevator, taking the stairs instead. But he knew that no matter how fast he ran, he might be too late. Like he would have been last night…

Rory was the one who'd saved her then. Was he with her now? Had he protected her again?

But at what cost?

His life?

Chapter Fourteen

Despite her size, Annie must have been part cat because she certainly had more than one life. Maybe even more than nine. Rory could relate. He'd had more than one himself.

Somehow both he and the dog had avoided getting hit despite all the bullets that had been initially fired at the steel door to the firehouse.

Someone must have called the police, though, and the gunfire stopped with the wail of sirens in the distance. The shooter didn't want to get caught.

So why take the chance of firing at them in broad daylight? How determined was he or she to kill…?

And who was the target?

Brittney or him? He'd been hit over the head, but nobody had shot at him and tried to run him down, at least not recently, like had been the case for Brittney.

He needed to make sure that Brittney was safe. He'd left her back at the firehouse when he'd run after Annie. The dog had kept running into the woods behind the firehouse. Was that where the shooter had been standing?

"Annie!" he called out.

Maybe the would-be killer was still out there. Waiting until he got closer to fire again.

Where had the dog gone?

Despite the unseasonably warm winter they'd been having, there were large patches of snow in the woods yet. There were also big sections of mud where the snow had melted and the ground had begun to thaw. If the shooter had been out here, maybe they would be able to track him through the snow and mud.

"Annie…" He lowered his voice now.

While she'd ignored his shouting for her, she turned now, at his whisper, and rushed back to him. Probably as scared as he'd been, she jumped up on him with her paws on his chest. The sudden weight of her body pushed him back, and he slipped and fell into that mud. At least it was mud and not wainscoting or asphalt like the night before.

But then he heard a gun cock, and he realized the fall and the mud wasn't what he should have been worrying about. And that he damn well shouldn't have assumed that the shooter had taken off with the sound of the sirens.

Because above Annie's big head, he could see the barrel of a gun pointing directly at him.

"WHERE IS HE?" Brittney asked, her heart hammering so hard with fear that her chest was starting to hurt. She paced by the door of the firehouse, the door that Trick and Braden were blocking as if they realized she would have run out after Rory by now if they hadn't stopped her. "Where is he?"

Braden shook his head. "The police are here," he reminded her. "They're searching the area."

"For the shooter," she said.

Braden said, "They'll find any victims—"

She gasped and slapped a hand over her mouth to hold back the sob that threatened to escape.

"I don't mean that they will find any, that Rory is one…"

"But he was a victim, not that long ago, in this very firehouse," Brittney reminded him. He'd been hurt so badly that he'd spent two weeks in a coma. He'd had no business running off like he had. After Annie or the shooter? "He doesn't have a gun. No way to defend himself..."

The door handle turned, and everybody whirled toward it. A trooper had been standing on the other side of it, so nobody could get inside to them. And probably so that they couldn't get out. She suspected she wasn't the only one who'd been tempted to run out to find Rory.

The door opened, but it wasn't the trooper who entered. Trent walked in instead. "What the hell happened?" he demanded to know. Then he rushed over to her. He clasped her shoulders and stared down into her face. "Are you all right?"

She nodded. "Thanks to Rory. He saved my life again." Even after how terribly she'd spoken to him...

He definitely cared about more than himself. He probably cared about everyone and everything else more than he cared about himself.

Trent peered around the garage area. "Where is he?" he asked.

She shrugged, knocking his hands from her shoulders. "He went after Annie."

Trent groaned. "I love that dog, but she doesn't have the sense to hide from shooters. Instead she races right toward them."

"Shooters?" Then she remembered the professional assassins that Jonathan Canterbury's brother-in-law had hired to kill him. They'd shot at the firehouse, too.

She shuddered. That had been her fault for revealing Ethan Sommerly's real identity. Was this her fault, too?

Had that shooter been after her or Rory?

"It shouldn't be taking this long to find him," Brittney said, her voice cracking with the fear that overwhelmed her.

Unless they'd found him and were working on him because he'd been shot.

Braden nodded. "We should have gone out after him," he said to Trick.

Trick pointed at her. "She would have gone out there, too."

"Brittney," her brother said, his voice gruff with emotion. "You've got to stop putting yourself in danger."

She held up a hand to stop his lecture. "Don't start. Just don't…"

"This isn't getting us anywhere," Braden said, and he opened the door to the trooper standing outside. "We can help you search—"

The guy touched the speaker in his ear. "Trooper Wells found someone."

Someone. Brittney wanted to demand to know what he meant. The shooter? A victim? The dog?

Who the hell had Trooper Wells found?

ETHAN HAD HEARD the gunfire and the sirens. And he knew he'd done the right thing. He'd come back for his team. They'd been there for him and for Tammy when his greedy brother-in-law had taken her hostage. Ethan had to be there for them now. But he wasn't allowed anywhere close to the firehouse.

He wasn't the only one being held away from the area, though. Pretty much everyone else had showed up at the scene. Stanley was sobbing.

"I don't hear Annie barking anymore," Stanley said.

Donovan Cunningham, who had two teenagers just a little younger than Stanley, wrapped his arm around his shoulders. "That dog is lucky, Stanley. She'll be fine."

"She's been good luck for all of us," Howie Lane said. He

was one of the newer hotshots and was probably just a few years older than Stanley, in his early twenties.

Howie and Bruce Abbott had shown up together. They were young and worked in the area, when they weren't working as hotshots, as arborists.

Sometimes just being around them made Ethan feel old. They were so young and full of energy.

Carl Kozak slapped Ethan's shoulder. "I thought you were gone on a cruise."

Carl was the old man of the team, but with his bald head and muscular build, it was hard to tell his age.

"I didn't feel right taking off when Rory isn't one hundred percent yet."

"He's the one who went chasing after Annie," Howie said.

"You saw him?" Ethan asked. "You were here when the shooting started."

Bruce nodded. "Yeah, we were just about to go to the Filling Station for lunch when we heard the gunshots. Then we saw Annie and Rory running toward the woods."

Stanley gasped. "Was that where the shooter was?"

Ethan and Donovan exchanged a significant glance over Stanley's curly-haired head. The dog had probably gone after the shooter.

And Rory had gone after her.

Had they gotten hit?

Where the hell were they?

Chapter Fifteen

Rory wasn't sure how he'd gone from lying flat on his back in the mud, staring up into the barrel of a gun, to here...

The shower in Brittney's hotel room.

The gun, fortunately, had belonged to Trooper Wells. Although he'd had a long uneasy moment of staring into the barrel before she'd finally turned it away from him.

Despite the warmth of the water washing away the mud, he shivered. Could *she* have been the shooter? Annie hadn't barked at her, so she could have even been the one who'd hit him over the head.

But why...?

Her former boss, Marty Gingrich, had hated the hotshots, but she had no reason to, even though she had spouted off at a few back at the firehouse. She'd warned them all to stop trying to investigate on their own or they were going to get hurt.

"Is that a threat?" Brittney had asked the question, of course, probably because it wasn't possible for her to not ask one.

She hadn't asked him back to her hotel room, though. She'd told him he looked like hell and that he needed to come back with her.

With everyone else at the firehouse, he'd been happy to

get away from the noise that had had his head pounding again. Or was his head pounding for another reason?

With fear and guilt?

Annie was fine. She hadn't even gotten as muddy as he had. She wasn't hurt.

But Brittney could have been. Those bullets had come so close to her. And to him...

Instead of coming back here with her, he should have headed where he'd intended earlier. To the island...

To his insurance.

But Brittney, and her quick talking, had gotten them both away from the trooper and her questions. She'd insisted that Rory was too weak yet from his concussion to answer any more questions and that she needed to drive him to the hospital.

But she'd driven his truck back to her hotel instead. Then she'd pushed him into the bathroom. "You need to wash off that mud," she'd insisted. "You're not making me lose my room deposit."

He'd chuckled but complied. The hot shower felt really good. But thinking about walking back out there to her had him cranking the faucet to Cold. He needed the blast of icy water to bring him to his senses. To remind him of all the reasons why he couldn't get involved with anyone. As if getting shot at and nearly run down with her weren't good enough reasons...

After turning off the water, he grabbed a towel and then looked around the steamy bathroom for the duffel bag he'd brought in with him. Hadn't he?

Where was his bag?

His clothes?

After drying off with the towel, he tucked it around his

waist and opened the door to the room, peering out through a crack. "Have you seen my duffel bag?"

He'd dropped it at the firehouse before rushing out the door after Annie. But he'd picked it up before rushing out the door after Brittney when she'd given them the means to escape from more of the trooper's questions.

Wells had already interrogated him when she'd found him in the woods, as if she'd suspected he was the shooter. And when he opened the door and found Brittney going through his duffel bag, he wondered if she suspected the same.

"You were with me when the shots were fired," he reminded her. "You're not going to find a gun in there."

"I'm not looking for a gun," she replied without even looking up at him, without looking at all embarrassed for getting caught rummaging through his things.

"Then what are you looking for?" And he was so glad that he'd stashed his insurance somewhere safe.

"Your cape," she replied.

"Cape?"

"You must be some kind of superhero since you keep saving me," she said.

He shook his head. "I'm no hero. Super or otherwise…" Or so many other people wouldn't have died.

"You've saved me," she said.

He gestured at her going through his duffel. "And yet you still don't trust me. What did you really expect to find?"

She shrugged. "I don't know. Maybe a bunch of passports with different names but your picture on every one of them."

"Now I'm a spy?" he asked, and he managed to keep his voice even so he didn't give away how damn close she was getting to the truth.

"Spy or superhero?" she asked. "Which is it?"

"You didn't find a cape or any passports, so I'm not either of those things," he said. And he wasn't. "But I am getting a little cold." The towel was damp from him using it to dry off, though he hadn't dried off completely. Droplets of water still streaked down his back and chest.

Her gaze seemed to track one of those drops sliding down his chest, and he wasn't cold anymore. Not when she looked up again and her topaz eyes had gone dark, her pupils dilated.

"Can I have my clothes?" he asked, reaching out for the bag with a hand that shook slightly. The way she was looking at him was testing his self-control.

Could he contain the attraction he felt for her?

"You are cold," she murmured, but instead of handing over the bag, she reached over it and touched his chest, pressing her palm flat against where his heart was beating so hard and fast.

He shook his head. "This is a bad idea, Brittney."

"Why?"

"You and those damn questions," he murmured before gritting his teeth.

Her hand still on his chest, she stepped around the chair where she left his duffel bag, and she laid her other hand on him, on his abs. "Give me a reason this is a bad idea," she challenged him.

He couldn't hold back a slight grin at her audacity. "Uh, let's see. We won't have to worry anymore about who hit me over the head, tried to run you down and took shots at you and at us. That's because your brother will kill me. My team members will help him. And yeah, the police could show up anytime."

"The police?"

"Yeah, what do you think Trooper Wells is going to do when she checks with the hospital to see if we're really there?" he asked.

"Well, hopefully the police show up before my brother and the rest of the team kill you," she said, and she was smiling now, her topaz eyes sparkling.

"You are probably more dangerous than whoever is after us," he said. Because she was making him forget all the reasons why he couldn't have a relationship, why he couldn't care about someone...

But it was already too late for that. He cared about her.

He groaned, his body aching with the need for hers. And he hadn't even kissed her. He wanted her so damn badly. But he wanted even more to keep her out of the mess that was his life. He didn't want her getting hurt or worse.

EITHER THE MAN wasn't attracted to her or he had incredible willpower. Because, despite her hands on his bare chest, Rory didn't wrap his arms around her and pull her close. He just reached around her for his duffel bag.

So she drew in a shaky breath and stepped back, letting her hands drop away from him. "Guess I'm not as cute as my producer tells me I am..."

Rory turned back to her then, and his pale blue eyes were intense as he stared at her. "You're not cute."

"Ouch."

"You're beautiful," he said.

She'd been called that before. Beautiful Brittney. She knew she was attractive, but apparently to a man like Rory VanDam that wasn't enough to attract him.

Then he sighed and added, "Stunning, smart, stubborn, infuriating..."

She smiled. "I'm infuriating?"

He nodded. "And that's why. You can't stop asking questions."

"There are things I want to know," she said. "I won't find

out unless I ask…" So she drew in a breath and asked him, "Don't you want me?"

He groaned and closed his eyes. "So damn badly…"

"Then why aren't you kissing me? Touching me?"

He grimaced. "More questions…"

"And you're not giving me any answers."

"I don't want you to get hurt," he said.

"I'm not going to fall madly in love with you," she assured him. Not a firefighter. Not a hotshot…

Not someone she could lose like she'd lost her dad while he'd been deployed.

He grinned. "Good to know. That still doesn't protect you."

"You've been protecting me," she said. "And if I didn't already know how damn short life can be, I would have realized it after the close calls we've had. I don't want to regret not doing this…" She closed the distance between them again and looped her arms around his neck, guiding his head down to hers. Then she kissed him.

The second her lips touched his, her skin tingled and her heart started racing. It was like she was coming under fire again and the vehicle she was in was starting to roll over, to spin out of control. But she wasn't inside anything. There were no airbags to protect her and nothing to hold on to but him.

Then he was holding on to her, too, but he just didn't wrap his arms around, he lifted her up. And she wrapped her legs around his lean waist.

His body was so strong, so hard…so hot.

He kissed her back, his lips nibbling at hers, the tip of his tongue teasing hers. She parted her lips for him, and he deepened the kiss, making love to her mouth.

Then she was spinning again, or at least moving, as he

carried her over to the bed. She pulled him down with her, clinging to him. She hooked her finger in his towel, loosening it until it dropped.

And she whistled in appreciation of all his muscles. The man was perfect. Or he would have been but for a scar here and there, scars like the one on the back of his head. "Rory..." She touched her finger to one on his shoulder.

The bullets had missed him earlier today, but she suspected that one hadn't. At some time...that he had been shot. "Rory—"

Before she could ask the question, his mouth covered hers again, kissing her so deeply that she breathed him in, that his breath was her air. And their hearts beat in a frantic rhythm.

He pulled back and panted for breath. "Let me ask a question," he said, his voice gruff.

Unable to speak for the desire overwhelming her, she just nodded.

"Are you sure?" he asked.

She reached between them and wrapped her hand around his erection. It pulsated against her. "Very sure."

"Then you're overdressed," he said.

And the man moved fast, undoing buttons, lowering zippers, pulling off her shoes until she lay as naked on the bed as he was.

But his gaze covered her, moving over every part of her body. "You are so beautiful..." Then his hands and his mouth moved over her, kissing the side of her neck and the curve of her collarbone.

His hands moved to her breasts now, caressing them, cupping them. Then he lowered his mouth and kissed one taut nipple before turning his attention to the other one.

She arched against the mattress, her body writhing inside with the tension he was building. The demand for release.

"Rory..." She didn't want to wait.

But he took his time, flicking his tongue across her nipple. Then his hand moved lower, between her legs, and his thumb pressed against the most sensitive part of her body.

Pleasure shot through her with a sudden and small orgasm. It had been too damn long since she'd been with someone. Too damn long since she'd felt this kind of pleasure.

She touched him, sliding her fingers over his muscles and his scars. She would save her questions for later because right now there was only one curiosity she wanted to satisfy. How he would feel inside her...

"Rory..." She wrapped her legs around him again.

"I—I don't have anything..."

"No diseases?" she asked.

He chuckled. "No protection. But yeah, it's been a while, so no nothing else, either...and no control if you keep..."

She rubbed against his cock again. "I have an IUD," she said. "And it's been a while. We're good..."

He parted her legs, lifting them up, over his shoulders as he guided himself inside her.

And she nearly came again at just that, that feeling of him filling her. Then he moved, thrusting his hips against her. She arched up, meeting his thrusts, and they found a fast, frenetic rhythm, one that drove them both to panting and grunting and groaning and madness.

Then finally the tension broke, and her body quivered inside and out. The pleasure was so intense, so unending...

Then his body tensed, and he shuddered as he found his release. And her name slipped through his lips. "Brittney..."

He sounded awed.

She was, too, awed by the intensity of the pleasure and the feeling. Of the connection…

But she knew all too well that it couldn't last. That they only had these stolen moments to enjoy each other because whoever was after her wasn't about to give up.

But she wanted these moments to last, so Brittney reached up and kissed him again. Deeply, passionately, and she felt him move inside her.

He groaned and then chuckled. "Brittney…" He definitely sounded awed.

HOW THE HELL had every bullet missed? Sure, the shooter had fired too soon, the minute the door had opened. But with the dog rushing out, running toward them, there hadn't had a choice.

If there had been any hope of hitting the target, the shooter had to shoot fast and then get the hell out of there before someone saw where they'd been standing in the woods.

Did anyone see them now? Where they stood in the shadows outside the hotel?

The shooter might have tried to take them out when they'd left the firehouse, but there had been so many police there. And while the shooter had followed them back here, other people had, as well.

The shooter wasn't the only one watching them. They weren't even sure if they were the only one who wanted them dead. And now the shooter wanted them both dead.

Him even more than her…

Chapter Sixteen

Rory knew Brittney was dangerous. To his secret…and to the life he'd built in Northern Lakes with his hotshot team. But he hadn't realized how dangerous she was to him personally until now.

Even as she lay sleeping next to him, he felt as if he couldn't escape her, that he was connected to her in a way he had never been to anyone else.

Not even Amelia…

Which was strange because he'd trusted Amelia and he knew he couldn't trust Brittney. She cared more about getting her story, or the truth, than anything else. She didn't really care about him.

At least Amelia had pretended to. Maybe she even had, but in the end her greed had been greater than her love. And that greed had proved the end of her…

The twinge in his shoulder wasn't just because of how he was holding Brittney but from an old wound. One that tended to remind him of all the reasons he shouldn't take another chance on a relationship.

Brittney didn't want one any more than he did, though. Maybe less than he did. But instead of reassuring him, that had him panicking now. He wasn't about to fall harder for someone than they'd fallen for him. Not again…

He'd intended to stick with her, to protect her and to figure out the truth together. If the saboteur had come after both of them or if someone else had.

But if it was someone else, someone from his past, then he might get sucked back into it. And she might, too. She deserved to know the truth, but would she believe it...?

Without proof?

He could bring her with him to get his insurance, but he needed some distance, some room to breathe, or he might lose his head and his heart completely. So he slipped out of the bed with the tangled sheets and the sleeping woman. But as he did, he felt a twinge in his heart, and he wondered if it was already too late.

If he was already starting to fall for her...

He had to protect himself now, but he wanted to make sure she was safe, too. Who else would stop Brittney from getting hurt? He dressed quickly and quietly and grabbed up his duffel bag. He'd charged his cell last night at the firehouse, so he had it with him now. Once he got into the hallway outside her room, he would call Trent and make sure that he would protect Brittney better than he had and that he would make sure she didn't slip away again and put herself in danger.

And he'd even wait in the hall until Trent got there, to make sure that she was never unprotected. He didn't want Brittney getting hurt. Not like Amelia had...

As he neared the door, he turned back to the bed to look at her one more time. Her hair had tangled across her face and across the pillow where his head had lain next to hers. He wanted to go back there, wanted to close his arms around her warm body and hold her close.

But it was that desire, that need burning inside him that scared him more than anything else right now. He needed

some distance, some time to clear his head, so he could figure out exactly how to finally take care of what he should
have five years ago.

He forced himself to resist the temptation of Brittney and
turn back toward the door. When he closed his hand around
the knob and just started to rotate it, she murmured in her
sleep. He glanced back over his shoulder, watching as she
settled back against his pillow. Once her body relaxed, as
she slipped back into deep sleep, he pulled open the door
and quietly stepped out into the hall.

He'd just closed it behind him when someone grabbed
him roughly, jerking his arms behind his back, preventing
him from fighting.

And if he called out...

Brittney might try coming to his rescue. But she had no
gun, nothing that would protect her and save him. He had
to figure out some way to do that, but he had a feeling that
he was outnumbered this time. It wasn't just one shadow
looming over him in that hall but two.

But he'd never given up before. Not when Amelia had
betrayed him or when that plane crashed.

He wasn't giving up now. Just like before, he wasn't giving up without a fight. And now he wasn't just fighting for
his life but for hers, too.

BRITTNEY JERKED AWAKE, her arms outstretched, reaching...

Reaching for Rory, but he was gone. The bed was cold.
How long had he been gone?

Snippets of a dream came back to her. Men's deep voices.
Sounds of a scuffle...

Had that been a dream?

Or had something happened to Rory?

She jumped up and hurriedly dressed. Then she searched

her room and the adjoining bathroom. Rory was gone, and so was his duffel bag. How long had he been gone?

The light was already dimming outside. How long had she slept?

Had the entire day slipped away from her? Just like Rory had?

A twinge of regret struck her heart. Not over what they'd done. She would never regret that. He was amazing in bed. Had brought her so much pleasure…

She had needed that. She'd needed him. Her regret was that he was gone now. And she didn't think she would find him as easily as she had earlier that day. He probably wasn't going back to the firehouse.

Where would he go?

That island where he was a forest ranger?

Or somewhere else? Wherever he was from?

Did he have a home? Family? He'd never said much about anyone but his hotshot team.

And yet, he didn't seem as close as the rest of them were to each other, either. Rory VanDam was a loner now, but had he always been alone?

Despite having dressed in a sweater and wool pants, she shivered. She wasn't cold so much as she felt alone. And despite the closed door, she had that uneasy feeling, that sensation that someone was watching her even though there wasn't even a peephole in the door.

Then the knob rattled, as someone tried to turn it. "Who's there?" she called out. "Rory? Trent?"

The knob rattled more and so did the door as someone tried to force it open. It definitely wasn't Rory or Trent. They would have answered her. They wouldn't want to scare her like this person obviously did.

But if this was the one who'd fired shots at her and tried

to run her down, this person didn't want to just scare her anymore. They wanted to kill her.

TRENT HAD NEVER felt like killing anyone more than he had Rory. When he and Ethan had caught the man sneaking out of his sister's hotel room, fury had coursed through him. And if not for Ethan stopping him, he wouldn't have killed Rory, but he certainly would have messed him up.

If he could...

His jaw still ached a bit from where Rory had nailed him the night before. Even with a serious head injury, the guy was strong.

And stubborn.

He'd resisted Ethan's efforts to encourage them to go somewhere and talk it out while Ethan stayed behind to protect Brittney. Rory had insisted there was nothing to talk about it.

And even though Rory had finally agreed to go to the Filling Station with Trent, he had yet to say much of anything. Trent wasn't sure what to say, either. He was almost too damn mad to talk.

From the way Rory had looked, sneaking out of his sister's hotel room, he could pretty much guess what had happened between them. That was bad enough, made Trent's empty stomach churn with disgust.

But then to sneak out like the man had...

Like he'd been trying to get away from her without waking her up...

A growl bubbled up the back of his throat, but he didn't want to think about why she would have been sleeping. Why she would have been with Rory at all...

Sure, the guy had saved her life. Twice. That Trent knew of. But what if he was the one who'd put it in danger?

He growled again.

"I don't speak Annie," Rory said. "So if you've got something to say to me, just say it." He squared his shoulders and leaned forward a bit, as if bracing himself.

After how Trent had pounced on him in the hall, he was smart to be wary. But Rory was always wary no matter what.

The first time Brittney had come to town, he'd worked damn hard to stay away from her. Why hadn't he done it this time?

But if he had…

She would be hurt or worse: dead.

He released the growl in a groan of frustration. Then he said, "Thank you."

Rory's forehead furrowed, and he leaned farther across the booth and peered at Trent's face. "What did you say?" he asked as if he hadn't heard it or, if it had, he didn't believe that Trent had said it.

"Thank you," he said. "You saved my sister's life. Twice. I can't thank you enough for that…"

Rory's mouth curved into a slight grin. "But?"

"I know she acts tough and all that," Trent said. "But she's got a really soft heart. She's hurt a lot more easily than you'd think. And she's been through a lot."

Concern filled Rory's eyes. "What do you mean? When?"

"We lost our dad when she was really young," Trent said. "Sometimes I think she doesn't remember him, and then sometimes I think she remembers him too much, that she remembers how hard it was for us to lose him."

"On *all* of you, I'm sure," Rory said with sympathy. "Especially your mom."

He shook his head. "My parents were already divorced when he died. He was married to Brittney's mom then."

A muscle twitched along Rory's cheek, and he cleared his throat and asked, "What happened to him?"

"He was deployed, roadside bomb," Trent murmured, and he felt that hollow ache in his heart.

"I'm sorry…"

The sympathy was genuine. Not for the first time, Trent suspected that Rory knew how it felt to lose someone and maybe not just because of that plane crash.

Trent nodded. "A few years later my mom died," he said. "Moe, Brittney's mom, had remarried by then, and Brittney convinced them to take me in, to foster me. She'll fight fiercely for those she loves, and she loves fiercely."

"Why are you telling me all of this?" Rory asked. "Why are we even here?" He gestured at the food untouched on the booth in front of them. "You should be back at the hotel with her."

"And what about you?" Trent asked. "Where are you going?"

Rory's gaze dropped down to the table then. That was clearly a question he didn't want to answer.

"Does this have anything to do with you?" Trent asked.

Rory shrugged. "I don't know."

"I think you know more than I do."

"You haven't had your detective girlfriend looking into this?" Rory asked.

Trent grinned at just the thought of Heather. Talking about fierce women, there was no one fiercer than her. Not even Brittney or Moe.

"What did Detective Bolton find out?" Rory asked.

"That a certain producer has been creeping on my sister."

That muscle twitched in Rory's cheek again when he clenched his jaw. "The one that calls her cute…" he murmured.

Trent bristled with anger over the thought of someone harassing his sister. "He's not been at work, either. Brittney's coworkers told Heather about him."

Rory didn't look as convinced of the man's guilt as Trent was.

"What?" he asked. "What do you know that I don't?"

"She got a couple of notes," Rory said. "One was shoved under her windshield wiper. Told her to drop a story or she'd regret it."

Trent groaned. "That would just make her more determined."

"The next was a text that told her she was going to die for not dropping it, or something to that effect, and after she got that somebody shot at her windshield. That's why she went off the road."

Trent cursed and jumped up from the table. "Why the hell didn't she tell me this? Why didn't you?" Then his fury turned back on Rory as he realized why. "The story she's supposed to drop… It's about that damn plane crash!"

"Or about the sabotage," Rory said. "She's still looking into both of those."

Trent cursed again. "Probably the sabotage even more now after what happened after the holiday party. Who the hell is doing this?" And he glanced around the bar all the hotshots frequented. Usually they would have been jammed into the big corner booth, but none of them were there now. They'd been at the firehouse earlier, though, so most of them were still in town.

Because Rory had been hurt? Or because Rory had recovered? Was whoever hit him worried that he was able to identify him?

"You really didn't see who hit you?" Trent asked him.

He shook his head. "Brittney wanted a list of all the hotshot team members. She intends to look into everyone."

"And I intend to stop her," Trent said. "Are you coming with me?"

Rory shoved his hands in his pockets, and his face got a little pale. "Damn. I must've left my keys…"

"You didn't have them," Trent reminded him. "Brittney drove you back from the firehouse." He wasn't happy that his friend had probably crossed a line with his sister, but it was clear that Brittney had been the instigator. Like she usually was.

But as she was learning from those threats, some people really resented the instigator and would do anything to stop them from meddling.

Even murder them…

Chapter Seventeen

Rory didn't know why his pulse quickened as he and Trent neared the hotel. Was it just because, in order to get his keys, he was going to have to see her again?

After...what had happened between them?

But the feeling churning his stomach was more than anticipation, more even than nerves. It was fear. Not of her but for her.

But Ethan was watching her room from the adjoining one that Trent had booked the night before. She'd locked the door on the other side, though, so all Ethan could really see was the hall through the open door of his room. And if he was focused on the hall, he wouldn't be able to see the fire escape...

The one Rory had gone out the night before when he'd sneaked up on Trent. He glanced up at it now and saw that the window to Brittney's room was open, the curtains and blinds hanging out as if someone had exited it in a hurry.

Or dragged someone out of it?

"Trent!" He grabbed his friend's arm and pointed up. "That's her room!"

Trent cursed and started running toward the hotel. While he went through the lobby, Rory jumped on the ladder dangling down from the fire escape and climbed up it. As he ran up the landings, he looked for blood or for any other sign of a struggle. Because he doubted that Brittney had just opened that window for some air...

Not with as chilly as the wind was now that the sun had dropped. It was cold. Too cold to leave a window open.

The escape swayed beneath his pounding feet as he hurried up the last landing to that open window. He leaned over, peering inside, before sliding his leg over the jamb. "Brittney?" he called out.

The door to the hall stood open, spilling light into her room. Into the empty room...

The door and the window were open? What the hell?

He climbed through the window and checked the bathroom. It was empty, too. And he noticed that the door to the hall hadn't just been opened, it had been kicked in, the wood cracked and the jamb splintered.

Hearing footfalls on the stairs, he stepped out into the hall and nearly fell over a body.

"Ethan!" He dropped to his knees and felt his friend's neck, checking for a pulse. It was there. Strong and steady.

But Ethan didn't move. And Rory was almost scared to move him. Had he been shot? Or stabbed? There was blood on the carpet near him.

"What the hell!" Trent shouted, standing over them in the hall. "Is he—"

"He's alive, but we need to call for a rig."

"And Brittney?" Trent asked, his voice cracking.

Rory shook his head. "She's not in there."

Trent stepped around him and looked inside, too, as if he didn't believe Rory. He unlocked the adjoining door from her side and looked in his room, too.

Maybe she'd gone in there. Maybe she was safe. But Trent

walked out of it into the hall. He was shaking his head, and tears shone in his eyes.

He was scared for Brittney, as scared as Rory was. He never should have left her.

But Ethan…

He was so damn big. So indestructible…

Then Rory saw where the blood was coming from, a wound on the side of Ethan's head. Someone had struck him just like Rory had been struck those weeks ago.

He hoped that Ethan recovered faster than he did. The man had already been through too much. The Canterbury curse couldn't claim him now, not when he was so happy.

"Owen, get a rig here to the Lakeside Inn," Trent spoke into his cell. "Ethan's unconscious—"

"He was hit over the head!" Rory said, speaking loud enough that Owen could hear him.

"And Brittney is missing," Trent added. "So we need to get Braden and Trick and whoever else we can find to help look for her."

Rory shook his head.

Trent clicked off his cell and asked, "What? Why are you shaking your head?"

"We don't know who we can trust," Rory said. "Besides you and me and Ethan—"

Trent pointed at Ethan's prone body. "He's hurt, man. And I trust Braden and Trick."

But Rory noted that he didn't add any other names. Not even Rory's…

Rory shook his head with disgust. How could Trent doubt Rory now?

Because of the damn story.

Because of the plane crash.

Was that what this was all about? If it was, Brittney was

right about getting the truth out. Keeping secrets certainly wasn't keeping her safe.

He needed to get back to the island. He rushed back into Brittney's room.

"She's not there," Trent said.

But Rory wasn't looking for her now, he was looking for his keys. They weren't on any of the tables or the desk. Not lying on any of the furniture...

He didn't have the keys, so Brittney must have taken them with her. Had she used them to get away? He rushed back to that open window and climbed through it. The fire escape shuddered beneath his weight.

"Rory!" Trent called to him. "You can't leave Ethan alone!"

Sirens were already wailing in the distance. Help was on its way. And there wasn't much Rory could do about Ethan's head injury when he was still recovering from his own.

Ignoring Trent, he continued clamoring down the escape and dropped off the end of the dangling ladder onto the sidewalk. Where had Brittney parked his truck?

Hadn't it been here, close to the hotel? He peered up and down the street and didn't see it.

Whoever had broken into Brittney's room must have taken her and the keys and his truck...

Taken her where, though?

And why? Why wouldn't he or she have just left Brittney in the hotel room like they'd left Ethan lying in the hall? Maybe Trent was right, maybe the person who'd been after her was her obsessed producer.

But then why shoot at her and try to run her down if he'd wanted to abduct her?

"Brittney, where are you?" he wondered aloud as he looked around the street again.

Lights flashed on and off. On and off.

And he noted they were coming from the alley where he and Trent had been standing the night she'd nearly gotten run down. But now there was a vehicle in it instead of two men.

He started down the street toward that alley, stepping in front of it just as the lights flashed on again and the motor revved up. He could see the US Forest Service insignia on the side door.

He'd found his truck.

But was it about to run him over?

BRITTNEY LOWERED THE driver's window and gestured for Rory to hurry around the front. To jump into the passenger's door. But he stepped up to her door instead and pulled on the handle. "Let me drive," he said with a quick glance around.

Brittney had already stayed longer than she should have. "He's probably out here somewhere—"

Rory reached through the window and unlocked the door and opened it. "Slide over, quick," he said.

She scrambled over the console. "I can drive—"

"You don't know where we're going, or you would have left already," he said, and he pulled out of the alley onto the street.

Obviously he knew where he was going.

"I couldn't leave," she said. She'd been so disoriented when she'd awakened *alone.* Had he snuck out after they'd made love? But she hadn't known if she was really alone or if Rory was somewhere else, if he'd heard whoever was at that door before she had. But that person hadn't been him or Trent or they would have answered when she'd called out to them. "I didn't know who was supposed to be *protecting* me and what had happened to them."

She'd been so scared that he or Trent had been hurt. Because how else would someone have gotten past them?

"What happened?" Rory asked.

She shivered as she relived those terrifying moments. "I heard some arguing earlier, but that didn't wake me up fully. I'm not really sure what did, but then I heard someone trying to get in the door. I grabbed your keys and my purse and went out the window onto the fire escape," she said.

"That must have been right before someone broke through that door. Did they follow you?" Rory asked, and he was glancing into the rearview mirror as he drove. As if looking for that SUV…

The person trying to get into her room must have been whoever drove that SUV straight at her the night before and who'd shot at her and Rory at the firehouse.

She shivered again.

So the lock and the door hadn't held, hadn't kept her would-be killer out. She'd been smart to run. But what happened…?

Lights flashed and sirens whined as an ambulance passed them. She knew where it was headed: the hotel.

"Who's hurt?" she asked, her heart pounding.

After going out the window, she'd pulled the truck into the alley, shut off the lights and hunkered down inside. But she'd seen Trent and Rory coming back from wherever they'd been, and relief had surged through her. Now she felt a twinge of guilt.

"Who is it?" She reached across the console and clutched Rory's arm.

It was already tense, like his tightly clenched jaw.

"Who's hurt?"

"Ethan," he said. "He must've gotten hit over the head. He was unconscious."

"Shouldn't we go back?" she asked. "Make sure he's all right?"

He drew in a shaky breath. "I want to," he said, his voice gruff with emotion. "But I don't think it's a good idea."

"Why not?" she asked.

"Because someone is trying very hard to kill you," he said. "And I don't think either of us want anyone else to get caught in the crossfire."

She sucked in a shaky breath.

"I assume that's why you didn't tell your brother about the threats you—"

"You told him?"

"Yeah, why didn't you?"

"Because I knew he would get crazy overprotective," she said.

"Like he's been since your van crashed?" Rory asked. "You think holding back that piece of information worried him any less than he's been worrying?"

She sighed.

"Holding back that information misled him," Rory said.

"What do you mean?"

"He had Heather checking out your coworkers and—"

"What?" she asked. "Not that I care…" After nearly getting killed and knowing that she was still in danger and putting others in danger, Brittney had a different perspective on her career. She still wanted the story, but it wasn't so she would be taken seriously as a reporter. She just wanted to make sure nobody else got hurt.

"She heard a lot of things about your producer, and he's been conspicuously off work since you left," Rory said with a glance across the console at her.

She shivered again.

And Rory reached for the heat, turning it up.

Despite the warm air blasting out of the vents, she was still chilled. "As big a creep as he is, I don't think he would go to all this trouble to hurt me. My career, maybe. But my life…" She shook her head. "And he has no reason to want to stop me from pursuing any stories. He doesn't even know that I've been trying to get enough information to do a follow-up to the plane crash and with the hotshots."

"Who does know?" Rory asked.

"I've tried talking to Mack McRooney," she said. "And I've called the FAA with questions about the flight path and the black box…"

"And?"

She shrugged. "Ethan. I'm always bugging Ethan for a follow-up," she admitted.

"Well, Ethan didn't hit himself over the head."

"He was hit like you? Do you think the same person hit you both?"

He shrugged. "I don't know what to think anymore, but I know this needs to stop."

"How are we going to stop it?" she asked.

He glanced across at her again, his pale eyes glowing in the dim light from the dashboard. Clearly he had some idea, but he said nothing, just kept driving. Rory had saved her over and over again, so he had to be heading someplace safe. But with how tightly his jaw was clenched, how grim he looked, he had obviously realized the same thing she had. No place was safe.

SOMEBODY WAS POUNDING. Hammering away at something…

Was it an axe chopping through a door? Or a wall? Or a tree?

Ethan breathed deeply, waiting for the burn of smoke, for

the tickle that would make him cough. But it didn't come. There was no burn. Did he have his helmet and oxygen on? He raised his hand to his face and found a mask over his nose. But not the kind that came with his helmet.

What was the pounding? Where the hell was he?

Ethan opened up his eyes to two guys leaning over him. Owen, with a pinched and serious look on his face, and Trent, who looked even more anxious.

But maybe not for him…

Ethan pulled the oxygen mask aside. "Where's Brittney? Is she safe?"

Trent grimaced, and Ethan reached up and grabbed his friend's shoulder. "What happened to her?" he asked, his voice gruff with concern. Despite her pestering him, Ethan had grown fond of Brittney, and he would always be grateful for her help in saving Tammy's life.

If he'd lost her…

That pounding intensified again, and he realized it was inside his head. He grimaced at the pain.

"We need to get you to the ER for a CT scan," Owen said.

He shook his head and grimaced again. "Where is she?" he asked. Then he glanced around the hotel corridor. "Where's Rory?"

"He went to find her," Trent said, "out the fire escape. The window was open."

The tension eased from Ethan, and he relaxed a bit against the hotel carpeting. "She got away."

Of course she would have. She was smart and resilient, like Tammy, which was probably why the two of them had become fast friends. He emitted a little wistful sigh for their missed cruise. He would have to reschedule once he knew everyone was safe.

"How do you know she got away?" Trent asked, his topaz eyes bright with either unshed tears or hope.

"The guy stepped over me again after he broke the door down."

"You saw him?" Trent asked. "Who was it?"

"I didn't see him when he hit me over the back of the head. I went down, but I didn't lose consciousness right away." But he hadn't had the strength to get back up after that first blow. "I just saw his legs when he stepped over me and headed back down the interior stairs."

"Why didn't he go out the fire escape after her?" Owen asked.

"He probably didn't want anyone to see him, in case someone was walking by, or Rory and I were walking back up," Trent said. "Rory saw that open window right away."

"Rory probably found her," Owen said. "I'm sure they're safe. So we need to get you to the hospital, Ethan."

While Owen was certain they were safe, Trent didn't look as convinced.

"Rory's smart and resourceful," Ethan reminded him. "He'll figure out how to keep her safe."

"What if she's in danger because of him?" Trent asked. "She got threats telling her to stop pursuing the story."

"What story?" Owen asked.

Ethan didn't have to ask. "The plane crash."

"Is there more to that story?" Trent asked. "Something someone else might not want made public?"

The pounding resumed inside Ethan's skull. But he didn't know now if it was because of the blow or because of the pendulum of the past swinging back toward him. He'd made a promise five years ago.

He and Rory both had. Rory had kept his promise all these years. And Ethan had, too.

But now…

He'd kept Rory's promise to keep him safe, but Rory was obviously not safe any longer. And Brittney wasn't safe, either, because she wouldn't give up the damn story. And Ethan was afraid that it might cost her more than her career.

It might cost her everything.

Chapter Eighteen

Rory kept glancing into the rearview mirror, looking for lights on the road behind him. Then he would know for certain that he'd been followed. Right now, he just had that uneasy feeling, that twisting of his stomach muscles that made him suspect that he had been.

But maybe he was just paranoid.

But his paranoia was for good reason after everything that had happened to him and had happened to some people who'd been unfortunate to be around him.

He glanced across the console at Brittney. Was he protecting her by taking her with him or was he putting her in more danger than she already was? Because she had something going on with her, too, and was it really related to him? Or was it her producer?

Or that damn saboteur…?

Brittney was digging inside her purse and cursing.

"What's wrong?"

"I must've left my phone on the charger," she said. "Can I use yours to call and check on Ethan?"

He wanted to know how his friend was, too, but he hesitated for a moment.

"What?" she asked. "Did you forget yours, too? I still don't understand what all happened at the hotel, how Ethan was hurt and where you and Trent were coming back from..."

"The Filling Station," he said.

"The Filling Station?" she asked. "Why were you...?"

He was trying to focus on the road, on finding the turnoff to what he was looking for, but that wasn't why he wasn't filling in the blanks for her. Recognizing the bend in the road, he turned onto the two-track road in the middle of the national forest. This was what he'd been looking for...

While she was looking for answers.

And with her life in danger now, she deserved those answers. "I snuck out when you fell asleep," he admitted. "Trent and Ethan caught me in the hall. Trent was probably going to kill me, but Ethan stopped him." And then might have lost his life, as well.

No. His pulse had been strong and steady, just like Ethan. The man was a survivor, like Rory, so he had to make it. He had to be okay.

"And so you two went to get a beer together?" she asked.

"We needed to talk."

"That was when you told him about those threats."

"You shouldn't have kept it secret from him," he said.

"Like you're *not* keeping any secrets, Rory?" she asked. Damn. She was smart. Too smart.

"I'm sorry," he said. If this was all his fault, if people were getting hurt again because of him...

"Don't be," she said. "I made the moves on you. I wanted what happened to happen. You didn't need to sneak out, though, so fast that you left your keys behind."

"I don't regret what happened," he assured her, his heart pounding fast as he thought of how amazing it had been, how they'd fit so perfectly, moved so much in sync and had

had such a mind-blowing release. "That's not why I took off like that. It's just..."

"What?" she asked. "What is it, Rory?"

"The last woman I got close to wound up dead."

She sucked in a breath then released it in a shaky sigh. "Well, someone was trying to kill me before we ever hooked up, so I can't blame you for that."

Even though there were other possibilities, he was not so sure.

"So did you leave your phone behind with your keys when you made your fast getaway?" she asked again.

"No, no, I have it," he said. "I just... I don't want anyone to know where we're going."

"Why not?" she asked.

"I'm not sure who we can trust," he admitted. He knew all too well how easily some people could be bought, people he'd believed had cared about him. People he had cared about.

The truck bumped along the rutted path between tall trees, but the lights shone up ahead on a clearing in the forest, then glinted off the metal of a big building.

"Don't worry about me telling anybody where we are," she said. "Because I have no freaking idea..." She leaned forward, peering around, but the sun had slipped away a while ago, leaving the area pretty much in darkness but for the lights of his truck.

He braked the truck next to the service door to the hangar. The overhead doors were on the other side of the building by the airstrip. One of his team would realize where he'd gone soon enough, but maybe by that time, he would have gotten what he wanted off the island and made it back already.

He reached into his pocket and drew out his phone.

"I have to get something ready," he said. "You can make the call…"

He would leave it up to her who to trust. He'd learned long ago that his judgment sucked when it came to that, or he wouldn't have been betrayed like he'd been.

So was he making another mistake trusting her?

Because that last woman he'd cared about had nearly gotten him killed.

BRITTNEY WATCHED THROUGH the windshield as Rory unlocked the door to the massive metal building in the middle of the forest. But there weren't as many trees around here, like they had been cleared away for this…

Whatever it was.

No, like she'd told him, she had no idea where he'd taken her. Then the headlights of the truck went out, leaving her totally in the dark. He'd shut off the engine, and he must have taken the keys with him.

To prevent her from leaving?

But then she couldn't blame him if he didn't want to be left stranded out here in the woods. She wouldn't, either.

Sitting like she was in the dark, she was very aware of the silence. There weren't even birds or animals making noises now. Then an engine started up, and light shone around the corner of the building and from beneath that door.

There was something in the metal structure that had an engine. So Rory wouldn't have been stranded.

She might be, though.

Something vibrated in her hand, and she jumped, realizing that she'd been holding his phone. She glanced at the screen that was lit up with Trent's name.

She accepted the call. "Hi."

"Brittney!" Trent exclaimed. Then he released a shaky sigh that rattled the phone. "Are you all right?"

"Yes, is Ethan?" she asked with concern. The guy wasn't just her brother's best friend, he was also the love of Tammy's life and a really good man.

"He regained consciousness right away, even before we got him out of the hotel hallway," Trent said.

Not like Rory, who'd spent those two weeks in a coma.

"That's good," she said. Hopefully that meant it wasn't a bad concussion.

"We're at the ER now, so he can get a CT and make sure he's as all right as he keeps claiming he is."

"Is Tammy all right?" Brittney asked. "Is she there?"

"She's here, with him," Trent said. "Where the hell are you?"

"I don't know," she answered honestly.

"You're with Rory, right? You have to be since you answered his phone."

"Yes, he's here," she said. She just had no idea where here was.

"You need to get away from him," Trent said with such urgency in his voice that Brittney shivered.

"What do you mean?" The man had saved her life. He wasn't going to hurt her. At least not physically...

Emotionally. She shut that down, refusing to think about that, about what they'd done and how he'd snuck out when she'd been sleeping.

"You were right," Trent said. "You've been right all along that there was more to that plane crash..."

"What?" she asked, her pulse quickening. "What did you find out about it?"

"Ethan didn't know a whole lot, just that when it first happened Rory was blaming himself..."

"Why would he do that?"

"He was the pilot," Trent said. "He went through hotshot training with Ethan, but he was also able to pilot the planes they were jumping out of. He already knew how to fly. And Ethan doesn't think his name is really Rory VanDam. Somebody else on that flight, somebody who didn't make it off the mountain, called him something else."

"What?"

"Mario."

Even though Trent couldn't see her, she shook her head. But she had no idea why she would deny it. She'd known there was more to the plane crash story and more to Rory VanDam.

"Mario what?" she asked.

"That was all Ethan heard, and when he asked him about it later, when they were stranded, Rory denied it, said he had to be mistaken."

"Maybe he was," Brittney said.

"You got those threats about dropping a story—"

"And Rory was the one who told you about those threats, and he wouldn't have done that if he'd been the one sending them," she reminded him.

"You should have told me."

"Why? So you could overreact?"

"Someone's trying to kill you, Brittney," he said. "So I'm not overreacting. You're underreacting."

She was scared to death, but she wasn't about to admit that aloud or she might fall apart. And she had to keep it together. The side mirror on the truck caught her attention through the passenger's window. She saw something…a flicker of light. But it appeared to be some distance back down that narrow driveway. But what was the message on the mirror? Objects are closer than they appear.

Someone had been following them.

"Trent, I have to go—"

"Where?"

The door through which Rory had disappeared opened again, and he gestured toward her.

Had he seen that light, too?

"Brittney!" Trent yelled. "You have to get away from him. You can't trust him."

"He keeps saving my life, not putting it in danger," she reminded her brother and herself.

"But your life might be in danger *because* of him, Brittney. You have to get away from him and stay away from him," Trent demanded.

The last woman I got close to wound up dead...

Rory stood there, gesturing toward her again, but he wasn't looking at her now. He was looking behind her.

Objects might be closer than they appear.

She pushed open the passenger door and jumped out. Trent might be right, but she didn't have a choice right now. Somebody else was out there, and it wasn't Trent.

It sounded like anyone else she could trust was at the hospital with Ethan.

So the only person left was Rory.

Or Mario…

"Brittney!" Trent called out again.

But she clicked off the cell and dropped it into her purse. And as she headed toward the door to the building, something pinged off the metal.

Someone was out there, and he or she was shooting at them. "Hurry up!" Rory said, and he reached out the door and grabbed her arm, pulling her inside with him. He slammed that door and locked it.

But she didn't know why he bothered—wide and tall

doors were open on the other side. And outside, a helicopter sat.

"Come on," he said, and he wrapped his arm around her, nearly carrying her toward that machine. "We have to get out of here." He cursed. "We were followed."

She'd been aware of how often he'd checked in his mirrors because she'd been checking, too. There was no way they would have missed someone tailing them unless…

Someone had guessed where they were going. Like a member of his team. Maybe they weren't all at the hospital with Ethan and Trent and Tammy.

"We have to go now!" Rory said. And he swept her around the helicopter, opened the door and lifted her up into it. Then he jumped into the cockpit or whatever it was called on the other side.

He touched buttons and switches, and the blades began to swish above them. Then he reached for some levers and the helicopter lifted. He pointed toward her belt and a set of headphones.

Her hands shaking, she buckled up and put the headphones over her ears. The sounds were muffled, but the noise was still there.

Even the pings as bullets struck the metal of the small helicopter. But it continued to rise above the metal hangar, above the woods.

The gun must have had a long range because it kept firing at them. And on the ground below, Brittney could see little flashes of light as the bullets left the gun. But she couldn't see the shooter.

As fear overwhelmed her, she closed her eyes entirely and hung on tight, terrified that they were going to crash.

Maybe to reassure her, Rory spoke to her, his voice coming through her headphones. "We're going to be all right," he said.

But she didn't know if he was lying to her or telling the truth...about anything.

Then he muttered, "I am not going to crash again."

THE SHOOTER WASN'T really worried about the reporter. Not anymore. Not now.

Because the shooter had finally realized the truth of what had happened five years ago and who Rory VanDam really was. They'd been worried about that damn woman, about the reporter, pushing others to look for that wreckage, to find out why it had crashed.

That helicopter needed to go down, or the shooter was the one who was going to suffer. So the gun kept firing; hopefully a bullet would hit the gas tank and that helicopter would blow up like they did in the movies when bullets hit them.

One of the bullets had to hit the target, if not the pilot then the gas tank. This helicopter had to go down like the plane had five years ago. But unlike that crash, there could not be any survivors this time.

Chapter Nineteen

The helicopter was going down...

Right where Rory intended to land it, on the section of rock that stood atop the hill on the island. No trees could grow out of the rock, and none of the ones near it were tall enough to stand above it. So this was the clearest place to land. Nothing to catch at the blades, and a solid place for the landing skids to rest.

Once Rory sat it down and shut off the engine, he waited for the blades to stop rotating. Then he turned toward Brittney. Her eyes were closed. He could see her face in the moonlight that streamed through the windows of the helicopter. Her eyes weren't just closed but squeezed tightly shut as if she was bracing herself.

Maybe for a crash.

He reached out and pulled off her headphones, and she jumped and flinched. "You're okay," he assured her. "We're okay." For now. "We're on the ground."

And none of the bullets that had struck the helicopter had caused any damage.

Brittney opened her eyes and peered around them then. "Where the hell are we?"

"Bear Isle," he said, and he opened his door and jumped down to the ground. Then he rushed around to help her out.

When she stepped onto the snow-covered rock, she slipped, and he caught her, closing his arms around her trembling body. Maybe she hadn't slipped. Maybe her legs had been shaking too badly to hold her. "We're safe here," he said.

She swung her head around, staring into the shadows of the trees and rocks. "How do you know that?"

"The only thing we have to worry about here might be a bear or a coyote," he promised her. "Whoever was shooting at us back there isn't going to be able to make it out here."

At least not for a while.

Rory's was the only helicopter within a couple hours' drive of Northern Lakes. And if the shooter tried to come by boat, there were still enough chunks of ice around the island to make it hard to get ashore.

As if on cue, a coyote howled somewhere close. Close enough to make Brittney jump again and to make Rory uneasy. "Let's go," he said, and he helped her down from the rock ledge onto the path that wound through the woods to a cabin. His cabin. His sanctuary, really.

"Your hideout," she presumed.

And she wasn't wrong. It probably was more his hideout than anything else. He'd been hiding for a long time. But he had a feeling that he'd been discovered. That the people he'd never wanted to learn the truth knew now that he wasn't dead. He hadn't died in that crash.

Rory opened the door to the cabin and stepped inside, looking around to make sure that it was as he'd left it. Empty. Not just of people but of animals, too. He lit a match to the kindling he had laid in the fieldstone fireplace, and flames flickered to life, illuminating the wood floor and log walls. He turned back toward Brittney, who stood on the outside of the door, hesitating like she had back at the hangar.

"What's going on?" he asked. Then his stomach pitched. "You called Trent. Isn't Ethan…?" He swallowed hard on the emotion suddenly choking him. He and Ethan had been through hell together. He couldn't have lost him, especially now when Ethan was so damn happy. He cleared his throat and asked, "Isn't he okay?"

"He's conscious," she said. "And he's *talking*…"

Rory tensed, waiting for it, because from her tone, there was clearly more to come.

"Mario…"

He could have denied that it was his name, like he had to Ethan all those years ago. And with Ethan assuming another name, he'd had no room to judge him.

Or so he'd thought.

After all, they'd both been afraid for their lives…just for different reasons. Ethan had been convinced that damn Canterbury curse was trying to claim him. And Rory had a curse of his own.

"I'm glad he's okay," he said, then released a heavy sigh of relief.

But she stood there looking all tense yet.

"He is okay, right?"

"They were waiting for a CT scan to confirm it, but he is conscious."

Which was better than Rory had been after the blow to his head. Maybe it hadn't been the same person who'd struck Ethan.

He shuddered, and not just from the cold, but from the thought that there could be two people that cold-blooded in Northern Lakes. But he knew, all too well, that anyone could be cold-blooded, especially when it came to money or their own well-being.

He'd even once been that way himself, when he hadn't

come forward with everything he'd known about the plane crash. When he'd let the people responsible for it escape justice.

But he'd done that for his sake, so that the people who'd wanted him dead had believed they'd succeeded. Playing dead was the only way he'd been able to stay alive.

The door slammed, and he whirled away from the fire toward Brittney. Had the wind slammed the door? Or...

She was bristling, her body tense. "I'm tired of this," she said. "Tired of being in danger. I want to know the truth, *Mario*."

"It's Rory," he said.

"Now. But it wasn't always, was it?" she asked.

He shook his head. "No. But it wasn't always Mario, either."

"So who and what are you really?" she asked. "A hotshot? A pilot?"

"Yes and yes," he said.

"And?" she prodded. Then she sucked in a breath and seemed to be holding it, waiting for his answer.

It had been so long since he'd told anyone the truth. So damn long...

His legs shook a bit, like hers must have from the helicopter trip, and he dropped into one of the big plaid easy chairs that sat in front of the fire. "I was... DEA," he said. "An undercover agent."

In a ragged sigh, she released the breath she'd been holding. She must have been convinced he'd been the criminal, not the cop.

Sometimes, with as deeply undercover as he'd gone, he had felt more criminal than cop. Which had reminded him of how he'd grown up.

"Mario was my undercover identity, my way into the organization," he said. "But I grew up with people like that, so it was easy for me to be Mario. Probably easier than it is for me to be Rory."

"Where did you grow up?" she asked.

"Baltimore."

"And where was Mario?"

"LA."

"And what is your real name?"

He leaned back in the chair and sighed. "When I woke up from that coma, with that concussion, I didn't even know..." He shook his head. "I couldn't remember who I really was. Mario was not my only undercover assignment, my only fake identity. And then there was the Special Forces ops and so many other things that I wanted to forget..."

"The woman?" she asked. "Who was she?"

"Someone who fell for Mario," he said.

"And did Mario fall for her?"

"She seemed sweet. Special. She was also the sister of the guy I took down."

"For drugs?"

"For murder," he said. "My undercover assignment, Mario, was a pilot for a drug cartel. While I was flying their private jet, I witnessed a murder." Remembering that murder, how he'd been unable to stop it, how the whole damn plane could have crashed if he hadn't stayed in control then even as everything had spun out of control around him. "It happened while I was flying, so I didn't have any time to react. I had no idea what was coming. This guy was so cold-blooded, so vicious. He shot this man right between the eyes." He shuddered as he remembered the scene, the blood, the...

But that wasn't even the worst he'd seen.

"Why?" she asked. "Why did he shoot him?"

"Because he thought he was a DEA agent," he said. "He knew someone had infiltrated their organization. He just suspected the wrong man." So that man had died because of him.

She dropped into the chair next to him then as if her legs had given out. "So you're talking about very dangerous people."

"Yes. People who don't forget," he said. "And damn well don't forgive that I arrested the killer and testified against him."

"You were just doing your job," she said. "And why would they go after a DEA agent, especially after you'd already testified and put him in jail?"

"Because the guy I arrested got shanked in jail before his sentencing."

"Then who's after you?" she asked.

"His father."

"I don't understand… You said the woman who got killed was related to them, too. Would the father have killed his own daughter?"

"She set me up," he said. "Got me to meet with her, swore she wanted to leave town with me, start a new life with me, when all she really wanted was to end my life." He rubbed his shoulder, but that wound was nothing in comparison.

"She tried to shoot you?"

He nodded. "She did. And it wasn't just for revenge. Her father had promised her a huge amount of money if she killed me. But a US Marshal killed her before she was able to finish the job."

"The scar on your shoulder?"

He nodded again. "Yeah, she wasn't a very good shot. The Marshal was."

She leaned back in her chair now and closed her eyes,

probably overwhelmed with everything he had told her. "I...
I don't know what to say..."

"Or what to believe?" he asked.

"It's a pretty wild story," she said. "If I wanted to sell this,
I would need proof. Corroboration of the facts."

"So you still want to sell a story?" he asked, his stomach
churning with disappointment. "Even though it might cost
you your life?" And him his.

He'd started to think there was more to her than ambition, that she genuinely cared about people. At least about
her brother. And Ethan and Tammy.

But she apparently didn't care about him.

"I want some proof," she persisted. "Some way to know
what the truth really is."

He sucked in a breath now and nodded. "You don't believe me."

"I don't know what to believe," she admitted. "That's
why I need corroboration."

He had proof. But for some reason he wanted her to believe him without it. He wanted her to see him for the man
that he was, instead of all the different men he'd pretended to
be. But how could he expect her to see what he struggled to?

"The person trying to kill us isn't corroboration enough?"
he asked.

"Why is that person trying to kill you now?" she asked.
"Why didn't that person go after you right after the plane
crash?"

"Because the pilot, at least the man who'd been listed as
the pilot, didn't survive," he said. "That's what all the re-
ports said. That man was really the US Marshal who had
helped set up my new identity."

"People didn't realize he was missing?" she asked.

"He went through the hotshot training with me as my protection. That's why he was on the plane, too, because everybody knew about the hit out on my life," he said. "And after the crash, his presence on the plane was kept quiet. Most people probably believed he'd taken money for killing me and that he'd retired on some Caribbean island."

"But there was coverage of the survivors," she said. "I dug up old articles and news coverage, although you and Ethan both looked pretty worse for wear..." She narrowed her eyes as she studied his face. "And you both did a pretty damn good job of not looking directly at the cameras."

He shrugged. "It wouldn't have mattered. Mario was the disguise. Dark wig, dark contacts, dark beard... I didn't have to wear a disguise for Rory."

"So this is how you really look?"

He shrugged. "Pretty much. I used to wear my hair longer except when I was in the Marines." He rubbed his hand over his short, spiky hair and felt that ridge of a scar beneath it in the back. Where he'd taken that blow.

Had that been the hotshot saboteur or someone who'd started digging a little deeper into the plane crash after Brittney had brought it all back up again? Could someone have realized what he would have looked like without the Mario disguise? Could someone have figured out who Rory VanDam really was? A wanted man?

She stood up and walked around the cabin then, pacing like she was nervous. Or searching? She glanced at the desk in the corner, at the filing cabinet next to it.

"You want to look for that collection of passports you searched my duffel bag for earlier?" he asked.

"Was that today...?" she murmured. "It seems like so long ago."

So long since he'd kissed and held her and made love with her. It seemed like a lifetime ago now. Like a dream that would probably never be repeated because she didn't believe him.

"I don't have any proof, any identification, anything to show I was ever anyone but Rory VanDam," he said. And no one, not even other US Marshals, had known about that identity. He'd created it himself after Amelia had tried to kill him because he'd known there was no one he could trust.

"But you must have something."

"Why do you want it, Brittney?" he asked. And he stood up then because she wasn't going to find what she was looking for without his help. He'd hidden it too well. But then he'd thought he'd hidden well, too, and someone had figured it out.

Or maybe they hadn't.

Maybe they were just trying to hide their involvement in the plane crash. Because that crash hadn't happened due to pilot error. Rory and the US Marshal had discovered a bomb in the cockpit. If they'd tried to dismantle it, it would have exploded. Not wanting to freak the others out too much, Rory had claimed that the engines were failing and urged everyone to parachute off. The timer had given them long enough for everyone to get clear before the plane exploded. But in the chaos, the US Marshal had urged Rory to go before him.

He wasn't sure even now if the plane had exploded. He hadn't seen it go down, and they hadn't found the wreckage. But maybe that was because the bomb had destroyed everything, leaving nothing left for anyone to find.

Except, if Brittney was being threatened to drop her story about the crash, someone must have been worried that the wreckage and the bomb would be discovered. Maybe that bomb could be traced back to the killer.

Rory had something else that could be traced back to

him, too. But that crash had proved to Rory that he couldn't trust anyone. Could he really trust Brittney? Because if he or Brittney put his insurance into the wrong hands, Rory had no hope of ever finding a safe place to hide where he wouldn't be found.

He had no hope of staying alive.

BRITTNEY HADN'T ANSWERED his question. And it wasn't because she was being petty over how many of her questions he left unanswered. It was because she didn't have an answer herself. Why did she want proof?

Because she wanted to sell the story? Could she do that if it would put him in danger?

But then he was already in danger.

He wasn't acting like it now, though. He was moving around the cabin, working in the small kitchenette area, opening soup cans, thawing bread that had been in the freezer. "There's electricity out here?" she asked.

He shook his head. "Power is solar and wind only, but it's enough to run some small appliances and lights."

"Any way to communicate?" she asked as she pulled his cell from her purse and held it up. There was no signal and the battery was draining fast.

He pointed toward a radio on the desk in the corner of the small log cabin. Besides the door to the outside, there was another that opened into a small bathroom. Then the cabin itself had the big stone fireplace with two plaid easy chairs pulled close to it. That fireplace and a king-size bed dominated the space. But there was also a kitchen table and chairs next to the short row of cabinets.

"Are you hungry?" he asked as he carried the food from a small gas stove to the table.

She nodded and joined him, pulling out the chair across

from him. He held out a bottle of wine he'd uncorked. And she nodded again, more heartily. But it didn't matter how much she drank, there wasn't enough alcohol to calm her fears or wash away the nightmares she was bound to have.

The only reason she was still alive was because of Rory. He'd saved her twice now. A third time on the helicopter. If they hadn't gotten away, they would have been shot for certain at that hangar in the woods.

No matter what he called himself, he was a good man. Only a good man would have jumped in front of a speeding SUV to rescue her and into the line of fire to save not just her but the firehouse dog, too.

She took a sip of the red wine, which was just a little sweet and a little dry. Kind of like the man sitting across from her, ladling stew into bowls.

"I trust you," she said.

He pushed the bowl across to her. "I didn't poison the soup or the wine," he assured her, his mouth curving into a slight grin.

"Not just about the food," she said. "I trust you about your story."

"It's so wild that it does sound like something made up," Rory acknowledged. "But I don't have a big enough imagination to make it up."

"You lived it," she said. She'd seen the scars on his body. But the real scars, she suspected, were deeper than his skin. They were on his heart. In his mind…

"And you trusted me with this information," she said, awed that he could trust anyone after what he'd been through. "You trusted me with the truth."

He shuddered a bit as if he was cold. The fire was dying down in the hearth. But then he said, "I didn't think I would ever trust anyone again."

"You didn't even trust your team with the truth or Ethan." And he'd been there with him. "Why me?"

"If it's because of me, because of this story, that you're in danger, you deserve to know the truth," he said.

She realized what he meant, that if she died because of this, she should know why.

BRADEN HATED HOW often he and his team had had to wait out here, outside the ER room, worrying and wondering about one of their own. Dirk was the only one who hadn't survived. But their luck was bound to run out again.

The more times they had to come here, the greater the odds that another life was going to be lost. Was this time because of that damn saboteur again?

"I'm not going to die," Ethan said as he stepped through the doors from the ER. Tammy was under one of his arms, her arms wrapped around him as if she was, with her slight weight, holding up the giant of a man. Ethan lifted one hand to his head and knocked his fist against his forehead. "Hard as a rock."

"More like full of rocks," Trent Miles said. His teasing him seemed like just a reflex. He was preoccupied, worried about his sister and Rory.

Braden was worried about them, too.

Ethan made his way through the crowd of concerned hotshots to where Braden and Trick stood near Trent. Owen had had to leave for another call. Dawson Hess, the other paramedic-firefighter-hotshot, was with his wife in New York City, so Owen was pulling extra shifts.

"Have you heard from Brittney?" Tammy asked Trent, her voice full of concern for her new friend. Tammy befriended everyone, she had such a big heart. But she also owed Brittney for helping save her life. She had been the one who'd put it in danger, though.

Trent nodded. "She called. She's with Rory."

"Where?" Ethan asked.

Trent shrugged. "She didn't say."

"The island," Trick said. "I checked the hangar. The helicopter is gone." A muscle twitched beneath the reddish stubble on his jaw.

There was more to the story. Braden knew it. Trick had already told him. But he must have been leaving it up to him to share or keep it from the others. Seeing the concern on Trent's and Tammy's and Ethan's faces, he was tempted not to share. But they deserved to know the truth, and they all damn well knew how much danger they were in.

"He found bullet holes in the metal walls of the hangar and spent shells."

Trent sucked in a breath. "So someone was shooting at them."

Trick nodded now. "Looks like it."

Trent cursed.

Tammy reached out and touched his arm. "But you talked to her," she reminded him. "She's safe. She's with Rory."

Trent shook his head. "She's not safe with Rory. Rory isn't Rory." He pointed at Ethan. "Tell them what you told me and Owen."

Ethan touched his head again, but he was holding it instead of knocking on it. While he was going to be all right, he had a concussion. Fortunately, it wasn't as bad as the one Rory had.

Rory hadn't just had that concussion, though. He'd had other scars. He was a man who'd been through a lot.

That plane crash. Ethan shared that Rory blamed himself for it, that he had been the pilot.

Trick nodded. "I knew he was a pilot from how he flies the helicopter."

"And he stepped in on previous wildfires, flying the plane when nobody else was available," Braden added.

"But he was here, in the hospital, when Brittney had her accident with her van," Tammy said. "He didn't hurt her, and I don't think he would."

"He wouldn't hurt any of us," Ethan said.

But one of them had. The saboteur. "We don't know that any of this has to do with that plane crash," Braden said. "Brittney was also investigating the things happening with our team. And someone hit Rory that night. Maybe Rory saw who it was and doesn't realize it. He's been so out of it since he regained consciousness."

But now Braden understood why the man hadn't even recognized his name at first. Because it probably wasn't his real name.

"Brittney was trying to talk to my dad," Trick said. "Maybe he knows what's going on, too. I tried calling him, but he didn't pick up."

Mack was a busy man, but he usually answered for Braden. "I'll try."

Trick chuckled. "You'll probably get more out of him than I could. I think you're his favorite son now."

"Son-in-law," Braden corrected him. "And it's easy to be his favorite since he only has one daughter."

One amazingly strong woman.

"I only have one sister, too," Trent said to Trick. "And I need to do everything that I can to make sure she stays safe. How can we get out to that island tonight?"

"Rory took the helicopter," Trick said. "So next best would be a boat, but it's dark and the water's rough with some ice chunks in it. It wouldn't be safe to go out until morning."

But from the look on Trent's face, he was afraid that his sister might not make it until morning. With how the attacks on her and Rory had escalated, Braden was worried about the same thing.

That the next hotshot he lost would be Rory...or whatever his name really was.

Chapter Twenty

The wind howled around the cabin, louder than the coyotes had been howling earlier. It would be too dangerous to try to fly back tonight.

Too dangerous for someone to try to fly out here tonight or even to take a boat. Knowing how protective Trent was of his sister and how worried he was about her, Rory pointed to the radio. "You need to talk to your brother," he said. "Make sure he doesn't try to get out here."

Brittney wrapped her arms around herself and nodded. "It sounds like a storm's coming."

"The storm's been here," Rory said. Ever since she'd done that story about Ethan and the plane crash, the storm had been brewing. Then it had just been a far-off rumble of thunder, a warning of what was to come.

The past.

It had come back to get Rory.

He had to make sure that it wasn't out there now. "I need to make sure the chopper is secure." And that nobody had made their way onto the island already. "But first I'll connect you with the firehouse radio where someone should be able to get patched through to Trent's cell," he said. "And I'll give you some privacy."

Brittney narrowed those pretty topaz eyes and studied his face. "Can I tell Trent what you told me?"

He nodded. "It's fine." It was all going to come out, anyway. Because probably the only way to protect her...was to put himself in even more danger...

Once the truth got out, nobody would have any reason to try to stop Brittney anymore. But him...

He still had that hit out on him. So he'd have to go back into hiding, have to leave this life as Rory VanDam and the people in it behind him because he didn't want any more lives lost because of him. "And tell Trent to sit tight on the mainland," he said. "He can't try to get out here tonight. It's too dangerous."

So was staying here with her...

Staring at her across the table as they'd eaten and drunk wine had had Rory hoping that it wasn't just one night, like the aberration making love with her had been.

A one-off.

A dream.

Something he wouldn't be able to repeat...even if he didn't get killed. If his old enemies didn't come for him, Rory was making new enemies among his team. They wouldn't like that he'd kept the truth from them.

And Trent probably wouldn't accept it as easily as his sister had. Hopefully he wouldn't risk his life trying to get out here, though, trying to get to her.

Now if the killer had...

Maybe it would all be over tonight.

Rory turned on the radio and connected it to the firehouse, then he handed the speaker and headphones to Brittney and walked to the door. When he opened it, cold air and icy rain rushed in, soaking him.

"Rory!" Brittney called to him.

But he ducked his head down and headed out into the storm. It was the lesser threat of all the ones he'd recently faced, like his feelings for Brittney. He didn't just trust her, he was beginning to fall for her.

And he couldn't do that…not when they both had so much to lose: their lives.

THE DOOR CLOSED behind Rory, but the cold stayed inside the cabin, chilling Brittney deeply. What if that person who'd been shooting at them had managed to catch up to them somehow?

What if he or she was out there, waiting for Rory? He wasn't armed.

As a former lawman, wouldn't he have a weapon somewhere around? Some kind of gun or taser? Something to protect himself, especially when there was a hit out on his life…

No. On Mario's life.

"Brittney!" Trent's voice crackled through the headphones she'd slipped on.

She pressed the button on the microphone and leaned forward. "Trent."

"Stanley said he patched the call through the radio. Are you on the island with Rory?"

"Yes."

"Sit tight. We're trying to figure out how to get there tonight—"

"No!" she shouted, and her voice echoed in her headphones, making her flinch at the volume. "It's too dangerous."

"Why? What's happened? What has he done?"

"Rory hasn't done anything." But save her, protect her, feed her and make love to her.

She sucked in a breath as she realized she was falling for him. And she had only his word that he was who and what he said he was.

What if she was wrong to trust him?

What if he was lying to her?

But why?

Unless he had been the one responsible for the crash.

"Rory's not even his real name," Trent reminded her.

"No, it's not," she agreed.

"He admitted that to you?"

"Yes, he told me all about his past, and the plane crash," she said.

The headphones crackled. Brittney didn't know if that was just static on the line or her brother trying to talk to her. "What?" she asked. "Are you there?"

"Yeah, I'm waiting for you to tell me what he told you," Trent said.

And Brittney hesitated. Dare she share Rory's secrets?

"Maybe it's better that you don't know," she admitted. For Trent's sake, but mostly for Rory's.

Trent groaned. "If it's that bad, you shouldn't know, either."

"Rory is not the bad guy," Brittney insisted. "But there are some dangerous people after him." She didn't want her brother to be one of them.

"You need to get away from him," Trent said. "Now."

The wind howled so loudly that the windows rattled. Then sleet slashed across the glass. Rory shouldn't have gone out in this, not even to secure the helicopter.

Was that all he was doing?

Or had he taken off and left her here?

"Rory won't hurt me," she said, but she felt a pang in her heart even as she made the claim. He wouldn't hurt her physically, but if he'd taken off, even with the intent of keeping her safe, she was going to be hurt.

He'd already left her once, at the hotel.

And this time they hadn't even made love first.

"The weather's bad, Trent. Don't do anything stupid," she said.

Instead of being offended, he chuckled. "I'm not used to you talking to me like this..."

"Like I'm the calm sensible one and you're..."

"You," he teased.

She wasn't calm and sensible, either. She was scared to death. Not of what she'd learned or even of that killer.

She was scared that something had happened to Rory. He'd been gone for a while. Maybe she needed to go and look for him...

Make sure he hadn't fallen on the rock when he'd gone back up to the helicopter. Or that the killer wasn't out there, that he or she hadn't hurt Rory or worse...

"I need to go, Trent," she said.

"Brittney! You can't go anywhere, either."

"I meant off the radio." But she intended to go somewhere, wherever she had to in order to find Rory.

"Brittney, you need to be careful," Trent said in his best big brotherly voice of concern.

"I'm always careful," she said. But even she couldn't say it without smiling.

Trent snorted. "I mean it. I don't like this, any of it."

"Rory's a good guy," she said. But she wondered now if she was trying to convince her brother or herself.

"Even if that's true, that doesn't mean he's good for you," Trent pointed out.

And it was a valid point.

One Brittney chose to ignore as she'd begun to ignore

most of the unsolicited advice she received. "Stay where you are," she told him. "Don't worry about me."

She wasn't sure how to sign off the radio. But she pushed buttons until the headphones stopped crackling and whatever lights had been lit up went dark.

Just like the cabin had begun to do as the fire died down. She needed to find Rory, make sure he was all right. But she didn't even make it across the room to the door before it opened.

The wind swept into the room along with the hard pellets of sleet and rain. Had the door blown open? Because she didn't see anyone.

Then a dark shadow stumbled across the threshold, his arms laden down with wood. Rory's hair and jacket were soaked, some of the ice clinging to his hair and his chafed skin.

Brittney rushed forward and closed the door behind him, shutting out the wind and rain.

"It's getting cold," Rory said. "We're going to need more wood than this…" He dropped his armload near the hearth and headed back toward the door, as if he intended to go back out into the storm.

But Brittney stood in front of the door, her heart hammering. She'd been so scared that something had happened to him. That he wasn't coming back…

"What's wrong?" he asked with concern, and he slid his cold fingertips along her jaw. "Did Trent upset you? Is he coming out here anyway, despite the storm?"

She shrugged. "I don't know. I tried to talk him out of it."

"Did you tell him about me?"

"I told him you're a good man," she said.

He closed his eyes then and leaned forward, pressing his

forehead against hers. "If I was, I wouldn't want you again like I do..." he murmured, his voice gruff with desire.

Her heart hammered even faster and harder. And she reached up to wrap her arms around his neck, to pull his head the rest of the way down to hers.

He kissed her deeply, and she tasted the beef stew and the wine and her desire. It rushed up, overwhelming her with its intensity.

"I was so worried about you out there," she admitted. "Worried that something would happen to you."

He stared down into her face, his pale blue eyes so intense. "You were worried that I wasn't going to come back?"

She nodded.

"Did you think I'd take off and leave you here?"

"If you thought it would keep me safe, you might," she said.

He nodded, and rain droplets sprayed from his hair to her face. He wiped them away like he was wiping away tears. "I might," he agreed. "But I'm not sure either of us will be safe anywhere until..."

"Until what?" she asked. Then she stared up at him. "You have a plan?"

"Yeah."

She should want to hear it, want all the details, but at the moment, she just wanted him. "Tell me later," she said. Then she rose up on tiptoe and kissed him. She reached for his wet flannel jacket. After unbuttoning it, she pushed it from his shoulders. Then she reached for the bottom of his sweatshirt, tugging it up over his washboard stomach.

He was undoing her buttons and zippers, too, pushing down her jeans, pulling off her sweater...until she stood before him in only her bra and panties.

And even that was too much. She wanted nothing between them. So she unclasped her bra and let it drop onto the clothes that littered the hardwood floor around them. And she slid her panties down her hips.

Rory shoved down his jeans and boxers and stepped out of them and his boots, so that he was as naked as she was.

She shivered, a delicious shiver of anticipation for the pleasure she knew he could give her. But he must have mistaken it as cold because he picked her up and carried her to that big bed.

"Get under the covers," he said. "And I'll add more wood to the fire..." As he threw in a couple of logs, sparks hissed and sprayed back at him.

"Don't get burned!" she said with concern.

"I'm a hotshot," he reminded her as he walked to the bed wearing only a slight grin. The firelight played across his skin, turning it gold, making him look like the painting of some mythical god. "I'm used to playing with fire."

"You jumped out of the frying pan of your old career literally into the fire when you chose your new one, your new identity..." When he neared the bed, she reached for his hand, tugging him toward her. "Why?"

"Fires are more predictable than people," he said with a heavy sigh.

"Trent says that they're anything but, that they can shift and turn at a moment's notice."

"But you know they're always capable of great destruction, of harm," he said. "You can't always tell how badly a person might hurt you, but a fire leaves no illusions." He stared down at her intently, as if he suspected that she would hurt him.

She didn't want to. That was why she hadn't told Trent any of the details yet. Maybe not ever...

This would have been the story to make her career, to

take her permanently off the fluff pieces, but if it cost Rory his life, it wasn't worth it. Nothing was worth that...

But everything was worth this...

Making love with him again. Even though she was putting not just her life but her heart in danger, too.

She tugged on his hand again, pulling him down with her, onto her. His body covered hers, naked skin sliding over naked skin.

"I told you to get under the covers," he reminded her.

"I don't need them," she said. "I need you."

He groaned then kissed her, his mouth making love to hers. And as he kissed her, he touched her, sliding his fingertips in light caresses along her side, over the curve of her hip. He pulled back, panting for breath, and said, "You are so beautiful. So sexy..."

He was the sexy one. She touched him like he'd touched her, just gliding her fingertips along his skin. First it was cold, damp, from the sleet and the wind, but it heated as she touched him.

Then she lowered her hand and wrapped it around his erection, and he began to sweat, beads forming on his upper lip.

"You're dangerous, Brittney Townsend," he said. "You can hurt me more than anyone else."

Before she could ask what he meant, he kissed her again. And his hands continued to move over her, caressing her breasts, cupping them.

He brushed his thumbs over her nipples, and she moaned. The tension was winding up inside her, twisting her muscles into knots. Making her desperate for release...

Then he was inside her, filling her, and they moved together like they'd choreographed a dance. She arched and he thrust. Then finally the tension broke, and the orgasm moved through her with such force and pleasure that she had to cling to him.

Then he called out her name as he came, too. And she knew that he was just as dangerous to her as she was to him because she was definitely starting to fall for him.

And she hadn't ever wanted to fall for anyone, let alone someone in a dangerous career, someone she could lose like she'd lost her dad.

Way too soon...

Way before their time and way before she was ready to let them go...

THE KILLER WAITED inside the SUV, which rocked and shuddered as the wind battered it. Rain and sleet swept across it so thick and fast that the wipers couldn't keep the windshield clear.

And the driver had to peer through the rain and the darkness to see the dock by which they'd parked, waiting for the boat that was supposed to be coming, that would take them to where the reporter and the hotshot must have gone.

That island, which was part of a national forest, was where the hotshot firefighter also worked as a forest ranger. They'd asked around the bar in Northern Lakes about the helicopter and the man who flew it.

Rory VanDam.

The tall, lean blond guy didn't look anything like dark-haired burly Mario Mandretti. But Mario had been a disguise, a cover for the DEA agent. For the former special ops Marine. With the expert flying and that ability to escape death over and over, Rory VanDam had to be Mario.

The killer had been worried about the wrong thing this whole time, that the reporter's quest to delve deeper into the plane crash would have the FAA and the US Forest Service resuming a search for the wreckage. And DNA had been left behind when the bomb had been planted in the plane they'd known Mario would be flying. They just hadn't realized why he'd been flying it, that he'd gone through hotshot training. That he was a hotshot now.

How the hell hadn't *anyone* known that the DEA agent hadn't died? Why the hell had the DEA agent been hiding out here all this time, posing as some hotshot firefighter?

Why hadn't he gone to anyone? Let the authorities know he was alive?

Was it because he'd realized there was no one he could trust? That the people who wanted him dead were just too rich and too powerful to be stopped?

Chapter Twenty-One

Rory wanted to stay on the secluded island, in the cozy cabin, in that warm bed with Brittney forever. But he'd realized long ago, with the careers he'd chosen and the enemies he'd made, that forever wasn't possible for him.

Especially now.

The sun was shining. The storm had ended with the break of dawn. While the water was calmer now, there was still ice in it that could make it hard to get a boat to the island. But there had been time for someone to get another helicopter.

So they couldn't stay. They had to leave as quickly as they could before the shooter found them. But Brittney seemed as reluctant to go as he was.

She was making the bed that they'd messed up so many times last night, kicking off the blankets, tangling the sheets...as they made love. His pulse quickened just looking at it, at her, and his body hardened.

He grunted and shook his head. "We have to go, Brittney. Now."

She must have heard the urgency in his voice because she stepped back from the bed and pulled on her jacket and hooked her purse over her shoulder. "Okay..."

But instead of heading toward the door, Rory walked over to the desk in the corner. He didn't open any drawers, though. What he wanted wasn't inside it. He pulled it back from the wall to reveal a small safe between joists in that wall. His hand shook a bit when he twisted the lock and opened it.

There was a gun inside, his old Glock. It had come in handy while he and Ethan had been stranded those months in the mountains. But he hadn't used it since.

And the other thing. The small USB drive beside it, he hadn't used it at all. And he probably should have.

But in order to use it, he would have had to come out of hiding. He would have had to blow up the life he'd made for himself here in Northern Lakes with his hotshot team.

"You do have a gun," she said.

He nodded. "This will do more damage, though," he said as he handed the USB drive to her.

"What is this?" she asked.

"This is the proof," he replied.

"What?"

"This is a recording of the US Marshal who was with me on the plane. He gave it to me when he gave me a parachute to get off the plane before the bomb we found on it went off. He said it was my *insurance*. This will prove what I told you is true. It's the corroboration you need for that big story you've been chasing," he said. "Even bigger than Jonathan Canterbury IV."

She shook her head. "I don't want it."

"What?"

"The big story," she said. "I don't want to put you in danger because of it. If that family is still paying people to try to kill you, you will be in terrible danger."

"If someone is after you because of that damn plane crash, because of me," he said, "the only way to make you safe is for you to tell the story, the whole story. Then there is no reason for anyone to try to stop you anymore."

"But those people, that family, want revenge on you," she said.

"They don't want revenge on you," he assured her. "You won't have to worry about losing Trent, like you lost your dad."

Tears suddenly filled her eyes, either over the loss of her dad or maybe the thought of losing her brother.

"Nobody will die because of you," he assured her.

"You might," she said, her voice cracking. "If I do this story, those people will know you're alive."

He sighed. "Yeah, they won't like that…" But who were they anymore?

He didn't even know what had become of the Falcone family. Amelia's dad had sworn out the hit on him, the vendetta, but he'd already been pretty old five years ago. That was why he'd had his son take over his business interests.

The drugs. Then after Felix Jr. had died, Felix Sr. had promised the empire to his daughter if she killed Mario. He'd thought she was different than her family, like Rory was different from his.

And just as he'd left his family for the service and never looked back, he hadn't wanted to look back at the Falcone family. He also hadn't wanted to draw any attention to his past, to himself. Until now…

"I think it's already too late for that, Brittney. You need to go with your story." He pointed to the flash drive she held. "With that."

Her brow furrowed as she stared up at him. "I don't understand you…" She shook her head. "You wanted nothing to do with me, with the press…and I understand why that was. But why did it change?"

Because he'd fallen for her.

He couldn't tell her that now, though, not when he was probably going to have to go into hiding again soon. And she wouldn't be able to hide, not with as famous as she was becoming. She was on the verge of the career she wanted, that she deserved. He couldn't take any of that away from her.

"Somebody's trying to kill us," he reminded her. "That's why everything changed, and it's why we have to get the hell out of here."

This time, he didn't wait for her to move. After tucking the gun into the waistband of his jeans, he grabbed her hand and urged her toward the door. As they headed up the path to the rock and the helicopter, he heard another motor.

Someone was coming.

"We have to hurry," he said. If they didn't get away with that tape, Brittney would never get her story. Nobody would probably ever learn the truth about what had happened.

But he wasn't sure that he knew the whole truth now. Maybe there was more going on than he'd even realized. Because was it really some minions for the Falcone family that were after them both?

The threats to Brittney and the blow to his head. Or had the saboteur been responsible for some of the things?

BRITTNEY HAD BEEN on edge ever since they'd left Bear Isle. He had proof. And he'd given it to her.

The responsibility of it weighed on her, making her bag heavier as she'd carried it from the helicopter to his truck. The entire flight, the entire drive…they'd both been so on edge, so certain that another attack was about to come.

Someone shooting at them.

Who?

Would she find out from playing that flash drive?

"You can play it," Rory said. Somehow, he'd known exactly what she was thinking. But they'd already pulled up to the firehouse.

Other trucks and vehicles were parked in the lot. A lot of the team must have been there. The side door opened and Trent walked out, Trick close beside him. Trick hit his shoulder and looked up, meeting her gaze through the windshield.

"Play it," Rory said.

But Trent was opening her door, pulling her from the passenger's seat into his arms. "Oh, my God, thank God you're all right," he said, his voice gruff with emotion. "I was so afraid I was going to lose you."

"I'm right here," she assured him as she pulled back. His weren't the arms she wanted around her, comforting her, holding her.

But Trent didn't give her a chance to reach for Rory again. Nor did Trick. He was standing by the driver's side. "Braden talked to my dad."

Rory's breath had a catch in it. "Your dad is a good man."

"Mack knew you were more than you were saying you were," Trick said. "He knew because you know my brother Mack. My brother vouched for you with my dad."

Rory's lips curved into a slight grin. "Mack…"

And Brittney didn't know which one had brought out that affectionate smile, the father or the son who were both apparently named Mack.

Trick continued, "My dad said that he kept quiet because Mack told him you had your reasons, whatever they were, for laying low."

Rory turned toward her again. "Play them that recording. That's what's on the drive."

"Recording?" Trent asked.

Brittney pulled the flash drive from her purse with a

shaking hand. "This. His proof... But I need something to put it in."

"Let's use the computer in Braden's office," Trick said. "Let's play it there."

Brittney got swept up between the big red-haired hotshot and her big dark-haired brother. They hurried her toward the firehouse, as if worried that someone might shoot at her again, and once inside, they rushed her to Braden's windowless office. He glanced up from his desk then widened his eyes and released a ragged sigh of relief.

"Thank God you're all right."

She smiled. "I never expected you to be happy to see me."

Braden chuckled. "Well, I am, very happy that you're all right."

Trent, with his arm wound around her, tugged her closer. "Me, too."

"You're not too embarrassed to claim me now," she murmured.

He hugged her now with both arms. "I'm really sorry, Brittney. Very sorry that I've given you a hard time."

"Not just me," she said. But she couldn't see around her brother to Rory. All she could do was grant his wish. She pulled back from Trent and held out the flash drive to Braden. "We need to play the recording on this."

Braden took it from her hand and pushed it into the side of his desktop. Then he pressed his fingers on the keyboard. "There's just one file on this. An audio file."

Her stomach flipped and dropped. Did she want to hear this? Did she want to know everything about Rory?

"Why do you want to play this?" he asked.

"It's proof." Trick was the one who said it now, not Rory.

She glanced back over her shoulder. But he must have been standing behind Trick. She couldn't see him.

"Proof of what?" Braden asked, but instead of waiting for an answer, he pressed a key and a voice emanated from the speaker on his computer.

"Your DEA agent crossed the wrong family," a male voice was saying. "Felix Falcone is not going to forgive or forget that this Mario whatever cost him his son and his daughter."

"She tried to kill him," another male voice remarked. "She would have if I hadn't been there."

"It wasn't supposed to be you there."

The man gasped. "Who was it supposed to be?"

"Me. I've been paid for this job. To make sure that Mario dies."

"You're a federal agent…"

Brittney held her breath, waiting for a name. But neither of them used each other's.

The federal agent continued, "You can't help him start over with some new identity."

"Why not?"

"Because you're on Falcone's hit list, too, for killing his daughter. The only way for you to stay alive and keep your family alive is to give him up."

"I don't have any family," the man replied.

"What about your life? Don't you care about that?"

"Sounds like I'm a dead man anyway."

"Be a dead rich man. Start over yourself, someplace warm and far away."

The US Marshal sighed. "Sounds tempting…"

Sounded sickening to Brittney, that the people who were supposed to protect Rory had given him up instead. But the woman who was supposed to have loved him had given him up, too. No. She'd tried to kill him herself.

"He's flying you somewhere, isn't he?" the agent asked.

"Make sure that plane goes down and the pilot with it." He chuckled. "Like the captain going down with his ship."

"Do you recognize those voices?" Brittney asked, and she tried peering around Trent and Trick again. "Rory? Do you recognize those voices?"

Trick and Trent both turned around, but Rory wasn't there. He'd slipped away. To go where?

Then she remembered what she'd heard as they'd headed up to the helicopter. The other motor.

But that hadn't been Trent heading toward the island. He was here. So who was there?

"We have to stop him," she said, and she tried to get around Trent to head out the door, too. But her brother held on to her arms, keeping her between him and his boss's desk. "He's going back."

"Back where?" Trent asked. "To his old life?"

She shook her head. "Back to the island. Someone was heading there when we were leaving. It was probably that person who's been shooting at us, trying to stop us."

"The US Marshal or the agent?" Trick asked from behind her brother.

"I think the Marshal died in the plane crash. There was a bomb in the cockpit, and he made Rory and the others parachute out. Before he did, he gave that recording to Rory, maybe so he would know not to trust anyone."

"What do we do with it?" Braden asked. "If we hand it over to the authorities, we risk this agent getting it or destroying it."

Brittney turned around and reached for the USB drive, pulling it out of Braden's computer. "I know what to do."

"This isn't just some story," Trent said. "This is Rory's life."

"Yes, it is, so go after him!" she said. "Don't let him face that killer alone!" She wanted to go, too, but she knew that since her brother wouldn't even let her out the door there was no way he would let her go back to that island, back to danger.

To the danger that Rory was facing alone.

He had a gun. But did it even work anymore? Would he be able to save himself like he had her so many times? Or was he determined to go back and confront the person in order to protect her once and for all?

FBI AGENT BARRY SHELTON had a trace on Felix Falcone's landline. But he'd had to get far enough away from the damn island before he got enough reception on his phone to play the call that had come in.

"Falcone? Felix?" a familiar voice said.

"Uh, yeah, this is Felix," the old man replied, his voice weak.

He was weak now. But he still paid. He had no power anymore, but he had money. And nobody to give it to...

"Felix, this is Mario," the former DEA agent told him.

"Mario?"

"Yes, Mario Mandretti," he said. "Do you remember me?"

"Uh, I... I don't know..."

"I was a friend of your son Felix's, and I was close to Amelia, too," he said.

"Felix?" Felix asked, and his voice was muffled, as if he was calling out for him. He chuckled. "I don't know where that boy is off to. Probably down at the basketball courts. And Amelia... She'll be playing with her dolls..."

"Yes," the man replied. "Yes, she will be."

"What's your name again?" Felix asked.

"Mario."

"I don't remember you," he said.

"What about any federal agents?" the man asked. "Do you remember them? Paying them?"

"Paid a lot of them…paid a lot of them…but I don't remember why…"

"I know," the man calling himself Mario again assured him. "I know why, and I know who. I have a recording of his voice. You don't have to pay him any more money, Felix. He didn't earn it."

Barry cursed. A recording.

He'd figured the Marshal might have recorded him. Barry hadn't trusted him. That was why he'd followed him and figured out he was getting on that plane with Mario. So, while they were at that training center in Washington, Barry had planted the bomb in the cockpit of the plane. He'd watched Mario inspect it, and then when he'd gone back inside the building, Barry had acted fast, planting the bomb he'd brought along.

But he'd had to move so fast, he wasn't sure it was going to work. Or what evidence he might have left behind. But when he'd heard about the crash, he'd figured his plan had played out how he'd intended. But the pilot hadn't gone down with the plane.

He was alive.

He was Rory VanDam.

And he had evidence.

It should be gone now, though. If it had been on the island, it would be gone soon.

Unless…

Unless Rory VanDam had already done something with it…

Had already given it to someone?

That reporter. She hadn't dropped the damn story. After she'd run the first story about Jonathan Canterbury, Barry had tapped her phone line. He knew what calls she'd been making, who she'd been trying to contact and question. And she hadn't stopped reaching out, trying to follow up and find out more about the crash.

If she'd gotten that damn recording...

Barry had to do whatever he could to get that recording back. He'd made too much money, but he'd also advanced too far in his career to give it all up for somebody who should have died five years ago.

Chapter Twenty-Two

Rory figured the FBI probably still had a tap on Falcone's line. When he'd gone undercover with the DEA, they'd co-ordinated with the FBI on the investigation.

After talking to the man, who obviously had dementia or Alzheimer's disease, Rory wasn't sure if his calls were still being monitored. But just in case, he'd made certain to mention the recording. But would his plan work how he wanted it to?

Would it flush out the killer toward him or toward…?

Rory sucked in a breath as he realized what he might have done. And his hand slipped a bit on the control of the helicopter, making it dip toward the lake below. Through the windows, he could see the smoke.

The son of a bitch had set the island on fire.

And that had been even before he would have heard that wiretap, if there was even still a tap on the line. The son of a bitch had set Rory's sanctuary on fire.

His heart ached for the animals and the cabin and all the trees and nature. Then he noticed through the window that a boat was heading toward the island.

A US Forest Service boat. His team members were heading out there. They would save what they could.

And Rory had a feeling, since that other boat was already gone, that he had someone he needed to save, too. If he wasn't already too late.

If he hadn't just made a horrible mistake by baiting a murderer...

BRITTNEY WAS SUPPOSED to lock herself into Braden's office and open the door to nobody until Heather got there or the hotshots got back from the island. That was the order that Trent had given her before he left with his crew.

But she'd had things to do.

A promise to keep to Rory.

She should have made him make her a promise, as well. A promise to stay alive.

Where the hell had he gone?

Straight to danger? Or maybe he'd taken off entirely, knowing that his secret was soon to be revealed. It was what he wanted, she reminded herself, as she wrapped up and sent off not just the audio file of the recording but also a video of her coverage of it.

She wasn't sure if her station would play it. But she knew somebody who would. And she didn't even care if she took all the credit for it. Avery Kincaid had done the first story about the hotshots back when the Northern Lakes arsonist had been terrorizing them and the town. Avery had once worked out of the news station in Detroit where Brittney worked. But after that story, Avery had been offered a job in New York City and had moved there. She was Brittney's idol, who Brittney wanted to be. Career-wise.

Maybe even personal-wise.

Avery had married one of the hotshots. Dawson Hess. Not that Brittney intended to marry a hotshot. She just wanted to make sure that a certain endangered one of them stayed alive. And because Avery knew the hotshots well, Brittney trusted her to do the right thing with the recording and the video she'd sent her. The video she'd taken outside Braden's office but still inside the firehouse, in the conference room on the third floor in front of the podium the superintendent used for hotshot meetings.

While waiting for the large file to finish sending, Brittney walked over to the windows and peered down at the street below. A black vehicle pulled up outside the firehouse. A long black SUV.

A chill rushed over her.

Then a man stepped out of the driver's door. His hair was salt-and-pepper, and he wore dark shades. He just had that look…that federal agent look to him.

Her pulse quickened. Was this the guy who'd tried running her down? Who had shot at her?

She rushed to the door of the conference room, intent on locking it to keep out the federal agent. But then she heard Annie's bark echo up the stairwell from below.

Annie and Stanley were down there, in the garage area. Stanley was polishing the trucks. Maybe the guy wouldn't hurt him. It wasn't as if Stanley understood anything that was going on, he just knew that people he cared about were frequently in danger.

But then he worked in a firehouse, so everyone he worked with put themselves in danger. Stanley hadn't signed up for that job, though. He was just a sweet kid.

A kid that Brittney needed to protect. But how…?

Maybe she was overreacting, maybe this person driving that black SUV wasn't the same one who'd tried running her down, who'd shot at her and Rory.

She slipped out of the conference room and started down the stairs to the ground floor.

Annie's bark got more frantic, and then she growled. This

person was a stranger to her, unlike the person who'd attacked Rory the night of the holiday party. So maybe there had always been two different threats to them.

"I'm sorry," Stanley said, and his voice sounded strained, as if he was wrestling with Annie. "She usually likes everybody."

"I'm not really a dog person," a man replied. And his voice sent a chill running down Brittney's spine. She recognized it all too well from that recording.

She hadn't been paranoid to think he might be that FBI agent—she'd been right. And now she had no idea what to do...

"If you're here to talk to Braden or any of the hotshots, they're not here," Stanley said. "They probably won't be back for a couple of hours."

And Brittney nearly groaned. The teenager had inadvertently let the man know exactly how much time he had before he might be caught. Because she was absolutely certain that he intended to commit a crime...

Especially when he asked, "What about Brittney Townsend, the reporter. Is she here?"

"Uh..."

Annie barked louder, as if the dog knew Stanley shouldn't answer this man's questions.

"She's supposed to be locked inside Braden's office," Stanley said.

The kid was sweet, too sweet to realize that he shouldn't always tell the truth, especially to strangers.

"Why would she be locked up like that?" the man asked with amusement in his voice.

"She's in danger," Stanley replied. "Somebody's been trying to hurt her."

"Why?" the man asked. "Has she been putting her nose where it doesn't belong?"

Had he seen her shadow on the stairs? Did he realize that she was standing there, listening?

Stanley chuckled. "That's what some of the guys say. Rory used to say it the most..."

"I bet he did," the man remarked.

"But now he seems to like her..." Stanley muttered as if he was confused about Rory's turnaround.

Brittney was, too. Had Rory developed feelings for her? Feelings like she had for him?

Where was he?

Had he gone back to the island?

Or was he around here somewhere? Ready to rush to her rescue again?

She couldn't count on that, though. She had to figure out how to save herself and Stanley and Annie, too.

"If he liked her, he wouldn't have let her keep pursuing her story, and he certainly wouldn't have given her what I think he gave her..."

"I... I don't know what he gave her," Stanley stammered. "I... I don't know anything..."

But from the fearful crack in his voice, Brittney knew that he'd figured out that the man he was talking to was not a good man. Annie had already figured it out because she kept barking and growling.

"Shut up that dog!" the man yelled. "Or I will!"

"Annie," Stanley whined at the dog.

And Brittney could hear the struggle between the kid and the animal. He was trying to hold on to her leash. He was getting out of breath, and Annie's nails were clawing against the concrete as she tried to drag him closer to the man.

They needed to get farther away. Out of the line of fire...

Out of the damn firehouse…

Brittney edged down a few more steps until she could peek into the garage area. The big doors were closed, and the man stood between Stanley and the side door he'd entered. It was closed now.

They were all shut inside with this man unless Brittney could figure out how the overhead doors opened. If it was possible there would be witnesses, the agent wouldn't try to hurt Stanley or Annie.

But as she peered around, she saw that the controls were on the other side of the garage. Not far from where Stanley stood. If only she could catch his attention…

But he was focused on his dog, on trying to pull her back from the man. Brittney had caught someone's attention, though, as the man stared up at her. Then he drew his weapon and pointed it, not at her, but at the kid. "You know why I'm here," he said. "So hand it over."

"How…" Her voice cracked. "How do you know about that?"

He smirked. "How do you think?"

Her pulse quickened even more, and she hurried down the last of the steps to join them in the garage area. "Rory told you? What did you do to him?" She wanted to hit him, to shove him back, to shout at him for hurting Rory. Because surely he would have had to hurt him to get him to say so much…

The man chuckled and nodded. "Uh-huh, I was right."

Brittney swore. He'd tricked her into confirming his suspicion. He hadn't known for certain that she had the recording until she'd just admitted it. This was a trick that, as a reporter, she knew and shouldn't have fallen for herself.

"Hand it over," the man said.

She lifted her empty hands. "I don't have it."

He pointed the gun barrel at Stanley, and she edged between it and the kid. Annie jumped on the back of her legs, nearly knocking her down. She turned and pushed the dog back along with Stanley, trying to steer them behind one of the engines, out of the line of fire. And as she shoved, she looked at those controls for the overhead doors, hoping that Stanley would notice what she was looking at...

That he would understand what she needed him to do.

"Get that dog under control or I will shoot it right now!" the man shouted.

And Stanley pulled harder on Annie's leash, pulling her behind the engine.

Some of the tension eased from Brittney. She didn't want them getting hurt. She didn't want anyone getting hurt but this man.

"You damn well have that recording!" he yelled at her. "And you need to hand it over or I will shoot you right in the head. And I'll kill that kid and the dog, too."

"Then you won't find the recording," Brittney said. "I hid it." In plain sight on the third floor, but hopefully he wouldn't make it that far.

At least not before the recording and the video file finished sending to Avery Kincaid.

"You're going to get it now," he said. "And bring it back down here or I'll shoot the kid and the dog."

"You're going to shoot us all anyway," Brittney said. "We've all seen your face. I know you have no intention of letting us live."

Stanley let out a little cry of fear, and Brittney glanced at him to see tears in his eyes. She tried to make eye contact with him before she looked at the controls again. *Please, Stanley, open those damn doors...*

If only he could read her damn mind...

The agent laughed. "You're not wrong, Ms. Townsend. I am going to kill you all. I guess it just matters how you want to die. Slowly and painfully or quick and relatively painless."

She snorted. "I don't want to die at all." And she certainly didn't want Stanley's young life cut short. If only he would move toward those damn doors...

"Get that recording," the guy threatened.

She shook her head. "It's too late anyway."

"What do you mean?" he asked, his body tensing.

"You don't think I would share that kind of bombshell recording the minute I received it? You don't think I got that out to as many news sources as possible to pick it up and run with it?" she asked. "Your voice is going to be played on every news program at every station in the country. It's over for you, Agent. It's all over."

He lowered his brow a bit. "You don't know my name. It's not mentioned on that recording?"

"You don't think someone will recognize that voice as yours?" she asked. "I recognized it the minute I heard you talking to Stanley. You don't think it can be voice matched to yours? That your coworkers and the US Marshals won't start pulling your financials and figure out that you took money to carry out a hit on a DEA agent?" She laughed and shook her head. "Then you're not as smart as you think you are."

"Neither are you, Ms. Townsend," he said. "Because you just pointed out to me that I have nothing to lose. I might as well just kill you and the kid right now." And he raised the gun and moved his finger toward the trigger.

Brittney moved, shoving Stanley and Annie farther back behind the engine as the first shot rang out.

Chapter Twenty-Three

He was too late. Rory had known it the minute he'd seen the black SUV parked outside the firehouse. And he'd made a horrible mistake on that phone call.

He'd thought mentioning the recording would get the agent to come out in the open, to come after him, or at least get him to leave Northern Lakes, to leave the whole damn country for one with no extradition. Then Brittney would be safe.

But he should have known that the guy was smart. Or he wouldn't have gotten away with his crimes for as long as he had. So the guy had figured out to whom Rory would have given that recording.

The reporter.

Brittney.

And somehow he'd figured out she was here, at the firehouse. Or maybe he'd just wound up here after checking the hotel and other places in town.

Rory had snuck up to the firehouse, to that side door, since none of the big ones were open. But when he touched the knob, it didn't turn. It was locked. He doubted Stanley had remembered to do that since he rarely did.

And the kid was here. His car was in the parking lot.

And Annie was here. Rory could hear her barking.

She sounded ferocious for once. But underneath that ferociousness was an element of fear, too. Fear probably more for her people than for herself.

Annie was a protector.

And for years, Rory had been, too. But he hadn't done everything he could have the past five years to protect people. He should have tried to figure out who the hell this agent was earlier. He should have made sure he would never hurt anyone else again.

Rory pulled his keys from his back pocket. Thank God he had one to the firehouse. All the hotshots did. He slid it into the lock now and slowly and softly pushed open the door a bit.

Annie barked louder, but she didn't give him up. Maybe she hadn't even noticed him. She was focused on the man with the gun.

But Brittney stood between that man and the teenager and the dog. She had made certain that barrel was pointed at her, not the kid.

And Rory's heart swelled with more love for her. She was so damn brave. So strong. So smart.

He listened as she tried to talk to the agent, as she tried to buy more time for her and Stanley and Annie. Had she really done with the recording what she'd claimed?

Was it really all over for the agent?

He must have thought so because he flicked off the safety and began to squeeze the trigger. And Rory squeezed his, firing off a shot.

He got the guy in the arm, spinning him around...toward Rory. But when Rory fired again, there was just a click, as either the gun jammed or it was out of ammo.

He hadn't checked it when he'd grabbed it out of the safe. He hadn't checked it once during the nearly five years it had been locked inside the safe because he hadn't wanted anything more to do with guns. He'd wanted to leave that life and that violence behind him and just be Rory VanDam, a hotshot firefighter.

But he'd always known that it would catch up to him someday. He'd just hoped that nobody else would get hurt because of him.

"It really is you," the agent murmured as he stared at him. "These past five years, I thought for sure you were dead, just like Mitchell."

"I'm not dead," Rory said. "You didn't kill me the first time you tried, but you killed some other people, some innocent people."

"You think Marshall Mitchell was innocent?" The FBI agent snorted. "He was willing to take bribes. He was willing to kill."

"He only said that because he was setting you up, getting you on that recording," Rory said. "He was going to deal with you once he got me safely established in my new life."

The agent snorted again, then grimaced as he moved his shoulder. But he grasped his gun tightly in his other hand, the barrel pointed at Rory now.

Not Stanley and Brittney…

But had they been hit?

Rory couldn't even see them now. They were behind one of the engines. And all he could hear was Annie whining…

Had the dog been hurt?

Or was she whining because one of the humans with her had been hit?

"He recorded me to get more money out of me," the agent replied. "He probably wanted a bigger cut."

Rory shook his head. "Not everyone is as greedy as you are…"

The agent laughed. "God, you're an idiot. Everybody has a price. Money. Or fame. With this reporter here..." He gestured behind him with the gun, but at least he wasn't pointing at her any longer. But maybe that was because she wasn't moving...

His heart hammered with fear that she'd already been hit. That she was lying there bleeding...

Needing help.

Rory had to help her.

"She couldn't wait to send that recording out everywhere," the agent continued. "She used it, used you, just for her career."

A little jab of pain and doubt struck Rory's heart. Was the agent right? Had Brittney been using him for her career just like Amelia?

While Brittney's job meant a lot to her, people meant a lot to her, as well. Her brother...

And even though she didn't know him, she'd put herself between Stanley and that gun. She'd been doing her best to protect him and his dog.

The dog continued to whine.

"You're wrong about Mitchell," he said, just trying to stall for time now. While he couldn't fire his weapon, maybe he could find one close enough in the garage that he could use. Like a wrench or an axe. "Why do you think he didn't tell you my new identity?"

"It doesn't matter," the agent said. "He died. He's gone. And soon you will be, too."

"Why?" Rory asked. "Felix Falcone doesn't even know who I am let alone want me dead anymore. He's senile. He doesn't even know his kids are dead let alone want to avenge their deaths. You don't need to do this. To do any of this..."

The agent glanced at his bleeding shoulder and shook

his head. "It's too late now. Too late. She already sent the recording. It's all over, and I'm not going down alone. I'm taking everyone with me that I can."

And he pointed that gun directly at Rory's heart.

BRITTNEY WAS HURT. But it was more her heart than her body. She would probably have bruises from how hard she'd hit the concrete when she'd pushed Stanley and Annie back and flung herself behind that truck.

The bullet the agent had fired had struck the rear bumper of the rig and bounced back. But another gun had fired, too, the shot echoing so loudly in the garage that it had scared Annie. And Stanley...

While the dog whined, the teenager cried. With his eyes closed, he couldn't see the gestures Brittney was making at him. So she crawled closer, while the two men talked, and she whispered in Stanley's ear.

And finally he opened his eyes and met her gaze. There was fear in his brown eyes but also resolve. He knew what he had to do.

She listened to the men's conversation, waiting for that moment, that distraction that would give Stanley time to get to the controls and get him and Annie out of the garage. And she heard what the agent said about her using Rory just for fame, for her career.

Would he believe that?

Would he think that was all she'd wanted from him, to further her career?

Or would he know that she'd fallen for him?

She didn't dare speak out now. It was better to be as quiet as they could be, so that the agent would forget about them for now. But he hadn't because he said even more, that because she'd sent that recording out nothing mattered anymore.

And she knew in that moment that he was going to kill Rory.

She nodded at Stanley, who moved surprisingly fast toward those controls. He smacked all the buttons, sending the doors up, the motors grinding.

But over that noise, she could hear the gunshots. The bullets pinging off the metal. She hoped that Stanley had followed through with the rest of her plan, that he and Annie had gotten out through one of those big doors.

That they were safe at least. Because she could hear shoes scraping on concrete, could see feet moving toward her. And she knew that she wasn't safe.

And Rory…

She was so damn scared that he'd been hit or worse. That he was dead…

For real this time.

TRENT WAS EXHAUSTED from sleepless nights and worrying and that damn futile trip out to the island. He'd seen the helicopter. Rory hadn't even landed. Maybe he hadn't been able to because of the smoke and the flames.

Or maybe he'd realized what Trent had…that Rory's would-be killer wasn't there any longer. He must have set the fire and taken off.

For where?

Northern Lakes.

Brittney was there. Heather on her way. Two of the people he loved most in the world. Two of the smartest, most resourceful people he knew. Surely, they would be all right.

And yet he had this sick feeling, this chill that he couldn't get rid of. He made his team leave early and head back.

And nobody had argued with him, as if they'd all realized what he had.

That something wasn't right.

That people they cared about were still in danger, and it wasn't just Brittney and Heather, but Rory, too. He was the one the killer wanted dead the most, the one he thought he'd killed years ago.

Until Brittney had started digging up the past, pursuing a story that the agent hadn't wanted anyone to pursue.

The closer they got to Northern Lakes, the more anxious everyone got. Braden and Trick kept checking their phones.

Trent checked his, too.

He had no messages from Brittney. But then he wasn't even sure she had her phone or if she'd left it in that hotel room when the killer had been coming for her.

When he'd hurt Ethan…

Ethan was back in Northern Lakes, too, but he was supposed to be resting. Tammy had promised that she'd take care of him, that she would make sure nobody hurt him, including himself.

He smiled a bit at how his friend had met his match in the salon owner. And Trent had met his match, as well, with Detective Heather Bolton.

A text came in from her:

I'm here, heading to the firehouse

She'd sent it several minutes ago, but it probably hadn't come through until the boat had gotten closer to land and cell reception.

He wasn't the only one who'd gotten a message. Trick was staring at his phone and murmured, "I'll be damned…"

"What?" Braden asked.

Hopefully it wasn't something from Trick's significant other. Henrietta "Hank" Rowlins was a hotshot, too, but she and Michaela had been busy at their firehouse up in St. Paul, nearly an hour north of Northern Lakes. Hopefully they were safe.

"I think Mack's in town," Trick remarked.

"Your dad?" Braden asked.

Trick shook his head. "My brother..." There was awe and surprise in his voice, like he couldn't believe it, like he hadn't expected to see him.

Maybe his relationship with that sibling was strained or strange. Trent's relationship with his only sibling had been strained, too. He'd been so angry with her for investigating his team, for running that article about them and Ethan and that damn plane crash.

He'd barely spoken to her lately. And when his life had been threatened, he'd pushed her away instead of pulling her closer. He'd thought he was doing the right thing, protecting her.

Just like she'd tried protecting him when she hadn't told him about those threats. She hadn't even told him about that creepy producer of hers.

That was his fault, that she hadn't trusted him to respect her, to protect her without trying to smother or control her. Not that she'd ever listened to him...

So no doubt she hadn't locked herself in Braden's office like he'd ordered her to do.

As the boat pulled up to the dock, Trent jumped off before even tying it off. He needed to get back to the firehouse, to make sure Brittney was okay.

To find out where the hell Rory was...

And Heather...

Braden and Trick caught up to him, running alongside

him as they rushed toward Braden's truck. They'd ridden with the hotshot superintendent to the dock.

Braden clicked the locks, and they all jumped into the vehicle. The boss must have felt his urgency because he drove fast, making the trip to town and to the firehouse in record speed.

But the lights that flashed weren't behind them. No officer followed him. They were already at the firehouse. Lights flashed on police cars and an ambulance. And parked alongside one of the curbs was that black SUV that had nearly run down his sister that night, that would have if not for Rory rescuing her.

Trent had been right to be worried. Something bad had definitely happened here. Had he lost anyone he loved? Everyone he loved?

Chapter Twenty-Four

Rory felt like he was in that coma again. He was caught somewhere between consciousness and sleep. And Ethan was right. He could hear voices around him.

"I'm so sorry, Trent," a female voice was saying. It wasn't Brittney's, though. It was huskier. Heather. The detective. "I got here too late."

Too late?

Too late for what? Was Brittney okay? Had she been shot like he'd feared? Then he'd been too late, too. He hadn't saved her at all.

Where was she?

He dragged his eyes open and peered around. He could see concrete and people's shoes. He was on the ground. He reached out, trying to shove himself up. "Brittney..." he murmured.

Big hands caught his shoulders, holding him down. "Take it easy," Owen said. "You've been hurt."

"Me?" He shook his head. "Brittney..."

Where was she?

He had to find her. She had to be here somewhere.

He turned his head and noticed what he'd missed before. The sheet. There was a sheet lying over someone. Blood stained it. He couldn't see who was under it.

The sheet covered the face of the person. Whoever it was hadn't survived.

"Brittney…" He coughed and gasped for breath as fear and grief overwhelmed him.

"You're aspirating, man. You've got to stop fighting me. Let me treat you."

"Help her…" he murmured, but he could see that it was already too late. Brittney was gone.

FURY COURSED THROUGH BRITTNEY. She'd never wanted to assault an officer before, not until Trooper Wells insisted on interrogating her instead of letting her go back inside the firehouse to check on Rory.

Was he going to make it?

How badly had he been hurt?

Those were the only questions she cared about, not the ones Trooper Wells was asking her. "Did you see the shooter?"

"What shooter? I saw that agent. He shot at me and Stanley and—" her voice cracked with fear and dread "—and he shot Rory. I need to check on Rory." She tried to step around the woman, but she'd trapped her between her body and the side of her state police SUV. She'd acted like she was going to put Brittney in the back seat and arrest her.

For what?

For trying to see the man she loved? The man who might be dying on that firehouse floor.

The blood had been spreading across his shirt when she'd scrambled over to him. And she'd tried stopping it with her hands, tried helping him. But then other people had rushed in. The police. Owen and another paramedic.

And she'd been pushed and pulled aside, taken away from him. And now he was being taken away from her. Over the trooper's shoulder, she saw Owen and that other paramedic carrying him toward the open doors of the ambulance.

"They're taking him away," she said. "I have to go!"

"I need to get your statement while everything's fresh in your mind," the trooper insisted.

Was this how people felt about her when she kept firing questions at them that they had no time or inclination to answer?

"I need Rory!" she cried.

But the ambulance didn't wait for her. It sped off, lights flashing and siren wailing. Rory was alive, but they obviously needed to get him to the hospital fast.

And that was how Brittney needed to get there, too.

"Please," she said, her voice cracking with a sob now. "I need to see how he is."

"You can't do anything for him," Wells said. "He's getting the help he needs."

Was she implying that he didn't need Brittney?

Maybe he didn't. All she'd done was turn his world upside down. But it didn't matter if she couldn't help him medically, she still needed to be there for him emotionally.

"I need to be with him," Brittney insisted.

And the woman just stared at her.

And Brittney's fury turned to pity. She understood now why Wynona Wells didn't understand her. "You've obviously never been in love."

Brittney could have said the same for herself until recently. But even before that, she'd known what love was like from watching the people she loved. Her mother and her father had loved each other so much. And her mom and her stepdad...

And Trent and Heather.

They walked up to her now. "You've asked enough questions already, Wells," Heather told the other law officer. "Brittney needs to be checked out, too."

"She hasn't been shot."

Trent pointed toward the torn sleeve of her shirt and her jeans. "She's been roughed up." And his voice was rough with emotion when he said it. "She needs to be checked out at the hospital."

She shook her head. "I need to make sure that Rory is all right."

"I have questions about him, too," Wells persisted. "I don't understand what's been going on here."

Heather snorted. "You're not alone in that, Trooper, but we'll figure it out. Right now, we need to get Brittney to the hospital."

Heather was smart. She knew Brittney wasn't hurt badly, but she must have figured she needed to be at the hospital for another reason. For Rory.

But was Heather's urgency an indication that his condition wasn't good? That he might not make it...?

Tears sprang to her eyes, blinding her. But Trent wrapped his arm around her, guiding her toward Heather's vehicle. And Heather, ever the law officer, put her hand on the top of her head as she helped her into the back seat. Brittney could have felt like a perp again, like Wells had made her feel, but there was affection and understanding in Heather.

She knew how upset Brittney was because she was in love. She understood. Brittney needed to be with Rory for however long he had left.

Braden's firehouse was a crime scene. Again.

Blood spattered the concrete and the side of one of the rigs. Lives had been lost.

At least one...

He wasn't sure about Rory. He'd regained consciousness for a minute, but then he'd lost it and his ability to breathe on his own.

Owen had done something with a long needle and rushed him to the hospital. The man had already spent three weeks there. Had already cheated death recently and then again five years earlier.

Braden stared down at the dead body. A sheet covered him, but his black pants and shoes stuck out from under one end of it. The gun that had been clutched in his hand had already been bagged and taken into evidence along with his badge.

FBI special agent Barry Shelton. His was the voice on that recording. Brittney had verified it to Trooper Wells, but according to the trooper that was pretty much the only question that the reporter had answered.

Braden couldn't blame her. She wanted to be with Rory. Just like Braden wanted to be with Sam.

But she was gone. On a case out west.

He needed her here.

But he had her brothers. Not just Trick.

Mack was here. He'd sent the text to his younger brother, and he'd made his presence known even though he hadn't shown himself yet. Braden gazed around the area. Where was he?

Why hadn't he come forward yet?

He had to be the gunman. The one who'd shot the FBI agent and saved Brittney and Stanley and hopefully Rory, as well. Heather had said she'd gotten here too late.

So why hadn't Mack stuck around?

What was the deal with Braden's mysterious brother-in-law?

Mack knew Rory. No. He'd called him something else

when he'd told his dad to talk to no one about that plane crash. But at the time he'd thought the man he knew had died. Mack hadn't been in the country then.

He very rarely was. What the hell was Mack? Not that it mattered much right now. He'd taken out the bad guy. Unfortunately, Braden suspected Agent Shelton wasn't the only bad guy who was messing with his team.

There was still the saboteur among them. Too many things had happened to them, too many things that hadn't been accidents. And Braden doubted the FBI agent had had anything to do with those incidents. He probably wasn't even the one who'd started up the trucks and hit Rory over the head, because he would have made damn certain he'd killed him then.

Stanley rushed up, away from the officer who'd been talking to him. And Braden closed his arms around him. "You're okay," he assured the kid. "You did good."

Annie jumped up, as if wrapping her long legs around them both, as if she thought this was a group hug.

"Brittney told me what to do," he said. "To open the big doors. She thought it would stop the man from shooting us if there were witnesses. But he shot Rory anyway." He started shaking. "He shot him anyway…"

Rory had to make it.

He had to. He'd already been through too much.

Chapter Twenty-Five

Rory could hear her voice in his head. She was talking about how a man who'd risked his life for others had had others give up his life for money. How people he should have been able to trust in law enforcement and even in his personal life had betrayed him...

How a hero had had nobody to turn to, and yet he'd continued being a hero, working as a hotshot firefighter. And his name was Rory VanDam.

"Cory..." he murmured. No. Not anymore. Cory was from a long time ago. A few lifetimes ago. Cory didn't matter. Even Rory didn't matter.

Only Brittney did.

That was her voice. She had to be here. But when he opened his eyes, he found himself alone but for the TV. It sat across from the bed where he lay with tubes and machines hooked to him.

"Déjà damn vu..." he murmured, but this time he didn't have a tube down his throat. He was breathing on his own. But his throat was dry as if he'd been asleep for a long time again. How long had he been out this time?

And why?

He felt his head, but he had only that ridge of a scar on the back of it. The stitches were gone now. So his head hadn't been injured again. Then he patted his chest and felt the bandage between his heart and shoulder.

"Damn…"

He must have gotten shot. He remembered the agent raising that gun, pointing it at his chest.

And he remembered the body with the sheet over it.

"Brittney…"

He'd heard her voice earlier. Or had he just imagined that? Then he focused on the TV again and saw her on the screen. She looked to be standing at Braden's podium, talking about Rory, playing that recording…

She had gotten it out just like she'd told the agent she had. Agent Barry Shelton. The reporter covering her, Avery Kincaid, showed his picture and reported about his life and his death.

Rory didn't recognize him, wasn't sure he'd ever met the man until that moment in the firehouse. The moment he'd been afraid the man had killed Brittney.

Was she alive?

That video from the firehouse, of her standing at Braden's podium, had probably been shot before the agent had showed up. Before Rory had.

He fumbled around, looking for a remote, a way to turn up the TV. What about Brittney?

He waited for more coverage but the program switched to a commercial. And he cursed.

"You're awake," a woman said, her voice cracking with emotion.

And he turned to find Brittney standing in the doorway. Was she dead? She looked like an angel with her brown curls and pale brown eyes. She was so beautiful.

Or maybe he was dead and he was just imagining her.

But the machine beside the bed recorded his blood pressure, which seemed to have gone up at just the sight of her.

"Are you all right?" he asked.

"I am now," she said.

He glanced at the TV. "Yeah," he agreed. "You're famous. You're on the national news now."

She had everything she'd wanted. The respect. The career. So what was she doing here? With him...

His heart seemed to shake in his chest, trying to swell, to warm, with hope. But Rory had never had much luck with love or anything else, really. Everybody who'd ever claimed to care about him had betrayed him.

Even a member of his hotshot team was willing to hurt the rest of them, kept sabotaging the damn equipment. So if he couldn't trust them, how could he trust her?

Maybe Agent Shelton had been right. All she'd wanted was the story.

"Are you here for a follow-up interview?" he asked. He gestured toward his door. "Got a camera crew out there?"

Her topaz eyes widened and she sucked in a breath. "Wow. Screw you. I can't believe you listened to what that creep was saying. That all I care about is my career."

He pointed toward the TV. "You got your big story."

"I gave that story to Avery Kincaid. I just did the video to let her know what was going on. I wasn't counting on her to use my part of it."

He sucked in a breath now. "You gave it up? It nearly got you killed. Why would you give it to someone else?"

"Because it didn't matter anymore who covered the story, it just needed to get out there," she said. "The truth needed to get out there."

"And you should be the one getting the credit for it," he insisted. She'd worked so hard that she deserved it.

She shook her head. "I thought you got shot in the shoulder, not the head. But you're not making any sense. First you act like you're mad I did the story, and now you're insisting that I should be the only one getting the credit for it. What's wrong with you? What do you want?"

You. Just you.

He wanted to say those words, but he couldn't bring himself to utter them now. He had no damn idea what was going on, how badly he was hurt. And how much danger he might be in now that the truth was out.

But Felix Falcone had dementia. "Is that FBI agent dead?" Was that who'd been covered with that sheet?

She nodded.

"Who killed him?" he asked. His gun had jammed. He hadn't been able to protect her and Stanley or even himself.

She shrugged. "I don't know."

"You haven't been investigating?" he asked.

She cursed again. "I told you that I'm not here for that damn story," she said. "I'm here for you. To make sure that the man I love wakes up."

"You love me?" he asked, and his heart swelled now with that hope as warmth flooded it. Was it safe for him to tell her how he felt about her? Would she be safe if he told her?

SHE'D BEEN SO happy to open that door and see him sitting up in bed, awake. It had been a long week since he'd been shot. And of course, he woke up when she was gone. When she'd finally given in to Tammy and Trent's nagging for her to get a shower and some sleep.

But the way he'd been acting since she'd walked in...

"You really believe what that agent said about me, how all I care about is my career?" she asked, her heart aching. But did she have a right to be upset about that? For so long that was what she believed, too, what she'd wanted to be true. She'd wanted to only care about her career so that she wouldn't love someone and lose them.

Like she'd nearly lost Rory.

Maybe she had.

Not to death but to his own doubts about her. Did he even believe that she loved him?

And if he couldn't believe that, he probably didn't return her feelings. Tears rushed to her eyes, and she turned toward the door but was too blinded to find the handle. She fumbled around, searching for it.

Then strong hands gripped her shoulders, turning her around. She blinked her tears away to stare up at Rory. "You shouldn't be out of bed." He'd dragged some of the machines with him. Hell, he'd dragged the bed behind him in his haste to stop her from leaving.

"I love you," he said. "I love you so much that I don't want to be around you if that will put you in danger." His hands moved from her shoulders to her face now, cupping it. She could feel a tremor in him, moving through him. "I love you so much."

"I love you," she said. "And the only danger I am in is getting my heart broken if you try to push me away."

He pulled her close to him now, wrapping his arms around her. "I'm not going to push you away," he said. "I'm tempted to never let you go. But I know you have your job—"

"I don't care about—"

"I do," he said. "It's your career. And you've worked too damn hard to walk away from it now. Take the credit and the opportunities that come up with that story and know that I will always be here for you."

"What about you?" she asked. "What are you going to do now that the truth is out?"

He shrugged. "The truth was always out that I'm a hotshot and a pilot. That's what I intend to keep being once I'm medically cleared to return to duty."

"You don't want to go back into law enforcement?"

"I think I lost my touch for that," he said. "I haven't figured out who the saboteur is, and I've probably been working right alongside whoever it is."

She shivered as she realized that he and her brother were still in danger. "I don't want you getting hurt again," she said.

"I wish I could promise that I won't, but we both know how unpredictable life is," he said. "It's not just officers and firefighters who get hurt. Anybody anywhere can have an accident or become a victim of a crime, even children. So loving anyone is a risk that you might lose them."

She closed her eyes on a fresh wave of tears. "I know you're right."

"You survived losing your dad," he said. "And you were a kid then. You're strong, Brittney, so much stronger than you give yourself credit for being. You can handle anything."

"Even loving you?" she asked, opening her eyes to stare up at his handsome face.

"Am I worth the risk?" he asked.

She nodded. "You're worth every risk. I love you so very much."

"I love you," he said, and he pulled her even closer to his madly pounding heart.

Hers was pounding hard, too, but with love, not fear this time. She wasn't afraid of falling for him like she'd once been. She knew that he was a survivor, too. He'd already survived so much and was still here. She wasn't worried about loving and losing him. She wasn't worried about anything anymore. Not even the saboteur, because so many people were determined to figure out who he was and stop him, that he wouldn't escape justice much longer.

A WHILE AGO the saboteur might have felt guilty over how hard they'd struck Rory over the head. But Rory might have seen them leave the bunk room before the trucks started. VanDam had been the only one not snoring or breathing hard like everyone else.

But the saboteur didn't even feel guilty anymore, didn't feel anything at all anymore except for anger and resentment. And the only time they felt less angry and resentful was when something went wrong or somebody got hurt.

Somebody was going to have to get hurt again.

Soon.

* * * * *

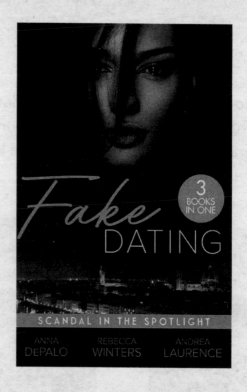